Your Reserves
Or Mine?

To Sam;
with very best
wishes from
Jim.

[signature]

This book is dedicated to the Good Guys

It is hard for thee to kick against the pricks.
Acts, ch. 9 v. 5

Your Reserves
Or Mine?

James Platt

First published in Great Britain in 2004 by Creighton Books
Email: jim.platt@planet.nl

© 2004 James Platt

ISBN 90 807808 2 0

The moral right of James Platt to be identified as the author of this work has been asserted by him in accordance with the Copyright, Designs and Patents Act 1988

British Library Cataloguing in Publication Data
A catalogue record for this book is available from the British Library

Designed in the UK by Special Edition Pre-Press Services

Printed and bound in Great Britain by Lightning Source UK Ltd

Also by James Platt

*East of Varley Head – Stories from Port Isaac,
North Cornwall, 1945–1959* (Creighton Books, 2003).

Contents

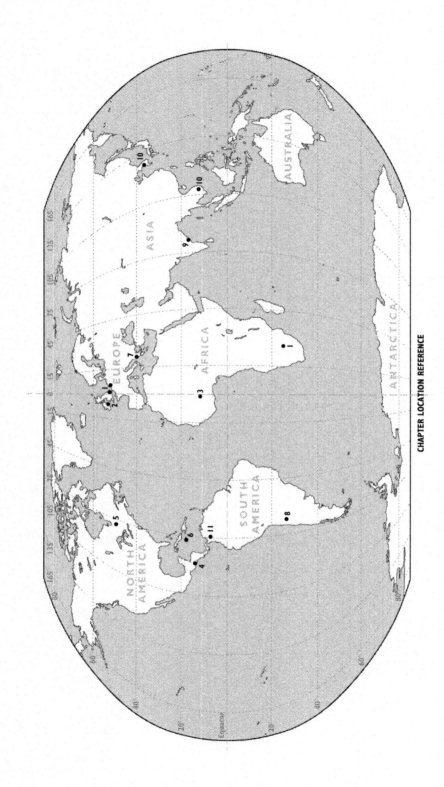

CHAPTER LOCATION REFERENCE

Acknowledgements

I have kept a daily diary through most of my working life. Dates and times for appointments, flight itineraries and an occasional reminder note formed the bulk of my entries. Although thinly sown, such information was generally enough for me to be going on with. That at least was the situation until a day arrived (in mid-1986) when thoughts of continuing to suffer the slings and arrows of outrageous corporate politics were no longer ennobling to my peace of mind.

From then on I formed an unfailing habit of writing up a daily account of my experiences. With the exception of parts of Chapter 2 of this book, the events, adventures, descriptions, conversations, attributions, perceptions and assessments on offer in the book are directly drawn from diary entries that I wrote as and when the said events and adventures *et cetera* were actually taking place.

My heartfelt and grateful thanks are due to each and every colleague that I associated with, at all levels, during the years in which I worked for the "Company" under two consecutive masters. Many of my colleagues are mentioned in the pages of this book. I appreciated them then and I continue to value them now. My working life was the better for knowing them. Of the very many hundreds of people that I associated with around the world in the course of my work, whether in work-related relationships or chance encounters or in friendship, I can list no more than half a dozen that I would rather not have known. That's not bad!

Mr John Maher of the Institute of Latin American Studies was my expert guide along the rocky path leading me into the world of authorship and self-publishing. John laid out a road map and gave me inspiration and a direction along which the only publishing pitfalls I fell into were those of my own making.

This book, as also my first book, was designed and prepared in every detail by Corinne Orde and Romilly Hambling, who together form Special-Edition Pre Press Services. Their kindness, style and expertise and the patience they showed me were all exemplary. Corinne's skill in editing and improving the text and the finished work as a whole added so much to the final book and could not have been of greater benefit to me.

The book was digitally set and registered for print-on-demand orders with key trade and Internet booksellers and distributors by Lightning Source UK Limited of Milton Keynes. LSUK's total commitment to its clients demonstrated consistent professional excellence and personal consideration that could not be bettered.

My publisher's mark, Creighton Books, was named for my grandparents, Jim and Eleanor Creighton, who hailed respectively from Toxteth in Liverpool and Port Isaac in Cornwall. May they ever rest in peace.

The lines of verse that open each chapter of this book, apart from those for Chapter 1, were inspired by timeless masterpieces of English literature. I didn't so much have to adapt the originals as to let them adapt themselves to the subject matter of the chapters they head. It would be impossibly pretentious of me to hope that the authors of the original gems of universal quality might look kindly on my use (or misuse) of their masterpieces – I can only trust that if they do turn in their graves it will be so that they may sleep more comfortably. I am grateful to them all, from the deep heart's core.

The sources for the adaptations (chapter and verse) were made as follows: Chapter 2 – "If" by Rudyard Kipling; Chapter 3 – "Home-Thoughts, from the Sea" by Robert Browning; Chapter 4 – "Daffodils" by William Wordsworth; Chapter 5 – "Jerusalem (from 'Milton')" by William Blake; Chapter 6 – "Spring and Winter (ii)" by William Shakespeare; Chapter 7 – "Ozymandias" by Percy Bysshe Shelley; Chapter 8 – "Ode to a Nightingale" by John Keats; Chapter 9 – "On first looking into Chapman's Homer" by John Keats (again!); Chapter 10 – "The Green Eye of the Yellow God" by J. Milton Hayes; Chapter 11 – "Morte d'Arthur" by Alfred, Lord Tennyson. "Genesis", with which the book commences, took its motivation from the first chapter of the Bible, the Old Testament book of the same name. "Revelation", with which both this and the Good Book conclude, sprang from the sixth chapter of St John the Divine's New Testament musings.

Any qualities that my book has are to the credit of everyone mentioned above. Its shortcomings are entirely to the detriment of me.

James Platt, July 2004

Genesis

In the beginning God created the heaven and the earth.

2. And the earth was without form, and pierced through with voids. And the spirit of God moved upon the face of the earth and through the bowels of the earth to consider the voids, and make the form of the earth whole.

3. And God said, let the voids be filled up with deposits of minerals, yea and let oil be not among the least of their host.

4. And God saw that it was good.

5. And God said, let Me not hide My deposits of minerals (not least among the host of which is oil) under a bushel, let there be a mighty horde of mining companies to exploit their substance.

6. And there was a mighty horde of mining companies.

7. And God beheld among the mighty horde of mining companies that some of them were good, but that others did not walk the paths of righteousness for His name's sake. And God divided the wheat from the chaff, and He cast the chaff into outer chaos.

8. And the evening and the morning were the first day.

9. And God decreed that all among the mighty horde of mining companies yet abiding in His firmament should be created equal,

and it was so for them all, apart from those holding that their measure of equality was greater than that of the others by many cubits.

10. And God was not happy. And He said, let there be a great organisation set in the midst of the mighty horde of mining companies to divide the one from the other and to seek to rule them all.

11. And God created that great organisation, and He gave it in charge to His peerless Uncle Joe who hitherto had toiled mightily (and in God's opinion to little effect) in endeavouring to solve the far formative riddles of God's mysterious universe.

12. And it was so.

13. And that was about it for the second day.

14. And God said unto His Uncle Joe, make the earth bring forth its bounty, make all the rocks bring forth gold, gems and baser metals, make the depths yield rich oils to move nations.

15. And this time it was not quite so.

16. For the great organisation of God's Uncle Joe went forth and produced oil, and more oil, and even more oil. And God's other minerals languished in neglect, and God saw that it was not good.

17. And that made not quite so nice an end to the third day.

18. And God said unto His Uncle Joe, it is not in thy best interests to neglect My other minerals, unless thou wilt return apace to thy hitherto ineffectual solving of the far formative riddles of My mysterious universe, therefore go forth and diversify.

19. And God's Uncle Joe pondered overlong on it, as was his wont.

20. And the highly charged atmosphere of the morning of the fourth day had not improved by a single jot or tittle by the evening of the fourth day.

21. And it came to pass that on the morning of the fifth day God took His Uncle Joe up unto a high place and showed him all the mighty horde of mining companies of the earth in a moment of time. And God said unto His Uncle Joe, all these I offer thee, choose but one, and with thy great organisation take it over so that My mineral

deposits about which thou knowest little, other than My oil about which verily thou knowest far too much, shall languish no longer in darkness.

22. And God's Uncle Joe did choose but one from among the mighty horde of mining companies, and his great organisation did take it over. And God's Uncle Joe, being less imaginative than his Nephew, named this acquisition the Company.

23. And the fifth day ended a lot more promisingly than the first as far as God was concerned, even though at the end of the day God still had a few doubts that it really was as promising an end to the day as all that.

24. And God said unto His Uncle Joe, make thee the Company in the image of thy great organisation and shape those who administer it after thy likeness, and make the Company have dominion over all the minerals of the earth, saving oil, which is for thy great organisation alone.

25. And God's Uncle Joe installed into the Company a legion, for they were many, of executives in his own image. In the image of Uncle Joe installed he them.

26. And the Company executives installed in Uncle Joe's image comprehended the exploitation of oil, but of the techniques of mining of all other minerals comprehended they not a lot.

27. And God called them each one to a meeting, saying unto them, let thy profit be as fruit on the trees, subdue and replenish the earth, for wherein there are mineral deposits, these I have given unto thee to use wisely.

28. And God saw everything that He had done, and behold, He thought, perhaps, it was very good.

29. And for God, that made not such a bad evening of the sixth day.

30. Thus should God's works have been finished, yea the very multitude of them.

31. And it was on this personal understanding that on the seventh day God rested from all the work that He had done.

32. And while God rested the legion of executives installed in the

Company by God's Uncle Joe in his own image were left to their own devices.

33. And that was not good.

34. Oh no, that was not good at all.

With apologies to His Majesty King James I and his diligent translators of AD 1611
(Not appointed to be read in Churches)

– I –

The Absolutely Mandate

Does anyone know why the subject of ore reserves
Makes the executive management of mining companies nervous?
Mining company executives don't have many endearing facets,
But they ought to know that ore reserves form a company's
  most important assets.
Certain of them are prigs to kig against in ivory castles.
God's creatures! A grey smoke conclave of astles
Who see themselves as chequebook-wielding rankers,
And are seen by those who serve them as a wunch of bankers.

A BSOLUTELY!
     I couldn't have got a more positive personal endorsement. However, let me backtrack a little and tell you how such an Absolutely positive mandate came about before I get accused of being too enthusiastic for my own good.

Trust me, I'm from head office and I'm here to help!

I ALWAYS IMAGINED that if I had ever had the courage to throw open one of the imposing Company boardroom doors behind which a heavily attended and onerously pointless meeting would inevitably be taking place, so as to stick my head in and call out, "Hey, asshole!", pretty much every one of the executives sitting around the over-polished oval table that was the mandatory centrepiece would have woken up and given me his immediate attention.

Meetings in those boardrooms, doubling up as bored rooms, created a slough of despond well able to bar the progress of any eager pilgrim. Summoned once to a boardroom at short notice to present my opinions to those gathered within on why a project was failing, I was at once confronted by the cited array of suited-up indolence. All present were united in a vested interest to ignore whatever I was going to say while veiling their hostility to me and to one another as thinly as they could. As it was, I had nothing much to impart, as the shock of the sudden encounter with the implacability of the audience infected me with a form of stage fright from which I was not sure I would ever recover.

The Company may not have been any more blessed in the asshole department than any other outfit of similar size carrying equivalent multinational aspirations. For that matter, the Company may not have been quite as overburdened – as were some of its competing peers – with know-it-all, over-promoted gentlemen who were more than capable of manifesting the great art of arrogance with an air that was as high-handed as it was condescending. Maybe not, but I wouldn't have wanted to bet on it.

What I did know was that the Company had at least its fair share of people who suited the appellation of asshole as well as if they were contained inside tight and occasionally skid-marked underpants. The yardstick by which they judged the success of their appointed jobs was how much fault they could find in whatever was presented to them. They were masters of negative spin. No detail was too trivial for them to overlook in a hunt for a scapegoat to pin the blame on.

"Hey, asshole!" Yeah, they would have looked up all right.

THE COMPANY'S CORE business was mineral exploration and mining. Worldwide, anywhere, you name it, the Company was ready to chase after any relevant project or opportunity that came up. In that very pursuit the Company regularly sent out a team of self-alleged technical experts to probe the perceived merits of project acquisition. The team was referred to, not inappropriately, as the Flying Circus. The stock in trade of the Flying Circus was to evaluate or perform a due diligence routine – it was all one to them – on a specified project. The Company's executive management group then scrutinised the Flying Circus's recommendations for a period of time long enough to give an impression of industriousness to observers so that, when it ultimately took no action, the abortive result smacked of decision.

Boardroom assessments of project evaluations were all too often directed at cutting optimism down to size and trampling promise into cynical dust. There was always some form of escape ruse for the Company's officious executives to fall back on when the routine approach to withdrawing interest looked even flimsier than it generally did. An excellent copper project in northern Greece, which it seemed that no amount of executive management slash-and-burn discussion could devalue, was finally thrown to the wolves on the grounds that, "We don't want to work with Greeks."

The wheels of the Company's ponderous decision-making process creaked in protest as they turned. Final destinations were rarely reached, since the competition out there habitually overtook the Company cart and picked up the project on offer, burning Rome while the Company fiddled. The Company's executive management was then left to wallow in a luxurious bath of simulated disappointment.

The members of the Company's executive management committee were exposed to open view so infrequently that the appearance of any one of them became something of an event in which volition must have played no part. They were usually only to be seen scurrying through corridors, either individually or, preferably, in small groups (as there was safety in numbers) in the manner of white rabbits on their way to Wonderland. The elusive passage of these corporate pimpernels was conducted at a sufficient pace not only to rattle the works of outrageous modern art hanging on the corridor walls but also to successfully avoid their persons being buttonholed by lesser mortals anxious to air grievances. Of lesser mortals there were many, and of the alleged grievances of lesser mortals there were even more.

When bustling along in a group, Company executive management huddled together in close enough proximity to one another to suggest a pantomime horse minus its costume. Raucous laughter emanated from their tight rank. It was the kind of laughter designed to ward off a frumious bandersnatch in a tulgey wood. The volume of executive guffaw was inversely proportional to its perpetrators' perception of the future economic prospects of the Company.

THE COMPANY'S HEADQUARTERS were located in, of all good places, the Netherlands. In a former life the Company's endeavours had been directed at the exploitation of minerals in some of the far-flung reaches of the Dutch colonial empire. The home base made a well-nigh natural

3

process of the eventual acquisition of the Company by a celebrated multinational oil giant with supposedly deep pockets, a diversification compulsion and a home of homes, also in Holland.

The Company's operating philosophy, put simply, was that if enough of the money contained in the deep pockets of its almighty owner could be thrown consistently in a specific direction for long enough then some of the dough was bound to stick to something. In other words, under such well-heeled circumstances, achieving success could be only a matter of time. Success was always going to be there, just around the corner. The only problem was to find the corner.

The owner was revered as the Company's affable Uncle Joe, who, no matter what scrapes his nephew got into, was a safe bet to put up the bail. Uncle Joe was a good guy with a chequebook. The people that Uncle Joe created in his own image were usually with him, body and spirit, from cradle to grave. The great range of remunerations that they received, and not infrequently took advantage of, guaranteed their allegiance to him. There were, of course, many among them for whom money wasn't everything and for whom pride of association with Uncle Joe was of chief account. It was a matter of regret that certain of these did not always receive from their executive management the desirable level of moral support that their loyalty merited.

More than a few of those who toiled to promote the Company's best interests believed it to be rather unfortunate that Uncle Joe had shoved so many of his own people into Company positions where, what the hell, they were equipped with all the authority to cause as much damage to Company aspirations as their limited understanding of the mining industry could sustain.

The darned thing was that the Company employed so many people of its own stamp who were genuinely competent at what they did. Assholes aside, on a cumulative assessment of talent, the Company was more than able to stand tall among its mining industry peers. Had the talented ones been provided with the proper guidance and encouragement from above to gel as a team pulling in one direction, teamwork being of the essence, there is no accounting for what success they might have achieved. The proper support fell short all too often, in spite of the availability to the Company of more Uncle Joe sponsored in-house courses on team building, teamwork and the development of high-flying leadership skills than you could shake a sledgehammer at.

Competition between the high flyers was a finely honed black art. Any one of them who could not succeed by rising above the skills of his or her peers on his or her own merits did so by surreptitiously chopping the peers off at their knees.

And the plaintive cry of "Et tu, Brute?" was heard in the land.

It was a painful fact of life that the Company's skill in placing the right people in the right place at the right time to grab at an immediate project opportunity was not always obvious. All too often when the Company's people were in the right place at the right time they tended to be the wrong people. If fate did conspire to set the right person in the right place at the right time, the boardroom *habitués* could always be counted on to winkle out some means of avoiding making a decision on doing anything with the waiting opportunity. Being in the right place at the wrong time was more the Company's lot.

Based on that sometimes deficient level of support that the head-office executive management types provided to some Company representatives in the field, the former could be deemed as being unworthy of the quality and calibre of its people sitting out at the hands-on end of its business. Uncle Joe looked on for quite a while with benevolent tolerance at a growing shortfall in Company progress, but there had eventually to come a point when the depredations of certain of the wall-to-wall bullshit artists in the Company's corridors of power began to wear a little thin on even Uncle Joe's patience.

When it came down to dealing with bullshit, Uncle Joe had no shortage of captive in-house exponents under his own banner to practise his technique on.

INEVITABLY, DAWN ARRIVED on a day of reckoning. Uncle Joe shook his head and decided that enough was enough. He made haste to scrape the bullshit from his boots. Uncle Joe's dominion over oil ensured that when push came to shove he would choose to go the way of some other big (but never bigger) oil companies whose combative dalliance in the dark arena of the mining industry had come to a bloody end. A towel was thrown into the ring.

Uncle Joe declared his readiness, as immediate as it was unexpected, to negotiate an unsolicited takeover bid for the Company from a prominent South African mining house. The latter, having unbundled its assets in South Africa (whatever unbundling actually meant, it sounded serious enough), was anxious to acquire a suitable platform in Europe to further its aspirations for international expansion. Or something like that anyway.

The takeover negotiations were nothing if not protracted. Then, as if that weren't enough, they dragged on some more. Foot-dragging technique was all very much a highlighted feature on the Company's list of prime skills. Due diligence evaluations on the mining properties that the respective parties that were the Company and the South African mining house had incorporated in the deal were not only carried out but also taken to a conclusion by highly priced organisations of international technical consultants retained for the purpose.

In an attempt to define an acceptable face for the takeover negotiations, the Company undertook frequent open forum briefings for its people at head office. Referred to as information meetings, the briefings, in the view of rather a lot of those in attendance, peddled disinformation as if it were a virtue. Truth was a constant hostage to the power of implication, held in chains and gagged into the bargain. Had it not been for the assurance of the good old corridor-located rumour mill, with its established nexuses at each coffee machine and photocopier, none of those whose security of job tenure was most likely to be affected by the takeover might ever have learned anything of substance until it was too late.

At long last a deal was done. The South African mining house handed Uncle Joe the monetary recompense that, as far as many of the host who had thereby been taken over against their wishes were concerned, no doubt contained a very specific thirty pieces of silver.

To the regret of far too many, Uncle Joe folded his Company tents and stole away. To the regret of far too few among those he stole away from, he took his former Company assignees with him. Uncle Joe might from time to time have been regarded by all of those who were subservient to him as being of canine parentage, but even those whom he abandoned to the mercies of a new master could not help but still see him as their son of a bitch. They watched him go with the kind of reluctant compassion generally reserved for the loss of a slightly suspect family member.

ALTHOUGH there were many nice guys among the South Africans who descended on the Company scene following the takeover, their complement included some who could easily have enhanced Uncle Joe's education in the science of behaving arrogantly. The new CEO of the Company was reputed to be an autocratic South African swashbuckler to whom the taking of prisoners in the pursuit of a deal was an unknown quantity; asking questions may have counted for far less with him than did shooting first. For all that, he was seen as a quintessential man of vision backed up by a genuine talent for business that was capable of either making or breaking any outfit he controlled. It was never clear to me on which side of a thin line separating success from disaster his propensity for making ever more perilously grandiose deals might fall. I always viewed the new CEO as a pugilist who would assuredly step into the ring once too often, unable to recognise that it was well past time to hang up the gloves.

I was not too willing to remain with the Company under the unfamiliar auspices of South African management. Resigning my position was one option, but I didn't feel quite so strongly about the situation to use it as the motivation to take such an irrevocable course. I couldn't help noticing, however, that following the takeover a fair number of my Company colleagues were rapidly enabled to pick up handsome early retirement or redundancy packages of the gold-bound kind usually reserved for executive managers who had screwed up a project in a big way, and so I thought I would chance my arm on joining them. Unfortunately my new masters wouldn't permit me to follow that route.

The new CEO and his band of executive and non-executive director buddies, none of whom seemed to experience any misgivings in affirming the new CEO's decrees, then changed the name of the Company to that of the South African mining house that had successfully taken the Company over. To the victor and his yes-men belonged the spoils. I could barely bring myself to associate with the amended Company name and was hesitant to flash the new business cards fitted with my job title and the South African mining house's logo. Unless I did it an injustice, the logo, a stylised "G", looked suspiciously like the profile of one of those pointy hats worn by practising members of the Ku-Klux Klan.

That which genuinely pissed me off to an extraordinary degree was the announcement that a former Company CEO, an alleged gentleman cast in the image of Uncle Joe, was to become a non-executive director of the newly taken-over Company. I took his appointment as a personal affront beggaring belief. The unspeakable had returned to take up full pursuit of the unbeatable.

Once upon a time I believed that this corporate pillar hadn't the wit to recognise a good thing in the context of the mining industry even if it jumped up and bit him, but I could judge from his reappearance on the Company scene that I erred in thinking that way.

Then, for reasons not unrelated to considerations of sustaining the Company's international credibility, and after having wiped out, sold off, given away or otherwise destroyed all items and objects bearing the original Company name and logo, the new CEO and his executive acolytes elected to revert to the original Company name and logo once more. So, it wasn't all bad, even if the process of reinstating the original name and logo, in the great tradition of so many projects, took more time than it ought to have done and was probably far more costly than it ought to have been.

UNDER THE COMPANY'S new executive management I was designated to report to an executive vice-president for exploration and development who was based in Johannesburg. Given the geographical disparity of our reporting relationship, a certain amount of debate took place, aimed at resolving whether or not I should relocate to live in the fair city of my appointed boss, or otherwise move to London, where the Company had just set up a plush corporate centre at an address somewhere in the lower Strand. As if to prove that irony was not yet dead, the Strand address was only a figurative stone's throw away across the road from South Africa House, although any decision to throw stones between the former and the latter would depend on who might be visiting South Africa House at the time.

The discussions dealing with my ultimate domicile generally excluded any contribution from me. I didn't want to live in either Johannesburg or London, which implied that those conducting the process on my behalf deemed that I was quite incapable of saying anything worth listening to.

In the course of the debate, however, I was instructed to take a phone call from one of the Company's less pleasing South African executive directors who was evidently keen to demand a firm decision from me on the proposed relocation. At the time of the call he was in London and I was making a technical visit to a small gold mine in which the

Company had a significant share, located in the historic depths of the state of Minas Gerais in Brazil.

The timing for the call was five o'clock in the morning in Brazil, arranged to suit the executive director's convenience and not mine. Perhaps he wanted to catch me off guard at a vulnerable hour before he had his lunch. His opening remark to me, delivered in tones as abrasive as they were aggressive, was, "What are you doing there?" It seemed that the health and well-being of either of us was not in question.

I told him what I was doing in Brazil and he told me we would speak of it again, although as it happened, and to no regret of mine, we never did. Nor was any decision on my relocation reached during the call. I hung up at the end wishing that I had had the courage to tell him to shove his partly configured proposals up his well-configured ass.

The final outcome of my relocation question proved to be an anticlimax worthy of comparison with the closing scenes of *The Browning Version*. Since my work involved extensive travelling to visit Company projects and mining operations around the world, it was reckoned not to matter where I was located and so I simply stayed where I was already. This result might well have come about by default, but it might also have been a small victory for me – an ill-favoured thing sir, but it was mine own for all that.

Because it couldn't be avoided for ever, the day came when I had to make arrangements to meet my new executive VP boss in his suite of offices in the imposing Company headquarters building in downtown Johannesburg. The building was uniquely and prestigiously fitted on top with a helicopter-landing pad, thereby ensuring that the CEO could arrive in style. As the helicopter bearing the CEO touched down, those forced to access the building by more conventional means looked at one another and commented, "The Ego has landed".

I took advantage of an arranged visit to a couple of the Company's mines in South Africa to obtain an appointment to call in and see my new boss. His secretary assigned me an appropriate time slot for the appointment. The secretary was a blonde dumpling whose manner, efficiency and over-zealous attention to her boss's agenda evoked the words "Third" and "Reich" in a linked sequence. Her office adjoined his, a castle keep guarding his door against unauthorised entry. His office door, securely closed behind the bulwark of her desk, exuded an air of some reluctance to being opened.

The secretary doled out the VP's time to supplicants like myself in fifteen-minute increments when he was actually in residence, and he wasn't in residence all that often. His presence in the Johannesburg building, fortuitously coincident with mine, was either a stroke of destiny or a misjudgement on the part of one or both of us. I was allotted a specific fifteen minutes, and no more, for my initial encounter with my august new supervisor.

The ensuing meeting was a minute late in starting, then overran at the end by five minutes. To the secretary's great displeasure I was a thief of time – four minutes of the said commodity to be precise.

If my boss's secretary's demeanour was not exactly militaristic, it at least had para-military overtones. Welcome to life in the mining houses of Johannesburg! Although a purist could have alleged that the secretary lacked a few elements of regulation crispness of bearing, this shortfall was not obvious to a less experienced observer like me. In any case, her boss more than compensated for it by managing to look like an erect ramrod even when he was sitting down.

Her boss – my boss – was slim, trim and smilingly grim, offering an impression of having been carved from a block of ironwood with all the minute attention to detail that excision of slivers by a cutthroat razor might guarantee. Not a hair on his head was out of place. He spoke English to me with a brittle accent which suggested that his personal sympathies did not lie with the side that allegedly won the Boer war.

He wore a blue striped shirt fitted with a stark white collar and bulky cuffs of the same hue held closed by chunky, gleaming cufflinks and a whole lot of starch. His corporate tie, decorated with a set of colourful splotches that must have constituted some kind of esoteric design symbolism but managed to make it look more as if it had been hard hit by falling bird shit, had clearly been fastened around his neck by an expert. The creases in his trousers were so sharp that had he sunk to his knees he might have been in danger of wounding himself. Somehow, however, given that he was a recognised protégé of the Company's new CEO, I couldn't quite visualise him on his knees before anyone other than the CEO for the time being.

He greeted me without evident warmth. His adjutant-like secretary brought in a couple of cups half filled with an opaque brown liquid that came as close to masquerading as coffee as any such beverage ever did in the context of South African office life.

With the formalities completed, we were free to commence our working relationship.

"What do you do?" he asked me.

"Well…," I replied, and then told him what I did.

"Hmmm," he mused for a while as if he were thinking of something meaningful to say and couldn't for the life of him figure out what it ought to be.

"Is that what you want me to carry on doing?" I asked him.

"Absolutely," he said.

"So that's what I should carry on doing?"

"Absolutely," he said.

It appeared that our interview might be at an end.

"Could you write it all down for me now?" he wanted to know.

"Oh, absolutely!" I told him.

I quickly scribbled out a list of my current activities, taking care to add to it all of the things that I thought I ought also to be doing and hadn't been altogether encouraged to do under Uncle Joe's ministration of the Company. I couched as much of the list as I could in terms that were broad and general enough to give me an impressive latitude of technical flexibility. I had nothing to lose from it, and I thought that the Company, under its new management, had everything to gain.

I handed the list over to him. He gave it a cursory glance and, right on cue, his secretary materialised through the connecting door from her bunker to whisk the manuscript away and disappear back into that redoubt. I sipped at the *ersatz* coffee, doing my best not to grimace, and realising how completely in keeping with the occasion the coffee was. After no more than a very few of her precious minutes the secretary returned, with my job list now typed up and photocopied in triplicate. This was efficiency of a breathtaking calibre. She handed the three copies of the list to our mutual boss, who signed them with a flourish and without as much as an unfocused gaze at what they contained. He wrote using a chunky fountain pen trimmed with enough gold to buy food for the population of half a street in Soweto for a week. Clearly in the boss's mind his secretary did not make typos, even when faced with interpreting my handwriting. That was a first. And so it was.

Each of us – boss, secretary and me – received a copy of what was now my formal job description, permitting me, within the field of activity covered by the technical disciplines of mining and geology, not to mention mining geology, to do more or less whatever I believed was the right thing to do from that moment on.

It seemed too good to be true.

"So this is what I will do for you?" I asked him again, holding up my copy of the list.

"Absolutely," he said.

It was the last word of our meeting.

It was the first word of the Absolutely mandate.

The Absolutely mandate may not have given me absolute *carte blanche* in the work that I did, but it felt as if it came pretty close to handing me an acceptably blank sheet. Within reason I was enabled to plan my own travel schedule and consider that all the Company's mining operations were worthy of my unsolicited attentions.

UNDER UNCLE JOE's auspices, in most cases local management ran the Company's mining operations as if they were island fortresses under siege. The local managers were Uncle Joe's appointees as often as not, and as such were politicians to the core who were not expected to know much or care less about the process of mining. Their primary objective seemed to be to present an optimistic front to the rest of the world and to bury bad news behind the wall of this façade. As a consequence, certain of the mining operations came to resemble teeth decaying from the central nerve outwards. It was necessary to drill through the glossy enamel on show in order to perform urgent remedial root canal surgery in order to avoid the need for an extraction. The Absolutely mandate gave me an inroad to tackle any recognised technical defects related, no matter how loosely, to the triplicate list.

The Company's mines were a disparate collection. Under the Absolutely mandate I attended to bauxite mines in Brazil, Suriname and Australia; gold mines in Indonesia, Brazil and Ghana; a nickel mine in Colombia; lead zinc mines in South Africa and Canada; manganese mines in South Africa; and chromite mines also in South Africa. In addition, from time to time, there were projects and opportunities to be looked at in, among other countries, Bolivia, Burkina Faso, El Salvador, French Guyana, Guinea, India, Jamaica, Mexico, Peru, Vietnam and Zambia.

It required a certain amount of skill in time juggling for me to manage the twin priorities of visiting the mining operations and fitting in work on identified projects between mine visits. I determined that each mine justified an initial visit from me, taking in at least two and as many as three weeks on site if I were ever going to develop an acceptable understanding of how the operations really worked and thereby define where I could make a positive contribution to them. The essential path to progress lay in my getting on close personal terms with as many as possible of the people involved in the mining operations by sharing their working lives and gaining their trust. The rapid same-day (even same-morning) in and out visits favoured by executive management simply didn't ever accomplish anything durable.

It took the best part of a couple of years for me to make the entire circuit of all the specified Company mining operations and with it to achieve a basis of acceptable working relationships from the general manager down to the miners at the face. I felt much more at home among those people who did the real work and whose job functions were to be retrieved somewhere in the obscurer lower boxes of organisational charts.

ULTIMATELY, THE THRUST of my endeavours was directed into installing a standard policy for ore reserve reporting practice at all of the mining operations. Mining activity was impossible in the absence of ore. There were no circumstances under which ore and profit could be considered as mutually exclusive. Ore was measured as reserves in the ground, specified in terms of available quantity (tonnage) and production quality (grade).

I chose to standardise the cited policy in compliance with what I believed to be the world-best code of ore reserve reporting practice as devised by the Joint Ore Reserves Committee of the Australasian Institute of Mining and Metallurgy et al.

This code of practice, popularly known as the JORC Code, required the assurance of rigorous professional ethics and scientific integrity in its application. The JORC Code took into consideration a comprehensive range of external (local, national and international) and internal (short- and long-term) influences on the ability of the mining operations under scrutiny to exploit their ore reserves successfully and profitably while living up to the Company's highly vaunted and much trumpeted "good citizen" ideals in conjunction with social and environmental responsibility. Success and profit in the mining industry were essentially synonymous.

Once ore reserve estimations could be competently declared

compliant with the terms and conditions of the JORC Code, virtually all other related technical and human aspects of the mining operations supported by the estimations could be expected to be equally in order.

A Company-wide standardisation of ore reserves was never destined to be an easy task. It involved the co-operative attention of a multiplicity of nationalities, cultures, operating techniques, institutionalised practices, styles of mineral deposits, commodities and contrary facets of plain human nature. Then again, few such worthwhile projects were ever completed without meeting obstacles to progress along the way.

I APPROACHED THE Company's London-based executive technical director to solicit his support for a Company-wide implementation of the JORC Code. I didn't feel that his endorsement was necessary in the light of the Absolutely mandate, but I was induced by a certain amount of arm twisting to accept that it would be "good politics" to get it. The willingness of the executive technical director to make a positive response was about as muted as I expected it to be. He demonstrated all the enthusiasm of a politician pressed by an interviewer to provide an honest answer. As I had feared, nothing happened on his side for quite a while.

By pushing my suit with him, I finally managed to obtain his written letter of authorisation to "investigate the possibility of implementing the JORC Code", something that in my opinion was already done to its limit. The grudging lines of the executive technical director's letter to me were described by one of his close associates as representing a "commission" to implement the JORC Code as a corporate standard. My first impulse was to reject the so called "commission" for the inadequate cop-out that I thought it was, but that would have got me nowhere, and so I decided to press on regardless, think Absolutely, and do what I thought needed to be done in the first place.

THE DUE DATE established for the completion and confirmation of Company-associated mine ore reserve statements was the turn of the calendar year. With a little bit of luck, this meant that the statements would be assembled and agreed to in a consistent JORC Code compliant format in time for publication in the Company's Annual Report at the end of the financial year on the subsequent June 30th.

The Company's Annual Report was thick, glossy, and produced quite as handsomely as it was expensively. Its endless pages of dense text and tight columns of figures were relieved here and there by colourful photographs of employees who were encouraged to be caught in the act of looking cheerful at least at the moment when the camera was pointed at them.

The Annual Report's lead page consisted of a supremely optimistic message from the CEO, who was moved to pay particular attention to the vital contribution of all the Company's employees to the so-called "bottom line". Most of the said employees could then be cheerfully forgotten about until next year's report was due. The information alluding to the CEO and his close henchmen's bonuses, fees and share handouts was buried in small print somewhere in the heart of the report. Hunting it out was an eye-blurring process that usually collapsed from tedium well before completion.

Tracking down the published figures for the ore reserves in the Annual Report made, if anything, an even more onerous task, notwithstanding that the whole corporate edifice stood or fell on their foundation. It was a function of the Absolutely mandate, I thought, to ensure that something got done to rectify this deplorable shortfall.

It would be wonderful to record here that my "commissioned" investigation into the implementation of JORC Code-compliant ore reserves exercised the minds of the Company's CEO and executive directors. Unfortunately, to assume that it did would be to confuse these executive types with a bunch of guys who actually gave a shit about a whole lot more than their personal agenda motives. In their shit-giving capacity, some of the executive directors were about as continent as Pinocchio.

THERE THEN CAME a day, albeit following a certain amount of further lobbying of the case from my side, on which a colleague and I were summoned to the corporate centre in London to make a short presentation on the JORC Code and its application to the assembled gang (or gangue maybe) of executive directors under the CEO at one of its regular meetings. It seemed that at long last a main chance had arrived for the ore reserves policy to impress itself on executive imagination.

The meeting of executive directors was an all-day affair. My colleague and I were in place at the outset, ready to step into an appointed time slot for our presentation. We hung around, waiting for a summons to perform for the delectation of the executive directors, sitting right outside the door to the boardroom in which their meeting was taking place. Our slot was rescheduled no fewer than three times before it was cancelled altogether when the board meeting ran out of either time or willpower in the late afternoon. When it came, the announcement of the cancellation of our presentation was unsurprising. Its corpse sprawled under a shroud of inevitability.

My colleague and I remained seated outside the boardroom door in the manner of just-in-case mediaeval petitioners when the executive meeting broke up. The first executive to emerge was the CEO, appearing to be about as smug and as self-satisfied as anyone with his bank balance and share options might well be. He looked at us from beneath a Neanderthal-styled fringe of greying hair and asked, "What are you doing here?" I had heard that one before. We told him what we were doing there, addressing our response to his back as he was already on his way home, having disregarded us in a instant.

The executive technical director, the man of the "commission", was the fourth in line to exit the boardroom (numbers two and three ahead of him had not spared us as much as a glance). He did acknowledge us, however, although whether or not that was to his credit was a matter for later debate. "Oh," he said, "there you are. We did consider calling you in, but we thought we weren't competent as a group to discuss ore reserve policy at this point in time." Then he too swept grandly on, having said it all.

Hey, asshole!

I wish I could record that I gained no pleasure at a much later date when that particular technical executive director was reported to have "resigned" from the board and the Company under circumstances which suggested that he was helped on his way with an almighty shove. The press release announcing his departure was a small masterpiece in the art of damning with faint praise. A golden handshake of the almighty six figure variety, reserved for types who, like him, least merited it, may have eased his departure qualms, although a kick up his ass with a dirty boot would have been more appropriate.

NOT ALL THAT long after my so near and yet so far day spent sitting outside that closed boardroom door in London, the cover of the Company's in-house magazine featured a photograph of the CEO in close proximity to none other than HM Queen Elizabeth II. The one seemed to be in awe of the other, and the CEO looked a little bit impressed as well.

Their two majestic heads were so close together, they seemed conspiratorial. I imagined that the Queen was asking, "Pray inform me on the status of the ore reserves, your Excellency." To which the CEO was replying, *sotto voce*, "Pray don't ask me that, your Majesty – I'm not competent to comment."

The Company's magazine was never found wanting in taking an opportunity to publish pictures of the CEO in any situation, let alone this one. As a publicity hound, he was as consummate as he was insatiable.

ANOTHER DAY DAWNED, as it simply had to, when the Company's ore reserves, all commodities included, were to have their hour, one far fierce hour and sweet. The glory revolved around a corporate plan, now that Uncle Joe was history, to float Company shares on the London Stock Exchange. A prospectus, in support of the Company's stature justifying the float, was formally required to carry certified statements of ore reserves with respect to each of the mining operations.

For the purpose of completing the prospectus, a few more high-priced firms of international mining technical and financial consultants were retained to make the rounds of all of the mining operations. Their representatives flew in, stayed on the ground as much as a couple of days and then flew out again. On that short-stay basis, allegedly informed technical reports, inclusive of ore reserve figures, were compiled.

IN CONNECTION WITH the LSE share float, great squads of nominally independent business analysts, borne in aircraft chartered by the Company, also charged around the world from mining operation to mining operation, setting down in one country for as much as a few hours before zooming on to the next one. I watched such a squad, twenty to thirty strong, arrive at the Company's nickel mining and refining operations in Colombia. To a man – even though the group included a couple of women – they were in an advanced state of disintegration from fatigue and so disoriented that they didn't know if it was Christmas or Easter. The identity of the country they were in was so immaterial to them that it made just another facet to their dull limbo.

The classic process of going through the motions was never more adequately demonstrated than by the visiting analysts' cumulative disinterest. If they were indeed providers of the fundamentals for underpinning a prospectus, the foundations they created were going to be as coherent as wet toilet paper.

ALTHOUGH I HAD covered most of the Company's mining operations and produced JORC Code compliant ore reserve statements in each case, I was not initially invited to contribute the fruits of my work to the prospectus. Then the eleventh hour arrived, featuring the discovery not only that the high-priced international technical consultants' contributions to Company ore reserve reporting lacked overall consistency but also that the cited consultants, in their customary way, were not altogether willing to take direct responsibility for the ore reserve figures they had allegedly estimated.

My unbridled admiration for such mining industry consultants disappeared on the day the chief geologist of a large bauxite mining company, active at the time in Jamaica, told me that such awe was wasted. "Consultants", he said, "are people who have been fired from their jobs."

AT THE ELEVENTH hour I was working on the technical assessment of a chromite mining operation set in the western Bushveld of South Africa, located not far from the town of Rustenburg. I was accommodated in a little thatched roofed rondavel a few kilometres from the mine. The rondavel was one of many such dwellings within a tourist complex that catered largely for families of the Afrikaans-speaking persuasion who were addicted to weekend barbecuing of large pieces of meat and vast spirals of home-made sausage.

During my two-week stay at the tourist complex I dined mainly on the contents of tins of curried items bought from a lonely supermarket run by an Indian family out on the Rustenburg road. There was such a restricted menu on offer in the tourist-complex restaurant that I had been there, seen that and done the red meat-overburdened lot all in three days.

All through a full week, both during working hours at the mine and additionally afterwards back at the rondavel, I found I was required to take and respond to very frequent phone calls and faxes from an unholy assortment of merchant bankers, analysts and lawyers who were simultaneously engaged in assembling the prospectus from various locations in England, in Johannesburg and in Canada. If it sounds clichéd to say that the left hand didn't know what the right hand was doing, well boys, that was how it was.

It seemed that someone, somewhere in the Company, had linked my name with ore reserves and had tracked me down. A phone was specially installed in my rondavel to facilitate the ability of many to contact me at will. I quickly lost track of who was who among them. Consolidation of the Company ore reserve figures for insertion in the prospectus was their order of the day for me. I was instructed to get in touch with certain of the pricey consultants and agree the ore reserve figures with them, and in this process to check and confirm for consistency the respective figures for all commodities, including coal, manganese and some other creatures that I had yet to work on.

It made for a nerve-wracking week. I was confident about the ore reserve figures that I had produced, but in rather more than a few cases the consultants' versions were somewhat different and I couldn't agree with them at all. With regard to mining operations on which I had not yet worked I was fortunate in having forged good personal relationships under the Absolutely mandate with colleagues who were in the know, and via that route I was better able to draw those strings together.

My *impasse* with the consultants was seemingly insoluble. Attempts to reach suitable compromises without affecting the integrity of my own ore reserve figures went nowhere.

On the Friday of the week I was informed that the following day, Saturday, was the deadline, as on the Sunday afternoon, in only two days' time, the CEO was to present, in an auditorium of the Johannesburg office building, an outline of the prospectus to an assembled mob of business analysts, stockbrokers, press hacks, peers and anyone else who had nothing better to do at the weekend. A final accounting of ore reserve figures was therefore needed by late Saturday afternoon for insertion where relevant on the CEO's overhead presentation slides. Once the figures were committed to the overheads, they could not be subsequently changed.

Throughout the Saturday morning I tried to make a last attempt to establish a joint position of agreement with the consultants. From the lack of success that I encountered, I assumed that, high-priced and even over-priced though they may have been, their service fees did not buy weekend availability.

I could only go with what I knew, and so, at the hour of reckoning on Saturday afternoon, I put together a list of my own ore reserve figures, signed it in compliance with the JORC Code and faxed it off from the tourist-complex office to those who were waiting for it in Johannesburg.

That was the finest hour for the Company's ore reserve estimates.

As the fax went out I was left feeling that there was a great whirring fan out there somewhere, waiting for a big pile of shit to hit it and come flying back in my direction, but no such thing happened. A disgruntled representative of the high-priced consultant clan rang me up a few days later and tried to bully me into changing my ore reserve figures for the bauxite mining operations in Brazil and Suriname, but since the prospectus die had by then been cast, his complaints were all bluster and I took them as such.

I was right and he wasn't.

Absolutely.

Joining up with Uncle Joe

If you can guard your ass while all about you
  Are stabbing backs, and blaming it on you,
If you can trust no one (since all men doubt you),
  And plot their downfall well before it's due,
If you can wait, and bide your time while waiting,
  And being lied about – tell bigger lies,
Or being hated, double deal the hating,
  Make them look bad; ensure your own stocks rise.

If you can scheme – and use those schemes to master
  The way they think – control their thoughts your aim,
If you can make your triumph their disaster,
  And have them seem impostors in the game,
If you can twist in knots the truth that's spoken,
  Bind up the knaves and hang a noose for fools,
And watch the things they gave their lives to broken,
  And kick 'em out to grass, like worn out mules.

If you can scam your cut of all the winning,
  And grab huge fees and never give a toss,
And take, and start again at the beginning,
  Adjusting books to paper over loss,
If you can force their nerves and minds and sinew
  To serve your case long after they are sacked,
And hold their closet skeletons within you,
  To dampen rashness, should they dare to act.

If you can bullshit crowds, pretending virtue,
  And walk with kings — forget the common touch!
If neither foes nor one-time friends can hurt you,
  If no men count with you for very much,
If you can fill an unrelenting minute
  With sixty seconds of self-serving fun,
Yours is the pot, and everything that's in it!
  You'll have become a CEO, my son!

With apologies to Mr Rudyard Kipling

I JOINED THE Company, when Uncle Joe owned it, in the seventh year of his reign. This is how it came to pass.

The Company invited me to be interviewed for a job. I knew the Company couldn't possibly have been less enthusiastic about the prospect than I was. I shrugged, thought, "What the hell", and let it go at that.

I didn't have a suit, and if I was to be interviewed properly it became a pressing priority for me to buy such a garment. The suit that I purchased was of the variety that came off the peg, which meant that it was guaranteed to fit me wherever it touched. When I put it on I appreciated how a snake about to shed its skin might have felt.

The suit was cut from a bolt of prickly cloth dyed in either a muted bluish colour or some kind of neutral grey. I don't remember the precise colour; not that it matters much, as I gave the suit away to a deserving cause a long time ago.

The draper's shop that sold me the suit was located somewhere down towards the bottom of that steeply inclined section of road that thrust into the commercial heart of the town of Arklow in County Wicklow in Ireland.

The road came into Arklow out of the Vale of Avoca, through which it more or less followed the right bank of the Avoca river. The Vale of Avoca, regarded as a scenic gem, was commemorated for ever more as "that vale in whose bosom the bright waters meet" by the Irish bard Mr Thomas Moore in a seminal piece of verse entitled "The Meeting of the Waters".

A collective group of small copper mines, the property of Avoca Mines Limited, straddled the Vale of Avoca a few miles upstream from Arklow. At the time that I was invited by the Company to attend an interview, and as a result forced to upgrade my wardrobe with a suit, I was working as chief geologist at the copper mines.

Downstream from the mines and as a direct consequence of mine-generated effluent known as acid mine drainage (or AMD), somewhat less than bright waters coursed over the pebbles and boulders of the Avoca riverbed and deposited on the same a significant crust of a substance that owed much to the tendency of AMD to precipitate unpleasantly brown oxides of iron. This ochre palette would almost certainly not have excited the poet Moore's fertile imagination.

Since the year in which I purchased my suit was 1978, Mr Moore was long past caring about the depredations of mining on the quality of water in the Sweet Vale that he immortalised. At an equally low local ebb as that of Moore's alleged unconcern for present-day sacrilege, at least in the province of those like myself who worked at the copper mines, was elegance of dress code, and it was that reality rather than Moore's outdated vision that drew me to follow the riverine course of AMD all the way down to Arklow in search of a tailor.

When I forwarded an application to the Company in response to an advertisement for technical staff that the Company had placed in an issue of the weekly *Mining Journal* trade publication, I did it as a matter of routine, and not with the anticipation of any positive result. I made such applications once in a while when an interesting-looking job advertisement came up and promptly forgot about them as soon as I dropped the envelopes containing them in the post box.

Responses received, if any came at all, offered a salutary comment of the type, "Don't call us, we'll call you", or "Thanks but no thanks", or "We have placed your application on file for possible future reference". "On file" was a euphemism for being binned with extreme prejudice.

The *Mining Journal* was a topical periodical that offered essential reading for those who were serious players in the worldwide mining industry. As often as not, any news printed in the *Mining Journal* that related to mining properties and exploration projects of which I had first-hand knowledge rarely coincided with my own hard-earned perceptions. It begged the question as to how reliable the *Mining Journal* was in reporting news of properties and projects of which I had no direct experience. The *Mining Journal* was an impeccable source of job adverts, however.

In applying for a new job I was not doing much more than placing a symbolic iron in an equally symbolic fire to be pulled out in the not unlikely event that the ailing operations of the Avoca Mines should fall terminally ill. It was a popular adage that mines didn't close down easily, but, as with any activity relying on waning natural resources, the song of the fat lady would eventually screech out, and in the case of Avoca Mines that corpulent diva was already running through a few practice scales.

It came as a complete surprise to me, not to mention a shock, when my job application to the Company resulted in my being invited to come along to the Company's head office for an interview.

IT WAS THEN that I found out that Uncle Joe owned the Company. The Company was Uncle Joe's corporate metals sector subsidiary, involved in mineral exploration, mine development, mining and processing, and metals smelting and refining. Uncle Joe's preferred natural resources interests were of course vested in oil and petroleum products. I had heard of Uncle Joe – in fact, who hadn't? He was a multinational behemoth whose humble beginnings involved selling seashells by the seashore, but that was then and now was now.

I had of course never heard of the Company before I responded to its *Mining Journal* advert, but then, neither had the Company ever heard of me, so the honours were about even for us both prior to round one.

SUITABLY CLAD, I accepted the Company's invitation to be interviewed. The venue was to be the Company's head office, located somewhere in the centre of The Hague in the Netherlands. It was a daunting prospect for me to have to travel that far, especially since I didn't really want to. And yet, travel I did.

MR. THOMAS O'TOOLE was a genial resident of the riverside village of Avoca, and a man of many parts. Not only did he act as the somnolent security gateman lodged in the tobacco smoke-impregnated interior of the entry gatehouse to the Avoca Mines Limited office and processing plant facilities, but he also had a role as the provider of an independent local taxi service.

Thomas drove me in his taxi to Dublin airport where a scheduled Aer Lingus flight, on which a seat had been booked for me by the Company, was waiting for its appointed hour of departure for Schiphol airport outside Amsterdam. I was accompanied by my new suit, which was temporarily hidden from view in an appropriately named suitcase.

FOLLOWING MY ARRIVAL and the completion of landing formalities at Schiphol, I journeyed south to The Hague in a bus painted all over in the striking blue-on-blue livery of the Royal Dutch Airline, KLM. The interior of the bus was so spotlessly clean and the timing was so precisely punctual that I knew for sure that it did not belong to the CIE bus fleet that plied the highways and byways of Ireland in a manner that made a virtue of informality.

The Company arranged a comprehensive interview process for me over the full day following my arrival in The Hague. Overnight accommodation was booked for me in a hotel that it would be unfair not to describe as being much smaller than the Royal palace sprawling nearby. The hotel stood, feigning anonymity with reasonable success, in the depths of a narrow street located in the confusingly rabbit warren-like maze surrounding the city centre. A cat in search of a corner to crap in could have crept into my hotel room in the confident understanding that there was insufficient space available in which it might be swung before it crept out again.

I checked in at the hotel on a Thursday evening, which meant that The Hague's weekly late-night shopping experience was in full flow all around and about. The lights were bright, and there was movement in abundance. No street was too strait to attract either would-be shoppers or those who were simply out for an evening of ambling around in the comfort of a crowd. I came to learn at a later date that on every other evening of the week, when office hours drew to a grateful close, The Hague came appreciably close to resembling a ghost town.

I felt genuinely out of my depth, but I didn't so much mind that or for that matter give much thought to it, as being out of my depth was a situation that I was quite used to at that stage of my professional career. However, a sensed inadequacy to pit myself against whatever awaited me at the Company's interview on the following day made the sinking feeling somehow plumb a little more depth than usual.

A COUPLE OF months later, when I moved from Ireland to live in the Netherlands and commence working for the Company (from which it may be deduced that the interview had a successful outcome), my struggle to hold even a static salmon-like position in the diurnally flowing tides of new revelations became even more difficult to sustain. It so happened, in those days when Holland was new to me, that I waited at an automatic boom-controlled railway crossing over a road for an approaching train to pass. Once the train had gone by I ducked under the boom and crossed to the other side of the track. A Dutch railway official immediately chased after me and berated me in tones both loud and long for not waiting until the boom had risen so as to permit me to negotiate the track in safety.

"What if another train had been coming from the opposite direction or following the first train when you crossed?" he yelled. As he was addressing his remarks to me in Dutch it wasn't too clear to me what I had done wrong until a helpful observer offered a translation.

On the basis of my experiences in Ireland it hadn't occurred to me that two trains could possibly show up anywhere in close succession. A single passing train once a day was sufficient to excite comment in the Vale of Avoca, the more so in the improbable event that the train was actually passing by on schedule. I wondered what I had got myself into.

THE COMPANY WAS like an over-inflated ball made slippery by the lubricant-dabbling hands of certain of Uncle Joe's assignees to the senior ranks of its executive management. The respective practices of mining ore and producing oil blended with one another as well as if oil were oil and ore were water.

The radically different operating philosophies of the oil and mining approaches to exploration and development were barely reconcilable. Oil and big money went hand in hand, mining and big money generally didn't. Grandiose plans by Uncle Joe to use his oil business know-how to build the Company into a mighty stalwart capable of standing at the forefront of the world's mining industry by virtue of a thick chequebook, a full fountain pen and a thin time perspective were always destined to realise disappointment.

To be fair to them, the management executives that Uncle Joe placed in Company driving seats did express a willingness to develop in themselves an improvement in the appreciation of the nuts and bolts of the mining industry. Achieving an improved appreciation was all that was really possible for them since their appreciation of mining to start with could hardly have been more dismal.

A prime *quid pro quo* required of the Company from Uncle Joe in return for his always-welcome handouts was that an Uncle Joe-type culture should instil itself within the Company to the greater benefit of all concerned.

The inability of oil and mining aspirations to fashion a smooth mixture resulted in the premature toppling of far too many promising mining-oriented careers. Mining men fell like the trees of a pine forest to the chain saw in a rout of early retirement campaigns as the attempts by Uncle Joe's men to address the dichotomy took regular advantage of the faithful cure-all corporate ploy of when in doubt or in trouble, reorganise.

Uncle Joe's desires for the Company's future moved along rollers thickly eased by repeated squirts from Uncle Joe's money-stuffed grease gun. However, the success of his mining interests needed to be based on so much more than merely how much cash increasingly desperate executive managers were empowered to spend in order to buy themselves out of trouble.

It took time for the realisation to dawn, if indeed the sun ever did rise in that east, that success in mining exploration and production could only be based on an informed knowledge of and experience in the mining industry, on initiative-taking, on a spirit of adventure, on persistence in the face of disappointment and, last but by no means least, on having the right people based in the right place at the right time.

But then, at the end of the day as it was, when push came to shove, Uncle Joe would be there to bail his Company nephew out – so, hey, no worries.

THERE WERE JUST too many layers of decision-making involved in an Uncle Joe-inspired culture to permit the Company to ever reach the real head of the world mining game. In the less than customary event that the Company should come to place that right someone in that right place at that right time to be first in line to pick up a bargain project, the tortuous process of running a proposal to go for the project through level after level of a stupefying corporate hierarchy, probably right up to the dizzy heights of Uncle Joe himself, offered the guarantee that any envisaged deal would fall by time-inspired default into the hands of a competitor.

YET, THERE IT was really. Under the modestly benign scrutiny of a seemingly endless array of Uncle Joe's executive management assignees, the Company was putting a major effort into the recruitment of appropriately disciplined technical staff in order to form a team capable of fumbling the acquisition and development ball forward. According to the *Mining Journal*, the range of technical disciplines involved in the Company's recruitment drive included geology, mining engineering, minerals processing and metallurgical engineering. Professions concerned with the care and protection of the environment in a close alliance with health and safety considerations had yet to emerge as the shiny veneer by which so many of the regular activities of the mining industry would ultimately come to be judged and found wanting.

There was not an active mining operation that I knew of anywhere in the world in which the separate proponents of such a range of technical disciplines as those advertised were not regularly clawing at one another's throats in principle if not in practice. Conflicts at a technical level arose more or less as a matter of course. It was possible that, up in the more exalted levels of executive management, as with those of the Company, inter-disciplinary co-operation might be better (although I doubted it).

The mantra "Health, Safety and the Environment", or "HSE" in buzz-word terms, was something of a trickle-down institution. Great lip service was always paid to HSE policy in the highest corporate ranks while leaving those lesser mortals charged with implementing the policy down the line to suit their own devices in getting on with the job. The sharp and dirty end of mining operations tended to be left to stew in its own juice. As long as the monthly safety statistics reports didn't look too bad, all would be well, and since everyone knew that statistics could be used to present whatever those who produced them wanted to prove, all appearing well was what it usually was.

THE ENGAGEMENT BY the Company of so many new technical staff made it imperative that there should be a Personnel Department in place, as large as possible and the larger the better. The Personnel Department was intended to organise, administer and manage the welfare of the newcomers. That, naturally enough, spawned a Finance Department to allegedly keep all dealings above board. Neither the Personnel nor the Finance people were expected to know anything at all about the practice of mining, and so they could cheerfully be drawn directly from the eager ranks of the host that owed primary allegiance to Uncle Joe.

The Personnel Department was ultimately re-christened "Human Resources", or "HR" for convenience. HR was a title that must have been devised by someone with a well-developed sense of irony, as the chief characteristics of the self-indulgent way in which HR functioned were neither human nor resourceful towards those who came to it seeking a warm embrace but who too often found only a cold shoulder.

The Finance Department carried out its allotted duties on the clear principle that when money had been disposed of, irrespective of the propriety of the transaction, the money was "sunk" and therefore no longer worthy of further consideration. The sub-text to the principle of sunken money called for making a real go of it and spending a lot more. The talent of the Finance Department was vested both in turning minor cock-ups into major catastrophes and in rewarding the perpetrators with farewell golden handshakes of breathtaking proportions.

If only the Company's technical staff could have been as imaginative as the Finance and HR people were.

I WAS A mining geologist – or, not to put too fine a point on it, a geologist who worked in mines. In my case the mines I had previously worked in were chiefly of the underground variety. Mining geology was an applied science and thereby conferred on me the fortunate blessing of being unencumbered with any pressing need to worry about the more scientific or academic aspects of the geological profession in general.

My *modus operandi* was hands-on. The keystone of my work was the estimation and verification of what I considered to be the most vital assets possessed by a mining company – namely, the reserves of ore and resources of minerals.

As far as I was concerned, "ore" was a poorly understood word. Ore had been defined and redefined far too often by too many self-appointed experts accomplished at springing onto bandwagons. A rampant succession of such definitions had been subject to lively and broadly acrimonious debate for a century or more. In essence, ore comprised naturally occurring aggregations of minerals capable of being mined and processed to generate a product that could be marketed and sold at a profit.

Ore and profit were like love and marriage. They went together like a horse and carriage. You couldn't have one without the other. Together they made up an "institoot" you couldn't disparage.

With the constraining factors on the profitability of mines taken into account, not least those involving governmental, environmental, economic, technical and legal considerations, if there was then no profit to be made for a product eventually processed from estimated ore, then whatever material was mined to generate that product was not ore. If it was not ore there was no viable mine, no work available for mining people and, in the unkindest cut of all, the likelihood of no fees for avaricious executive directors.

As applied to executive directors in general, the term "avaricious" could be construed as redundant since it went without saying that a fondness for money of their very own was a characteristic widely spread through their ranks. On the other hand a declaration of redundancy was something that executive directors were well versed in evading, especially when it was applied to them. If, apart from banking money, there was one thing that a run-of-mill executive director was good at, it was hanging on to his lucrative position for dear life.

Of course, on the matter of such money, the existence of a creative pathway of verisimilitude leading well-reimbursed executive directors out of the valley of the shadow of dearth was never going to be in any doubt.

THE COIN-OF-THE-REALM appetites of executive directors notwithstanding, I believed that most of the technical professions related to the mining industry were not without honour. They stood out with distinction in a world in which the more traditional legal, medical, educational, political and financial professions were increasingly being shown to possess feet of clay.

I would not have wanted this to imply that the mining industry's technical professions were not noteworthy from time to time for their reliability in throwing up charlatans characterised by a staggering ingenuity to defraud, not least with respect to their uncanny prowess in manipulating ore reserve figures. Tight professional control of ore reserve reporting codes and standards was essential to constrain such egregious intentions, stay the clutching hands of executive direction and management, and so ensure confidence in the mining industry's integrity.

IT WAS ON the strength of being a mining geologist that I found myself about to be interviewed by the Company in connection with its imposing plans to grow into and dominate the mining world. If I approached the interview with reluctance, I came away from it only with a near euphoric relief that it was over. I bore not one shred of residual preoccupation as to the eventual result of the interview or its consequences, having already written my chances off to the legacy of much prior experience of rejection.

My interview occupied a full working day. It took place in a continuous sequence of half-hour segments, with an intervening break for lunch.

The half-hour segments were all one-on-one affairs, with a different interviewer participating each time. After the third segment, the line of questions directed at me took on a repetitive familiarity. All those who interviewed me were drawn from the Company's Technical Divisions and Personnel Department. I sat with them in a confusing plethora of individual offices scattered through a couple of floors of the Company's crammed head-office building. There were enough suits on view around the building to suggest the expert dissection of several hectares of cloth.

After a while I became bewildered as to who was who and what was what as I was shuttled from one pillar to another post and then on again. Although I had always had the ability to instantly recall faces (once seen always remembered), the face subjects' names invariably slipped from my mind a split second following the very instant that I heard them. An overriding impression, growing ever stronger through the interview sequence, was that I was being exposed to a level of operating skill so advanced in comparison with that which I was used to that its majesty was obscured in clouds a very long way above my head.

All those whom I met in the half-hour interview sessions impressed me with possessing genuine warmth. They came over as rather decent professionals. I estimated that only about a third of them were practised exponents in the art of bullshitting. Uncle Joe may have been proud of them all.

They were at their most confident in talking to me on the subject of budgets, with particular reference to how rapidly and by how much any budget could be increased and spent in the pursuit of projects.

Sums of six or seven figures and counting were tossed about with an air of casual abandon. That worried me. At the Avoca Mines, our budget allocations were of a truly anorexic nature. We regarded single and double figure sums with reverence and three figures with a sense of longing that Tantalus would have envied.

Big numbers were to me nothing if not a turn-off. If the least vestige of a mathematical formula should chance to appear in any technical paper I picked up to read, it would be a sure-fire certainty that my eyes would not be destined to feast on any other part of the balance of that paper, irrespective of whatever else of value it might contain.

Finance and cost figures, of the operating as much as of the capital variety, always numbed my mind. Merely grasping at the significance of the massive figures that I was being regaled with by my Company interviewers, let alone what the figures implied, was never going to be within my personal remit.

Remit – now that was a good buzz-word I picked up somewhat later, when I was in Toronto on Company business. A peripatetic type demanded to know what my remit in being in Toronto was, and I didn't know what my remit was, largely because I didn't know what remit meant. I had to go away and look the word up. Had he asked me what I was in there to do (a familiar question) I could have told him, but that would have made it too easy for him, I supposed.

ABOUT A YEAR or so after the fateful interview, I was sent by the Company to pursue my ore reserve estimation remit in Australia, at a mining property that the Australian subsidiary of the Company wished to acquire. I found the formally declared ore reserves for the mine in question to be unviable for mine production purposes owing to the very unstable and hitherto very undeclared geological conditions in the immediate vicinity of the overlying wall rocks adjacent to the mineral deposit. I reported accordingly that the reserves weren't ore.

The Company's local executive manager, who was known by the title of Metals Manager, was a dyed-in-the-wool flinty antipodean who appeared to see the acquisition of the mining property as a not unimportant step in the furtherance of his career. He was therefore unwilling to accept my report. An Uncle Joe man from his chip-laden shoulders to his supercilious core, he requested, or demanded was more like it, that I must report more favourably on the production prospects than the facts allowed me to. He went on to refer to me, in the open comfort of a pub of his choice, as a "bastard" when I politely declined his entreaty.

A colleague of this forthright Metals Manager then took me to one side and advised me that in this Uncle Joe-inspired hierarchical context my opinions could never be permitted to prevail.

"How much budget do you control?" he asked me.

I told him, none at all that I knew of.

"Well," he said, "in this Company, anyone who controls as little as one dollar of budget will have their opinion valued above yours!"

Control of budget created kings from those who filled the ambitious court of the technically incompetent. The more budget anyone controlled, the more important he was in the grand scheme of things. It appeared that the attainment of personal success was not about saving Company money; it was not even about spending Uncle Joe's money wisely; it was entirely about spending any available money purely for the sake of spending it.

That made it simple enough for me to rationalise why managing the disbursement of big budgets was prized above all other considerations by all Company executive managers riding eagerly on a direct, and hopefully fast, track to personal fame and fortune. Fame and fortune had to abide, these two, but the greatest of these was fortune.

THE COMPANY'S CAREER development policy for its employees was an Uncle Joe clone. Career planning was layered like jam on to the daily bread – fresh or stale it made no difference – of all professional disciplines. The planning mainly involved moving the favoured so-called fast trackers and high fliers from assignment to assignment on the basis of approximately three years per assignment. The actual duration of an assignment depended on the closing proximity of any posse in pursuit.

Three years was just about the optimum amount of time for anyone to spend on an assignment in order to ensure that the Company's best long-term interests could be sacrificed to a short-term expediency aimed at ensuring the personal advantage of the assignee. Those to whom assignments of this kind were handed saw them as the essential stepping-stones, or alternatively as crosses to bear, between successive promotions.

As a direct result of a new managerial broom regularly assigned to a local scene at three-year intervals, longer-term continuity of tenure counted for just about nothing. A great expertise in reinventing the wheel over and over again on a three-year cycle was established as a matter of course. Forward momentum was at best sluggish, even if the reinvented wheel was round and well able to rotate in the unlikely event that the right assignee might come along to push it. The re-creation of identical mistakes was a more or less mandatory feature of each triennial cycle. If any defects were eliminated along the way it was purely by accident involving a probable oversight.

A dozen years of experience in working on the mines of the Zambian Copperbelt were described to me by a well placed Company man (in a rare departure from bullshitting for a living) as, "one year's experience performed a dozen times over". The Company's three-year assignment cycle was not so very different from the Zambian model: two steps forward and two to three steps back probably summed up the results of a typical career-building assignment period reasonably well.

The assignees moved from one berth to another with all the verve and vigour of Samson emerging from a temple within which he had recently torn down a few key pillars. The edifice of whatever they had wrought in the preceding three years tottered and collapsed behind them as they strode onwards to greener pastures. The more monumental the ensuing cloud of dust rising over the sorry pile of debris and the greater the amount of money euphemistically sunk into the debacle, the more lucrative were the future rewards to be reaped by the perpetrators. Or so it seemed.

Blunders on a scale that could not be suitably covered up, irrespective of protective shields held by executive mentors in high places, were rewarded by severance settlements incorporating more than enough associated gold to set the miscreants up for life. The ordure of responsibility slid from their shoulders when they moved on as easily as if their neatly tailored suits were made of pure Teflon. If accountability for their actions ever chased after them, it never quite managed to catch up.

The troubled waters that they left in their wake as they steamed towards the next three-year island of personal advancement were usually smoothed out by a snake-eyed Company hatchet man, sent in to pour boiling oil on the waves, persecute the innocent, sack witnesses to the truth and reconstruct the shattered organisation to allow budget building to recommence all over again like *déjà vu* on a nailed-down platform of sunk costs.

THE ACQUISITION OF the Australian mining property for which my unfavourable report led to the legitimacy of my birth being questioned went ahead regardless. The ultimate financial loss to the Company was (allegedly) in the order of a couple of hundred million US dollars. That was the way it was. The Company's central filing system in The Hague was the graveyard in which embarrassing reports were buried to protect the culpable.

IT WAS INEVITABLE that attempts to construct a viable mine on the unfortunate Australian property would fail. The Company withdrew from the misadventure without batting an eyelid. The Metals Manager who presided over the whole sorry show was then awarded the position of CEO for Uncle Joe's down-under coal interests, thereby placing his feet even more firmly in budget heaven.

Even at an early stage of my employment by the Company it was not difficult to recognise that this kind of standard cock-up and mop-up equation could only balance out for just so long. In the absence of a radical change of direction the Company was eventually going to disappear up its own ass, no matter how ready Uncle Joe might be to cough up "Get out of jail free" cards.

TO GO BACK to my Company interview, in the cumulative time made available for the sequence of half-hour interview slots, I imagined that the day progressed as well as it could. The Company asked me to stay on for a second day of similar treatment, but their request rang no bells in my heart. Enough had been enough. I possessed a ticket on an Aer Lingus flight to return to Dublin that same night, and any question of changing the flight to the following day was not open to debate.

My flight back to Dublin was delayed by some mid-autumn fog around Schiphol airport, but I thankfully got away at long last. Thomas O'Toole picked me up in his taxi at Dublin airport. I reached home, hung up my new, off-the-peg suit, and left the garment to fend for itself.

A MONTH LATER, closing in fast on the festive period of Christmas, there were few things further away from my mind than thoughts of either the Company or Uncle Joe. Then, right out of the blue, I received a letter from the Company and started to think about it and its good old Uncle Joe once again.

It had been an odd December all round. There were days of such closely enveloping heat that the air seemed to have a liquid quality about it. A few strawberries grew to ripeness in my garden. The earthmoving contractor with whom I worked at the Avoca Mines was not infrequently accused by those who knew him well of "promising strawberries at Christmas", and lo and behold, there we were in the exceptional year that proved the rule.

Then the subsequent months of January and February elected to take counter measures by bringing in an elongated period of cold of a peculiar intensity. Ponds lay under thick ice, and snow flurries scuttled like white rats in blind corners.

AT THE COMMENCEMENT of all these vagaries of climate I received the letter from the Company offering me a job. The shock of having an actual job offer in my hand was much greater than it would ever have been had the Company, as I expected, turned me down.

The job offer placed me on the horns of a dilemma as to what to do. I had no wish to sever my association with Avoca Mines, to the extent that I would not even have attended the interview in The Hague had not the Avoca Mines General Manager, a much-respected long-term mentor, advised me to give it a try.

He followed this up by additionally counselling that I should accept the job offered by the Company, given that the future prospects for Avoca Mines did not have time on their side. After much soul searching I followed his recommendation. Avoca Mines actually closed down its operations about three years later.

THE DATE THAT I was due to commence work with the Company was the last day of January in 1979. It was a date auspiciously timed to coincide with the apogee of the dreadful winter's bite.

One single off-the-peg suit, no matter how ably resurrected, was unlikely to be sufficient to satisfy what my interview had led me to perceive to be the sartorial norms of the Company's head offices where I was to be based, according to the job offered me. It therefore seemed sensible to get hold at least one extra suit.

Mr John Flood, a master tailor from the tight little town of Wicklow, obliged by making me no fewer than three suits, three sports jackets and three pairs of trousers, one in blue, another in green and the third in brown. With these made-to-measure additions to my wardrobe I thought I was ready for just about anything.

Subsequently to the acquisition of these garments I never again purchased another suit. Moreover, if I counted up the total number of times between then and now that I was moved to don one or other of John Flood's creations, I would be able to count through all my fingers but would have to stop counting well before I reached the limits of my toes.

THE INITIAL JOB title awarded me by the Company was Senior Mining Geologist. By virtue of this, although I was directly assigned to the Company's Mineral Exploration Division, I was given at least a figurative handhold on the knob of the door barring access to the Mining Division. The job title offered me a dual allegiance akin to serving God and Mammon at the same time while walking on a sagging tightrope over a pit filled with sharp stakes. At Avoca Mines my job description according to the General Manager was "Do what you think is right!" Doing what I thought was right in the Company's head office generally satisfied neither of the two stools, Exploration and Mining, that I fell between.

The Company could actually boast of three technical divisions, although it didn't have the motivation to brag about it very often. "Division" was an appropriate way to describe each of the three, Exploration, Mining and Processing, as they were not only divided by internal conflicts but also totally committed to pitting themselves against each other given the least excuse.

Exploration was classified as an "upstream" activity and processing as "downstream". Whether or not that made mining "midstream" never came to be clarified. Without recourse to buzz-words, there would have been life in the Company Jim, but not as I came to know it.

The three divisions were respectively referred to in Company jargon as MTE, MTM and MTP. Since no one was in a hurry to tell me, I assumed (correctly as it turned out) that the empty part of the trio of initials had some association with "metals". Each of the three divisions employed an office-based staff complement about forty strong.

In terms of technical people, a combined total of a hundred and twenty could be considered by some to be close to scary. They may or may not have frightened the competition, but they certainly frightened me. An assembly of their combined tri-divisional might made a sight that was not so much impressive as overwhelming.

Every member of each of the divisions was labelled with a "reference indicator" related to his or her divisional acronym. Reference indicators were diagnostic of job descriptions. The construction of a reference indicator followed the guiding principle that although its current owner might change (or, given the Company's three-year assignment turnover routine, inevitably *would* change), the reference indicator would always be there to provide the illusion of continuity. This principle was, in its own right, a variation on the theme of "The King is dead, long live the King!" Reference indicators offered a most satisfying means of depersonalising the consequences of incompetence, particularly in cases where the consequences (although not necessarily the incompetence) were avoidable.

The first reference indicator that I was tarred with was MTE/215. The respective letters and numbers, not forgetting the forward slash that separated them, determined that I was employed in Section 2, Subsection 1 of the MTE Division, and that I had at least four colleagues in the same section, all of whom were more important than me.

I was informed – by none other than MTE/322, I believe – that one's status and salary level were in inverse proportion to the number of digits in one's reference indicator. The bigger the number, the less you got. On the strength of that advice, the top tip of the Company's totem pole was clearly towering high above my head.

The Company's CEO (Uncle Joe version) was equipped with the reference indicator MT, which gave me an impression that some shadowy type in the heart of Uncle Joe's outfit might very well bear the reference indicator M. Sometimes life followed art. To be fair, however, Uncle Joe's licences for Company kills were issued against projects rather than people.

If we entertained any doubts in our hearts over the love of the CEO and his executive disciples for the Company's people, we could always turn to an annual report and read about it there in black and white.

THE COMPANY'S HEAD office was spread through what was originally two adjoining buildings occupying one side of a secluded square. The united buildings were characterised by long, narrow and rambling corridors that presented something of a safety hazard to negotiate wherever they broke through and stepped up or down from one building into another. The lines of individual offices occupied by the MTE and the MTM Divisions were located on appropriately opposing sides of the first floor. The members of the two divisions sat at their desks behind an array of closed and blank-faced office doors and waited for something to happen.

With little more than a short hop, let alone a skip or a jump, it would have been possible to make an immediate transit across the corridor from the domain of MTM to that of MTE (or vice versa), had any two facing doors been open at the same time. Had the doors even been left a little bit ajar it would have helped. For all the lack of constructive trans-corridor contact that there actually was, the corridor might well have been a yawning abyss, at the bottom of which were large creatures with sharp teeth.

Members of the MTE Division seldom referred to the MTM Division by invoking the appropriate reference indicator. According to those who sailed under the MTE flag of convenience, the MTM Division was "those people across the corridor". I never managed to discover how the disparagement fared in a reverse context, if indeed anyone in the MTM Division ever really thought about the MTE Division at all.

Had I been pressed to do so, and regrettably I never was, I expect I could have made a few suitably impolite suggestions for the MTM people to take up *vis-à-vis* (as the expression went) some of the MTE types.

THE COMPANY APPEARED to me to marshal its forces in the manner of a colonising crusade. It demonstrated an almost compulsive intent to set up a subsidiary in as many of the countries of the world as was feasible in the shortest possible time. Uncle Joe had an established presence in most of those countries already, and so the basic support structures were understood to be in place. The leader of the MTE Division was a smoothly urbane Uncle Joe man fitted for the purpose with the reference indicator MTE (no surprise there). He had walked so many miles in a pair of shoes provided for him by Uncle Joe that no other footwear could fit him any longer. He envisaged that success in finding appropriate projects and making newsworthy discoveries lay in increasing annual budgets by geometrically proportioned leaps and bounds. That way, something positive had to happen, somewhere, probably, next year maybe.

North, south, east and west, all points of the compass were grist to the Company's mill, from the heights of Baffin Island in the far Arctic down to the insular arrow point aimed towards Antarctica at the bottom end of Tasmania. Every continent except Antarctica – and the Company was probably already working on invading the latter – formed part of the accepted fiefdom for exploitation. Company envoys operated at temperatures ranging from sixty above to sixty below. They mined gold at the foot of underground shafts 2,000 metres deep in South Africa, and developed open-pit copper deposits at altitudes up to 4,700 metres above sea level in the Chilean Andes.

In the process, no extreme of climate, geography, conduct or pattern of executive behaviour was ruled out.

One executive director of the Company favoured setting up subsidiaries only in English-speaking countries. Another would not consider favourably any proposal related to a country in which Spanish was not the mother tongue. Between the two they managed a pretty wide global spread. French-speaking countries were anathema to both.

THE KEY CRITERIA applied by the Company in targeting projects in those countries in those regions procured and occupied by those assigned to manage the occupation seemed to be vested in the *prima facie* assurance of the local availability of an acceptable range of five-star hotels and high-quality restaurants. Of equal importance was access to an unlimited supply of fine wines, and airline connections featuring aircraft equipped with first-class cabin sections.

To qualify as a regional manager the chief attributes for an incumbent were a demonstrated inability to speak the local language, a disdain for the local culture and a penchant for breaking eggs to make omelettes. These qualifications would never fail to set a Company regional manager apart as someone very special indeed and would, moreover, be sure to get him noticed by those who mattered in ensuring the furthering of his career.

In pursuit of the said objectives, the establishment of an elaborately furnished and appropriately overstaffed regional office served as the priority foundation stone of the Company's embassies in countless capital cities. It helped a lot that Uncle Joe already had his own well soled and better heeled foot in many of the influential doors of the same fair city. Uncle Joe and ubiquity went hand in hand.

If some of the capital cities were a little on the ratty or decrepit side, the regional manager could take comfort from knowing that he would be moving on to a more amenable setting in about three years' time, well before the organisation that he would by then have created commenced to fall apart under the burden of his screw-ups.

Once the apartments of the regional office were satisfyingly engorged with staff specified with indicators all suitably referenced and formalised within an elaborately constructed organisational chart, only then was it considered opportune for the regional manager to seek out business opportunities. The chart formed a tool vital to the regional manager's cause, since he could shuffle and prune it at will to provide the Company's head-office phone jockeys with a steady impression that dynamic things were happening in the region, even when they weren't.

As long as decisions were not pending which might – though heaven forbid that they actually would – result in moving a project from an upstream vantage point to a downstream development destination, the regional managers were content. They wanted to avoid the winds of progress that could shake the trees of complacency and thereby make their sinecures feel insecure. They countered any worries by adhering, as the ever-appropriate South African expression had it, "like shit on a woollen blanket" to projects that were perceived by outside observers to be of small account even at their inception and on which nothing subsequently happened to alter the colour of such crusty expectations.

THE SINGLE-MINDED zeal of the MTE Division and its closely affiliated regional managers to defend and protect their shared territorial imperatives at all costs, particularly when it came to preventing an intrusion from those people across the corridor, was buttressed by one supreme ace in the hole.

In the event that – in spite of everything humanly possible that could be done to delay or prevent its progress – a project reached a point when development and a likely role for the MTM Division were in the air (since, in the absence of the prospects of working with Greeks to deride, some projects actually went ahead on merit alone), the exploration manager on the spot was normally appointed to take charge of the development. The exploration manager was invariably a geologist, swearing fealty to the MTE Division. Possession was nine points of the law.

This fortunate circumstance guaranteed the retention of power in the hands of the MTE Division. It made, in its way, a natural succession from exploration to development, notwithstanding that a geologist of any stamp rarely (if ever) made a competent manager where development, construction and mining activity were involved.

The Company seemed to have a genuine talent for such right man/wrong job, wrong man/right job and wrong man/wrong job assignments. The assignments were part of a standard process of project evolution along a convoluted and anguished path ending in a "Lessons Learned" exercise. The path was paved with the dull tiles of inexperience, indecisiveness, arrogance, cover-up, budget escalation (not to say explosion) and economic meltdown.

Lessons Learned investigations always had a negative connotation. They were carried out only on the coat tails of failure and ostensibly designed to define what went wrong and why it went wrong so as to ensure that the same mistakes would never be made again. The investigators tended to be either those responsible for the debacle or, at the very least, the cronies of the same. Lessons Learned reports were prepared with what for the Company could be construed as unseemly haste, to be then briefly flashed to an eager public before being interred in that deep Central Files archive, impervious to the light of future day.

THE USUAL EVOLUTION of a project was best summed up in a Seven Stages list that once enjoyed a brief life posted on a Company notice board. The list, which spoke for itself, was set out on a single sheet of paper, meticulously lettered by someone experienced in the use of plastic stencils and a Rapidograph pen. The seven stages of a project were:

       1. Excitement
       2. Euphoria
       3. The dawn of reality
       4. The arrival of disillusion
       5. The search for the guilty
       6. The punishment of the innocent
       7. The distinction of the uninvolved

The seven stages formed a standard menu supporting the feeding frenzy of all involved in all too many projects sponsored by MTE Division. To the seven stages I thought might be added an eighth, namely "The rewarding of the real perpetrators", not to mention a ninth, "The inability to benefit from lessons learned".

WITHIN THE COMPASS of its three technical divisions, the Company employed many highly proficient individuals, although the vital glue that might have fastened and combined the various facets of their talent into an effective team never really seemed to be generated. As far as the regional managers were concerned, the common good was a sacrificial lamb at the altar of their personal ambition. There would always be somebody else for them to pin the blame on. Indeed, Uncle Joe's Company-imposed culture implied that this should be so, and so it came to pass.

It was then perhaps something of a personal delight for me that, in all the scrambling for power that typified so many of the internal machinations of the Company, and for all its corporate politicians who were prepared to play both ends against the middle and piss on the rubble of so many demolished careers, I met up with very few people in my years with the Company that I didn't like. The extent of my liking was not always accompanied by the level of respect that some of those concerned might have felt they deserved, but it was genuine for all that.

THE REGIONAL MANAGERS all came along to the head office in The Hague for a regular annual sequence of presentations spread over about a month and a half just prior to the commencement of the financial year. The respective presentations included proposed budgets for the following year, together with associated strategies, scenarios, schemes and scams, all delivered for the consideration of the executives occupying the killing fields at the centre of power. Like it or not, that was it. In this battle the regional managers had no high ground to command, whether of a strategic or of a moral character.

The annual budget presentations were garlanded about with sufficient masking generalities in the form of platitudes, obsequiousness of delivery and brightly coloured overhead slides to, as a rule, cover up the reality that the discoveries and worthwhile project acquisitions of the preceding year were few and far between and likely to remain so. In any case, the all-important control of budget was what it was all about, and the system in place decreed that there was really little danger of any grandiose proposal being turned down.

The overall process of the presentations, as regional managers came and went in their allotted revolving-door sequence, was carried out in an increasingly intensifying atmosphere of forced optimism that would have been familiar to Prince Prospero briefing his caterers on the eve of the Masque of the Red Death. The Emperor's new clothes were hanging in the Company's closet, and the closet door was clearly ajar, exposing at least some of the ethereal garments to public view.

The co-ordinating framework in which the grab bag of combined regional budget presentations formed a strut was a Master Plan controlled from the head office. Persistent delays in the execution of the demands of the Master Plan were vaguely acknowledged prior to being dismissed with a languid wave of the hand as mere bagatelles.

Failure of the Master Plan was not an option that was ever mentioned, at least in any open forum. If Great Discovery 1 was not made in Year 1 of the Master Plan, it was simply assumed that Great Discoveries 1 and 2 would take place in Year 2. When Year 2 joined Year 1 in the wasteland of sunk money, then confidence was expressed in making Great Discoveries 1, 2 and 3 in Year 3. And so on.

THE BUDGET PRESENTATIONS were held in one of those imposing boardrooms furnished with an ultra-long and rather narrow elliptically shaped table made of some form of light coloured and highly polished wood. It wasn't important to know the type of wood involved. As long as the wood looked expensive, which it did, it was sufficient unto the day.

The boardroom table could seat about thirty people around it if everyone edged their chairs together and drew in their stomachs, the latter requirement forming something of a challenge in several well-fed executive cases. However, such seating arrangements only accounted for the first thirty to arrive.

It required no more than a rumour that a budget presentation was about to take place for the hordes to be immediately drawn out of their individual offices or any of the other cubbyholes in which they chose to keep their heads down during working hours. The grander the scale of a presentation, the greater was the consensus of acknowledgement that it offered a great way to pass the better part of a morning or an afternoon, or preferably both. Whether the subject of the presentation was of interest or not was immaterial to the cause.

Such mass gatherings featured an unlimited flow of coffee, against which inspiring incentive to be there the formal agenda of the presentation paled into insignificance.

Once the thirty or so seats around the boardroom table were taken up, chairs were commandeered from other parts of the head-office building to seat the latecomers. The good, the bad and the ugly took up their positions. The boardroom table lay like a piece of flotsam in a rippling sea of faces.

A TYPICAL BUDGET presentation was designed to be drawn out over a lengthy enough period of time for the regional manager making it to be sure that the vital comments he made at the outset would be swept out of mind under the spate of the turgid overhead slide-dignified deluge of dross that followed afterwards.

Questions were nominally permitted at the end of a presentation, although most of the questions asked had such a prearranged feel about them that they were almost certainly engineered to comply with the requirements of minutes that had been written before the presentation started. An occasionally perceptive question, of the type that threatened to expose an uncomfortable truth, was quickly shot down in flames by one or other of the upper echelon executives present. They were trained to have both a vested abhorrence to boat rocking and a love of big budgets for their own sake.

ONE SUCH PRESENTATION, in setting out a budget for a large development and mining project at a tin deposit in Nova Scotia, extolled the technical merits of the project to such an over-the-top extent that those sitting around the oval table could be forgiven for thinking that even sliced bread came no better than this. On the other hand, the presentation seemed to take great care in avoiding making any reference to the status of the project's mineral resources and ore reserves.

Seeing this as an omission with a sun-like glare about it, I thought I had better ask the presenter for an appropriate comment and did so, rather timorously given that the audience was at a minimum count forty strong. "How should I know about ore reserves?" the Canadian presenter replied to me, "I'm only a fuckin' mining engineer!"

I think that in all the budget presentations I attended – and, let's face it, I found myself equally ready to put in coffee-drinking time around the oval table in order to discuss whether or not support should be given to budgets that had already obtained all the support necessary behind closed doors elsewhere in the building – that this was the most honest answer to a technical question that I ever heard.

As a mining geologist it was my stock in trade to know that within any naturally occurring mineral deposit the portion of the said deposit that could be developed and mined as ore was a function of its geological characteristics. Wherever I had worked prior to joining the Company, my task in the general scheme of things had been to render the geological contribution to the assurance of mining production into a form couched in as many monosyllables as possible so that even a fuckin' mining engineer could understand it.

To perform the task of simplification effectively, the great barrier that I usually had to surmount was the fact that most of the others in the cast of characters primarily involved in mine production – albeit those fuckin' mining engineers, or mine captains, or shift bosses and miners at the working face – all loathed mining geologists. They had no greater liking for geologists of any stamp, pure or applied, of course, but that brought me no comfort at all. All it did was to give me a feeling that I was being despised for my profession even before the opportunity to demonstrate how I practised it came along.

All of which was fair enough, I supposed, since a majority of geologists, mining or whatever, could without fear of contradiction easily be classified as dyed-in-the-wool smart-asses. Geologists were normally university-educated and, as such, were more than ready to use their lettered qualifications as clubs to suborn those among their fellow workers in the mining industry whose educational opportunities had been more restricted. The higher the class of geological degree and the greater the propensity to academic orientation, the more pronounced was the insufferabilty of character of geologists in action on the mining front.

In my early dealings with underground miners I was misdirected and misinformed by them as a matter of course. It was quite odd, as I held their fund of practical experience and know-how in such regard that it was a privilege to rub shoulders with them. For their part they refused me co-operation, and among other delights at their hands I was spat at, openly cursed, ignored, physically menaced, threatened with dismissal, deliberately sent a few times into harm's way, reported to management in adversarial terms, bypassed, and, well, the list went on. As Al Read's signature tune ran, it was necessary to "Show them you can take it, on the chin, with a grin". Such was life. Life with real mining people was what you made it.

I resolved that whenever I might attain a position senior enough (which seemed doubtful in itself) to have the authority to do so, I would act to break down the barriers of distrust. As far as I was concerned, conflictive relationships would not be permitted to exist within or without the scope of any mining geological group that I should have responsibility for.

Although the traditional conflicts were probably not about to be wiped out overnight, attrition through persistence and example was the best route to success. I insisted that every contribution made to a project or a mining operation, no matter who made it or how great or how humble it was, deserved a consistent measure of respect. That went as much for the man carrying the honey bucket as for the Head of Personnel. Both of them moved shit for a living in any case.

It was all about goodwill. The demonstrated capacity of anyone to move well beyond the halfway point to strike a compromise was a jewel to be coveted and worked on every time.

All types of people responded in kind to a genuinely warm and open hand. I wondered why the corporate politicians that Uncle Joe and the Company loved so much seemed to be so unaware that this was so. Treating everyone in a consistently friendly and positive manner opened doors everywhere. I found that I came to relate much better and more comfortably to the middle and lower levels of organisations of all kinds than I did to those occupying the top, who were by and large, and I meant it most sincerely, a bunch of overweening prigs. I hope I spelt that last word correctly.

I quickly discovered that in all instances where there were endemic problems in inducing people to work together in a co-operative environment the indifference of top management was almost invariably one of the root causes.

IN THE COMPANY'S head office I took steps in my intrusive territorial dealings with the MTE and the MTM Divisions to try to promote a spirit of cross-corridor co-operation. It was no easy task when faced with a situation where not only was there precious little of the co-operative commodity to build on but the lack of the same was palpable.

For my opening salvo I decided to visit those people across the corridor and talk to them. My action might well have established a Company record for in-house pioneering. Interestingly and to some extent incredibly, the fourteen years of underground mining experience that I had accumulated up to that time exceeded the combined total of years of similar experience for all head-office members of the MTE and MTM Divisions put together.

What this disparity implied to me was that even though I was incapable of relating to the array of vast dollar figures being constantly voiced around me with so much throw-away nonchalance, there was a hands-on skills gap in the organisation that I could readily fill. That was just about all I knew on earth and all I needed to know.

Filling the gap required me to ride out the many rebuffs that my spirit of initiative drew from both sides of the MTE/MTM divide. In the business context, I thought, virtue didn't bring along rewards in the short term, but for those like me who were willing to play the long game it could be another matter. Barriers always collapsed under steady pressure, provided that the exerted pressure came from a credible direction.

A COMMON CHAIN linking many members of the MTM Division was time spent in Suriname working at the Company's open-pit bauxite mining and associated alumina refining operations. Bauxite was a sack term describing a deposit of residual soil of shallow depth but great areal extent, carrying ripely hydrated oxides of aluminium, and more than enough silica, beneath a durable ferruginous crust. Suriname was a former Dutch colony on the Caribbean coast of South America and appeared, from the nostalgic tone that those who had been former expatriate assignees to the bauxite mines put into talking about it, to represent a flowering field in Elysium.

My own feeling about Suriname, following an initial visit, was that the best means of seeing the country was from a window seat in a departing aircraft.

THE HEAD OF the MTM Division, whose reference indicator was MTM, was a dour and fussy professorial type whose association with the front end of the mining industry was as cursory as his smile and as thin as his lips. His gentlemanly attributes were, however, many, and far too well developed to permit him to function with success in front-end mine management. He not infrequently invited me to "refresh his memory" on aspects of mining practice. Where underground mining was concerned I had the feeling that I could have told him anything and he would have believed it without compunction.

On each occasion when we met in his personal office, the Head of the MTM Division routinely opened a side drawer in his desk, from which, with an air of great solemnity, he took out a pad of A4-sized paper. He flicked through the pad until he came to the first blank page, on which, with a thick-nibbed fountain pen, he drew an impressively straight line down the centre, from top to bottom. Then he wrote the relevant date in the top right-hand corner of the page.

As we talked, the Head of MTM Division took notes steadily, sometimes writing on one side of the vertical line, sometimes on the other. On reaching the bottom of one page he turned over to the next, drew another vertical line and continued with his hip-hopping sequence of notes. At the conclusion of our meeting he placed a horizontal line, just as straight as any he had so far drawn, directly beneath his last entry.

The Head of MTM Division must have had a vast collection of such notebooks filled out in this way and filed away somewhere, all of them probably in chronological order. They formed an archive that might have served as a *bona fide* monument to futility. I didn't know when, or if, he ever referred to his notes on our conversations and I suspected that he didn't. Note-taking was perhaps the Head of MTM Division's security-blanket manifestation.

THE DEPUTY HEAD of MTM Division, as fine a burden sharer as was ever created for just that purpose, sat in an office adjoining that of the divisional Head himself, behind a desk piled half a metre high with tottering stacks of paper, files and trade magazines. The Deputy Head's presence at his desk in his office could, on the rare occasions when his office door was open, be confirmed either by a glimpse of the top of his head cresting the paper battlements or, when the sheeted piles were at their ultimate height, by the curls of tobacco smoke rising from behind them.

Had anyone dared to excavate down to the base of the Deputy Head of MTM Division's ascendant stacks of desk-bound documents, I was sure that it would have resulted in the discovery of tomb-like archives lurking there, compressed into a time-dependent compact solidity.

THE COTERIE OF mining engineers in the MTM Division that these two paper tigers supervised, with or without the association of forgotten and forgettable documentation, were for the most part placid hirelings who believed that if bauxite was not a feature of any project then the project was unworthy of their critical attention. They were masters in the art of turning run-of-the-mill routine into a virtue. They guarded the exclusivity of their interest in all Company matters related to bauxite, irrespective of how tenuous the association might be, with a tenacity that would have been almost religious in its zeal had it not been trussed up in so many overtly political overtones.

In the book of rules of the mining engineers of the MTM Division, the questing eyes of any member of the MTE Division were not destined to feast themselves on the mysteries of bauxite exploitation.

I didn't take it too much to heart. People who were accustomed to hard-rock mining regarded the mining of bauxite as little more than glorified earthmoving – or, more aptly, mud shifting. Since bauxite deposits had the unfortunate habit of occurring in parts of the world in which tropical deluges were commonplace, not for nothing were they described as "bauxshite" by some of their less dedicated proponents.

CAUGHT UP ON the dilemma-generating horns of my mining geologist's job title in that long corridor of MTE and MTM contestation, it was inevitable that I was drawn – not too long after I joined the Company, as it happened – into becoming a member of the so-called "Flying Circus".

Oscar Wilde might have described the Flying Circus as "the unspeakable in full pursuit of the unfeasible", although unfortunately Oscar wasn't there to be able to do that. It was Oscar who described work as being "the curse of the drinking classes", thereby implying that the concept of what the Flying Circus did best was not entirely foreign to him.

The Flying Circus was not all that inappropriately named. To justify one aspect of its name, it flew, making use of aircraft, rather frequently in fact. The Flying Circus was additionally adept at going around in circles, and moreover its members included many who conducted precarious balancing acts and others who, when in restaurants, demonstrated the feeding habits of animals. It was especially celebrated over the years by featuring much more than its fair share of clowns.

IN PRINCIPLE THE Flying Circus was set up as a multi-disciplinary technical team, capable of mobilisation at short notice for travel to any part of the world where its services might have been required, although not necessarily accepted. Those who required the Flying Circus to be despatched to specific destinations were almost invariably to be found amongst the more elevated executive ranks at the head office. The regional managers tended not to want, not to need and definitely not to welcome the administrations of the Flying Circus, so it was just as well for the regional managers that they had little choice in the matter.

The regional managers tended to think of the Flying Circus as a flock of seagulls that flew in, shit on any exposed surface and flew out again. Head office and assistance were a contradiction in terms as far as the regional managers were concerned.

Not to put too fine a point on it, the attention of the Flying Circus was a near certainty to place the kiss of death on pretty much any project that fell into its multiple-faceted hands. Flying Circus troubleshooting was carried out from the hip. Its recommended solution to most mining operational problems involved spending far more money than the relevant regional manager was willing or able to stand.

The absence of a ha'p'orth of tar meant far more to the Flying Circus than did the existence of a sturdy ship.

THE TECHNICAL DISCIPLINES that went into the construction of a typical Flying Circus team (or perhaps "group" would be a more relevant word to collectively describe such a varied bunch of guys following entirely personal agendas and placing their best endeavours into undermining one another) were vested in the persons of a mining geologist, a mining engineer, a metallurgist, a processing engineer, an environmental engineer, an infrastructure man and an economist or finance man.

A few other characters might also enlist themselves in a Flying Circus group, especially if the intended destination was an exotic location.

When Rio de Janeiro was the port of call, for example, the regional manager on the spot could always count on the arrival of a suitably extended Flying Circus group, with at least one member's set of personalised luggage containing scuba-diving equipment.

On a Flying Circus visit to Whitehorse in the Yukon Territory of Canada in the late spring of one year, the group's infrastructure expert stepped out of a taxi into a sidewalk snow bank that, oddly enough, no animal, whether four or two-legged, had yet peed on, and he remarked, "Snow! It must get cold up here!"

It was in Whitehorse that the real glory of the Flying Circus was best characterised. The visiting group, at least eight strong, was walking along in the vicinity of the Whitehorse River, close to a derelict stern-wheeler that had once graced the passage down to Dawson in Klondike gold-rush days but was then marooned on the riverbank. A pickup truck, encrusted with salt derived from the winter sowing on the Yukon roads, approached the group. The driver gesticulated from the window open on his side. The group waved back at him to offer him the warmth of its greetings as well. As the pickup sped by, the driver shouted from the window "Go home, ya fucken tourists!" It was a moment that even Shakespeare could not have improved on.

The Company required all employees intending to travel internationally on its business to complete a requisition form for the trip and submit it to the executive director designated to sign off and authorise the travel costs. Such requisitions were delivered to the no-doubt eager executive director in ream-like sheaves, one pile for requisitioned intercontinental travel and another for journeys within Europe.

The way the system worked was that the executive director assumed that anyone wanting to undertake intercontinental travel must have had a good reason to do so, otherwise he wouldn't have filled out the form.

Intercontinental travel requisitions were therefore signed off by the executive director without as much as being glanced at, other than to locate the dotted line on which his signature would be scrawled.

Travel within Europe, however, was quite another matter. There was an enhanced executive awareness of the existence of fleshpots in European cities. European travel requisitions were therefore subject to intense scrutiny. The executive director knew something about reading between lines to seek out the underlying motivation for European business travel, perhaps through recalling either his former experiences in a lower-ranking life or his current predilections.

It was the assigned economist who normally led any Flying Circus group. As a numbers man, such a leader didn't need to have any technical understanding of exploration and mining at all, equipped as he was with all the necessary skills to arrange the numbers to make a project look either good or bad, or both of the above at the same time. One or other of the Company's executive directors would most probably have slipped the word to the designated leader on the nature of the preferred outcome to a Flying Circus evaluation. The final result might well hinge on that great imponderable as to whether or not the locally spoken language was English or Spanish.

There were few members in any given Flying Circus group who were not concurrent members of one or more frequent-flyer schemes run by certain of the world's better-known airlines. Accumulating a massive inventory of frequent-flyer points was first and foremost the true beauty of air travel for most of them.

Those entitled by virtue of rank (not to mention the pulling of a well-connected string here and there) to fly in the ostentatious setting of first-class cabins were prepared to settle for no less than first class all the way. If ever first-class seating was not available to them, well, they didn't fly. It was as simple as that. They were first-class people to the limit of their own personal satisfaction. Being fawned over in the air was their stock in trade. Hubris it was. They were caught up in life, liberty and the pursuit of self-gratification.

Bringing ingenuity to the design of an itinerary, and being blessed with a squared-away associate in the Company's travel department, the more experienced Flying Circus travellers were generally well able to follow preferred routes on their selected airlines in their cabin of appointed class and never be forced to suffer the ultimate indignity of having to associate in flight with those members of the public who were actually reduced to paying their own fares.

The great unwashed mob destined to occupy the rear end of an aircraft was equally avoidable by members of the Flying Circus during transit stops in the confines of airports through the expediency of repairing to the hushed hallows of first-class airline lounges. A wave of a boarding pass and a slapped-down frequent-flyer card, and the Flying Circus was in.

They strolled disdainfully past the trolley-garnished, static check-in lines of the common man. Not for them came the need to struggle with heavy luggage and hot frustration on the shore of a sea of unsuppressed tantrums. They could relax in a smarmy world of polished chrome fittings and garish furniture and partake of snacks and coffee of indifferent enough quality to make it a blessing that they were gratis, while basking in the gleam of fixed, full-toothed smiles from a string of wary-eyed flight attendants.

The Flying Circus was at home with opulence, although since its members were not in their own homes when they travelled, they were easily able to overlook any necessity to be tidy. Magazines and newspapers were for slinging around and leaving wherever they fell, crumbs were for dropping on the floor and treading into the carpet, drinks were for spilling on upholstery, towels were for throwing in a sodden heap on hotel bathroom floors. This was first class! Someone would always be there to pick up after them, and if the menials didn't like it, that was just too bad.

THE MOST INVENTIVE traveller in the Company's employ was a senior geophysicist of Polish extraction, whose declared lifetime ambition was to set foot in every country in the world at least once. He might typically route himself to Australia via the Azores, Namibia, Mauritius, the Seychelles, Sri Lanka, Singapore, Vietnam and Indonesia. It would have been no surprise to find Fiji and Tahiti included in the same itinerary, but he probably held on to those cards pending a visit to Chile via Easter Island and Juan Fernandez. He never forgave me for making a business trip to Albania.

A senior executive whose main focus of interest lay in matters relating to the acquisition for the Company of properties underlain by the well-nigh unavoidable bauxite so beloved of MTM Division, was addicted to making comprehensive changes to his personal itineraries, commencing from the very moment that his first-class ticket was delivered into his ever-willing first-class hand. His penchant was for arranging to land himself in an airport so as to make his period of transit coincide with that of one of his peers from a competitor company in order that he might hold a meeting for as much as a couple of minutes. He might equally endeavour to meet up with a dignitary related – at least between *coups d'état* – to the government of a republic hot enough and wet enough to lay claim to both the ownership of bauxite resources and the extensive cultivation of bananas, although he wouldn't rule out meeting anyone else that he could try to impress with just how pretentiously important he was.

For the duration of his visit to any country in which the Company had set up an outpost, this worthy carried the twin guarantees of keeping at least two secretaries permanently busy on rearranging and then re-rearranging his forward journey and of generating a telephone bill for the Company's account offering no change from a thousand dollars or more.

That no regional manager was motivated to present the said senior executive with a first-class kick up his first-class ass said as much about the regional managers as it did about him.

TIME SPENT IN the air was what the Flying Circus craved. Time in flight reflected a great corporate dynamic. According to more than one regional manager, the more time the Flying Circus could spend sitting in an aircraft at 35,000 feet, the less time it had available to it to inflict damage to projects on the ground.

Encapsulated in the first-class cabin, the members of the Flying Circus were the recipients of airline bounty wrapped in a routine of vainglorious behaviour. Elaborate menus dignified in-flight meals for which presentation counted for a lot more than palatability, and style strove against substance and lost out every time.

THAT GREAT PROFESSOR of geology at Imperial College, H. H. Read, once wrote that there were "granites and granites". In the golden realms of corporate first-class travel, there were, to borrow from the professor, bullshitters and bullshitters. Some of the goodly Flying Circus members could bullshit better than others maybe, but the elite among the practitioners of the art were those who saw themselves as wine fanciers.

When I was a small boy I overheard a story told by a customer in my village barber's shop about a hillbilly who entered the lobby of the

Waldorf Astoria hotel in New York carrying a rifle and a bucket brim full of some form of shit. The hillbilly placed the noisome bucket on the lobby floor, aimed his rifle at the bucket and fired a shot into it. Officials ran to gather around him to demand an explanation for his conduct. "Well," said the hillbilly, "I was told that if I wanted to get ahead in New York I had to come to the lobby of the Waldorf Astoria and shoot shit!"

It was only when I came to acquire a seat on the fringe of a bunch of corporate and Flying Circus types discussing a wine list that I finally understood the punch line of that gag.

AIRLINE SLIPPERS, TOILETRIES and in-flight souvenirs were handed out to Flying Circus members by a rotating succession of cabin crews. The hallmark on the silver cup of international business traveller experience was stamped in accordance with the degree of indifference with which such largesse was received. It was unclear whether or not thanks from the receivers to the donors were necessary, as none were ever given.

The Flying Circus soared over wars, poverty, famine and natural disasters, taking the whole lot in its stride. That was all down there and they were all up here. They sat in comfort, waited on while they slugged vintage wines, watched movies that for the most part the word mediocre was coined to describe and deluded themselves that this was all going to last for ever.

THE DOWN SIDE was that their cosseted travel arrangements occasionally fell a little way short of what was desirable when the need to actually visit a project site became unavoidable. The first rule of visiting a project site was to eschew the kind of overnight stop in which the only view of the accustomed five stars was to be obtained through a hole in the bunkhouse roof.

Projects and mining operations had an unfortunate tendency to be located in remote places, and as such could only be reached by virtue of a journey of some hours duration over a road that, no matter how bad it may have seemed on the way in, was going to feel a great deal worse on the way back. Unless, that is, there was a nearby airstrip long enough not only to land a twin-engine aircraft on but also, much more importantly, to allow the aircraft to take off from soon afterwards.

Company safety regulations for its roving executives called for the availability of two engines on any light aircraft transporting them, with both a pilot and a co-pilot in the cockpit, one for each engine presumably.

THE POLICY RELATED to site visit reports was that they should be avoided in the first place, but if they couldn't be avoided then as little as could be got away with should be written in them. The best way for the Flying Circus to get away with not writing a site visit report was not to visit the site.

Certainly, nothing should ever be written into a visit report that would do anything other than reflect credit on the Flying Circus to the total detriment of the regional manager as a first preference, followed in close succession by invective directed at the project or mine operators on site in order to add the icing to the cake of disparagement.

In any case, when the Flying Circus was on site, both the regional manager and the mine operators could be mollified by being told exactly what it was that they wanted to hear. The brickbats could always be saved for insertion into the Flying Circus's subsequent visit report, traditionally written on the far side of an advantageous barrier of great distance.

And that, my boys, was a job well done!

But of course, it wasn't.

– 3 –

Dinner at the Golf Café Bar

Coldly, coldly to the north-east we bade farewell to Marseille,
The sea ran, one glorious blue-green, leaking into Algiers Bay,
Brown on the burning landmass the Atlas ramparts lay,
In the dimmest south-east distance stretched the desert, gaunt and grey.
There lay Tamanrasset, Timbuktu and Niamey,
And here and there the Niger flowing slowly, slick with gley,
While Ouagadougou trembled yonder, silent in Africa.

With apologies to Mr Robert Browning

IT WAS AROUND mid-morning on an April day when I was startled to hear my name announced over a public address system. I was at Terminal 1 in the Paris Charles de Gaulle airport, having recently arrived from Amsterdam as a passenger on one of KLM's species of the smaller Boeing aircraft.

Being paged made a new and not altogether satisfying experience for me. Whenever I set my feet to ground at a French airport I needed to dig deep into my stores of goodwill to uncover a scrape or two of bonhomie, and the crackly echo of the PA announcer's voice did little to make the excavation process seem any shallower.

I felt exposed to public scrutiny, as if I had been caught in the sudden beam of a roving searchlight. The cloak of anonymous reserve under which I preferred to travel seemed to drop in shreds around me.

An acquaintance who once occupied a fairly senior position in the Geological Survey of Canada and who flew around a lot (in Canada at any rate) developed the practice of always having himself paged at any airport in which he found himself at liberty and with time to spare. His fervent hope, he told me, was that in casting the hooked bait of his name into the great pool of loose-ended bored and idle fellow travellers that lapped into every last corner of most airport facilities, he would reel in someone who might have heard the paging announcement and be motivated to seek him out as a consequence. There might also, much more importantly, be a free drink in it for him.

Whatever the Charles de Gaulle pager's metallic assault on my celebrity portended, I was sure that a complimentary beverage was unlikely to be involved. Being paged was not normal, and I was never comfortable with deviations from the norm where air travel and its trappings were concerned. Air travel was all about doing things by prescription. Anomalies damaged my over-developed sense of personal insecurity. Since I had to contemplate a later connecting flight onwards with Air France, an airline that some of my colleagues were not reluctant to refer to as "Air Chance", the paging didn't help matters at all.

Faced with no other alternative, I duly presented myself at the specific checkpoint designated by the pager. Trepidation was unfounded. I was introduced to an airline attendant who expressed an eagerness she may not really have felt to escort me from Terminal 1 to Terminal 2A where I was due to join the Paris to Ouagadougou leg of that afternoon's Air France flight to Abidjan.

The first-class ticket that I was clutching in my hand may have encouraged the deference that I was shown by the attendant in our joint journey to Terminal 2A through a weird and essentially unwonderful maze of plastic-tubed escalators and rough concrete passages.

On the way, the attendant advised me that the Air France flight was full, or at least would be full as far as Ouagadougou. I had never previously visited Ouagadougou, or Ouaga as it was referred to (not without affection) by those who claimed to know it well. I knew that Ouaga was the capital city of Burkina Faso in French-speaking West Africa and – well, that was about all I knew on earth and possibly all I needed to know about it for now.

Burkina Faso was formerly named Upper Volta, in which capacity its international reputation was chiefly distinguished, in a 1966 edition of *Encyclopaedia Britannica* that I once consulted, as the country with the world's lowest average life expectancy.

On this claim to enduring fame, Burkina Faso offered me a portrait of an ultimate pit of deprivation and despair. I could but trust that the change of name from Upper Volta to Burkina Faso had served to improve the social situation. It could hardly have made it worse. When place names change in Africa, recent *coups d'état* are never conspicuous by their absence.

Why an entire plane-load of people was going to Ouaga was a question that begged to be answered. What they would all do when they got to Ouaga was another question equally pressing. Most likely, I thought, I would be the only passenger to disembark in Ouaga as the balance of my fellow passengers sat out the stopover *en route* to the greater delights of a final destination of Abidjan, down in the Côte d'Ivoire.

I WAS OF course well versed in my own motives for flying to Ouaga. My journey was a means to an end. My ultimate destination was the bush town of Poura and the associated gold mine of the same name located in the southwest of Burkina Faso. Poura was reached by travelling for a couple of hours out of Ouaga by car along the main road linking Ouaga with Burkina Faso's second city, Bobo Dioulassou, and then turning left on a broad dirt track. Those worthies who liked to refer to Ouagadougou as Ouaga were equally apt to speak of Bobo Dioulassou as Bobo.

Having reached Poura, I was due both to undertake a technical examination and appraisal of the gold mine and its ore reserves and to assess the mineral exploration potential of its surrounding property. The fact that the spoken language of Burkina Faso was French didn't seem to have made any impression yet on those who sent me thither. I assumed they were saving that card to play as part of their eventual exit strategy.

THE FLIGHT TO Ouaga from Charles de Gaulle took off only half an hour after its scheduled departure time. On the scale of customary delays, that was close to punctuality. The first-class cabin ambience supported a notion that Air France had recently discovered "business class" and had added fractionally more leg room to effect the upgrade. Lunch was served, a meal that owed much more to the way it looked than to how it tasted.

The duration of the flight to Ouaga was to be five hours, an amazingly short bridge to the third world, with no second world on the way to soften the suddenness of the gradation. Poverty increased and multiplied in silence all the way down beneath a barrier thirty thousand feet high.

As the flight progressed, I looked in my briefcase for some scope of work documents in order to go through a semblance of reviewing the tasks that faced me at Poura. The documents had been right there in a pocket in the briefcase when I left Amsterdam that morning, since I took a look at them on the way down to Paris. However, that location was no longer true of the documents. It occurred to me that I might have left them on that first flight of the day, which meant that they were most likely to be on their way back to Amsterdam, showing a better sense of preferred direction than I had done. The loss of the documents was not a disaster, but for all that it was hardly auspicious.

There was some small consolation in there having been not all that much in the strayed documents to look at, as the contained details could only have been described as comprehensive by someone dedicated to the art of hyperbole. Unfortunately, their absence left me unable to perform the mandatory business traveller routine of exposing credentials in the flight cabin in order to create a suitable image of self-importance to impress fellow passengers. It was not that the routine did actually impress anyone, but you never could tell, and it was always worth a try.

The prolific application of a highlighter pen, preferably of the fluorescent yellow variety, to colour in large swatches of business documents provided vital support in the endeavour to convince fellow passengers who sat and stared that a critical mission was in progress, with sums riding on it from seven figures upwards. Further bonus points were accrued from having a chunky, hand-held calculator accessory, although for the ultimate self-esteem of the terminally conceited, an open laptop computer on the tray table was sure to carry the day.

The golden key to acquiring business kudos was not that the in-flight business traveller should genuinely be doing any work but rather that he or she should present a strong impression of appearing to be working to those who patently were not. The critical agenda was to make oneself feel good by making others feel guilty.

Faced with a lost-document-generated inability to read what I was supposed to do when I got to Poura, I was reduced to doing my best to recall it from memory. First and foremost, I remembered that the Company's representatives based in Accra down in Ghana claimed to have despatched, a couple of days previously, a four-wheel drive vehicle (not forgetting a driver) to meet me on my arrival in Ouaga. The state of Ghana's roads decreed that both the two days and the four-wheel drive elements were essential if the vehicle was to reach Ouaga in good time.

If Accra to Ouaga sounded like a pretty long drive, it was all of that. Some time later when I followed the route in reverse and came to appreciate the shattered, junk-lined battlefields that masqueraded as roads in Ghana's infrastructurally challenged interior, I realised just how far it was, although that was another story.

The driver of the Accra-based vehicle was reputed to be bringing with him a supply of Burkina Faso's national CFA currency (always referred to by those who handled it as the seefa) to cover expenses. He would also carry some items of technical equipment and background reports needed for the gold mine appraisal. From Ouaga airport I was due to be taken by the driver and vehicle to a hotel for the night. The journey to Poura was scheduled to commence early on the following morning.

THE COMPANY'S INTERESTS in Ouaga, such as they were, were sheltered under the parasol of Uncle Joe's local organisation, the attentions of which were directed almost exclusively towards marketing Uncle Joe's brand products in a joint venture with a state-sponsored organisation. The joint venture called itself Burkina et Uncle Joe, known in short as Beejay. Whether or not Beejay could, had the question been asked, have come up with a Ouaga-based vehicle and driver to take me to Poura was doomed never to be known.

Beejay's people in Ouaga had done their level best to assure me that they either weren't geared up to receive visitors from foreign parts or, better yet, weren't really interested. I made several attempts to advise them that I was coming to Ouaga, only to receive in reply a telex written in French that read so cryptically that it gave away much less than the cost of sending it. My avenue of contact with Beejay seemed at the outset to lead in the direction of cold comfort.

As the Air France flight neared Ouaga, I felt as if I were a fragment of wood about to be thrown into a rip tide. Although I had no doubt that I would ultimately float, I was equally sure that there would, along the way, be substantial unexpected turbulence intent on dragging me down.

Far beneath the line of flight, the land was made featureless by an overlying dun mat of fine, hanging dust. There were no clouds, but for all that the sun had lost any fight it could put up to place the direct light of its countenance on the ground. In the final approach to Ouaga the dust closed a cloying fist around the Air France aircraft. The sun turned blood red and ultimately dimmed down to a grimy brown circle. The landing gear bumped once or twice in a touch-down that felt less precise than I would have liked it to be.

The aircraft stopped at its parking space at Ouaga airport's one and only terminal. A flight of steps was run up to the front cabin door, and the door was opened unto the ambiance of Burkina Faso, which hung as a dense veil of baking heat, thick enough to swim through. It was late afternoon.

Across the way, the terminal building lurked like a sunken hulk, its smeared glass doors beckoning, with little suggestion of invitation, from behind a stretch of concrete pavement that had seen less than its fair share of patch-up repairs.

I wasn't sure how many people lived in Ouaga's urban sprawl, but however many it was, a sizeable proportion of them appeared to be gathered in, on and around the terminal within easy hailing distance of the newly arrived Air France flight. Prolific was an apt description for them. They made up in volume and presence what they appeared to lack in terms of sense of purpose.

I disembarked and commenced threading my way through the gathered masses in a route that had little of direction about it. I was surrounded by chaos overlain by clamour, a tumult pierced with teeth flashing like a battalion of press cameras and beset with the pungent odour of well-united wood smoke and sweat that was such a basic feature of crowd life in Africa.

The Ouaga customs officials were kinder in their treatment of me than were their immigration authority counterparts, although even the latter were reasonably tolerable. I assumed that if I had filled in my arrivals form correctly in the first place, immigration would not have elected to send me to the back of the line to fill it in again.

When I emerged from the front entrance of the terminal I was immediately enveloped in a further seething mass of Ouaga humanity, rank upon rank, cumulative gallons of pungent sweat running under the weight of the still heat. Hundreds of hands presented themselves, offering to relieve me of the burden of my suitcase. They were good hands, kind hands without aggression. I was given no cause to feel anything other than pressured, but I held onto the suitcase all the same with a grip that was tightly white-knuckled.

One face amidst the furrowed sea of glittering grins had to belong to the Company's driver from Accra, assuming that he had run the gauntlet to Ouaga and lived to tell the tale. Finding him in the mob would be akin to finding a needle in a haystack, but in this case it was fortunate that I could take the role of needle as, for various reasons related to the local context, it was a lot easier for the driver to find me than vice versa. The driver didn't have all that many white-faced options to cover, and even if he was wrong in his first choice he would get to me eventually, and so he did.

THE DRIVER'S NAME was Kwashi. He was a short, thickset man who looked much younger than he actually was. He was personable, friendly and polite without being obsequious, all very acceptable qualities in my book. He told me that his journey from Accra to Ouaga had taken him the best part of two bone-crunching days, but he had arrived on schedule, was conversant with at least the rudiments of my lost scope of work and was ready to proceed onwards to parts unknown to either of us.

Kwashi's vehicle was a hard-top Nissan pickup truck. The vehicle was assumed to be fit for anything that the state of a Burkina Faso road could throw at it – a safe enough assumption in the dry season, probably.

Kwashi and I pushed our way through the madding crowd towards the spot where the Nissan was parked. We loaded my suitcase onto the back seat and sat in the cab in front. In the space behind the back seat rested a large, lined polystyrene cooler. Kwashi pointed out that the cooler was laden with bottled water. The Company seemed to place a high priority on providing bottled water for travellers.

On leaving the airport the Nissan was immediately surrounded by large expanses of Ouaga. The air conditioner with which the interior was fitted fought against incursive heat and took second place. Our destination was the Hôtel Indépendance, not so very far away from the airport and situated more or less in the dustier centre of the dusty city.

Kwashi's driving style was of the kind described by experts in the craft of piloting motor vehicles as "defensive". One of the many courses sponsored by Uncle Joe for both his willing and his not-so-willing underlings treated of defensive driving, and it was not improbable that Kwashi had been a one-time course participant. Observing Kwashi's technique, I made a private bet with myself that if the trip with Kwashi to Poura and back should be completed without the Nissan in Kwashi's hands hitting someone or something, I would acknowledge that the age of miracles was alive and well. It was a bet that I did not expect to win.

The architects responsible for the sprawling accumulation of Ouaga appeared to be accomplished in the design of low-slung edifices faced with either flaking concrete or crumbling mud. The edges of every street were jammed with citizens eager to sell the staples of life to one another from baskets, buckets, rickety tables and rustic stalls that looked as if they had been constructed from purloined wood. The vendors plied their wares along the rims and in the bottoms of otherwise currently redundant trenches that might serve as gutters in the event that rain, a distant memory on that day, should fall.

Hagglers overflowed into the streets, intent on conducting ritual business transactions and demonstrating the power of liberal gesticulation. Children chased around and about adult legs ending in a prolific variety of dilapidated footwear, and emerged to dart from side to side of the streets, heedless of motorised traffic. An itinerant goat, or it might have been a sheep, ambled slowly along the centre of the street and stood in head-hanging, traffic-defying obstinacy. Scrawny chicken and guinea fowl scratched dirt and tried to evade, with sometimes more and often less success, the calloused feet stamping around them.

Through this shifting obstacle course, traffic chose to move at its own pace, which was to say rapidly, directly, and as if it were totally unhindered. It was clear to me that in this institutionalised game the onus was on the people, children, animals and poultry to avoid being hit by traffic rather than on the drivers to avoid hitting them.

Perhaps for the sake of the underprivileged of Ouaga, it was as well that the city was not especially overburdened with four-wheeled motorised vehicles. In addition, of such vehicles that did ply the teeming streets of Ouaga and the roads of its environs on a regular basis, the majority looked as if they had genuinely passed their prime of life and were left with any capacity to speed diminished by senility.

Every now and then the traffic featured gliding examples of cars manufactured by the Mercedes Company. These were big and usually black. Their polished bodywork was a magnet attracting an impressive dust patina. It could be cheerfully assumed that the furnishings of any one of the coolly air-conditioned interiors comprised much in the way of soft leather on which was seated a somewhat less flexible politician whose arrogance, penchant to accept dashes of any size, shape or form and total disregard for the welfare of the common man were well matched by the magnitude of his lack of integrity.

The vital form of private transport for the populace of Ouaga was mounted on no more than two wheels. Bicycles flowed in streams and mopeds surged in floods. I looked on with a sense of wonderment and decided that Ouaga must be the moped capital of the world. The principal thoroughfares were rife with mopeds of a bewildering array of makes and colours, ridden alike by the ragged, the elegant and the merely suave. Rush hour was a never-ending feast as the mopeds ran like rivers in spate, breaking away from the few traffic lights in waves of dust and choking clouds of exhaust fumes. The mopeds circled Ouaga's Central Square of the Revolution and made of it a churning maelstrom.

The moped riders of Ouaga appeared single-mindedly intent on reaching an eventual, if undisclosed, destination. They looked straight ahead and went for the main chance, edging out to the side of the current when required to turn and popping up from the sucking swirl in the manner of wave-discarded jetsam.

KWASHI DROVE US to the Hôtel Indépendance employing a driving technique that owed much to a heavy foot on the accelerator and a heavier hand on the horn. I had already identified the horn as an essential local vehicle accessory. In the absence of its repetitious blare, driving in Burkina Faso, and assuredly in Ghana as well, would have been no more than a pale shadow of the pale horse that reality made it.

THE HÔTEL INDÉPENDANCE was a tumbling, battered-looking establishment. From the outside it appeared to be devoid of the least element of charm. From the inside it was clear that the impression gained from the outside was not without validity.

The street on which the hotel fronted bore the rather ominous name Avenue de la Résistance du 17 Mai. The resistance and the date both had the ring of truth about them, but for the title of Avenue to be authentic there should have been a few trees around, and there were none of those. Perhaps it was the intensity of the resistance on the seventeenth of May that took the trees out.

From the level of that strikingly unlovely treeless street, a short flight of wide steps led up to the broad, glassed-in entrance to the lobby and reception area of the Hôtel Indépendance. The steps were fully occupied by a tiered host of vendors of local artefacts, not a single one of whom was prepared to accept *"Non, merci"* as a response to his entreaties to buy an item of his wares.

On the steps the vendors drew their ranks into a tight array, penetrable only by the brave. Their host bristled with and waved carvings of animals, printed textiles, knives, paintings, tribal masks, statues, bronze busts and stone sculptures. Whether guests were trying to enter or to leave the hotel was immaterial to these princes among salesmen. Fair game was fair game to them, irrespective of the direction in which it moved.

I felt that I had no alternative other than to yield to the pressure of sales tactics if I were ever to reach the hotel entrance at the summit of the packed steps. I threw out a request for postcards. A handful of grimy-edged postcards bearing views of some of Ouaga's starker architectural gems was instantly thrust into my face. I desperately pulled out four from the array, and then realised I had no money in my pocket to pay for them. Kwashi was the one with the pocket full of seefas, fifty of which, it was officially advised, were equivalent to one French franc.

At my entreaty Kwashi reluctantly produced a 500-seefa note, evilly wilted to the touch. I forwarded the limp currency to the vendor of postcards, who grabbed it and disappeared into the maw of the hawking crowd as if he were a stone swallowed in a bucket of Uncle Joe's engine oil. Ah, well, I thought, if our roles had been reversed, I might well have done the same.

I re-entered the affray of the steps and won through to the comparative quiet of the Hôtel Indépendance foyer with a feeling of accomplishment mixed with relief. The Hôtel Indépendance claimed that it was of the three-star variety, and thus far it was clear to me that one of the three stars was possibly merited. The other two would have been visible at night – dust, moped fumes and the press of vendors permitting – through the bleary glass of the entry doors.

A kindly Beejay operative had arranged a single night's reservation at the Hôtel Indépendance for me. All that was then formally required of me was to complete the check-in formalities and sign the bill on departure. Or so I supposed. It was standard practice for Flying Circus hotel accommodation accounts incurred in less-developed countries to be paid for directly either by the local branch of Uncle Joe or by that of the Company (if there was one). Unfortunately, at the time of my arrival for check-in, Beejay had yet to submit a guarantee to the hotel that the bill would be paid by them on my signature. This lapse of protocol was not much to the liking of the clerk on the reception desk.

The clerk looked as if he occupied a state of permanent harassment. He went about his desk duties with all the enthusiasm of one who was contemplating a pressing appointment elsewhere but would be prepared to reconsider his priorities if the prospect of a dash in hand should enter the equation.

Kwashi, whose willingness to provide me with seefas would have met with a nod of approval from Mr Ebenezer Scrooge, was cajoled into parting with a meagre wad of the flaccid currency. He withdrew the notes from his pocket, one by one, making no attempt to disguise a mounting displeasure. The notes adhered to each other, held by skins of grime and slime. I didn't want to think about where they had been in their obviously lengthy history or, for that matter, what nameless things they might have purchased or been exchanged for.

The trouble was, there were not enough seefas in Kwashi's entire stash to cover the cost of my room. The check-in impasse was solved by the production of my credit card, which the reception attendant was not only ready to accept but quite appropriately seemed to think would do nicely.

A hotel porter took my suitcase and set out to lead the way to an allocated room. As we were heading off there came a shout from the hotel entrance. Someone, oddly enough in a city where I was unknown, was looking for me. Lo and behold, it was the postcard vendor who had previously made such an effective exit on the steps with 500 seefas in his hand. He was back, bringing me the change from the transaction, correct to the last seefa.

It was a rare and deeply touching moment, made even greater by its unexpectedness. Not altogether to Kwashi's wholehearted approval, I told the vendor to keep the change. If this vendor was typical of the people of Burkina Faso, I thought, this country would endure in spite of itself.

The guest rooms of the Hôtel Indépendance were established in blocks built to surround a large open courtyard, the centrepiece of which was a long, if narrow, swimming pool. The lobby adjoined one corner of the courtyard. Around the pool was set an array of battered metal tables and equally battered accompanying metal chairs. A few of the tables were shaded by tattered, sun-bleached parasols.

On the far side of the pool directly across from the lobby, a pair of ornate gates fronted the entrances to a couple of enclosed restaurants, one of which claimed to be a grill. The boast of the other was that it was a pizzeria. I imagined that a pizza of Burkina Faso construction would be quite something – something worth avoiding, that was.

The harshly open glare of the courtyard that I crossed with the porter on the way to my room served to make the interior of the room (cubicle would have been a better description for it) appear deeply gloomy by comparison. An alternative explanation for the sombre hue of the room may have been that I forgot to take off my sunglasses when I entered, although it was much more likely that the deep gloom was real.

The porter switched on a small television set residing on a high shelf in one corner of the room and left before the twangy tones of CNN were able to insinuate themselves through the snowy image on the screen. I went into the adjoining bathroom, but although it was getting late, the Ouaga water supply was evidently still trying to regenerate its forces against the demands of the day. The air conditioner was also putting up a fight – noisy but equally ineffectual – against the encroachment of heat.

I LEFT THE room and rejoined Kwashi in the courtyard, where we sat at one of the metal tables and ordered a couple of bottles of Ouagabrewed beer. The beer was named SOBBra, which those who favoured it pronounced "Sew-bee-bra". It was served cold, but since it was contained in very large green bottles, the inherent coldness didn't survive the consumption time. Sewbeebra was designed to be purchased one bottle at a time, and shared out between a group of drinkers.

A white-shirted, moon-faced man approached us as we sat. He held a sheaf of papers under one arm and was enveloped in the demeanour of officiousness. He enquired after my name. It was not a difficult question for me to answer, even after the better part of one bottle of rapidly warming Sewbeebra. I responded truthfully.

The new arrival informed us that he was the senior administrative assistant to the marketing manager out of Beejay's Ouaga office. Moreover, he had been specially delegated to meet me on arrival at Ouaga airport. His name was Camille. That he had failed in his mission to find me so far was a matter of some concern to him. Camille made it clear that he did not blame himself for the missed encounter. I was given to believe that it was my prerogative to shoulder the burden of guilt.

I was glad enough to do that. It emerged that the Company's representatives in Accra had omitted to liaise with the Beejay people in Ouaga and, not to put too fine a point on it, vice versa as well. Since communication shortfalls were fairly standard features of Company practice, I should have anticipated them.

Camille's self-important indignation, real or imagined, soon turned into a relieved bluster as I apologised to him as profusely as I could. I stopped only just short of grovelling, but it was all in a good cause. A Sewbeebra was ordered for Camille. The brew and a couple of items of Company public relations memorabilia that I had brought out with me – namely a decorative plate and a corporate tie – served to mollify Camille's hurt feelings even further.

The corporate tie was about as inappropriate an item of apparel to hand over to a member of Ouaga society as could be reasonably imagined. Somewhere, perhaps, it might come to fulfil a useful function in which it, or the remnants of it, would bind up a load of wood, support a pair of ragged trousers or tether a donkey to a bush.

In order to cement our genial new relationship and augment its scope I declared myself ready to accompany Camille to the Beejay office building, where an appropriate larding of gratuitous compliments could be spread over Camille's superiors, of whom it seemed there were many. We sank the Sewbeebras and then made the journey to the Beejay nerve centre in Camille's car, an off-yellow Renault that could be described as being clapped out without any fear of misrepresentation.

Ahead of a noxious wake of exhaust fumes, the little Renault allowed itself to be pulled into the torrent of mopeds, gushing along thoroughfares and barely escaping being drowned in the whirlpools of roundabouts.

At the Beejay office building, security appeared breachable by no more than a smile and a mere hint of a sense of purpose. This gave me a good feeling that all was not as bad as it might have been. Camille introduced me to the Beejay general manager and the marketing manager, two gentlemen who conspired to hide their undoubted enthusiasm for my presence in Burkina Faso with great expertise.

It required little time in the presence of either, not to say the pair of them together, for me to be well aware that, although Uncle Joe's Beejay associates were prepared to give me moral support for my visit, material considerations were unlikely to be appended.

The Accra-sponsored wad of seefas of dubious provenance, secreted somewhere among Kwashi's personal effects, shaped up as the miserly virtual limit governing my expectation of incidental expense money. On the positive side I knew that the Hôtel Indépendance accommodation costs were already covered by my credit card. Once I reached the gold mine property at Poura I could anticipate being the guest of the mine operator, and whatever lack of largesse that might or might not imply it shouldn't cost me anything – well, not much anyway.

I could do no other than make the best of the situation as it presented itself. I was used to doing that, although travelling in an unfamiliar country without ready access to funds to cover any emergency, even the type of funds that made me shudder to touch them, could not but give rise to some unease.

Camille, prior to returning me to the Hôtel Indépendance in his creaking yellow Renault, invited me to view his own office quarters in the Beejay building. The tidiness displayed was of a kind less suggestive of efficiency than of not an awful lot happening. Camille showed me a small blackboard nailed to one of the walls. On the blackboard my name and the day's date were both inscribed in white chalk. No greater proof could have been provided to establish that Camille had indeed been expecting me, and as a result I was moved to photograph Camille standing alongside the blackboard in order to place the moment on permanent record. Camille adopted a pose that would not have been out of place on the front of a flyer for a political party.

I WAS NOT entirely bereft of money as such, since I was carrying a few American dollars with me, as I always did when travelling. Single dollar bills generally made a universally acceptable response to the entreaties of the underprivileged. When an elderly lady approached me following my departure from the Beejay offices with Camille, her thin hand extended in the customary manner, I gave her two such dollars at once.

I was something of a magnet for beggars wherever I went. I often wondered why this was so when I had seen beggars avoid so many of my Flying Circus colleagues that the latter might have been bearers of a contagious disease. I was told that I had to avoid eye contact with beggars, something I was quite unable to do. Many beggars were people down on their luck, but that didn't mean they had forfeited the right to be respected.

The elderly lady went away with an air of apparent satisfaction, only to return within a minute, thrusting the two dollar bills at me and demanding "real money" to replace them. The irony of the moment was not lost on me.

I worked for a Company that believed it strode the world, its executives scattering millions into the wind and squandering as much again in failed self-serving ventures. Yet on that day in Ouagadougou, Burkina Faso, one of the Company's accredited representatives was not equipped with the wherewithal to dispense alms to a deserving beggar.

By the time Camille's yellow Renault came to a gasping halt outside the Hôtel Indépendance, it was growing dark, although not quite dark enough for me to enter the hotel unobserved — not that a white man could have done that kind of thing in any part of Africa, no matter how dark it was.

The hawkers, souvenir vendors and opportunists homed in on me as I set my foot on the first step of the flight leading up to the entrance of the Hôtel Indépendance. I struggled through the horde, which did not smell of roses, advising its members that I had no money to buy anything (which was true), but that I would have some tomorrow (which might or might not have been true) and would see them tomorrow for sure (which they would remember even if I tried to forget it).

KWASHI, THROUGH THE mixed blessing of necessity rather than choice, was not a registered guest of the Hôtel Indépendance, and hence he left me to pursue my own devices for the balance of that evening. I was faced with making a weighty decision on where to seek sustenance, impelled to make a selection between the grill on one hand and the pizzeria on the other. That was on the assumption that I could afford to pay for the bill of fare in either one of them.

I was strongly tempted to sample the delights of a pizza Burkinabé, yet when the crunch moment arrived as I approached the entry to the pizzeria, I found myself able to resist the temptation without too much trouble. My feet appeared to turn in the direction of the grill by a process that fell short of being involuntary.

The dining facilities of the Hôtel Indépendance grill were arranged beneath a spreading roof of thatch. The drapery on the tables was white enough and more or less clean, twin qualities shared by many of the restaurant clientèle. The waiters were friendly and attentive, supervised by a Maître D' who epitomised the strength of character and consummate professionalism that were so often found in African establishments, great or small, where the public gathered in the anticipation of being served.

The menu of the day – or more likely of any other day – offered a number of dishes of interest to the discerning palate, but the most popular selection was grilled chicken, perhaps because everything other than grilled chicken was off.

I seated myself at an empty table and ordered a bottle of Sewbeebra, which was delivered at the very moment that the portion of chicken designated to become my dinner was dropped to hiss and fume on a charcoal grill over to one side. I was moved to ponder the nature of the ingredients included in the pizzas concurrently under construction not so far away from where I sat. It did not take me long to conclude that the principal pizza ingredient was very likely to be chicken.

Something brushed against my legs under the table. I lifted the edge of the tablecloth and looked down to investigate. There stood a grey cat, gaunt and emaciated. The cat lifted its head towards me and creaked out an accusing demand for food, evidently a commodity with which it had had little recent association.

My appetite, which had not been desperately keen in the first place, fell back a few notches. I advised the cat to come back later when my grilled chicken was available and in place. The cat heeded me and slipped reprovingly away in the faint hope of discovering a more reliable benefactor.

The grilled chicken came along. It was an entire bird split open and grilled on both sides to a variety of incendiary shades linking dark brown with carbonised black. Its bones exceeded its meat in volume. The meat was perhaps stringy but delicious in flavour. I placed some of it on one side of my plate for the prowling cat, although the cat did not return.

As far as dessert was concerned, the chicken was, in more ways than one, a tough act to follow. I elected to take only coffee. The coffee was of genuinely first-class quality. I was so pleasantly surprised by this that I ordered a second cup to confirm, as it did, that the first cup had not been a one-off aberration. Any country producing such excellent coffee, I thought, had to have something going for it.

One consequence of the coffee might have been to reduce my ability to sleep well that night, although the mattress on my bed, a conglomeration of lumps that refused categorically to match the contours of my body, didn't aid slumber too much either. The residual heat in the air, plus a rogue mosquito that revelled in its embrace, formed additional sleep-repellent criteria.

An army of people had almost assuredly slept (or tried to sleep) in that bed before me, several of them having almost certainly elected to do so without first taking off their boots.

IT WAS NOT without a sense of some relief that I approached the front desk of the Hôtel Indépendance in the only relatively cooler conditions of the following morning to go through the check-out routine. No wake-up call had been necessary. Camille phoned me at 6.30 a.m., and Kwashi came along to hammer on the door of my room not long afterwards.

In preparing my account for settlement by credit card, the hotel cashier managed to convey an air of total bewilderment over the requirements of the process. He made it seem evident that he might just have performed the task once before, but that had been a long time ago, long enough to erase most of the routine actions from his mind. Time in his book was clearly not of the essence.

My account payable included a few bar bills supported by signatures that were not mine and was weighted beyond the point of imbalance by a monumental charge for a short telephone call to Europe that I had made on the previous evening. The phone call cost so much as to virtually make it a cost-competitive alternative to fly to Europe, economy class of course, in order to hold a proper conversation on a face-to-face basis.

Querying the multiple errors on my hotel bill only served to increase the cashier's confusion. The option of paying the bill as it stood, solely to avoid the tortured hassle of sorting out the intricacies of the mangled itemisation, became one worth considering. However, in a change of heart the cashier decided to relent on the bar bills, and then, in no more than thirty minutes, my account was settled.

THE FRONT STEPS of the Hôtel Indépendance may have been slightly less thronged with the cream of Ouaga street life when I left the hotel after checking out than they were when I had arrived on the previous evening. It was hard to tell, really. I felt that I was stepping onto a stage set, with the same people in the same places waiting for the same cues and calling out to me with the very same plaintive cries.

I boarded Kwashi's Nissan for the journey out of Ouaga and onwards to Poura. Camille was present for the occasion and led the way, a pathfinder in a yellow Renault weaving through the rising haze of dust and smog and the swelling tide of mopeds. Ouaga looked just about as decrepit in the light of day as it had done in the dimness of evening. It seemed to be run down far enough to demonstrate that the point of no return was an ever-present spectre hovering around in anticipation of being reached.

Camille halted our convoy outside a coffee house, not far from the Hôtel Indépendance, but far enough for all that. The fittings of the coffee house were faded and dingy both inside and outside, but the atmosphere was vibrant and alert. It was Ouaga in microcosm. Excellent coffee was available once again, ably supported with freshly baked croissants, bread and sweet pastries in piles on the counter. The experience was close to being uplifting. The kind of faintly coloured tea, prepared from a soggy tea bag undergoing at least its seventh steeping, that characterised such establishments just across the border in Ghana was always going to be an unknown quantity in Ouaga.

Bread vendors were out on the Ouaga streets in profusion, small boys hawking armfuls of French-styled baguettes and risking life and limb on every corner and in every location in which traffic stopped either simply for the fun of it or, more rarely, because a traffic light required it.

Camille left us after successfully guiding us to the outskirts of Ouaga, whence the main road to Bobo stretched west into the distance, obscured only by a multitudinous populace and a constant stream of two-wheeled traffic through all of which four-wheeled navigation was much more of an art form than a science.

Kwashi's impressive expertise in leaning heavily on both accelerator and horn had not lost any of its flair overnight. No African politician engaged in contemplating his next bribe from the back seat of a chauffeur-driven Mercedes could have been driven more aggressively than I was. Pedestrians not only didn't count on the roads of Burkina Faso but were also not far removed from being declared legitimate targets for motor vehicles to seek out.

Kwashi blasted the Nissan along the Bobo road in the manner of a biblical scourge. The crowd scattered sideways ahead of the vehicle like chaff before the wind, only to regroup in the wake of passage with a surprising air of nonchalance as the Nissan moved on.

The Bobo road had a fully paved surface. It thrust through a succession of small towns and villages for which sticks, grass and mud formed the construction materials of preference. In every village the Bobo road crawled with people and domestic animals, all oblivious to the foot-down disregard for a reasonable speed limit that was an evident feature of the training of just about every driver in the nation.

The surrounding country was a severely parched scrubland. Scattered clumps of trees, looking stunted and abandoned, were surrounded and linked by yellow, flaking vestiges of grass. Here and there dry earthen dams were rimmed about with bone-jutting cattle and sheep hoping to survive until the next rains.

After 150 kilometres or so of such sameness, albeit with a progressive diminution of moped traffic as distance was placed between the back end of the Nissan and Ouaga and a reduced speed enforced on him at my behest, Kwashi brought the Nissan to a junction with an adjoining wide and hard-surfaced dirt track leading south from the Bobo road to the town of Poura.

The Mohoun River, otherwise known as the Black Volta River, lay close to the right-hand side of the Poura track. It slid with thick and soupy green perennial water. Over on the left, a peppering of small, dark hills seasoned the dry plain.

I asked Kwashi to stop the Nissan. He did. We both got out and walked down to the bank of the Mohoun. A number of ragged sheep were strung out along the edge of what remained of the river, all of them drinking with the kind of urgency which suggested that one drink a day was about their limit of expectation. The sheep were watched over by a small boy dressed in the tattered remains of a khaki shirt and little else that was obvious. The boy stood like a stork on one leg, his other leg curled behind him, maintaining his equilibrium with the help of a long and gnarled staff of wood.

Set in the hard-baked clay along the receding edge of the Black Volta, I saw a line of elephant tracks, their integrity preserved until some far distant rain might cause the river to leap up and reclaim them as mud. The elephant responsible must have come, seen and moved on, and who, I thought, could blame him.

A kilometre or so before we reached the town of Poura, the road began to rise a little. Signs of civilisation then commenced to manifest themselves. On the left of the road bulked a decaying concrete slab bearing an inscription carved on it by someone unlikely to have been famed for either the precision or the style of his curlicues. The inscription declared, in terms that might have suggested a cavalier attitude to both local and national priorities, "*Les Mines Poura – La Patrie ou La Mort, Nous Vaincrons!*"

Near the head of the rise, on the other side of this stirring exhortation, a Beejay service station profusely decorated with Uncle Joe's logo was sitting like an abandoned outhouse of dusty empire. It exuded an air of under-utilisation. A surmise that the service station's petrol tanks were empty, gazed at no matter how wildly, would no doubt have been close to the mark.

78

Beyond the service station lay the sprawling town of Poura. It stretched down along the left-hand side of the road and tumbled off into the heat-shimmering distance. The town stood as a monumental tribute to what could be achieved with an apparently unlimited supply of mud and straw under conditions of stupefying aridity.

Poura seeped like a brown blot surrounding the gold mine and its adjacent staff village at centre stage. The gold mine site was dominated by a tall, sentinel-like head frame constructed with steel girders. The town almost threatened to engulf the mine but seemed to have relented at the last minute. The magnetic lure of the town for the mine was probably vested in endeavours by town dwellers to tap into the mine's utility system. Electricity, running water and the admittedly basic provision of sewage disposal were, to judge from appearances, less elusive quantities in the immediate vicinity of the mine and staff village than they were in the more distant reaches of the town.

ON THE FINAL approach to the mine's entry gate, Kwashi halted the Nissan outside a mud-walled edifice, bidden to do so by a sign warning that this was a designated police post, at which visitors to the mine property, not to say to the town of Poura as well, were required to report not only their presence but also the reason for the same.

A gentleman whose uniformed attire suggested that he was the duty police officer acknowledged our arrival with a reasonably perceptible gesture from his prone position on a mattress, where he seemed to show more interest in anticipating the heat of noon than in worrying about mad dogs and Englishmen. We were then free to proceed.

The well-trampled ground immediately outside the mine gate was occupied by a large number of people. There were enough of them to have constituted a small mob if they could only have worked up enough energy to protest about something. From the limited earnestness of their demeanour and the understated animation of their conversation it could be judged that they had not reached the point of rebellion just yet, even though the prospect of jobs for any of them was denied on a sign that appeared to have been hanging on the gate for some time.

Our Nissan was waved into the mine yard by a somnolent gateman for whom formality was of little account. The tyres bounced over dust-inundated ruts as we scouted for a parking space. In between the ruts oil had been spilt plentifully and probably not entirely by design.

Poura gold mine was equipped with all the standard cosmetic outer trappings of its genre. The surface buildings had been sturdily constructed at a time when money was less of an object than it clearly was at the time of our arrival.

Open conveyors snaked up and down above us on steel-latticed frames linking an ore crusher to the processing plant. The mine's clinic appeared to have been sited with a view to trapping copious quantities of the fine dust that floated across to it from the primary conveyor given the excuse of the slightest breeze. The impressive red cross painted on the clinic's roof served as a target for the streams of dust to aim at.

The administrative office block was built as a square enclosing a central garden. The garden looked as if it had been watered on a regular basis, although the arts of pruning, weeding and removing dead vegetation had still to gain any momentum.

It was in the administrative block that I was introduced to the four-man directorate of the operating company, respectively embracing the grand titles afforded the mine manager, the technical manager, the geological manager and the finance manager. There seemed to be no shortage of managers around.

I recalled an occasion in Peru when I flew as a passenger on a privately owned local company jet from Ilo in the south of the country up to the capital, Lima. A Peruvian army general and his wife were fellow passengers. I couldn't remember which of the two was the fatter. However, I was impressed at having travelled with a real live general and voiced that opinion to a Peruvian colleague. "My friend," said my colleague, "Peru has got lots and lots of generals."

The mine had lots and lots of managers. I began to think of the directorate as the "gang of four", but when it became clear that the finance manager was generally conspicuous by his absence from site, the "three stooges" was the only reasonable collective sobriquet under which to classify those who remained.

The complete gang of four, consisting of Shemp, Moe and Larry plus one, were not a bad cadre of professionals in their own disciplines. They anchored the operations, in fact forming a veritable bunch of anchors. Most if not all of them were educated at universities in France. It was certain from the outset that the three stooges at least were doing a difficult job more or less as well as the fiscal resources, so exceedingly constrained by the finance manager, would permit.

My ARRIVAL AT the mine property took place shortly after that of a crew from Burkina Faso's national television station. The crew were there to capture something of the essence of current activities on video-tape for subsequent transmission to those residents of Burkina Faso who either owned or had access to television sets and who were either not disposed or otherwise unable to feast their unbelieving eyes on CNN's version of the news.

The cameraman was not there to record my visit. The more was the pity, I thought, as whatever I might manage to do on site could have been just as lacking in newsworthiness as anything else happening in the whole country on that special day.

The presence of a national television crew at the mine was, however, a cause generating some excitement in the breasts of each of the gang of four, assembled *en masse* for the occasion. Each of them considered that any opportunity for any one of them to be captured in a panning shot to be subsequently broadcast to an admiring nation on television was a more pressing priority than coping with a non-national visitor like me. So it was that I was despatched on a tour of the processing plant with the process plant manager, a gentleman named Toussaint, who had obviously drawn the short straw.

TOUSSAINT GAVE ME a broad overview of his sphere of managerial influence and shed some revealing light on the nature of the technical and personal infighting between the mining and processing interests of the operators. This was somehow comforting, as in my experience there was no mine worthy of its name anywhere in the world at which, for reasons which no one knew or cared about, the mining and processing departments were not at loggerheads. Mutually dependent, the two areas of interest co-existed on a shared policy of cutting one another down to size.

For my purposes, a visit to the process plant at the very outset was most valuable. The state of process-plant housekeeping and mainte-nance made a sound yardstick that normally characterised the quality of the operations as a whole. On that basis of extrapolative measure-ment the process plant on the Poura gold mine was shabby and exten-sively patched up, but acceptably tidy.

To complete the tour of the processing plant, Toussaint took me to the so-called gold room, in which a pour of a small bar of gold was reputed to be imminent and, as such, was to be stage-managed for the benefit of the television camera. The heat in the gold room was raised to dramatic levels by the roaring inferno of the small furnaces, roaring not a little, I suspected, in reaction to a long-delayed arrival of the television crew. The gold room, for those who stood and sweated in it waiting until the television people deigned to show up, bore more than a passing resemblance to whatever hell was in Burkina Faso.

The television crew put in an appearance at long last, bringing with them an impression of recent largesse greatly enjoyed in whatever at Poura passed for *la chambre verte*. The cameraman wielded the tools of his trade like an expert in the relevant craft, but the bulky muscularity of his physique was much more indicative of one who had more than a passing familiarity with the interior of a professional wrestling ring. He bore his camera on his right shoulder as if he wished it were a rocket launcher. If his exposed skin contained one or two blocked pores that were not yielding more than a fair share of rank sweat it was not obvious, but then, as coursing sheets of perspiration characterised the epidermis of everyone else in the gold room, such a condition was common.

The pour of the gold bar was a piece of pure theatre incorporating elements of triumph, tragedy and farce all at the same time. The lengthy delay in the pour had raised the contents of the furnace to temperatures considerably in excess of design levels. When a technician (who might well have been another titled manager for all I knew) clad in heat-reflective gear came to the fray do his bit in tilting the furnace so as to disgorge the molten gold into a mould, the very same superheated molten bullion bored straight through the mould, hit the floor and froze in a sheeted congregation of auriferous clumps and splashes as the surrounding onlookers leapt for cover.

The riches of Poura lay decrepitating on the floor of the Poura gold room under the scrutiny of a national television camera. As far as the crew were concerned, this might have been standard gold-pouring practice, and there was no one present who knew otherwise who was about to disillusion them. It was fortunate that hard hats formed the universal style of headgear as not a single hair could then be observed to turn.

As the spectators and television crew filed away in retreat from the debacle, the gold-pouring technician (or manager maybe) was endeavouring to pry the main sheet of spilled gold loose from the floor using a steel crowbar.

Not to be found wanting in the zealous exercise of his responsibility, one of the security attendants at the gold room exit sprang at me, flourishing a hand-held metal detector, and flicked the instrument up and down, fore and aft of my person. The attendant was intent on ensuring that none of the spilled gold had bounded my way to lodge in either a fold of clothing or a secret pocket.

The metal detector made not a single beep, which may have meant on the one hand that I was clean or on the other hand that it was not equipped with batteries, or alternatively (allowing for the fact that there was no third hand, even in Burkina Faso), both of the above at the same time. That last option seemed the most likely.

During this verification of my honesty, the television camera pointed in my direction, seizing the moment in its electronic grasp. It gave me a marginal brush with fame, which might have been worth amplifying further had it not been time for lunch. Getting out of the calefactory gold room, given the imminence of lunch, somehow seemed more pressingly important than posing in front of a camera for posterity.

LUNCH WAS SERVED in the Poura Mine Senior Staff Club, more commonly referred to in rather less grandiose terms as "The Club". The gang of four, the entire television crew, myself and one or two others from the mine who might also have achieved managerial status (although they didn't allude to it one way or the other) were included in the luncheon party.

The Club was a low building established on the near edge of the staff village. In keeping with the dwelling houses that surrounded it, the Club had clearly known better days. Within its newly shabby interior, the ghosts of glittering social events could be sensed lurking in dusty corners.

Behind the Club, a meticulously maintained swimming pool stretched in a sparkling blue oblong towards a tennis court, the surface of which was studded with brittle weeds and in a clearly advanced state of decay. I assumed that for Club members, tennis was a rather less popular recreational activity than was swimming.

A large mural painted on the back wall of the Club's dining area offered a bird's-eye impression of the Club and staff village as they might have looked in the dearly departed days of good expatriate living, when neat bungalows were screened off by groves of stately gum trees and interspersed by well-watered green and pleasant lawns.

On the mural a paint-cast single-engine aircraft flew above the staff village, forever in the company of a startled-looking vulture. The pilot of the aircraft, whose nationality was whatever any observer wanted it to be, appeared to be exceedingly irate, possibly because a ball rising like a rocket from the tennis court far below had torn a hole in his aircraft's left wing.

Lunch was a three-course meal served under the steady gaze of the mural. A range of strong alcoholic beverages, ably flanked by an apparently unlimited supply of bottles of Sewbeebra, was available for lunch participants who wished to partake of the same. Those who did thus wish formed the overwhelming majority of those present.

The three courses consisted of a potato salad to start with, then a vegetable casserole accompanied by couscous and a hearty stew of mutton and guinea fowl, and finally an excellent *crème brûlée*, sheeted in vitreous caramel. There was precious little of third world exigency about the bill of fare.

However, all was not lost in the field of deprivation, since with subsequent meals that I partook of at the Club in my own company, when the gang of four and the national television crew were no longer a factor for the chef to reckon with, quality galloped appreciably downhill. The pickings eventually became as thin as the aeronautical joke on the Club mural came to seem once its novelty wore off. All Club meals were prepared for me, however, by a chef who was as kind as he was generous and were accepted by me with gratitude.

The chef, who was also the waiter, the dishwasher and the general custodian of the facilities, and who may well have rejoiced in the knowledge that he was not designated a manager (not yet anyway), was tall, heavily rotund, obliging and beaming. His name was Pascal. He normally wore a dark, short-sleeved safari suit that had once been new, but exactly when was open to debate. He sported a skullcap of rather more daring design on his head. Pascal's face was lightly but geometrically ploughed with ritual tribal scars.

Following lunch, served always on the stroke of noon, it was the custom of all who either worked or pretended to work at the mine property to retire to rest from the rigours of the morning until precisely

3.00 p.m. Given the heat of day and a not inconsiderable load of heavy food to digest, the three hours of siesta could be judged to cover barely enough time to properly renew the bodily resources in order to ensure that the subsequent three hours at the workplace, right up to 6.00 p.m., would be productive.

FOR THE PERIOD of my sojourn at Poura, I was provided with accommodation in one of the village bungalows, situated not far away from the Club. The bungalow was in modest disrepair, although serviceable. Someone for whom luxury was an unknown word and to whom the definition of comfort was still open to debate had almost certainly selected the furnishings.

The bungalow's refrigerator worked, but lacked only contents to refrigerate. The shower unit delivered hot water in abundance. There was a table that could be used as a desk, and an accompanying wooden chair to sit on. An air conditioner fought yet another losing battle to cool the interior of the bungalow, emitting a thumping beat that any discotheque would have been proud to claim as its own.

The trees surrounding my bungalow were mainly the variety of eucalyptus enshrined on the Club mural. All were engaged in the long-term shedding of a profusion of leathery leaves that formed a crunching carpet underfoot. In front of the bungalow a solar heating unit stood like a monument to vanished hope, its broken panels choked with dust and dead vegetation. Here and there on the ground, fluffy speckled guinea fowl feathers stirred in anticipation of a cooling breeze that failed to materialise.

AT THE WITCHING hour of three o'clock, the staff of Poura gold mine rose from their respective beds of repose in the manner of vampires sensing dusk. The remnants of a dust cloud marked the route taken by the national television crew, vanishing in the direction of Ouaga.

My tour of the mine surface facilities was then ready to be taken up again. The tour was conducted earnestly, with guides trying hard to impress me and me trying even harder to be impressed, but with neither party quite succeeding in being unduly influenced by the other.

The highlight of the afternoon was a visit to the mine's analytical laboratory. The operating environment of the laboratory was as sterile as it was clean, although it was not really very clean. I was met at the entry door by another quartet consisting of three middle-ranking technicians under the command of a fourth whose title was chief chemist. I was glad to note that the latter wasn't yet flaunting managerial pretensions. All four were clad in spotlessly white disposable laboratory dustcoats, replete with the manufacturer's creases imposed from the original packing. On the front pocket of each dustcoat was printed the inscription "Kimberly-Clark", on which the light of day had never before cast its welcome gleam.

As I approached the three technicians and their chief, each of them was busily involved in completing an already impressive wardrobe by respectively pulling on pairs of rubberised surgical gloves and demonstrating in the act that this was no easy matter when attempted for the first time and the Marx Brothers weren't around to offer advice.

THAT NIGHT I slept well, even after dining on a plate of tough beef and bullet-like peas at the Club. The meal was washed down and held down by the liquid volume of two cold Sewbeebras.

With the onset of darkness the climatic conditions inside my bungalow moved in the direction of the temperate without actually getting there, but the effect of moderation was a tribute nonetheless to the tenacity of the ever-battling air conditioner.

I ROSE ON the morrow and strolled along to the Club for breakfast. The town site looked a little more presentable in the early morning sunlight than it had done in the harsh glare of the previous day, although for all that, the little more was little enough.

Pascal was ready and waiting for me at the Club. He had fried two eggs for me, of variety unknown, although it could be surmised that the eggs had been laid by a guinea fowl (or two) as there was not much substance to them. The yolks were marginalized, but the flavour was good and greatly welcomed.

I was rapidly being induced to realise that the flesh and other products of guinea fowl were not the least feature of the staple diet of residents of Burkina Faso. It was rare not to see guinea fowl scuttling around wherever people gathered and to come across errant drifting vestiges of the birds in the way of shed or plucked feathers. Oumar, an exploration geologist working at Poura mine, told me that in the order of ten thousand unfortunate representatives of the species were slaughtered every day in Ouaga to satisfy urban culinary demands.

AFTER THE TWO-EGG breakfast, Kwashi drove me over to the mine's administrative office block. The schedule called for me to make an underground inspection of the mine workings, accompanying a shift supervisor on his morning beat.

I was supplied with a clean overall to change into. It was a few sizes too small for me but I struggled and heaved and managed to button it up eventually. I then received an ancient and much-abused hard hat in which the leather sweatband had so lived up to its name that it had all but disintegrated. The rubber safety boots that I was provided with were in a more acceptable condition. Once I decided not to think about the state of the feet of many of those who might have worn the boots previously, they fitted me well enough.

Had there been a lamp belt available, I could have considered myself fully kitted out for an underground visit, but since there was not, full kit was a claim denied me. I fastened the lamp handed to me onto the side of the overall, where a couple of fabric straps were dangling, presumably placed there for just that purpose. The lamp in place dragged and thumped heavily and uncomfortably on my hip, riding on a curve of my tightly strained overall.

ENTRY INTO THE underground mine was made through a portal opened up at the bottom of a steep-walled, disused open pit about a hundred metres deep. From the portal an inclined tunnel, known as a ramp, zigzagged its way to depths as yet unknown to me. The descent to the portal within the pit was made down a steeply inclined track. Huge, fragile-footed rocks were Damoclean threats resting on the pit walls above the portal.

The shift supervisor and I were driven into the mine in a cut-down Toyota pickup truck that offered the appearance of having been recently attacked by a frenzied mob wielding sledgehammers. The accessories of the pickup did not include either seat belts or a roll bar. It would be too kind to the vehicle to describe it merely as an accident waiting to happen. I sat in the passenger seat at the front, secured from falling out sideways by a length of rusty chain stretched across where the door would have been if there had been a door.

The Toyota was driven down the ramp at a pace that was so excruciatingly slow that it could only have been put on for my benefit. The driver's foot must have itched to give the motor its accustomed gun, but he resisted the temptation with aplomb. That particular excursion underground may well have been unique in being uncommemorated by either a dent or a scrape on what remained of the vehicle's bodywork.

The housekeeping in the underground mine made a favourable impression on me – an unexpected surprise. The basic elements of a planned operation were in place. The mine working places appeared sound and reasonably secure. The gold-bearing quartz vein structure that the mine was designed to exploit was wide, strong and handsome. What was totally lacking was advance forward development in the vein and the availability of any decent mechanised mining equipment to carry out the same. The standard was characterised by hand to mouth techniques.

My exit from the mine was made via the main shaft, straight up to surface from the lowest working level established at 267 metres below the shaft collar. The cage rose smoothly up the shaft, perhaps slowly, but it took a lot less time to ascend in this manner than it did to descend into the mine in the Toyota. The residual heat at surface had not dissipated at all while I was underground.

I never discovered whether or not the Toyota returned to surface in one piece, if indeed it was genuinely in one piece when it went down with me in the first place.

I SPENT THE afternoon of the day, naturally enough after 3.00 p.m., with the Poura mine geologists. They showed me the nature of their combined scope of work with good humour and a spirit of co-operation that the gang of four could have chosen to adopt without fear of censure. The geologists maintained copious records of their activities, although their approach to organising and systematising the same fell some distance short of being either organised or systematic. The records were in essence not dissimilar to the vein that the miners were pecking away at underground, consisting of small nuggets of value contained in a mass of sterility.

The mine's administrative staff, prompted by one (or it may have been more) of the three stooges, kindly agreed to contact the Air France agency in Ouaga on my behalf to ensure that my return flight from Ouaga to Paris a couple of days hence was safely reconfirmed. Air France, and even the Paris Charles de Gaulle airport, were assuming a more attractive aspect in my mind almost by the hour. Late that afternoon the administration office informed me that my return flight was all in order. All I could wonder was why I didn't altogether believe what they told me.

ON THE CONCLUSION of work at 6.00 p.m., I was invited by one of the geologists to partake of a cooling bottle of Sewbeebra by visiting an open-air bar in the middle of the part of Poura town governed principally by mud-based edifices. The open-air bar rejoiced in the name of Golf Café Bar. Any visitor would not take long to appreciate, however, that if there was a sporting connection to the establishment, this was not reflected in the name. There was barely a blade of grass of any passable shade of green within two kilometres of its location. The nearest golf ball was probably lying in the rough somewhere in the outskirts of Abidjan.

The Golf Café Bar stood on an elevated mound, looking across crumpled ranks of mud huts and narrow thoroughfares stuffed with people. The smoke from cooking fires rose from all around and hung in the air like a pungent veil, forcing the Golf Café Bar to fall a little short of justifying any claim to an *al fresco* ambiance. Over to the west, the twin minarets of a small mosque that demonstrated a rather precarious dependence on even more mud were thrust like a defiant gesture up against the stark red face of the setting sun.

The redoubt of the Golf Café Bar was partially enclosed around its rim. Some chairs and low-slung tables were grouped around a central hub-like counter from which drinks were dispensed from storage in a paraffin-driven, heavily scarred refrigerator.

What the establishment lacked in creature comforts it made up for in the warmth of its hospitality. Food was available for those wishing to eat, and the fact that at least two creatures, one of which was almost certainly a chicken, were noisily slaughtered close behind the table at which I was sitting suggested that some orders for dinner had been placed.

At the foot of the mound in front of the Golf Café Bar, a small party of entrepreneurs were engaged in firing up a pile of charcoal inside a cut-down oil drum that might at one time have had a close association with Uncle Joe. An evil-looking pile of meaty material, evidently destined to be barbecued over the charcoal, was being hacked for the purpose into small chunks by certain machete-wielding exponents.

A cloud of flies rose and fell on the surface of the meat in concert with the machete swipes.

The meat might have originally been part of a goat, but beyond that generality it was perhaps wise not to think too much. Gleaming gobs of a species-defying grey-green stomach appeared to represent a locally favoured delicacy. Invited to indulge, I felt able to decline an offer of food for once without the least prick of conscience that I might be hurting someone's feelings.

Later that evening at the Senior Staff Club, Pascal served me some sliced sausage of indeterminate provenance as a starter. It would have been a safe bet that the sausage was neither made nor cured in Burkina Faso. Then came what might or might not have been a small piece of pork, travelling incognito in the presence of potatoes. To finish with, the remains of the *crème brûlée* from yesterday's lunch were placed on the table. I renewed my acquaintance with the dessert and was back on familiar ground.

ON THE MORNING of my third day at Poura, I once more joined forces with the geologists, two in number this time, just as the sun was casting its first long beams across the mine and town. Warm already, the air promised to become much hotter before noon presaged the by now almost customary three-hour break.

Our objectives for the morning were to make a field visit to areas of potential interest for gold exploration in the property surrounding the mine, and then in the course of the trip to examine the opportunity for extending the future of mining in the district.

We were driven into the field in the Ghanaian Nissan with Kwashi at the wheel. Kwashi's manner, now that he had no mopeds to threaten, appeared deflated, although he could take some comfort that there was still a return journey to Ouaga for which to plan a moped and pedestrian-threatening strategy.

Guided by the two geologists, Kwashi drove to the south of the mine along fairly well defined bush tracks lined by brittle scrub. A few kilometres brought us to an abandoned open pit, named Balago. The area covered by the open pit was at least a square kilometre. Vast quantities of waste rock had been excavated at Balago for the purpose of exploiting a single gold-bearing vein. The waste-ground to vein removal ratio would have been astronomical had it ever been recorded. Never in the field of mining endeavour could so much waste have been moved using so much effort to expose so little ore.

The bottom of the pit was flooded, about one-third filled with greenish translucent water. It made a small lake of sorts in a supremely dry land. Swallows – or maybe they were swifts – were skimming the surface of the water, in all probability thinking of heading for Europe. It was not difficult to empathise with them. The breeze across the water felt refreshingly cool as it rose over the lip of the open pit. We left Balago to its own devices, not without feeling some consequent breeze-related reluctance.

THE NEXT PROSPECT to be visited was named Larafella, located some ten kilometres to the south of Balago. At Larafella the excavation principles tested at Balago appeared to have been employed with an equally stunning effect. A number of lengthy trenches around five metres wide and twenty metres deep had been dug at Larafella for the purpose of exposing and sampling yet another vein that might or might not contain a little gold. The ground was yellow-brown and crumbling back into the trenches, the walls of which were unsupported. Some of the trenches showed signs of imminent collapse. One trench had caved in completely in a catastrophic manner that would have been a lot more unfortunate had there been people in it at the critical moment.

A positive inference to be drawn from the visit to Balago and Larafella was that all points in between could be considered reasonably prospective for potentially gold-bearing veins. This concept was reinforced by the widespread presence of ancient artisanal mine workings scattered all along the way adjacent to the tracks we drove down. It was such workings, referred to as *orpaillage* and worked by *orpailleurs*, that had originally motivated the discovery of the vein that came to be exploited by the Poura mine. However, whereas the *orpailleurs* had operated with surgical finesse, their modern counterparts had been more prone to wield a blunt axe.

The working practice of *orpailleurs* involved sinking pits through the hard laterite capping at surface down to the bedrock interface a few metres below and then to excavate the bedrock laterally to discover, follow and exploit vein material under a firm protective roof of laterite. There were many hundreds of the *orpailleur* pits. Each was perfectly circular in plan view, measuring precisely 0.8 metres in diameter. The pits constituted the most impressive examples of the art of mining that I saw anywhere in the Poura district.

We all returned to Poura in time to beat the noon deadline, and were back in the field again after 3.00 p.m. The temperature at noon was forty-two degrees Celsius in the shade, as fierce as it was unrelenting. Lunch at the Club should have compensated for the heat, but did not. A couple of tinned sardines preceded a dish of rice accompanied by semi-raw mutton swimming in an oily red sauce, the ingredients of which seemed to bear a distant relationship to tomatoes. Dessert was a pithy orange that was about as sweet as the mutton had been tasty.

Dinner that evening complemented the quality of the lunch menu, opening with a small piece of sliced ham and leading on to a leathery lump of what might have been beef topping a matted tangle of hard-boiled spaghetti. This was to be my last dinner at the Club as a return to Ouaga was scheduled for the following day. The one blessing at dinner was that the red sauce of lunch did not appear again.

Most of the essential goodbyes were said in the Club on that self-same evening after dinner when the gang of four and a few others came along to sample the Sewbeebra and whatever else was on offer and free of charge. That left only Pascal for me to bid farewell to on the following morning. In truth, Pascal was one of those that I was going to miss the most.

KWASHI DROVE BACK to Ouaga in his tried and tested style, with one hand on the horn and the other hand expertly jerking the steering wheel in order to miss pedestrians, domestic animals, mopeds and approaching traffic by as close a margin as was feasible without actually making contact. He appeared to have an ambition to judge avoidance margins by the width of a razor blade.

Our one stop on the return to Ouaga was at a police road block to pay what in principle was a form of road toll but in practice was not a long way removed from an extortion carried out with the best of casual humour on all sides.

OUAGA HAD FAILED to change much during my absence at Poura, although the absence did serve to edge me towards a more appreciative acceptance of Ouaga's faded gentility. I felt quite at ease in the midst of Ouaga's dusty vistas and teeming humanity, not least perhaps because I knew I was departing for Paris tomorrow.

I checked once again into the Hôtel Indépendance. The same clerk was in the same position at the reception desk as he had been when I checked out a few days previously. He might not have moved in all that time. If the clerk recognised me as a former guest he did a good job in subduing any enthusiasm. White faces all looked the same in Africa in any case. I was given a room in a block of the hotel on the far side of the swimming pool, a long walk from the reception desk, threading through gloomy, dank-walled corridors.

Kwashi made a trip to the Air France agency in Ouaga to ensure that my flight to Paris really was confirmed. Fail-safe systems were not part of the travel culture of Burkina Faso. The penalty for assuming that a flight confirmation, once made, meant that the flight was genuinely confirmed had, so I was given to understand, resulted in far more important people than myself watching their flights head north without them on board.

CAMILLE APPEARED AT the Hôtel Indépendance as if summoned by bush telegraph, since he had not been summoned by me. Since I was required to make a so-called debriefing visit to the offices of the president of the state mining organisation that owned and operated the gold mine at Poura, I was not therefore predisposed to entertain Camille for long.

On learning of my presidential mission, Camille advised me that he, Camille, was a personal friend of that very president, making it seem reasonable to him, Camille, that he should accompany me on the debriefing visit. There was no arguing with that, as Camille was intent on serving as the mouthpiece for Beejay for the occasion, as well as for carrying intelligence back to his superiors afterwards. As this took me formally off the immediate hook for directly informing Camille's superiors myself, I didn't protest.

With Camille at my side I walked the few hundred metres from the Hôtel Indépendance to the building in which the state mining company maintained its Ouaga headquarters, in the course of which I was accosted by not more than a score of beggars and hawkers. By Ouaga standards this was a relaxing stroll.

I had made another bet with myself that the president's office would be lushly decorated with status symbols and ornate furnishings. Fortunately no money passed from one of my hands to the other as, in common with the personal wager on Kwashi's ability to make the Nissan collide at speed with something or someone, it was a bet I would have lost. The president's office was too austerely appointed to give a visitor any feeling of comfort inside it. There was no window. An air conditioner worked overtime to the extent that the office was air conditioned to a fault. A few minutes inside and cold began to exercise a vindictive grip.

The president sat behind a desk featuring numerous scars of combat on its veneered surface. He was resplendently clad in robes of such garish colours and riotous design that the sun, a stranger to the room, might have felt outclassed had it ever managed to find a chink that it could penetrate.

If in Ouaga social circles being a personal friend meant that the extent of your acquaintance was so transitory that the person alleged to be your personal friend was unaware of who you were, then the president of the state mining company did, at our meeting, come to qualify as a personal friend of Camille.

Camille must have enjoyed a fair degree of personal ease in the office of his personal friend the president, since he elected to fall asleep in the course of the debriefing. This achievement was made even more memorable by being conducted in the full glare of the president's robes and the wintry blast of the air conditioner.

The president did not offer to provide us with lunch, and nor did Camille. The latter showed a continuingly impressive reticence to part with seefas. Insofar as money had not been a required commodity during my stay at Poura, I had forgotten that I possessed no seefas to move over in Camille's direction in any case.

By the time the meeting with the president was concluded, Kwashi had returned from the Air France agency, claiming yet another successful reconfirmation of my flight. Kwashi still held his wad of seefas and thereby established himself as a clear leader in the contest as to who would pay for lunch.

CAMILLE'S CONTRIBUTION TO lunch was to suggest a restaurant where Kwashi's seefas might be spent. The relevant establishment was located off a courtyard frowned over by a dingy block of cramped apartments. Camille said that he lived in one of them.

After the unprepossessing appearance of its exterior, the interior of the restaurant was a revelation. Tables were discreetly placed in straw thatch-shaded alcoves around a small, centrally placed pool and were awash with clientele. A large charcoal grill, larger than that at the Hôtel Indépendance, smoked and spat on the far side of the shallow end of the pool. The waiters were attentive and their service was crisp and splendid.

Kwashi, Camille and I seated ourselves at a vacant table. The first Sewbeebras of the day were placed on the table an instant later. We ordered grilled guinea fowl, accompanied by fried potatoes. The guinea fowl meat, what there was of it, was crisp on the outside and succulent within. We ate with our fingers, dripping with grease. Time, place and context made the lunch one of those great meals that live in and enrich the memory.

AFTER LUNCH, I visited the Ouaga market, an enormous complex of tiny vendor cubicles packed with trade goods and lined up one on the other through a labyrinth of narrow passages jammed with potential customers. Haggling over purchases was practised as an art form.

The Ouaga market was reputed to be the largest of its kind in West Africa. A hugely extensive flight of admirably stained steps led up to its imposing façade. I climbed the steps, entered the market, advanced a couple of paces, and that became the limit of my Ouaga market penetration. The balance of the market was forever going to remain a mystery to me.

I had the all too solid impression that the not inconsiderable number of traders that immediately surrounded me on my entry were all related to one another, and not only by tribal bonds. I was forced to retreat into the nearest cubicle. My way out was then blocked as effectively as if a mud brick wall had been thrown up.

A gentleman who was most likely the proprietor of the cubicle, clad in a coarse smock that had once been white, backed me into a corner where I found myself hemmed in by a range of goods that a large number of crocodiles had sacrificed themselves to generate. Belts, bags and briefcases crackling with scales blocked the rear.

Artisanal weaponry was waved in my face in anticipation of a sale. I was shown knives of a bewildering array of shapes, sizes and length, each one that came being seemingly wickeder than its predecessor. There were enough knives on offer to start a small war. I had the fleeting thought, at once dismissed, that I should buy one and endeavour to fight my way out.

I told the insistent proprietor that I had no money with me to buy anything. This was something that the proprietor heard from prospective customers at least a score of times every day so now was not his moment to start believing it. The more I protested poverty, the more the case for a sale at a good price was pressed. It finally occurred to me that the proprietor regarded me as possessing a high level of expertise in the art of haggling.

Left with no alternative, I enquired, rather timidly, if American dollars were acceptable at the establishment. The proprietor at once demonstrated a total lack of reticence. Unreal money had finally found its acceptable face in Ouaga.

AFTER MY ESCAPE from the market, the final task left for me was to depart from Ouaga altogether. I was equipped this time with a business-class ticket for an Air France flight from Ouaga to Paris. The ticket had so far been reconfirmed twice. The Hôtel Indépendance was not far away from the airport. Taken all together, these factors should have made for an orderly departure process, dignified if not stylish.

However, by all accounts Ouaga airport was characterised by many passengers and few flights. That was not a happy equation. The surplus of the former over the latter was balanced out by summarily bumping latecomers. Nothing should be left to chance.

I AWOKE VERY early on the morning of the day of departure with a pain in my stomach and a taste in my mouth that was, in line with an expression I had heard used in East Africa, not unlike "an Indian shithouse at the height of paw paw season". Nervousness played a part in the discomfort, although yesterday's guinea fowl might not have been blameless. I got up and walked around the inner precincts of the Hôtel Indépendance. The surface of the swimming pool was a still, black mirror. A blushing hint of dawn lay over to the east. The clerk at the reception desk was slumped in a chair, snoring loudly.

Checking out, when the clerk had completed his slumbers and the cashier was available to conduct his magic, meant yet another half-hour saga of who should pay what and why, but the bill was finally settled to the cashier's entire satisfaction. I was glad to pay whatever was asked of me so as to gain the privilege of being allowed to leave.

The scheduled departure time for my flight was 10.35 a.m. I had been instructed to report at the airport at least two and a half hours beforehand. Somehow this did not provide me with any comfort that the airport check-in process was likely to be efficient. I had heard a rumour that the flight check-in counters opened for business at 7.00 a.m. and was determined to be there in advance of the hour if that was what it took to be certain of boarding my flight.

KWASHI CAME TO the Hôtel Indépendance with the Nissan at ten minutes before 7.00 a.m., and so it was that I was at the airport precisely on time for the check-in counter to open for business. I was the only passenger, or would-be passenger for that matter, in sight. The deserted airport only served to emphasise its seediness. The facilities seemed to have been abandoned in a hurry. The airport looked like a set for a remake of the film *Raid on Entebbe*. The concrete walls continued to flake in silence. A janitor put in an appearance, passing a damp mop over cracked tiles that may never have been clean and surely never would be again.

The entry door to the check-in area was locked. News came from a passing official that the door might be opened at 7.30 a.m., although he didn't know for sure, but it wasn't, and at 7.30 a.m. I was still standing in a queue of one. There was then another suggestion that 7.50 a.m. was being considered for door-opening time, and this was subsequently extended to 8.00 a.m.

Luggage-bearing passengers then began to arrive behind me, at first in a trickle, then in a flow, and finally in a flash flood in spate. Clamour and gesticulation were the order of the day. A solid mass of humanity pressed forward at the locked door to the check-in area. There was no way to either advance or retreat, and still the passengers kept on coming.

The door was finally opened at 8.10 a.m., whereupon a portly resident of Ouaga, dressed in an immaculate safari suit and carrying both a crocodile leather briefcase of a kind that I was by then not unfamiliar with and a heavy burden of self-importance, pushed his way to the front of the queue. Ouaga was his city, and I held no scrap of envy for him.

This gentleman's luggage, carried by a hired hand, matched his briefcase, and its manufacture clearly represented a major diminution in the crocodile population in some unfortunate location. The proceeds from its sale would have enabled a very large number of its owner's less privileged fellow citizens to eat guinea fowl for an extended period of time.

I was the second in line to pass through the door and content at that. In a screened closet beyond the door a policeman made an examination of my personal effects that was as casual as it was perfunctory. I moved on. My luggage was checked in. My ticket was registered and then taken to a glassed-in area off to one side in which a number of bemused looking people were sitting in front of computer screens. All of them seemed to be doing their best to demonstrate to observers that this was their first day on the job and they had not yet worked out what the computer screens were for. Their job was to produce boarding passes. In due course, of a variety in which time meant little, they generated a boarding pass for me.

After check-in, I had planned to return to the body of the airport to meet with Kwashi, and although, if the imagination could be stretched to dramatic limits, such a return would have been possible, the developing melee inside and outside of the check-in area made getting out a too-daunting prospect to contemplate.

I therefore called my farewell to Kwashi through the check-in door, over the heads of those fighting to get through it. I would have liked to have given Kwashi something material, but since Kwashi already possessed all the seefas, that was not to be.

Passengers continued to push their way into the check-in area, which had become a holding pen as no one was yet being permitted to advance out of it in the likely direction of an aircraft. The quality of air was hot, humid and as thick as treacle, seasoned by newly shed sweat and the institutionalised body odour of a not insignificant number of low-budget European tourists whose itinerary in Burkina Faso must have taken in places where water was scarce and soap scarcer. They were festooned with wooden artefacts, tribal masks, drums and grime.

AFTER A FURTHER hour had elapsed, the atmosphere inside the check-in area was becoming unbearable. It was solid with people. The least movement on one side of the area created a Mexican wave rippling through the humanity to the far side in an instant. To add insult to injury it was announced that the Air France flight was forty-five minutes late out of Abidjan.

As if this announcement had triggered sympathy in the breasts of those in authority, a door leading to the official realms of emigration was opened on one side of the check-in area. The seething mob began filtering slowly through in that direction, at a snail's pace, but in blessed movement for all that.

My journey to Burkina Faso began with my being paged at an airport, and it was to draw to its close in a like manner. The difference was that my being paged at Ouaga airport was a lot more alarming than it had been in Paris.

On reporting to Ouaga airport's version of an information desk I was told that I had been bumped, although as it was from business class up to first class this was not unacceptable. I was provided with a new boarding pass, which I then had to resubmit to the emigration desk for endorsement. I struggled back through the crowd against the tide. It was a return to combat once again, but that was a small price to have paid for the result.

THE AIR FRANCE aircraft touched down at Ouaga at 10.12 a.m. All individually departing passengers who had, by whatever means, obtained a valid boarding pass were herded into another holding area. The people outnumbered the seating arrangements in the holding area by a long margin. The sun beat through the glassed-over front of what was fast becoming a limbo along the road to perdition.

The better part of an hour (more or less) elapsed before an announcement was made that boarding was about to commence. Eight to ten passengers at a time were released in the direction of the aircraft. There was a period of more than several minutes between releases. I felt much more than a little frustration in not knowing what was happening.

My turn came. The relief of stepping through the departure gate was profound. Air France had set up their own baggage check at the foot of the steps leading up to the aircraft door. Checked-in luggage required personal identification by the owner and was then searched and inspected in detail before being finally consigned to the aircraft hold. Carry-on luggage was similarly scrutinised. Air France was manifesting a level of confidence in Ouaga airport security that was shared by me.

I saluted Air France in my heart and resolved never to think badly of that airline again, although I supposed that that particular determination would go the way of most similarly good-intentioned resolutions that I made at the start of each New Year.

I turned around at the top of the steps before entering the aircraft and cast my eyes over what I could see of Ouaga airport. I raised my right hand to wave goodbye, resisting any temptation to make a V sign. Such a sign could equally have signified victory of course.

It had taken me almost as long to travel between the Hôtel Indépendance and my seat on the Air France flight as it would for me to fly from Ouaga to Paris.

The flight departed only an hour or so late. Guinea fowl was on the menu for lunch in the first-class cabin. I doubted that that particular bird was one of the ten thousand slaughtered that day in Ouaga.

The dun desert slipped away beneath as the aircraft headed north.

– 4 –

Secretaries' Day at the Tropico Inn

Each pondered, lonely midst the crowd,
  Brave campesinos, tortured hill.
Machetes drawn, the word came loud,
  They scattered, and the mine was still.
The guttered plant, the dumps of spoil,
Air shimmered on the sun-stroked soil.

Two adits blind, both belching smoke
  That rolled and boiled, and strung
          the breeze.
A heartbeat, then the powder spoke,
  Leaves pattered from the mango trees,
Ten thousand twisting at a glance,
A salsa beating deadly dance.

Bright gold of San Sebastian,
  Once pride of east El Salvador.
Guerrilla stations, man for man,
  The base pursuit of civil war.
Grim soldiers' faces, tautly grey,
Death squads paid by the USA.

For oft, when in the mud they die,
  Delivered lives for greater good,
They flash upon the tearing eye.
  Those bodies sprawled in solitude.
Then hearts with resolution fill.
Fight on, to cure the nation's ill.

With apologies to Mr William Wordsworth

M Y KLM FLIGHT landed at the airport of Guatemala City at precisely six o'clock in the morning. The airport concourses were lively even at that hour, and if the liveliness did not contain much of the quality of orderliness, well, that was Latin America, carrying one less burden and all to the good.

In the waiting lounges bright-eyed children scrambled over mighty accumulations of hand luggage of such a wondrous variety that the head of a live chicken, or the questing snout of a pig poking from a corner of any one of the creaking and bulging items that made the piles what they were, would have presented no surprise, even to the uninitiated.

A little boy, wearing khaki shorts and a faded tee shirt that in its prime might have had an association with Miami Beach, sat barefoot on the main concourse floor, sucking at broken chicken bones. The debris of a fried chicken meal unrelated to Kentucky was distributed around his stretched-out legs. The spread included the remnants of at least two French fries unwittingly smeared into a flat and streaky pancake by the heavy foot of a careless passenger. The fries, thus reduced, constituted a culinary loss of some severity to the bone sucker, whose attempts to scratch up and consume what was left of them had already reached the point of diminishing returns.

I threaded through the throng, taking great care where I placed my feet so as not to interfere with any other meal in progress as I made my way to the departure gate for flight GU 961 of Aviateca airlines. That flight was destined, when it ultimately got away, half an hour late in fact, to take me to San Salvador, the capital of the country of El Salvador over on the Pacific side of Central America. The Aviateca aircraft was a Boeing 737. It appeared, both on the outside and the inside when I boarded it, to be almost uncannily clean and well maintained.

I WAS ALLOCATED a window seat and was thereby enabled to observe some of the delights of Guatemala City unrolling beneath the aircraft as it tracked out to the east. The city was an overblown and sprawling congregation of island-like blocks of festering flats rearing up through a sea of rusting corrugated metal roofs. The side walls of the flats were strung, from window to window, with loaded washing lines bearing enough clothes in various stages of dampness to cover up most of the long streaks and blotchy stains on the rude concrete that they lay against.

In the near vicinity of the city's airport a shantytown formed a haphazardly cast dark blot. As I looked at it, it seemed to seep outwards, intent on consuming whatever lay in its voracious path. At its core the shantytown ringed a vast and smouldering garbage dump as if it were presiding over its own funeral pyre.

Beyond the city the land was, by contrast, green and pleasant. There was a scattering of small, bright villages placed in the midst of so many diminutive fields that I could not imagine where enough people to work such an infinite chequerboard could be found. Relief reared up in smooth hills. My eye was drawn to follow the twisting lines of placid rivers.

Coffee was served on the aircraft. It was fine coffee, its taste enhanced by association with the little cinnamon-flavoured bun that accompanied it. Quality of coffee was, in my experience, always directly proportional to the quality of the people in the country that produced and ground the beans. As measured by this coffee scale, things were already looking good, to some extent easing any sense of nervousness over what might await me over there in El Salvador.

FLIGHT GU961 TOUCHED down at the airport of San Salvador at 8.20 a.m. The airport was located close enough to the Pacific coast for aircraft to come in low over the sea near the little town of La Libertad when making their final approach. However, the airport was so far away from the city of San Salvador, forty-two kilometres to be precise, that any acknowledgement of direct association of the airport with the city seemed to be hardly credible.

The date was 23rd April, 1992. El Salvador's bloody twelve-year-long civil war, infamously fuelled and funded by alleged interests (both overt and covert) of the United States of America, had subsided into a tenuously holding ceasefire only a month or so previously.

In a situation of ceasefire, a month without a shot fired in mortal anger was an even longer time than a week in politics. United Nations monitoring agencies were by then spread out all over El Salvador to guarantee the alleged peace in their fortunately inimitable way, so that was all right maybe. At the very least the current state of play in the country was felt, in the judgement of those who knew about those things at the offices of Uncle Joe's subsidiary (better known as El Joe) in San Salvador, to have calmed down enough from what it once was for a representative of the Company's Flying Circus, namely me, to make a several times postponed visit.

El Joe didn't ask for my opinion on the matter, but there was nothing new in that. The Company didn't have an administration base in El Salvador as yet, but give it time, and in any case El Joe was there, so for all true believers there was nothing to worry about.

At the San Salvador airport immigration counter two of El Joe's representatives were waiting for me. Their names were Mauricio and Eduardo. They had come down from San Salvador for the purpose. Grateful for their assistance, I was raced through the immigration formalities without a single official murmur being directed either at me or at the validity of my travel documents. Mauricio and Eduardo seemed to be on highly familiar terms with just about everyone who worked at the airport, not to mention more than a few of those who hung around on its lesser fringes. The depth of familiarity with the scene that they displayed denoted a truly inside track.

Many major multinational organisations based in Latin American countries in the manner of Uncle Joe, whose El Joe business included the frequent passage in and out of the country of visitors from overseas, engaged so-called fixers such as Mauricio and Eduardo to run slickly greased trails through the dense jungles of local bureaucracy.

At any relevant airport or in any government department where filling in a mind-numbing array of official forms constituted an everlasting barrier to the progress of the hitherto uncorrupted, such fixers found their rightful place. Many were consultants for independent hire. They lurked as they waited for custom, circling the innocent arrivals in the manner of hungry sharks around a shoal of fish. They were sharply suited and favoured florid ties, and each of them invariably carried a leather-bound folder, fat-packed under one armpit.

Fixers were experts in circumventing queues and waiting lists, in knowing who to see and when to see them. Once, at Lima airport when travelling with none other than that prince of note-takers who bore the reference indicator MTM, I asked him how Uncle Joe's contracted fixers in Peru managed to perform their tasks so well and so instantly. "I don't know," he replied. "And I don't want to know."

As fixers went, Mauricio appeared to be quite at home in the seedier corners of the mould, although Eduardo didn't. Eduardo was sprightly and moved with a manner of clipped bearing suggestive of a military background. He was, it later emerged, a former colonel of the Salvadorian national army. Now permanently retired and as out of uniform as it was possible to be in El Salvador, Eduardo headed up El Joe's security department. Any questions as to what daddy Eduardo had done in the civil war were, I thought, best answered in accordance with MTM's comment as applied to the methodology of Uncle Joe's Peruvian fixers.

MY DRIVE UP to San Salvador with Eduardo and Mauricio took place along a fairly modern road half choked by the trappings of poverty. The day was hot and muggy, even at the relatively early hour. Ragged hawkers and vendors of flowers, fruit, yellow dusters, hub caps, newspapers, cheap necklaces and brooches, lottery tickets and garden tools, to name only a fraction of the wares on offer, swarmed around knocking on the vehicle windows at every road junction and tollgate. Having survived a civil war, their objective now was merely to survive the vicissitudes of post-war life.

The direction of the road to San Salvador led just about due north from La Libertad, on a line that came close to bisecting the battered rectangular box-like shape formed on a map by the international border of the country. The long axis of the El Salvador box ran more or less from west to east and was followed by the Pan American Highway, which entered El Salvador from Guatemala, traversed the nation, and exited into Honduras.

At the entry to the city of San Salvador, the road taken by our car passed a virtual skyscraper, a uniquely tall and isolated building rising like an incongruous finger from the otherwise clenched fist of lowly red-tiled roofs surrounding it. The building offered an impression of giving the bird to something, or hopefully someone, who might be extremely well placed at the peak of the current USA administration.

The exterior of the tall building was coated in sheets of one-way reflective glass of the kind that was a favoured choice for the sunglass lenses of thugs, bouncers and bullies, not that there was much to differentiate between such variations on a dregs-of-society theme. On one face of the building a ragged black gap looking like a mouth pursed open in surprise was surrounded by a radiant halo of shattered panes. It suggested that not too long ago a perspicacious individual, disillusioned with whatever the building stood for, had taken advantage of having a loaded rocket launcher in his possession and furthermore of knowing how to aim and fire the weapon.

San Salvador affected an air of being traumatised. Not only was the city badly run down but at first glance it looked to be well on the way to falling apart. Its downtown area teemed with aimless crowds consisting of randomly wandering collections of the dispossessed who wouldn't know what they were looking for until they found it.

A military presence was sown around the streets as thickly and as potently as slices of red chillies in a chicken stew. The automatic weapons that the soldiers carried, with a familiarity born of long experience in their use, were darkly metalled and menacing. Their camouflage-capped heads traversed in tight half circles, eyes ever alert for promising targets.

In San Salvador I was accommodated in the Hotel Presidente, set at the top of a steeply sloping road in a good residential sector of the city, a long way away from the downtown clamour. In front of the hotel stood an imposing monument to the revolution. The only problem was, Eduardo told me, that no one knew which revolution it was that was being commemorated by the monument: they had had so many revolutions in El Salvador that they had quite lost track of the sequence.

That afternoon Eduardo took me to El Joe's offices on the edge of the city to discuss and confirm my itinerary for the coming week. The arrangement involved my first of all travelling with Eduardo by car out of San Salvador and down along the Pan American Highway to the city of San Miguel in the east near the border with Honduras, a distance of a hundred and forty kilometres.

In the countryside to the north of San Miguel, not far from a bustling market town named Santa Rosa de Lima, the San Sebastian gold mine was located. Over a few days I was due to make an evaluation of the mine and assess any exploration or development opportunities that could be incorporated, with local support provided by El Joe's people, into a Company investment proposal to the current owners of the mine and property, assuming that such a proposal was deemed reasonable to make on the strength (or weakness) of my consequent report.

Eduardo set out the security rules for our journey to San Miguel. The civil war, he said, had laid a heavy hand on the road and the people who lived along it. He advised that if the vehicle in which he and I were to travel should perchance be detained *en route* by what he described as *bandoleros* he should handle all the talking. I could easily buy into that, although not with a happy heart.

I was collected by Eduardo for our trip to San Miguel at 7.45 a.m. on the following day. Such facilities of the Hotel Presidente as I had been able to appreciate during my short stay were excellent, although jet lag militated against my having used them to the full. But that was the way it went sometimes.

We travelled over to San Miguel in a convoy of two pickup trucks. I was the front-seat passenger with Eduardo driving in one pickup, and two euphemistically titled *ayudantes*, or helpers, followed in another, always keeping close to our tail. The helpers, named Carlos and Jesús (otherwise Chucho), were assigned by Eduardo to stay with me for the duration of the trip. I assumed that Carlos and Chucho might be bodyguards, and if so they were distinguished in being the first of that breed that I had ever been provided with on a Company-sponsored business visit anywhere.

The thing was, Carlos and Chucho didn't appear at all tough. They were not at all like the battering-ram-faced soldiers who were so prolific in urban El Salvador. They did not look to be any more threatening than the comfortable family men that they turned out to be. Carlos was a little tubby and more than a little cheery, and Chucho by contrast was slim and sombre. Together they came close to resembling a Salvadorian version of Laurel and Hardy.

They might very well guard me, I supposed, but who was going to guard them?

Carlos carried a small leather pouch in one hand, and if he ever put the pouch down it was only to have Chucho pick it up again immediately. The contents of the pouch were heavier than might have been estimated from pouch size considerations alone, suggesting that they consisted of something metallic. Possibly something like a gun.

Eduardo for his part was equipped with a snub-nosed pistol that was subject to much less secrecy. He placed the firearm under his seat in the pickup, where he could reach out and touch it without a tremor.

ALL OVER THE near and far environs of San Salvador that we drove through garbage was strewn on either side of the Pan American Highway, stretching as far off into the dwindling distance as the eye could see. It was venerable garbage of a most fundamental kind, sorted and re-sorted to the extent that it had achieved an imposing degree of barrenness approaching sterility. The garbage no longer contained any vestige of anything that could with the remotest stretch of the imagination be described as useful, even to the host of disadvantaged people that continued to rummage through it with such obvious assiduity.

The garbage had gathered in mounds. It filled up gullies and stood in shallow banks against dwellings and on any slopes that provided the least kind of positive inclination. It was the chief attribute of the wasteland it occupied. The local environment was so shattered by the civil war that the only real priorities for those who had lived through its daily thrall was to avoid being overwhelmed and to exist against the odds in the faint hope of meeting better days ahead.

The condition of the tarmac surfacing the Pan American Highway, apart from the drifts of sun-rotted plastic rubbish littered across it near San Salvador, was fairly good. Considering that the highway had traversed a war zone for more than a decade, there were fewer rough spots on it than might have been expected. The highway went on to run through relatively rugged volcanic terrain in which the volcanoes might have been extinct, but where, as San Salvador knew to its historic cost, unexpected earthquakes remained an ever-present danger.

Way off to the right of the highway the mighty cone of Volcan San Vicente (2,181 metres) served as an effective marker for the commencement of our journey to San Miguel. In between Volcan San Vicente and San Salvador the highway snaked through the little town of Cojutepeque and on around the north curve of Lago de Ilopango, a large lake occupying a bush-decked volcanic crater. Cojutepeque rejoiced in its dedication to the sale of oranges and orange juice pressed to order. The oranges were piled in glowing windrows and neat pyramids and cones a couple of metres high all along the verges of the town centre.

The slightly lesser peak of Volcan San Miguel (2,130 metres), close to the city of San Miguel, was the counterpart to Volcan San Vicente that made a fitting finishing post for our trip. Both of the extinct volcanoes were, not inappropriately given the times, memorials to an effective ceasefire, this one of a specific geological variety.

The vegetation on either side of the highway, once San Salvador's sea of garbage had ebbed behind us, seemed dry and scrubby where cultivation had yet to gain a hold. A goodly proportion of the land, however, was under commercial crops. Beans, maize, coffee, sisal, oranges and extensive sugar-cane plantations with a related scatter of artisanal sugar-processing mills offered up great swathes of intense and rippling greenery.

OUR CONVOY OF two pickups approached the outskirts of San Miguel after a journey characterised by a lack of any direct contact with *bandoleros*. That of course did not imply that there was never a time when there might not have been a *bandolero* looking at us, or we at him, somewhere or other.

Bandoleros, together with their guerrilla associates, had certainly been busy on the great bridge that took the Pan American Highway across the river into San Miguel. The state of that bridge suggested that among the talents of *bandoleros* and guerrillas was an expertise in the use of explosives for destructive purposes. Pending the reconstruction of the main bridge, a temporary bridge crossing had been erected alongside it to convey traffic to San Miguel, and on that happy basis we crossed the river.

My FIRST VIEW of the city of San Miguel provided a less than prepossessing impression of narrow, littered streets, crammed to near insensibility with people. The main street of the city was named Roosevelt, and on it was located the Tropico Inn, the hotel where I was to reside. The rooms and facilities of the Tropico Inn were established as a square on a single floor level enclosing an open-air dining and functions area within which coconut palm trees rose in elegant curves and purple bougainvillea cascaded.

At the Tropico Inn we were met by El Joe's San Miguel district resident manager. He just happened to be Eduardo's son, Eduardo Jr.

Luis (otherwise Lucho), the local manager of the US-based outfit that owned the San Sebastian gold mine and property, was not present to meet us as arranged, however. Eduardo Jr advised us that Lucho had come along to the Tropico Inn a little earlier, had waited for a while and had then departed, ostensibly for another engagement but more likely, as it emerged later, because that was just the way Lucho was.

I never found out whether or not Lucho had a second given name, but if he had I would have bet that it was not Reliability.

I checked into my room at the Tropico Inn, mainly to claim it as my own, since the availability of hotel rooms was at a premium owing to demands from the large contingent of UN ceasefire monitors invading the city. Eduardo Sr, together with his *bandolero* deterrent gun, prepared to make the return journey to San Salvador.

Attempts to make contact with Lucho fell as flat as the surface of the crater-bound Laguna de Olomega to the south of San Miguel. After a fruitless wait of an hour or so for Lucho, enough was finally enough for us all, and, prompted and led this time by Eduardo Jr, we decided to go and take a preliminary look at the San Sebastian property without him.

My first meeting with Lucho eventually took place at 8.00 p.m. that night when he deigned to put in an appearance at the Tropico Inn. If Lucho had set out from home laden with excuses for his earlier vanishing act, he had shed them all prior to his reaching the Tropico Inn, since if he ever referred to them I didn't hear him.

Lucho was a Peruvian national, which made him a genuine expatriate in El Salvador. His face might have exhibited the dark-skinned, hawk-nosed, piercing features of his Inca ancestors, had such features not been submerged beneath a burden of flesh. A kind classification of Lucho's figure would have seen him typified as moderately obese – for those who wanted to be kind to Lucho, that is. It was not easy to think of Lucho with benevolence for any extended period of time.

It took no more than five minutes in Lucho's company for me to recognise in him a reluctance to engage with society. Lucho was fully equipped with a severely limited appreciation not only of how to do the right thing by his peers but also, more importantly, as to why the right thing ought to be done by them in the first place. Lucho had come to adopt bullshitting as a way of life. I worked for a Company in which the fine-art exponents of bullshitting were almost as thick on the ground as was the garbage around San Salvador, and so I recognised a master of the craft instantly when I met one.

It was always said that it took one to know one, but I don't know about that.

The location of the San Sebastian mine property was forty-five kilometres north of San Miguel. The first forty kilometres out of the city made use of a road that was paved, although in poor repair, to reach Santa Rosa de Lima. The final five kilometres beyond Santa Rosa de Lima ground along a narrow and rough dirt track.

As a central feature, serving as a landmark to home in on, the mine property offered a rounded hill, rising to a couple of hundred metres above the surrounding terrain. In the heart of this hill coursed the gold-bearing quartz veins that provided the San Sebastian mine with its life-blood.

In its heyday of production the mine was accessed from a couple of entry adits driven into one face of the hill. The fact that both of the adit portals and a not insignificant extent of their immediately proximal tunnels had been blown in by guerrilla action during the civil war served to render their access application redundant. To all intents and purposes the mine was closed off to being entered by any conventional means.

A less orthodox option to gaining entry into the mine appeared to be provided by virtue of the work of a number of small groups of informal (not to say illegal) miners, who were burrowing in the manner of moles directly into the hill in at least four locations, although to what effect was not immediately clear on that first day.

These groups of miners, locally known as *wiliseros*, were conducting their activities with the tacit tolerance of the property owners, although presumably only for as long as the owner was prepared to be tolerant. I found the quality of their co-operation, right down to the very last man among them, to provide a marked contrast with that of the indifference of Lucho.

The *wiliseros* were mining men who, to quote Agricola, were blessed with a "peculiar dignity". They possessed little more than the tattered garments they stood up in and their daily lives were unimaginably hard, yet their hands were always warm in friendship.

During my first afternoon on the San Sebastian property I descended a narrow, ten-metre deep shaft with one of their cadre named Santander, lead hand of the two *wiliseros* who had sunk the shaft, and crawled behind him on hands and knees for twenty metres or so along a one-metre high drift that was cut laterally from the shaft bottom to engage with one of the San Sebastian veins. It was hot enough at the face of the drift to suffocate an iguana. I was glad to claw my way back out again to the more supportable heat of the surface.

Santander's shaft was sunk into the floor of a rudimentary open-pit mining excavation, which was in effect not much more than a shallow scour in the ground exposing a zone of dun-coloured rock with clay-type alteration. The open pit rejoiced in the somewhat overstated title of Casa Grande.

AROUND THE RIM of the hill into which the two hapless adits were driven, and on which the mine buildings formerly serving them were located, mine spoil dumps formed dribbling scars. All save one of the mine buildings had been reduced to dusty rubble following the explosive attention of guerrillas. The remaining standing building, which might at one time have been a storage shed for ore and process plant samples, was in use as a rudimentary office for a crew of half a dozen men employed at the site by Lucho on behalf of the property owner. The members of the crew were presumably presiding as custodians over the ruins. Why the guerrillas chose to let that building live on was a question that only the guerrillas could answer.

At the foot of the hill a dammed up area filled with grey tailings derived from the impressively wrecked ore processing plant reared up on the very edge of a substantial river that flowed onwards down to Santa Rosa de Lima. Acid drainage from the spoil dumps and tailings dam placed a tart yellow hand on the riverbed and pointed its fingers ominously downstream.

THAT NIGHT, WHEN Lucho finally put in an appearance at the Tropico Inn his lack of contrition knew no bounds. He assured me that he would definitely be along at seven o'clock on the following morning in order to honour me with his company for a full day's jaunt to the San Sebastian mine property. I could but take him at his word.

He arrived for this promised appointment no more than half an hour late to find me waiting for him, not exactly patiently, in the central courtyard of the Tropico Inn. Unfazed by time constraints, Lucho sat down at a table, ordered a breakfast of a dimension to match his state of corpulence and delayed our departure for an additional half hour. By then the outside temperature was already making healthy inroads on the 35°C that it was determined to reach as soon as possible.

Finally, we set off for San Sebastian. I travelled with Lucho in his pickup, with Carlos and Chucho following closely behind in theirs. On the way, Lucho launched into a rolling commentary that would assuredly have gained first prize in a boring-the-pants-off contest and received an additional certificate of commendation for its ability to take avoidable liberties with the truth. Much of what he had to say stressed the more negative aspects of the aftermath of civil war on the El Salvador and the San Miguel district and touched further on a related mountain of problems that in Lucho's perception militated against undertaking any form of mine development in the foreseeable future.

It seemed to me that if Lucho's corporate terms of reference included making a sales pitch for the property on behalf of his employers, as I had been led to believe it would, then Lucho was setting about fulfilling the task in a very oblique way. On the other hand, Lucho was behaving extremely rationally for one who might have felt that his comfortable little backwater berth at San Miguel was being threatened by a potential investor.

Within the walls of the one remaining building at San Sebastian Lucho produced a few property-related maps and recited over them a brief account of the work thus far carried out on the property, under his supervision, for the owners. The maps dealt mainly with the surface installations, layout and exploration sampling results. There was, however, one composite plan showing some of the underground development headings, no doubt presented as they were prior to the attention of guerrillas rendering them as they weren't.

Even allowing for the undoubted difficulties of conducting mineral exploration practice in a time of civil war, neither the content of Lucho's maps nor the quality of the work performed by Lucho and his crew could be defined as satisfactory under the circumstances. The crew had devoted a great deal of effort to digging trenches across the face of the hill for sampling purposes, which, at face value, was commendable. But on later inspection of the trenches I saw that none of the excavations had gone deep enough to expose any bedrock, which meant that the industry of the diggers was largely delivered in vain.

Such extremely arduous work and the not unreasonable technical principles applied to it were not helped by Lucho's foundered endeavours in the field of gathering information that was geologically valid. This situation of knowing what information was relevant and what was not was compounded at an analytical laboratory that Lucho had had his crew construct alongside the track into San Sebastian from Santa Rosa de Lima, down at the foot of the hill near the tailings dam. The lab was set up in just about the least sterile environment that could be imagined for the analysis of gold values in samples.

The reason for the lab being where it was may not have been unrelated to the nearby presence of a small bakery, a consummately localised little *panaderia* that served the surrounding and sparsely populated San Sebastian locality to great effect. When such a commercial establishment appeared in such an unusual context, faith in the future of the people who set it up and patronised it rode high in my estimation. The *panaderia* was run by a middle-aged *dueña* of cheerful demeanour, ably assisted by two young girls. Rolls of bread were baked daily. Cookies in various guises formed a speciality of the house, and sweet buns were a treat that sold out almost as quickly as a batch of them hit the counter. Lucho and his crew were regular customers.

Lucho's crew was additionally engaged in a laborious attempt to clear and reopen the portal of one of the dynamited adits. Their labour was honest, but their pick and shovel technique was about to take them nowhere quickly. I thought that the hiring of a gang of *wiliseros* for the task would have speeded up the clearance, but that might have been too much to hope for. Lucho lived in a state of uneasy truce with the *wiliseros*, as if by ignoring them he could pretend that they weren't really there. Any attempt by Lucho to insert his person into a *wilisero*-sized tunnel (and more critically to extricate himself again) would surely have found echoes in the story of a certain honey-loving bear named Pooh and a rabbit hole.

At the point where he judged his map-associated presentation to be complete, Lucho bade me farewell, at the same time failing to simulate reluctance for us to part company. His attention span was not able to spread itself across a full day. He departed in late morning for San Miguel, where even if he didn't have better things to do, life would certainly be less exacting for him than it would have been on a day out at San Sebastian. That was fine by me, as the flag of Lucho's ability to hinder my investigation of the property was by now in principle firmly nailed to the top of the tallest mango tree on the hill for all to recognise.

Before he left, Lucho assigned three members of his crew to me to serve as expert guides to the property and also to assist in taking any required geological samples. For once, Lucho did me a favour. The three men comprised two auxiliaries working under the leadership of a certain Don Juan. Don Juan was wafer thin, seemingly composed totally of weathered skin and tough sinew. He was a small man graced with the air of a giant, courteous and dignified, the equal of anyone and ready to face down any challenge. He had the drooping grey moustache of a grandee – a man who might sit easily on a horse if he had one. His sparing stature made the broad-brimmed straw hat that he wore seem to stretch as wide as a parasol, so that he carried shade with him on every part of his person.

From Don Juan's belt hung a long scabbard of tooled leather that barely avoided dragging its tip along the ground. The scabbard was home to a machete with a blade of blued metal, the double edges of which, when drawn, were honed to a gleaming keenness of the kind that could hold still and part a floating chiffon scarf. As Don Juan led the way through the tangle of brush on the hillside he had only to touch errant branches with the edge of his machete for them to give up and fall in an instant.

OUR NEWLY FORMED group, led by Don Juan and his two assistants with Carlos and Chucho guarding the rear, made its way up the hillside by way of one of Lucho's abortive trenches. At the top, where it was so sorely hot that I was already as wrung out as a twisted sheet fresh from being pummelled on the rocks on washing day in the river (upstream from the AMD, that is), I could see that the hill had three effective summits, or *cerros*, separated from one another by shallow saddles. The three *cerros*, advised Don Juan, who was something of a fount of information, were named Conseguire, San Juan and San Sebastian. We had arrived close to Cerro Conseguire. To return to the base of the hill we traversed along the summit ridge to San Sebastian via San Juan, on the way preparing a sketch map of the mine facilities spread out below us in all their decaying splendour.

I ARRIVED BACK in the welcome shade of the central courtyard of the Tropico Inn at approximately five o'clock that evening. There had been a few changes made in the courtyard during the preceding hours, not the least being the erection of a performance stage over on one side, which was incidentally the side of the courtyard on which my room was located. The stage was draped with cables and wires and stacked on either side with a collection of large black boxes, including a twin set of massive amplifiers. The arrangement suggested that a rather loud musical performance of some form was very much imminent. One of the amplifiers was positioned, with a semblance of absolute finality, in the near vicinity of the outer window of my room. Whatever my short-term options were about to be, any sleep for the duration of the expected musical performance was unlikely to be one of them.

The occasion about to be celebrated, I was told, was "Secretaries' Day". This explained why so many young ladies could be spotted in the streets of San Miguel clutching cellophane-covered single roses, tributes from their bosses to commemorate an elapsed year in which the dedicated secretarial services of the former to the latter had been not only taken for granted but also very probably received with thanklessness by the latter.

The Tropico Inn, so I was told, planned an evening (and for all anyone knew a night as well) of music delivered by a nationally well known salsa band to delight the hearts of those for whom Secretaries' Day might offer, to quote Robert Burns, "one cordial in this melancholy vale".

There, in that batter'd Caravanserai, the prospect of a few hours sans song and sans singer shaped up as being somewhat insecure. The brave music of a distant drum seemed to be an equally remote possibility. A night sans sleep and sans end was more likely.

I decided that as I was unable to combat this looming assault on the senses I might as well link up with it. I sat down at a table in the courtyard of the Tropico Inn at the appointed hour of eight o'clock, both to see what was going to happen and to eat dinner. I ordered some *camarones a la plancha*, grilled prawns without frills. The *camarones* were excellent, although fewer in number than was desirable. Perhaps their paucity was a symbolic precursor of the eventual outcome of the evening.

Time passed, and secretaries were as thin on the ground around the salsa stage as Lucho was broad around the beam wherever he was actually located at the same time. It was rumoured that a cover charge set for the event had acted as a deterrent not only for the secretarial population of San Miguel but, less surprisingly, for their bosses as well. A single flower and maybe a hastily signed card once a year might be one thing for the bosses to hand over, but forking out a cover charge for a secretary as well as themselves to attend an event at the Tropico Inn was quite something else and not to be considered lightly.

The salsa band mounted the stage and struck up its first number. The band outnumbered the audience, and so the demographic balance remained until 11.30 p.m. when the celebration died on its feet and Secretaries' Day at the Tropico Inn came to a premature conclusion.

I was then able to retire gratefully to my room in the sure knowledge that the opportunity to sleep was assured – unless, that is, the stage should collapse and cause one of the giant amplifiers to fall over and crash through my window.

ON THE FOLLOWING morning Lucho was again scheduled to appear at the Tropico Inn at the hour of seven-thirty to accompany me into the field. It seemed once more, however, that there was appointed time, there was Salvadorian time and there was Lucho time, and never the trio should meet. Lucho, amazingly enough, turned up five minutes early, but it was merely to announce that he needed to go and find a doctor to tend to his wife who had incurred a domestic accident involving a pressure cooker. This meant that Lucho would not be ready to leave for the mine site until 8 a.m. So far, so good, except for Lucho's wife maybe.

At 9 a.m. Lucho had still not fulfilled his threat to grace the Tropico Inn with his bulging presence. I phoned Lucho's house. The phone was answered by Mrs Lucho, who seemed quite bright and cheerful for one who had allegedly had a recent altercation with a pressure cooker. She told me that Lucho had left home for parts unknown about half an hour since.

I left a note for Lucho at the reception desk of the Tropico Inn in the event (unlikely though it seemed) that he might elect to show himself that morning, and then we – that is, Carlos, Chucho and myself – went out to San Sebastian without him. I could not quite suppress a sense of relief that Lucho was elsewhere. The sad thing was, I thought, that Lucho was much more of a liability to himself than he was to his employers. He could have accomplished so much if the great energy he directed at evasive pursuits could have been channelled into moving his project forward.

THE DAY PROMISED to be another hot one. We stopped at the marketplace of Santa Rosa de Lima to purchase for me a straw sombrero of the low-crowned, broad-brimmed type worn by Don Juan.

The market, even at a mid-morning hour, was very busy. There were quite a number of vendors of sombreros to choose from. I was a gringo and my presence not unnaturally attracted a fair measure of slightly hostile curiosity as to who I was, where I came from and, for that matter, what I was doing in Santa Rosa de Lima. I found that once it became common knowledge that I was not a citizen of the USA, where apparently the real gringos were supposed to come from, I met only with friendliness. All the same, there was a lesson to be learned insofar as being different in El Salvador meant being careful.

At the mine property, I was reunited with Don Juan and his two aides once more. Don Juan said he knew of an adit named the 300 Coco that was cut into the hill from around the side under Cerro

San Sebastian and that was still open for investigation. The tunnel allegedly had a gold-bearing vein exposed in the roof at its inner end of penetration and, moreover, offered a good transverse section of the hillside geology that could be sampled along its full length.

We worked our way through dry scrub, a journey eased by the gentle application of Don Juan's machete, to reach the portal of the 300 Coco adit. The adit, which had been driven using hand-held drill steel and sledgehammers, was approximately two metres by two metres in cross-section, allowing an adequate provision for standing room, especially in the case of Don Juan. We all entered the tunnel, illuminating its passage with the assistance of flashlights, courtesy of El Joe, held in the capable hands of Carlos and Chucho. The tunnel ran straight in for seventy-five metres, where it met with caving on one side that we needed to scramble around with care to get into the final fifteen to twenty metres leading up to the end face.

Beyond the caved area the atmosphere of the tunnel felt oppressively humid. Bats, modest in size but numbered in scores, resided on the roof of the tunnel and were evidently less than pleased at being disturbed. One or two of them gave me baleful red-eyed glares along a flashlight beam as they crawled and flopped over the rock like a Dracula team honing its descent skills on the outside wall of a gothic castle.

The bats wheeled and flapped around us, seeming to take up such space as was available to fill and dispelling for a while the understanding that they navigated using sonic radar, for in spite of squeaking like a corridor of doors in a haunted hotel, more than a few of them managed to collide with one part or another of my anatomy. To reduce their confusion the bats made their way to the portal of the adit, where they held position just inside, a fluttering and squealing mass that made a strobe of the square of sunlight framed by the portal.

On the floor behind the face of the 300 Coco adit's inner section, large and long-legged black spiders scurried over the not insignificant deposits of dusty bat droppings that they had colonised. Don Juan and his two helpers declared the spiders to be poisonous and were intent on stamping them out of existence until I asked them to put a stop to any further thoughts of such a heartless massacre. The foot-pounding activity raised great powdery puffs of bat shit that hung in hesitant motes in the artificial light.

Most of the stirred-up bat excrement made its way back to the floor of the tunnel for the further benefit of the black spiders. A definite balance of the suspended motes was no doubt breathed in by all of us.

Medical practitioners did not recommend the inhalation of powdered bat shit: it was not an ideal substance to sow on the inner surface of lungs, for elements of the unsavoury commodity were apt to take root there and grow in weird and not very wonderful ways.

An uncomfortable ripple of chest pains that I experienced a few days after my encounter with bat shit in the 300 Coco adit might well have formed a tribute of sorts to the capacity of inhaled bat shit to impede one who partook of it. I should have heeded the bat shit hazard but, purely through ignorance, I didn't. I was lucky to get away so lightly with the oversight.

APART FROM BATS, bat shit and spiders there should, according to that identified fount of information Don Juan, also have been some indication of a gold-bearing quartz vein at the face of the 300 Coco adit. However, there wasn't. That would have been too much to expect in any case. The fact that *wiliseros* had yet to pay any attention to the adit offered a sure guarantee that there was going to be nothing of value involving gold exposed in either its face or its walls.

All the same, ably assisted by Don Juan and his two helpers, I dutifully chipped a continuous channel of rock samples along both walls of the adit, from the face and its spider-ridden floor out to the bat-swirling entry. As we sampled outwards, so the bats moved back inwards. They went in ones and twos to commence with, but finally the whole flight of them whirled back in a disorganised flurry to the reassigned security of the inner face.

WHERE THE BRUSH commenced to thin out some way down the slope below the 300 Coco adit level, a *wilisero* camp stood in place, part of the brush in all but name. At the back of the camp, the ragged mouth of a wormhole-like tunnel entering the hill demonstrated proof positive that the residents of the camp were active in their arguably legal pursuits. The residential section of the camp consisted of a framework of cut branches supported at either end by stout poles sunk into the ground. Some of the branches still bore crisp leaves attached to annoyingly trailing twigs. A few ragged-edged sheets and torn fragments of black polythene were draped over the framework to provide a modicum of protection from dimly anticipated rain. Inside, net hammocks were slung, pole to pole.

The lead *wilisero* of this august operation was named Andrés. He was thin to the point of emaciation, even thinner than Don Juan. Andrés wore a pair of shorts so ragged that few of his masculine attributes were unheralded quantities. The shorts seemed to represent the full substance of his wardrobe. He was daubed in grey clay from the split ends of his hair to the soles of his feet, making him seem a ghostly figure lurking in front of the entry to his tunnel, which was no more than one metre high by half a metre or so wide. His naturally dark skin was exposed in tight streaks where runnels of sweat had eroded away the bodily deposit of clay.

A small boy, not dissimilarly attired and decorated, emerged on hands and knees through the tunnel entrance, dragging a wooden-wheeled trolley behind him. The trolley, attached to a rope around the boy's waist, was almost as long as the boy himself. On it lay a chunky mound of rocks which, on inspection, I was excited to discover were pieces of quartz vein. Andrés confirmed that his tunnel had intersected one of the San Sebastian veins and, moreover, that his crew was currently exploiting it. For me this presented an opportunity too good to pass by. Andrés agreed at once to a request that he might take me into the tunnel to see the intersected vein, although his accompanying air of amazement at the nature of my request would have been familiar to Dr Samuel Johnson. That great man once compared a female preacher to a dog walking on its hind legs, alleging that although it wasn't done well, it was a surprise to find it done at all.

So it was that I entered the *wilisero*-driven tunnel, my nose closely following the soles of Andrés' feet as there was insufficient height for us to do any other than wriggle and claw forward on our bellies. Andrés, whose standard means of underground illumination consisted of a stub of candle, this time pushed one of El Joe's flashlights ahead of him.

Behind me came Chucho, clutching the little leather case in which there might or might not have been a gun. Chucho had never been in any kind of underground mine tunnel hitherto, and it must have taken great courage for him to enter that very tightly restricted situation. Under El Joe's orders not to let me out of his sight, he was following such orders to the letter. Such men may form the warp and weft of legend.

I trusted that Chucho would show circumspection in relating his exploits to his colleagues back in El Joe's San Salvador offices, as what we were doing in Andrés' tunnel was rupturing El Joe's (not to mention the Company's) occupational safety norms to a point where all the king's horses and all the king's men would have been hard pressed to put them back together again.

Ah, but El Joe and the Company paid great service to considerations of safety in the field from the security of desk-bound comfort.

I squirmed forward along the tunnel floor, my shoulders scraping the walls, my back barely missing the roof. There was no remote possibility of turning around. The only option was to commit to the advance. The tight tunnel went on and on. Now that I was inside it, I travelled in the hope that it had to end somewhere and that when it did there would be a little more space available. The trolley-pulling boy had clearly gone in and then come out again and that brave lad had had to make a reversing turn at some point or other.

As we crawled ever inwards, the temperature within the tunnel reached for heights that rapidly threatened to exceed bearable limits. Even the spate of hot air emitted in Company boardrooms stood diminished by comparison. Breathing in the overheated air was an ordeal. I was familiar with temperatures in the elevated forties Celsius and knew with certainty that in this tunnel the temperature was very much greater than that. It must have reached at least 60°C. Its intensity magnified an already compelling sense of claustrophobia.

Andrés told me later on that his *wilisero* crew worked the vein at the end of the tunnel (there was an end to it after all) in twenty-minute shifts followed by two full hours of recuperation in the camp outside. I thought that the proponents of twenty minutes of rock-breaking hard labour in that ferocious atmosphere deserved the greatest of admiration.

For a stretch of what must have been twenty to thirty metres (although it seemed to be much, much more), the tunnel was driven along the line of a geological fault, taking advantage of the comparatively softer ground conditions. The fault formed the left-hand wall of the tunnel from which it scaled inwards in a long curl like a precarious raft of onionskin. It was impossible for the back of any crawler in the tunnel not to drag along the hanging ground and equally impossible when doing so not to contemplate its peeling descent onto the helpless bodies of such passers by. I edged below the overhang in what felt like centimetre increments. It seemed that I glided over the rough floor of the tunnel like a hovercraft resting on a cushion of fearful sweat.

At the working face, which I reached with a sense of relief tempered only by the realisation that it was still necessary for us to make a return trip, one of Andrés' mining crew was wedged into a tiny hollow, barely illuminated by a guttering candle, chipping at a narrow quartz vein with a hand moil and a short length of chisel. The vein was of tight white quartz spotted with the sulphide minerals pyrite and arseno-pyrite. There was no indication of visible gold, but for gold to be visible would have been asking for too much under the circumstances.

The *wilisero* up at the face broke out a couple of specimens of the vein for me, then, with my vote of thanks and a large measure of contortion involving Chucho, Andrés and me sliding over one another one at a time, we struggled the tortuous way back to daylight again. Daylight was a sight to gladden my heart.

THE ASSOCIATION OF the yellow pyrite and grey arsenopyrite with the quartz veins defined the cause of the desperate heat in the *wilisero* tun-nels. In the former San Sebastian mine at large, the complex of veins was riddled through with development headings, and the combination of consequent aeration and the flow of groundwater induced the vein sulphide minerals to oxidise and decompose. Oxidation was an exo-thermic reaction. The whole hillside was undergoing a kind of low-level combustion, a virtual casserole of contents stewing in their own juices.

I was hesitant to offer Andrés any gratuity for his kindness and enterprise, not knowing how such a gesture would be received. What I did was to leave fifty colones behind, ostensibly for Andrés to buy some beer for his crew. That appeared to satisfy honour for both of us.

DON JUAN LED us back to the vicinity of the Casa Grande pit, where, adjacent to some of the piles of junk that were once proud components of the San Sebastian mine facilities, there stood a huge mango tree that had in its time witnessed its fair share of enemy action. A few small boys had ascended to its summit and were rattling branches high up at the top where the mango fruits were already maturing, having absorbed the sun to its optimum.

The boys came down from the tree with a sack full of small mangoes, some of which were perhaps riper than others. Irrespective of their state of ripeness, to me, drained from the fiery underground excursion with Andrés, no fruits ever tasted so juicy, or so sweet, or were so opportunely welcome as those mangoes that the lithe boys gave to me.

Low DOWN ON the west flank of the part of the hillcrest known as San Sebastian, Don Juan knew of yet another adit, this one referred to by him as Miguel 300. Refreshed by the succulent mangoes, I went around with Don Juan to have a look at it. Miguel 300 did not penetrate the hill very far; however, two *wilisero* crews working close to it had either enjoyed better luck or, more probably, had worked a lot harder to get much further into the hill than had the instigators of Miguel 300.

The thought of crawling into the depths of the hill again with *wiliseros* was not altogether appealing to me, but at fifty colones a shot (the news of payment having travelled faster than we had) the respective *wiliseros* were willing to give it a go. On the grounds that if nothing were ventured nothing would certainly be gained, there seemed little else to do really but for me to get on with it.

One of the *wilisero* tunnels commenced on a slight downgrade and seemed to descend endlessly. Snags of rock jabbed and plucked by turns at my shirt from the roof and walls as I wriggled along, following the leader. This tunnel terminated in a cavity that was only barely broader than the tortuous tunnel itself. The floor of the cavity was littered with sharply abrasive rubble derived from the narrow vein under exploitation. The heat surged off the walls of the cavity in waves and turned the cramped confines into a cauldron. An egg might well have been fried on any chunk of rubble big enough to crack an egg over.

The second of the Miguel 300 *wilisero* tunnels was slightly easier for me to crawl into as it commenced at a level gradient. After ten metres or so, however, it entered into a succession of twists and turns as it wormed a passage through a perilously unconsolidated deposit of spoil dumped from the mine in better days. At the least touch on the tunnel perimeter, dust drifted out of yawning interstices between shivering blocks of rock. The way out of the loose spoil at the far end led through a jagged hole so constrained that I had to edge along on my flank, pushing with my feet, emerging from it on the far side in the manner of a cork drawn from a bottle. Beyond this hole, a blessedly cool (all things being relative) cross draft was encountered. Relief was instant. This particular crew of *wiliseros* had broken through into the foot of an old stope, a former underground working associated with the operating heyday of the mine.

Immediately ahead, a shelf of rock, too steeply inclined for any fallen or discarded debris to maintain a purchase on it, led up into the darkness. A bat flapped across the probing beam of an El Joe flashlight. The *wilisero* who led me in placed one of his hands – the one not holding the flashlight – on the shelf of rock, told me he was off to get me a specimen of vein, jerked himself forward, scrambled up the shelf as if he were a guerrilla in flight (which he may well have been in an earlier life), moved off to one side and was instantly swallowed up by the black void. I was left to imagine the worst in pitch darkness below, not forgetting Chucho behind me clutching the ubiquitous leather pouch. I could hear the rattle of the *wilisero*'s upward passage for a while, and then the rest was silence.

There was only going to be a problem, I thought, if the *wilisero* didn't come back. I had no alternative but to wait for him. I was not so much worried about making my own way back through the tunnel as I was about any requirement to search for the *wilisero* inside the mine at large if that should prove necessary. The thought of unseen bats drifting around me at that particular moment of darkness was not one that raised much joy in my heart.

It seemed to take an inordinately long time, but it was probably not much more than ten minutes before a vague glimmer from somewhere in the gaunt mine above signified the return of the *wilisero*, safe and bearing in his hand a promised piece of vein. It would have been good to see gold glittering in the specimen he brought, but that was not to be, even when the specimen was taken out into the advantageous daylight.

ON EMERGING FROM that second of the *wilisero* portal entries in the Miguel 300 area, the first thing I noted, once the immediate effect of the almost savage glare of sunlight had eased, was the bulky figure of Lucho casting a rotund pool of approaching mid-afternoon shadow on the dusty ground. Lucho was standing close to the portal, but not in such proximity that he would have to consider poking his head into it for the first time ever. He was accompanied by a few of his own crew and an eminently well dressed stranger. The latter was a thickset and heavily bearded Salvadorian gentleman who, it emerged, was named Jorge.

My first reaction to the sight of these visitors was to believe that I was about to reap a peck of trouble for making an underground foray with the *wiliseros*. It was not that I minded this for myself, but I didn't want to bring down any problems on the *wiliseros* from Lucho for their association with me, as for the *wiliseros* life was quite difficult enough already. However, such concerns were set at nought when, in the grand tradition of El Salvador, Jorge strolled across and greeted me like an old friend.

Jorge told me that he managed a local radio station and was keen to include a report on the developing situation at San Sebastian in his programming. Hence, he said, the reason for his presence on site. He was equipped with the glad-handing manner and slick bearing of a natural politician. His expertise in remaining at the top of his provincial game could be given no better recommendation than that he had come through the civil war in one piece.

Lucho's obsequious deference to Jorge indicated a clear intention by Lucho to utilise any (and for that matter all) facilities that Jorge could provide to present Lucho's much less than modest endeavours in a favourable light. The real agenda drawing Lucho to put in an appearance at the Miguel 300 site became clear when Jorge declared he was taking me, Chucho and Carlos to have a late lunch with Lucho and himself in Santa Rosa de Lima. A promise of lunch at any hour would certainly have provided a highly effective stimulus for prising Lucho's ass out of a comfortable chair in San Miguel.

Dust-stained and mud-streaked clothes notwithstanding, it would have been churlish of me to refuse Jorge's invitation, and with little more ado a convoy of three pickup trucks bore us, willing participants all, along the bumpy track towards Santa Rosa de Lima and lunch.

THE RESTAURANT IN Santa Rosa de Lima where lunch was taken was located in a secluded, almost secretive, part of town. Those seeking it in normal times, or in whatever masqueraded as normal times in El Salvador, would have had to know precisely where the restaurant was in order to find it. However, times were not normal, and under current conditions of abnormality it appeared that UN cease-fire observers had placed the restaurant firmly on their route map. The afternoon may have been waning, but a substantial fleet of white vehicles marked with the symbols of the UN hemmed the restaurant in as effectively as if a state of siege had been declared.

The restaurant was packed with clamouring diners, once again courtesy of the representatives of the UN. They were all impeccably garbed, either in uniform for the more conventional types or in safari-type suits for the bolder multinational spirits among them. On the fabric of their cloth and the light blue of their berets no speck of dust would ever have dared to settle.

Specialities of the restaurant's bill of fare were steaks and a range of shellfish dishes featuring the carapaces of crabs, *langostas* (small lobsters) and *camarones*. The steaks were of a size and thickness to rival the dimensions of any single volume drawn at random for the purpose of comparison from a leather-bound set of encyclopaedias. Enough blood oozed from the char-grilled and cracked surfaces of the meaty chunks to gladden the heart of a CIA-backed death squad.

My meal was selected for me by Jorge and was served by a sublimely efficient waitress. I received a large glass containing a delicious blend of pineapple and mango juice and a huge bowl of soup laden with a stack of crab legs and *camarones* in the shell. It was indeed a great meal. I pressed to pay the bill, but Jorge overruled me. More than that, and probably to Lucho's discontent, Jorge presented me afterwards with a paper bag full of sweet buns baked that very morning at the San Sebastian *panaderia*.

Throughout the meal Jorge kept up a running monologue focused largely on how much he was doing for the benefit of the local community. He was so emphatic about his personal greatness and the wide-ranging scope of his good works that he appeared to be trying chiefly to convince himself that what he was saying had some elements of truth in it. He spoke very highly of Lucho and the company that Lucho worked for, which as far as I was concerned cast a cold eye reflecting detriment on his otherwise impeccable politician's judgement.

We parted after lunch, and in spite of my making a number of efforts to contact him thereafter, I never saw or heard from Jorge again.

CARLOS, CHUCHO AND I returned from Santa Rosa de Lima to San Miguel by the direct route along the main road, making a detour on the way to visit the mothballed Divisadero gold mine property, which the San Sebastian mine owners were rumoured to be interested in acquiring, assuming Lucho hadn't already managed to deter them.

Prior to reaching the Divisadero mine we were required to make an unscheduled halt at a military road block. The barrier was manned by soldiers dressed in camouflage gear. They were rocky-faced men bearing fearsome weapons slung on webbing spanned across their shoulders. The weapons were of the kind that would have been all too familiar to anyone with an interest in movies starring Mr Arnold Schwarzenegger.

The soldiers were checking the personal papers of vehicle passengers and, given the proximity to the nearby national border with Honduras, searching the accompanying vehicles for anything that could be defined as contraband, no matter how loose the definition might be. These forces of so-called law and order distinguished themselves by providing for me the only moments in my entire visit to El Salvador when I felt genuinely insecure.

My worries about the intentions of the soldiers were compounded by thoughts of the supposed gun that I believed Carlos and Lucho might be carrying in the leather pouch. That useful container was no longer in evidence, having been pushed down into an interstice between the two front seats of our pickup at the instant the road block first hove into sight.

The soldiers examined my passport and business visa in nerve-wracking detail while directing the open ends of at least three items of heavy weaponry in my direction. I had the feeling that it would have taken very little provocation for the soldiers to open fire. They looked as if nothing would have pleased them more than to do so, and it may have been with no small degree of reluctance that they returned my passport and allowed our vehicle to continue on its way. The leather pouch went undiscovered. In any case the deterrent value against the soldiers of whatever the leather pouch might or might not have contained would have been worth about as much to us as one of Lucho's promises.

THE DIVISADERO GOLD mine was located about half way between Santa Rosa de Lima and San Miguel. It had closed a few years back and was slowly rusting its way towards an oblivion that was surely coming unless another company was prepared to get hold of it and carry out a salvage operation. The caretaker on the property was a fine elderly gentleman, and it would have been a privilege to have been able to get to know him better had there been more time.

There was food for thought in that the Divisadero gold mine had come through the civil war with all its facilities more or less intact. Such deterioration as had taken place in the course of time since mine closure looked to be all in the province of natural wear and tear under conditions of disuse.

Guerrilla action against the Divisadero was conspicuous by its absence. The San Sebastian gold mine had fared rather less well under the ministration of guerrilla interests. This probably said something about the level of regard in which local guerrillas held the San Sebastian owners when compared with their counterpart owners at the Divisadero.

I TOOK MY dinner that night in the courtyard of the Tropico Inn, from which, with gratitude on my part, the stage and amplifiers had been banished in the course of a day. I dined on *chancho* (pork) with *frijoles* (beans) and *guacamole* and enjoyed every morsel of the repast.

A strolling trio of guitarists came around and, at my request, performed the number "Perfidia" alongside my table ("Perfidia" was one of my favourite melodies). The trio played and sang so sweetly that my heart ached for the unfettered soul of El Salvador.

No VISIT TO the San Sebastian mine was planned for the next day. Instead, Lucho's San Miguel office was the targeted location for work. Once access was gained to that mysterious hallow of hallows, Lucho would (so he told me) make available for examination all the technical reports and supporting maps relating to the San Sebastian property and its history, past and present, that were in his possession. This intimation could have meant everything, or it could have meant nothing.

The one thing that was certain in my mind was that if Lucho were to be true to form, he would have to devise some means of delaying my visit to his office. The requirement to fetch his wife home from hospital provided the very excuse he needed to conform to type. Maybe Mrs Lucho really had come off second best in a tussle with a pressure cooker. The evidence relating to that accident was never going to be placed on the table (or on the floor either), as I never got to meet her. It would have been quite interesting to meet the kind of lady who had chosen to marry Lucho.

This not unexpected delay took up the best part of an hour, after which time Lucho must have run out of subterfuges and found it unavoidable to defer my visit to his offices any longer. His offices were located in his home residence, set in a dusty side street of suburban San Miguel. The residence comprised a collection of rooms that seemed to have been thrown together around a little courtyard in a hurry by a builder skilled in dealing with haphazard architectural arrangements. Ageing furniture sat in various rooms in an impersonal array on floors that were none too clean.

The courtyard held a swimming pool of restricted dimensions at its centre. The pool was perhaps broad enough to accommodate Lucho but would have been placed under great stress if Lucho had had a twin brother who wanted to get into the water with him. The pool was surrounded by an unkempt garden featuring a threatened-looking mango tree, a desiccated coconut palm and a somewhat withered banana plant. More leaves than were desirable floated on the surface of the pool, as if they were intent on participating in a foliated regatta before subsiding to the bottom to enrich the thick and blackening mat of fellow leaves that had already made the watery descent.

LUCHO'S OFFICE WAS equipped with an ancient wooden table flanked by four wooden chairs and a desk whose surface was decorated with ring-like features suggestive of a close association with a serious if careless aficionado of strong coffee. A further attribute of the top of the desk was a total absence of anything resembling paper. On one side there was a map cabinet boasting four drawers (or it might have been three – I couldn't swear to it).

From one of the drawers in the cabinet Lucho withdrew a couple of maps (what else?) relating to the San Sebastian property. From a deep well-like drawer on the side of his desk he extracted a set of reports related (he said) to the mining history of the property. He placed the inconsiderable pile of documentation on the ancient table with an air that fell significantly short of being enthusiastic, then departed with a somewhat less reluctant demeanour, no doubt assuming that he was through for the day.

There wasn't much to look at. I was reduced to prying around the office in Lucho's absence in an attempt to locate information more relevant to the task in hand, in which pursuit I enjoyed only marginal success. It was reasonable enough to accept that the San Sebastian gold mine offered a potential investor a decent opportunity to carry out further exploration, but the work that Lucho and his crew had carried out was too lacking in technical detail and insight to enable the mine to be seen as a development opportunity as yet.

Lucho's return appearance was made at 4.30 p.m. On my insistence he agreed to permit me to take some of the documentation with me back to the Tropico Inn, where I could continue with the review that night and complete it by the following morning, given that I was due to depart for San Salvador on the afternoon of the next day. Lucho's consent was made with the air of one who had just acceded to having his teeth pulled out in the absence of anaesthesia. It was clear that Lucho was as aware as I was of the real quality of his work.

When, burdened in more ways than one with Lucho's reports, I returned to the Tropico Inn, it was to find that Chucho and Carlos had acquired a genuine machete to give to me. It occurred to me that I shouldn't have admired Don Juan's machete as enthusiastically as I had done. However, with a straw sombrero on my head and a machete in my hand I would be able to take my rightful place in the ranks of the multitude of the similarly crowned and armed *campesinos* of El Salvador. There was only one problem: a gift being something not to be refused, whatever was I going to do with a machete now that I owned one?

The machete was a handsome – not to say a formidable – item, at least a metre long in its combined blade and leather handle, secured in a dark red leather scabbard bearing much decorative hand-tooling. The machete blade was fortunately blunt, although it was obviously begging for contact with a grindstone.

Chucho wrapped the machete in several sheets taken at random from a local newspaper, one or other of which might well have carried a story on the disaster of Secretaries' Day at the Tropico Inn. He placed and sealed the packaged weapon inside a heavy cardboard map tube, where it could reside for the remainder of my journey in El Salvador and home thereafter.

By virtue of there being a photocopying machine available and, more importantly, in working order at the Tropico Inn, certain segments of Lucho's documentation came to be copied on the following morning without Lucho being privy to the fact.

I finished with Lucho's documents at 12.30 p.m., had some lunch, and checked out of the Tropico Inn for my return to San Salvador at 2.30 p.m. During the check-out process I received a phone call from

Lucho to enquire as to my hour of departure. I told Lucho that I was just about to leave and had planned to pass by Lucho's residence to drop off the documents that I had borrowed.

Lucho would have none of that and declared that he would come to the Tropico Inn to pick up the documents himself. Evidently one visit by me to his residence had been enough for him. He said he would be along in five minutes. I decided to give him fifteen minutes. Lucho split the difference and came in ten. He was unshaven and looked intensely bleary eyed.

Lucho asked to see any copied maps that I proposed to take away with me. Fortunately he didn't ask about material photocopied from reports, thereby removing any obligation for me to lie to him about it. He reclaimed two of the copied maps, much as I had guessed he would, since I had to all intents and purposes removed one of the maps from his office in a clandestine manner after repeated requests for him to make a copy were ignored.

Lucho said that he would definitely get copies of the two maps made and would personally deliver them to Eduardo Jr to send on to me. It needed no intuition for me to know that that event would never come to pass unless Lucho leapt out of character, and that wasn't going to be on the cards.

Chucho, Carlos and I left San Miguel at 2.45 p.m. I thought that the visit to San Miguel and San Sebastian had been a good few days among wonderful people whose spirit was supreme. Lucho was not a feature of that sentiment.

There was plenty of traffic all along the road between San Miguel and San Salvador, with only one half-hearted police presence encountered a few kilometres out of San Miguel.

We made a stop along one stretch of road where vendors of dried beans plied their wares along the verges from an extensive rank of stalls that seemed to stretch on and on for so far that I wondered where so very many beans to sell could have been grown in the first place. I bought two bags of red beans, and there were also black and white beans on offer for the connoisseurs of that variety of *frijole*.

We stopped once more in Cojutepeque to sample the orange juice pressed to order from the range of citrus mountains crowding the pavements and casting their rolling foothills into the road. It was orange juice of such magnificent flavour that one sampling was not enough and a second was taken and a third became essential. Could there be orange juice anywhere else in the world to compare with that of Cojutapeque? I didn't think so and would have sworn to it on a stack of bibles.

SAN SALVADOR WAS, on our return to it, still seriously congested. The route that Carlos drove along to reach the Hotel Presidente went once again through the centre of the city. The traffic moved with all the inherent confidence of a Lucho assurance, past great swathes of split and broken buildings that still showed what Carlos and Chucho told me was the devastation of the 1985 earthquake. The damaged cathedral, where Archbishop Romero was slain by the usual suspects, was bristling with the scaffolding of reconstruction.

As if in memory of the fate of Archbishop Romero, a pianist in the dining room of the Hotel Presidente that evening murdered a succession of tunes as he smiled nonchalantly at the diners trapped within his range of influence. As one of the confined, I chewed through my chicken and chunks of boiled yucca in silence.

AS FAR AS the next day went, wrap-up time with El Joe's people was the order of business. This involved a little debriefing (omitting any reference to the *wilisero* tunnels), some further assessment of the options for a future San Sebastian project prioritising both investment and the appropriateness of eliminating Lucho's liability factor, a few phone calls and the cataloguing and packaging of samples (not least among which were the vein samples collected in the company of *wiliseros*) for shipment to a specified analytical laboratory.

That was about it for the whole visit as far as my part in it was concerned.

I was then ready to leave El Salvador.

ON THE FOLLOWING morning, Carlos and Chucho came at 6.25 a.m. to collect me from the lobby of the Hotel Presidente for transportation down to San Salvador's international airport near La Libertad. Security at the airport seemed a lot tighter than it had been when I first arrived. Merely getting into the departures area was akin to running the gauntlet of a bear garden. As far as the documentation formalities went, however, El Joe's fixers under the steady direction of Eduardo Sr still had that situation under efficient control.

Carlos and Chucho accompanied me as far as the flight departure gate, their orders to hang on to me at all costs holding fast to the very end. Their presence made a major deterrent to my ability to quietly lose the leather-scabbarded machete hidden in a map tube. It was vital not to hurt their feelings after all they had done for me. As a consequence, the fearful implement in the map tube came to be checked in as personal luggage for my TACA airline flight TA 310 to Miami.

I knew that I was eventually going to be faced with reclaiming the map tube and all that lay therein from a baggage carousel at Miami airport in order to conduct the item onwards for the succeeding stage of its travels. Well, that was a bridge to be crossed when it was reached.

FLIGHT TA 310 departed at 9.10 a.m., made a bumpy climb, a smooth run at cruising altitude and a good descent into Belize at 10.00 a.m. It left Belize half an hour or so later, and landed in Miami at 2.20 p.m. local time. Some excellent chicken was served for lunch on the second leg of the flight.

The route over the Caribbean crossed islands and stark white atoll-bounded lagoons set in water painted from a whole palette of startling shades of blue and turquoise.

I WAS DUE to connect at Miami with Delta flight 625 to Atlanta, scheduled to depart from that one fair city to the other at 4.05 p.m. In principle therefore, I had ample time to make the transfer. First of all, however, I had to enter the USA. Principle did not count for much where US immigration procedures were concerned.

A huge flow of recently arrived passengers from a host of flights choked a tightly meandering array of holding barriers and dammed up against a long bulwark of immigration desks. The obdurate immigration officials manning the desks created a desperately tight sluice through which the would-be immigrants leaked one by one with a slowness of pace that was as impressive as it was frustrating for those penned at the rear.

The immigration officials, I thought (not for the first time), must surely have been expertly trained in practising the quality of obnoxiousness. Time passed and it was barely possible to sense that the crowd was moving at all.

The hands on the clock in the immigration hall, which seemed to have been placed there to compound the misery of those whose perception of forward momentum was growing ever more indistinct, touched 3.25 p.m. I felt that I had barely moved more than a step or two forward through the holding area since I entered it, crushed in like one of a flock of sheep being driven to slaughter.

If I had genuinely wanted to spend time in the land of the free and the home of the brave I might have entertained a different view on inching forward, but I didn't want to spend any longer there than I had to – not at all. All I wanted to do was to get up to Atlanta to join my flight back home, but it didn't look as if I would be allowed to do that. The snail's pace at which the queue for immigration was moving and continuing to build up in an ever-assembling crush way back behind me made it clear that my stay in the holding pens would be prolonged to the extent that Atlanta that day was shaping up as a lost cause.

I voiced this concern to my nearest pent-up companion in suspenseful waiting and received the advice from him that I should, in the manner of a first namesake of mine who bore the surname Kirk, boldly go where no man had gone before and advance to the front of the line to present to the authorities a case for preferential treatment. With nothing to lose and as little to hope for, that was what I did.

A hard-faced female official ceased patrolling the front of the immigration pen for as long as it took her to relieve me of my airline ticket. She held the ticket at arm's length in the manner of one unwilling to believe that it might not be contaminated, glared at it as if it were a subversive document and then consulted with a second female official, the dimensions of whose figure suggested that she was no stranger to the consumption of large quantities of hamburgers. The first of the two said, "Well, if it was a domestic flight I wouldn't care, but I don't always like making people miss international flights." That implied that she was not averse to making people miss international flights on occasions when it pleased her to do so.

She flapped my ticket up and down with the hand that held it, and with her other hand she made a beckoning motion. I was, in living proof of the adage "nothing ventured, nothing gained", thereby summoned to present my passport and landing forms to an immigration officer, a male this time, sitting behind one of the levee of tall desks. He asked me the standard type of questions on the purpose of my visit and my eventual destination that were asked by immigration officials everywhere, although none of such worthies anywhere else ever asked the questions with a stronger intimation of dire consequences in prospect than did those of the great and grand USA.

He advised me that I was a form short in my application and therefore required to go to the back of the line to fill in that errant form and then make my way forward once more. The back of the line was at the moment in question so far away that it couldn't be seen. Things were not looking good.

Whereupon, in a sudden undertaking that was at best an aberration and at least contrary to the US immigration regulations calling for entry to the country to be made as difficult as possible for arriving passengers, the official relented. From a pile of blanks he selected and filled out the missing form himself. Thus it was that I found myself on the far side of immigration at 3.35 p.m., with thirty minutes remaining prior to the departure of my connecting flight to Atlanta.

FOLLOWING THE POSTED signs, I raced down to the baggage hall to collect my personal effects, which consisted of two bags and the map tube containing the machete wrapped in sheets of a newspaper published in San Miguel on a date assumed to be sometime around Secretaries' Day, although that was not certain.

It was absolutely inevitable that there were no baggage trolleys available in the hall. I carried the three items, a ponderous load, to a customs desk. There an official looked me up and down and, with neither question nor comment and to my great dismay, pointed at an adjacent x-ray unit equipped with a moving belt on which I was required to place the bags and the map tube. I trembled as I laid the items down and they moved away to be irradiated.

Sometimes, just when you don't expect it to, fate delivers the unexpected. All three of my pieces passed through the x-ray unit and emerged on the other side with impunity. I was free to pick them up and move on. The explanation must surely be that the x-ray machine was not working. Another possibility is that some kind of miracle involving the placement of scales over the monitor controller's eyes took place.

I grabbed up the three items and headed off at a run into the maw of Miami airport's ultra-long concourse, seeking the Delta Airlines check-in area, where I arrived at 3.47 p.m. on the dot. The gate for my flight was just about to close. The handle of one of my bags had broken *en route*, adding to the awkwardness of the three-piece load. A girl at the Delta Airlines desk checked me in, took the bags and map tube and told me that they might or might not make the flight and that the same consideration applied to me.

The departure gate was H11, out at the far end of the airport, quite as far away as under the rushing circumstances Murphy's Law said it really had to be. I reached the departure gate at exactly 4.00 p.m., when the flight attendants were preparing to close the aircraft door.

They let me board the flight, and as I set foot inside the aircraft, the door thumped shut behind me.

I SAT IN seat 38F, a lot further back in the aircraft than I would have liked, but whatever, it was a seat, wasn't it?

The passenger I was seated next to passed me a copy of that day's *New York Times* to read.

The front-page news dealt with riots in Los Angeles, inspired by the public release of a secretly videotaped altercation between a couple of members of LA's finest and a certain Mr Rodney King.

It was, I thought, a not dissimilar bunch of such good old born-in-the-USA boys that had sought, with a similar lack of success, to impose their own special brand of democracy on the people of El Salvador.

− 5 −

The Peeyay Strikes Again

And did those feet, scant decades since,	*Bring me a Caterpillar truck!*
Walk north from Joutel's	*Bring me the dozer I desire!*
muskegs green?	*Make me stockpiles of broken muck!*
And were there rigs of diamond drills	*Fetch me contractors for hire!*
Through Wawagosic's willows seen?	
	I shall not cease to break the rocks,
And did they countenance a mine,	*Nor shall chill winter stay my hand,*
Blunt head frame proud midst spruce-	*Till we have built a copper mine*
clad hills?	*In Quebec's blackfly-ridden land!*
And was an open pit builded here,	
Beside these concentrating mills?	**With apologies to Mr William Blake**

I T WAS MY second trip to that particular location in northern Quebec. A working open-pit copper–zinc mine stood there now as the natural, if lower-grade, successor to an already worked-out underground mining operation that once exploited the self-same commodities beneath it. Fifteen years previously when I had visited the area for the first time the open pit hadn't existed even in concept, and the underground development then in place was no more than part of the exigency of a development project.

In the interim linking the visits, presumably as a consequence of the switch from exploration success to mining activity, the operators of the new mine saw fit to make a significant local name change as well. What was formerly known as the Detour development project was transformed into the Selbaie Mines, or, with due deference to provincial linguistic preferences, Les Mines Selbaie, or, in the simplest rendition, just Selbaie.

Come to think of it, Selbaie wasn't located all that desperately far north in Quebec to justify the title "northern" in the strict sense in which elevated latitudes might have provided some justification. However, by Montreal convention, which in the province of Quebec was all that ever mattered anyway, anything up there on and above the left-hand side of the St Lawrence River corridor looking downstream was indubitably northern and well beyond the pale of civilisation.

Up there lay Shield country, an intricate mosaic of lakes, glacial moraines, swamps and muskeg bogs. Up there, countless swarms of black flies and mosquitoes made a misery of whatever part of the year wasn't classed as winter. If that wasn't enough, there was the real winter to cope with, temperatures of thirty below taking a much more substantial bite at any living thing other than the hibernating larvae ready to erupt into the next vicious generation of the said black flies and mosquitoes. No matter how deep was the winter cold, these merciless insects showed up again not long after the ice broke up. You could count on it.

Up there, people kept parkas on the rack, ready to break out at short notice throughout the year. There were two designated seasons in northern Quebec: winter and tough sledding.

Up there, trees covered the land and maintained its secrets under a deep green, almost forever sea of conifers that only broke when it surged onto the shores of the barrens. Dotted through flooding pines, archipelagos of deciduous hardwood cycled in fresh green, yellow, flame-red and grey by seasonal turns. The deciduous component of the mass of trees dwindled in intensity and influence as the south slipped away into memory. The immediate area surrounding Selbaie held on to a few patches of birch forest, but spruce was in the ascendancy, even if much of that mighty spread of ubiquitous conifers was typically more than a little stunted in growth.

My first visit to the region had taken place during the days of the Detour development project. It was a landmark visit for me, the essence of the first overseas business trip that I was required to undertake as an appropriately constituted member of the Flying Circus.

As justification for the occasion, the Flying Circus was called on by the then manager of the Company's Canadian subsidiary, based in Toronto, to assist in an evaluation of the Detour development project. (Let's give him the reference indicator TM.) He regarded the project as an attractive opportunity in an acquisition-related furtherance of his career.

TM was a glib and fast-talking individual, thereby equipped with the two prime qualities for making it big in Toronto. His presence was as familiar over on Bay Street as it was down in the lobby of the Royal York Hotel.

TM's single significant personal shortfall in the litotes-lacking society of Toronto-based mining promoters was that, although he may have been more than a little plump he was only modestly overweight when measured against local standards. The top players in the Canadian mining industry distinguished themselves as heavyweights not only figuratively but also in fact. However, a glass of any common or garden diameter, acceptably charged with a high-proof beverage of the amber kind, fit into TM's right hand as if it were to the manner borne, and an attribute like that could only help to get him known where it mattered in Toronto, irrespective of his relatively constrained physiology.

The Company office that TM managed was to be found occupying an opulent suite of rooms on the twenty-sixth (or it might have been the twenty-seventh) floor of an imposing high-risen tower on the corner of a block on Adelaide Street. For his technical staffing establishment, TM had gathered together an array of characters, some mediocre, some not, but all united in sycophancy. They were hired principally for the lack of challenge they were likely to attach to TM's position. Alongside many of them TM was always going to look relatively good. With due consideration to their capabilities as a whole, even the Flying Circus was an improvement. For TM, the great benefit of bringing in the Flying Circus was that he could avoid awkward questions by getting rid of it when its job was done.

THE CROSS THAT TM was forced to bear weighed down on his flexibility to acquire projects on behalf of the Company. The problem, which was not of TM's making, was caused by the Company setting up its Canadian subsidiary under TM with all essential trappings while overlooking (maybe inadvertently and maybe not) the reality that Uncle Joe happened to have a Canadian mineral exploration company of his very own already in place and highly active from a base over in Calgary.

To all intents and purposes this dichotomy turned Uncle Joe into a competitor with himself. Great minds were brought into play to solve the conundrum. At a given moment it seemed that one or the other of the self-competing concerns would have to go, and there were no prizes for guessing which of the two that would be. In any direct contest of wills in Canada between Uncle Joe and the Company, the result would always be an avuncular success in which Toronto would not feature.

Uncle Joe, however, would not have made his impressive way around both the oil-replete and the oil-hungry countries of the world if he hadn't possessed a talent to compromise. And so it came to pass that a tacit agreement was thrashed out at a suitably high corporate level to the effect that Uncle Joe's Calgary-based boys would handle exploration projects (what they called "grass roots" work), and the Company's people under TM in Toronto would look after development (or "advanced stage") projects.

Calgary and Toronto were in principle thereby designated as non-competitors. TM and his Calgary counterpart accepted the compromise, but they didn't have to like it. They just needed to be a little more circumspect in their attempts to undermine one another's aspirations.

The acid test of the compromise would emerge if ever Calgary managed to convert a grass-roots project into an advanced-stage development project. That eventuality would drop Calgary into the deep shit position of having to hand the project over to Toronto. Such a truly frightening situation once arose in the case of a Nova Scotia tin project, explored and assessed with a high degree of competence by Calgary up to the point at which a development decision was pending.

The fervent attempts made by Calgary to cloak the positive results of the tin project in secrecy were about as successful in holding the results *sub rosa* as were all other similar endeavours in the context of the Canadian mining industry. The assay results of drill-core intersections from all around the great nation of Canada were common knowledge in the bars along Bay Street almost before the split cores had cleared the assay lab.

Calgary managed to snatch glorious victory from the jaws of humiliation, however, by reining back progress on the tin project. Then, when it seemed likely that their project might well go ahead on its own merits in spite of all that could be done to delay it, Calgary acted to reduce expectations by invoking the fine political principle of talking much and saying little. A fortuitous *coup de grâce* to the tin project was supplied by an unexpectedly precipitate collapse of the international tin market when the manipulative international cartel controlling that market disintegrated like a house of cards. Clearly, where Calgary was concerned, fortune did not favour the brave.

THE PHILOSOPHY BEHIND the policy of division of projects between Calgary and Toronto envisaged that grass-roots opportunities were much more likely to be available in Canada than were good advanced-stage projects. On this basis Calgary assumed that Toronto would assuredly founder into and sink beneath a slough of comparative inaction.

However, and be that as it may, Calgary reckoned not with the emergence of the Detour development project. The Detour development project came along as an almost ideally heaven-sent evaluation opportunity for TM to chase up, allowing him not only to put Toronto in the ascendancy, where he thought it belonged, but also to deliver a metaphorical kick up the ass to Uncle Joe's guys over in cow town.

THE DETOUR DEVELOPMENT project involved the evaluation of a copper–zinc mineral deposit, and on that reckoning it was not to be confused with the nearby Detour Lake exploration project for gold. The respective project names could brag of having "Detour" in common, but the end-commodities that each was linked with were substantially different. Even more radically, Detour's copper–zinc was located in the province of Quebec and the gold of Detour Lake was over there across the quasi-international border between Quebec and Ontario. The two projects were therefore separated by a distinctive cultural and political gulf that was barely bridgeable.

THE FLYING CIRCUS in which I participated, accompanied by the ebullient TM and a couple of his fawning acolytes, flew up to visit the Detour development project in mid-March of the year 1979. The journey took place in two steps, the first of which involved a chartered aircraft between Toronto International airport and a provincial airport as tiny as it was lonely, located somewhere outside the mining town of Matagami in northern Quebec. From Matagami the visiting party flew onwards to the even more isolated Detour development project site using a cross-country helicopter transport link.

There were seven of us on the visit altogether, and it would need two separate helicopter trips to ferry us all over to the site. I was designated to travel on the first of these trips.

WE ARRIVED AT Matagami to find the shack-like airport terminal building thickly encased in recently deposited snow. The fresh snow provided a welcome gloss of clean white icing to coat the grimy cake of prior accumulations of similar precipitation. Any active, or for that matter barely active, harbingers of spring could not yet be sensed.

For all that, Matagami airport's landing strip was as clear of snow as were the patches of blue sky above, as seen between flurries. Someone offered the comment that Canadians didn't know a lot about much, but when it came to clearing away snow they were the knowledge masters of the world.

Snow tended not to age gracefully in the course of a Canadian winter. Snowploughs expelled snow from roads with a magnificent lack of discrimination as to where it would end up. Garbage was thrown onto snow. Dirt was spread across snow. Dogs crapped along its banks. Humans who should have known better, but never mind, pissed on it. All these delights were covered by fresh falls and destined to emerge to public view as unsung glories of the spring thaw.

I heard a story, allegedly true, of an angry Ontario lady who marched off to confront a neighbour in order to complain that the neighbour's son had peed her daughter's name into a fresh snow bank outside her house. The neighbour came along to view the work of art and shook her head in disbelief. "Your daughter must have done that herself," she exclaimed. "And in any case, it's not in my son's handwriting!"

THERE WAS NO ONE present in the snow-girt Matagami airport terminal shack, but fortunately the front door was unlocked. After a short period of kicking and pushing snow out of the way we were able to pull the door open sufficiently to gain entry and thereby replace the cold without by the cold within while we waited for the hired helicopter to show up.

A well-chewed tennis ball lay in a corner of the terminal shack. The ball must have been dropped and then forgotten by a dog that had been more interested in going out to paint the snow yellow.

Encouraged by the discovery of a ball, the Flying Circus economist, ably aided by the metallurgist, joined TM in setting up an impromptu cricket match in the shack, using a geological hammer for a bat and the chewed tennis ball for, well, a ball. The ball whanged around the walls of the shack, and it was fortunate that nothing got broken, unless it was my belief hitherto that the Flying Circus was a plausible outfit.

The helicopter thwacked in across the trees and dropped gently to the tarmac through a great blast of snow. As I departed in it on the first traverse to the Detour development project I realised that I was doomed to never know how the Matagami airport test match ended for those who remained behind to play it.

THAT WAS THE first time I flew in a helicopter. The pilot instructed me how I should duck down low to approach the cabin, always from the direction of the sides, never from the front, and absolutely never from the tail where the tail rotor formed an invisible trap for the unwary. Although I was a little nervous at the prospect of flying in a helicopter, I thoroughly enjoyed every minute of the half hour or so that it took the machine to fly from Matagami to the Detour development project site. I sat alongside the pilot in the front of the bubble-like cabin.

We sped across muted contours that owed much to deep snow, skimming over pointy-topped spruce trees draped with more snow, little lakes thick-set with ice, sporadic clearings carpeted densely white, and, close in to the project site, the ice-locked meanders of the Wawagosic river, bearing down on water that was no doubt anxious to shake off the chains of winter when, or if, break-up ever arrived.

The helicopter flew at a height of not much more than fifty metres above the determinedly flat terrain. The wash of the helicopter's rotors pounded the snow beneath into crystalline clouds and caused swathes of snow to slump from the taller trees as we sped on.

THE APPEARANCE OF the Detour development project camp was by no means suggestive of the last word in frontier luxury but it did indicate that it was much more than fit for purpose. The camp facilities were contained in an integrated cluster of small portable, trailer-like units, a couple of which served as bunkhouses, another as a cookhouse and canteen, and still others as office and administrative units.

A few hundred metres away from the camp along a bulldozed track heavily banked with dirty snow stood a rudimentarily covered head frame capping a development shaft. The head frame was linked to a combined change and hoist house of rustic construction by two dark threads of hoisting cable. White vapour rose in a long plume from the top of the head frame and leaked out in tendrils around the sheave wheels. On the far side of the hoist house a mighty array of racked-up boxes of diamond drill core was doing its best to stretch off into the distance while avoiding being crushed by the weight of snow piled on it. A further trailer unit stood strategically close to the racks of core, intended for use as a core-logging shack.

THE CLOSEST POPULATED settlement to the Detour exploration project was Joutel, a mining village located eighty kilometres down to the south, linked by a rough track. The two small underground mines that formerly gave Joutel its *raison d'être* were closed. Any future Detour mine construction was destined to assume considerable significance to the future of Joutel.

The Detour development project was owned and operated by the Canadian arm of a multinational mining company, known as Selco. Much to the gratification of TM, Selco was seeking a partner to share the risk of turning the Detour development project into a mine.

I knew Selco's multinational parent company reasonably well from certain of its African undertakings. In the late 1960s I had worked for ten months at its diamond mines in Ghana. Ten months was the minimum period that I had to put in to endure the non-work they gave me to do in order that I should be able to resign in good conscience.

Selco's parent was not my favourite company, but at least I didn't have to resign from it again, and there was always the hope that they did things differently in Canada – and in Quebec as well. Indeed they did just that. Ron, the Detour development project's resident geologist, had carried out a fine and successful exploration and development programme. It took me very little time to decide that the Company would benefit from partnering Selco in the succeeding mine construction phase.

This feel-good factor at the project camp was compounded by the quality of the cookhouse output, with particular reference to the glorious wedges of succulent blueberry pie that the cook was ready to hand over given the least encouragement.

With Ron I discussed the status of the project, looked over his reports, examined drill cores and took a couple of trips down the approximately one-hundred-metre deep development shaft. It was known as the "B-zone" shaft, given that its purpose was to engage with a geological zone or deposit of copper mineralisation referred to as the "B-zone".

There were three levels of headings driven off the B-zone shaft, the deepest being located about eighty metres down from surface. On all three levels impressive showings of chalcopyrite and lesser sphalerite mineralisation were exposed in all their glory of blobs, clots, veins and mere disseminations.

The thrill of the copper-spangled moment was to some extent offset by the fact that the headings were wet – rather more than wet really, as water poured and cascaded forcibly from each and every joint, fault and crack that opened up from the three B-zone shaft stations all along the respective development headings to the end faces. A trip through any one of the headings was akin to negotiating a passage beneath a pounding cataract. The submersible pumps down in the sump at shaft bottom had their work cut out to cope with the ceaseless attempts of groundwater incursion to overcome a fragile capacity to hold their own.

The B-zone received its alphabetic designation in order to distinguish it, both in space and in grade, from the nearby and geologically related "A-zone". The A-zone, as yet geologically interpreted only on the strength of the results of diamond core drilling, was characterised by being split up into two sub-zones, not unnaturally known as the A1 and the A2.

Although the near-surface A1-zone was a huge geological occurrence, it contained significantly weaker and appreciably more disseminated copper–zinc mineralisation than did the B-zone. At the time of my visit Selco regarded the A1-zone as representing not much more than an interesting curiosity with assessment pending.

The A2-zone underlay the A1-zone and shaped up as a probable collection of veins of chalcopyrite that, on the existing database, defied reasonable geological correlation.

In studying the information related to exploration of the A1-zone, I felt that it could be interpreted as representing a very big (if rather low-grade) opportunity for a potential open-pit development that could do none other than add value to any Company participation in the Detour development project. I was so enthusiastic about this possibility that I made it the focus of my contribution to the eventual Flying Circus report.

It was perhaps unfortunate that a further duet contributing to the same report, composed of the metallurgist and the mining engineer, were not as in tune as I was over the open-pit option and demurred in its acceptance, not to me but directly to their note-taker boss, MTM across the corridor. They declared that they wished to dissociate themselves from my assertion that the AI-zone had substance. The benefit of their back-door discord lay in the lesson learned that it provided me with as to the real truth about co-operation within the Flying Circus as a unit.

That story had a chapter or two to run, however.

As well as the Detour development project, Selco operated the small South Bay underground copper mine on the marge of Uchi Lake in western Ontario. South Bay was located a hundred kilometres or so to the north of the paper-pulping town of Dryden, itself more than one thousand kilometres northwest from Toronto, directly across Lakes Huron and Superior as the crow flew.

It was decided by TM at the close of the Flying Circus sojourn at the Detour development project, at which time the general feeling of all involved in the exercise was more or less rife with optimism, that three members of the Flying Circus – namely the aforementioned metallurgist and mining engineer plus me – must all go and have a first-hand look at South Bay Mine to develop an informed opinion on just how good a mining operator Selco was.

TM's inference was that if the Company was about to deign to honour Selco by joining Selco in a partnership to construct a mine at the Detour development project, then Selco would need to demonstrate to the Company that it was pretty damn good as a mine operator. That figured, because being pretty damn good at mine operating was an allegation that it was not so very easy to level at the Company, whether in Canada or anywhere else. It was essential that one of the two likely partners should know what it was doing.

The chosen three flew to Dryden from Toronto on an Air Canada flight, which was so far, so good. Dryden was a stunningly unlovely town that seemed to have been hurriedly plonked down nowhere and abandoned even more rapidly to the incursion of an infinite snow-gripped forest. Outside the town, although by no means far enough outside, sprawling paper-pulp factories offered dark satanic threats to the surrounding trees. Towering chimneystacks dominated the factory infrastructure. Each chimney belched out a great column of streaming fumes, dedicated to passing a noxious buck downwind under the flurrying sky. The stacks were sentinels guarding the grim town, giving Dryden the bleak semblance of a prison camp.

The surface of the streets of Dryden was caked with salt, winter's enduring municipally strewn legacy to any Canadian town. Dryden's sidewalks were crusted with filthy snow. Wind was a razor's edge daring pedestrians to test its chill factor if they dared. A sniff of Dryden's air, in or out of the cutting wind, evoked a mental picture of a lascar's armpit.

THE THREE OF US engaged a taxi at Dryden airport, and in that vehicle passed through the town to be dropped off at our intended destination outside the door of a sagging shack at the top of the sloping bank of a small frozen lake just beyond the town limits.

A small single-engine, four-seat light aircraft equipped with skis was standing on the lake ice at the foot of the slope below the shack. The aircraft was decorated with oil and grime and a mixture of the two. Both of the doors on the side of the aircraft facing me looked to be a little ill-fitting. The rear of the two doors was held closed by the expert application of a short length of haywire, which seemed almost symbolic. I couldn't see whether or not any elastic bands were also involved, although since elastic bands would have perished in the better than twenty-below cold, I shouldn't have expected to see them and should therefore have realised that haywire made an adequate substitute.

We were destined to fly up to South Bay Mine on Uchi Lake in this aircraft. All that was lacking was a pilot to fly it. Having seen the aircraft, I wasn't going to complain if a pilot didn't show up. I didn't know about any two-engine rule so was unable to wonder where it was when I needed it.

The shack at the top of the slope, which was presumably the head office of the outfit that owned the aircraft, was locked up. We crunched around to its leeward flank and huddled there, stamping our feet, to await the pilot's arrival. He appeared after about ten minutes, driving an open-backed, battered pickup truck on which the dents had dents of their own.

The pilot was a youngish man, probably somewhere in his mid-twenties. In spite of the deep lack of positive temperature his personage was covered only by scuffed leather cowboy boots, a pair of worn denim jeans, in which a vestigial hint of blue was only holding on by the skin of its teeth, and a black leather jacket, well-worn and cracked with age. On the pilot's head was a dark blue cap, the legend on the front of which suggested that he might have been a fan of the Toronto Maple Leafs ice-hockey team. It was only to be hoped that he wasn't as big a loser as the Maple Leafs were. Tufts of blond hair drifted from beneath the cap and did a little maybe to warm the tops of the pilot's ears and the back of his neck. The tufts also did what they could to droop over the mirrored lenses of the sunglasses he was wearing so as to obscure the view ahead.

I hoped that I might be forgiven for the misgiving thoughts I was entertaining with regard to both the pilot and his aircraft. The two looked to make a perfect match for each other.

PAUSING ONLY TO offer a greeting of some brevity, the pilot slid down the slope between the shack and the aircraft, only narrowly avoiding falling flat on his ass on the way. The furrows of multiple tracks on the slope indicated that he had descended on a number of occasions previously with less success. He opened the side doors of the aircraft, one of them by virtue of tugging at a handle, the other by loosening the piece of haywire. He moved to the front of the aircraft to unplug an engine heater and then beckoned the three of us down to join him. The moment of truth was nigh.

I was once again given the front seat alongside the pilot, an honour I could reasonably have forgone. My recalcitrant companions – namely the metallurgist and the mining engineer – were seated in the back of the aircraft. Once we were all aboard, the pilot secured the rear door with the useful length of haywire. No one was likely to fall out of that door during the flight. I couldn't speak for the security of the front door, however.

The pilot crunched his heels around to the rear of the aircraft where he pushed at the tail and thereby turned the end bearing the propeller to face out into the lake. He subsequently boarded the aircraft on his side, strapped himself into his seat, tapped his right forefinger on a dial or two, flipped a couple of switches and turned a knob, and his pre-flight checklist was complete. I wondered if he might consider submitting the checklist routine to *The Guinness Book of Records* for inclusion in the "most perfunctory" category, but I didn't like to voice such thoughts and kept them to myself.

The pilot fired the engine up. It coughed, emitted a great gust of smoke on one side and caught. The propeller flipped around, speeded up and settled down into a hazily transparent ring. We taxied slowly out into the lake to reach a point on the lake's long axis, and, with the engine roaring, the pilot took the aircraft down into the wind, gained speed and lifted up and over the surrounding forest without a single protest from the skis. I looked back through the side window and was glad to see that the ski was still there on my side.

There seemed to be few seams on the aircraft through which wind, some of it whistling in shrill protest, was unable to find its way. Even with the heater running the ambient temperature inside the aircraft would have needed to be raised by a great deal more than ten degrees Celsius to have stood any chance of approaching zero.

The nose-cracking assault by chill draft was accentuated by the incidence of prolific snow flurries that we encountered all the way up to Uchi Lake from Dryden. The pilot tried to dodge the aircraft around the flurries to start with, but regrettably there were too many flurries to cope with and so he gave up and flew through them. Before long, all of us inside the aircraft were dusted over by a rime of finely sifted snow.

For much of the flight to Uchi Lake the flurries obscured any view of the ground. I could but trust that the pilot knew where he was going. The flurries parted once to display a broad swathe of devastated forest directly underneath us, the consequence (said the pilot) of a tornado tracking through the area a few years previously.

At a given moment the pilot banked the aircraft and began to circle around, looking downwards across his shoulder with an appearance of rather more anxiety in his demeanour than I thought was desirable under the circumstances. As if by a miracle the flurries opened, and there was the ragged outline of Uchi Lake below with the facilities of South Bay Mine prominent on the edge: head frame, mill, dock, bunkhouses, administration buildings, warehouse, mine yard, all part and parcel of a self-contained operation located a long way from civilisation, provided it could be assumed that Dryden was civilised.

The pilot brought the aircraft down towards Uchi Lake in a stuka-like dive, no doubt aimed at beating any intention of the flurries to close up again. He levelled out much closer to the lake's surface than I found comfortable. As we touched down the flurries enveloped us in a virtual whiteout that hid the shoreline and seemed to leave the aircraft as effectively lost as was ever possible. The pilot's sense of direction, however, was fortuitously a lot better developed than that of his dress code. He sped the aircraft through the all-encompassing white, slowed and halted, and as the latest flurry thinned out we found that we were no more than twenty metres off the South Bay Mine dock. It was a *tour de force* arrival on the pilot's part.

The three Flying Circus passengers disembarked. I got out first, not unwillingly, there to undo the haywire holding the back door tight and then to fasten it up again when the other two were out of the aircraft. The pilot, who had barely throttled back on the engine and who remained in his seat, yelled at us that he had to be off back to Dryden to undertake another job and would return to Uchi Lake to collect us at noon tomorrow. With that he raced the engine, spun the aircraft through a half circle and tore out into Uchi Lake *per ardua ad astra*.

I sincerely hoped that we would indeed see the pilot tomorrow at the appointed hour. In the event of an airborne emergency in the meantime, he always had the option of dropping down onto any one of a myriad of small lakes in the region, but dressed as he was, he would assuredly freeze solid long before he was rescued.

WE WERE SELCO's guests at South Bay Mine until the pilot's return relieved Selco of that responsibility. We were to find the mine operations both creditably and tightly run by the general manager, named Doug, and his capable team. It was an excellent little mine, very much as I guessed it would be. Selco's credentials as a mine operator came to be much better than proven. Our guide in tours through the underground mine, and also the processing plant, was a resident geologist of oriental extraction who went under the name of Jim. There was nothing the Flying Circus trio could teach Jim on the subject of his professional discipline – not that that would be likely to stop them trying.

The South Bay bunkhouse accommodation was very comfortable. The food in the cookhouse was of high quality, if a little plain in character. The importance of food quality and quantity, as well as regularity of service, in sustaining morale in mining, development and exploration camps, and not only in Canada, could not be understated.

As it happened, our visit to South Bay Mine coincided with "Steak Night" in the canteen. Steak Night was a perennially and universally popular institution offering a menu built on a mountain of grilled T-bone steaks and governed by an all-you-can-eat principle. Each T-bone contained a pound or more of thick brown meat off the hoof, overwhelming and hiding from view any standard-size dinner plate on which it lay, and dripping puddles of bloody juice onto the oilcloth-covered table on which the charged plate sat.

There were underground miners working at South Bay Mine who were well able to eat their way through three or more of these monster T-bones at a sitting. The record for individual consumption was alleged to be seven. One of the T-bones provided far more than enough meat for me. A not uncommon local practice was to pile four or five T-bones on a plate, eat the rib eyes out of them and throw away what remained. The steak consuming contests between well-matched trenchermen were dramatic events. The deadly sin of gluttony may have realised some of its finest hours in the South Bay Mine canteen on Steak Nights.

APPROPRIATELY IMPRESSED BY the merit as much as the conduct of the South Bay mining operations, I took up station with Jim and my two Flying Circus associates at the head of the ice-riveted South Bay dock on Uchi Lake shortly before noon on the following day. There was not a cloud in the sky. The white glare searing off the snow-bound lake felt as fierce as an advancing wolf pack. The twenty-five below temperature made a far more solid assault on the person than any stack of T-bone steaks ever could. We stood encased in snow boots, ski pants, long johns, down-filled gloves and arctic parkas, eyes to the south, each perhaps wanting to be the first to spot a speck up in the blue and make the Tattoo-like exclamation, "The plen! The plen!" Although South Bay Mine did not altogether fit the mould of Fantasy Island, the Flying Circus might well have rung a bell with the proprietors of that famous resort.

A short distance from us on the left-hand side of the dock, its door facing towards the lake, was a small and very compact wooden shack of relatively new construction. This edifice, Jim pointed out to us, was the Uchi Lake sauna. A thick plume of smoky vapour rising from a metal chimney on its roof suggested that the sauna was currently occupied.

As we watched, the door of the sauna was flung open and a naked man emerged. He sprinted over the snow in the direction of a snow-mobile, an item of transport more commonly referred to as a skidoo, which stood with its engine idling some metres from the door. He straddled the skidoo, gunned the engine and raced the machine out onto the lake. He made a sweeping circuit of the littoral, shot back to the parking place, stopped the skidoo, leapt off it and rushed back into the sauna, closing the door behind him with a mighty slam. I wasn't sure if he left any of the skin of his ass on the skidoo seat — it's not for nothing that miners are a hard-assed bunch, I thought.

This action placed a new slant on the Scandinavian-originated tradition of leaving a sauna and rolling in snow in the immediate vicinity of the entrance. Perhaps rolling in snow at twenty-five below was seen as a bad idea, although it couldn't have been nearly as bad an idea as haring off on a skidoo trip. Jim said that there was one sauna *habitué* who was proficient in riding the skidoo from the sauna right over to the far side of Uchi Lake and back. I didn't like to ask Jim what might happen if the skidoo broke down or if the sauna regular fell off it on the way over — or on the way back, come to that. A brass-monkeys result would have been the least expectation. It seemed that where the sauna was concerned there existed at least one loophole in Doug's much vaunted safety policy.

THERE WERE A couple of false alarms to cope with during our plane-spotting exercise, caused by distantly soaring rises of crows, big black hardies that cast a vestige of life into the tightly locked landscape. Crows were a year-round presence, surviving against the odds, although aided greatly by the dispersal of mine garbage, inclusive of the excesses of Steak Night, by profligate humans.

We heard the aircraft long before we saw it. It landed on Uchi Lake with a flourish and sped in towards the dock tailed by a cloud of glittering and whirling ice crystals. The pilot hadn't shaved since yesterday, but then again, yesterday he hadn't shaved since the day before, and so his consistency was preserved. He also didn't seem to have changed his clothes since we last saw him, and for all I knew he might even have slept in them. The Toronto Maple Leafs was still featured on his headgear as the ice hockey team of choice.

We said goodbye to Jim and boarded the aircraft, each of the three of us occupying the same seats that we had held on the way up to Uchi Lake from Dryden. With the back door haywired shut it was time to go. We rose into sparkling clean air under the bright beam of a heat-deprived sun.

Then, somewhat precipitately, the air inside the aircraft did not seem quite as pristine in quality any longer. An odour so totally vile that it made a grievous bodily attack on the senses filled the cabin in a snap instant. My first thought, both figuratively and literally, was *Shit!* The metallurgist had complained of stomach problems earlier in the morning, probably related to an over-indulgence in the bounty of the previous Steak Night. To judge by the prevailing smell, I thought that he must have messed his pants. The unwelcome bouquet intensified to the extent that it came close to assuming a living presence around us.

The pilot looked up and advised us that what we could smell had its point of origin near Dryden. From our cruising altitude of around three thousand metres the Dryden pulp mill plumes were clearly visible a hundred kilometres away to the south. The drift of the noxious fumes out of Dryden that we were caught up in had travelled an astounding distance already, and heaven knew how much further north they might spread.

For the rest of the flight back to Dryden the options facing me in the desperately pestilential chamber that the aircraft cabin had turned into were to give up, throw up or jump out minus a parachute. Arrival at Dryden was a blessing, no moment more precious than the instant on the descent when we dropped through the noisome layer of atmosphere and the background odour of Dryden, relatively delectable by comparison, regained command.

THE REPORT OF the Flying Circus presenting its assessment of the Detour development project, including an account of the visit to South Bay Mine (but excluding references to Dryden, the aircraft pilot, T-bone steaks, saunas and skidoos), offered the select few who were prepared to read it a strong recommendation that the Company should bid to become a participant with Selco in an ongoing Detour mine development.

The Company accepted the Flying Circus's recommendation. Its bid was prepared in Toronto, masterminded by TM in his twenty-sixth (or it might have been the twenty-seventh) floor site on Adelaide Street. TM was more than content to slip happily into his most effusively unctuous mode in performing the task. The bid document was indeed well thought out and expeditiously presented. Its added-value characteristic, which perhaps went not unnoticed by both the metallurgist and the mining engineer who were involved, lay in the concept of developing a large open-pit mine in the AI-zone.

On the strength of such a creditable job, it was something of a pity that the Company was not the only horse in the race to bid for the Detour development project. Following the opening of received bids on the allotted date and at the allocated time, and allowing for a suitable period of reflection thereafter, it was announced that Selco's partner of choice was surely going to be a Big Oil connected outfit, but, horror of horrors, it was to be good old Cousin Beepee and not Uncle Joe's Company.

Whether or not the contest was a close-run thing, as TM suggested that Selco told him it had been, was immaterial. There were no prizes for coming second and no kudos whatsoever for Uncle Joe in being beaten by a Big Oil rival imbued with similar fancies of grandeur through diversifying its interests into the mining industry.

The merger of Cousin Beepee with Selco on the Detour development project resulted in the construction of a mine under the name of Les Mines Selbaie. This title was shortened to Selbaie for convenience. The name recognised the predilection of a workforce about to be dominated by French speakers for conversing with one another in French, or whatever masqueraded as French in the province of Quebec.

SELBAIE COMMENCED ITS operations as an underground mine on the B-zone. When the B-zone ore reserves approached exhaustion, attention shifted to the AI-zone and an open-pit mining option for the same.

TM, pursuant on the failure of the Company's bid, had passed the Flying Circus's assessment of the AI-zone opportunity to Selco. Whereas in the normal course of events Selco would eventually have figured out for themselves the potential of the AI-zone, I imagined that TM's generosity with our added-value concept had to be pretty useful to its beneficiaries.

TM told me that he had no alternative other than to hand over the information, as he had promised Selco that he would do so, irrespective of the outcome of the Company's bid. It had probably never entered TM's mind that the Company was destined to be second past the finishing post. All the same, it seemed to me to be a curious thing that TM did. It would have been interesting to find out just how closely the disclosure of the relevant information to Selco related to the timing of Selco's decision on a preferred partner. I had my view on the matter, but it was soon swallowed up in water under the bridge.

TIME MOVED ON. Cousin Beepee somehow managed to become the majority shareholder of Selbaie. A few years of this supposedly happy state of affairs elapsed before Cousin Beepee appeared to decide that for its Big Oil aspirations enough was enough, not only with respect to Selbaie but perhaps also with regard to the whole damn mining industry. In consequence, Cousin Beepee's majority share of Selbaie hit the market, open for sale to parties interested in bidding for the same.

The wheel had moved full circle. The Company was once again attracted into investigating the merits of acquiring a participating share in Selbaie and therefore evaluated, prepared and once more submitted a bid, the value of which was rumoured to have been excessive enough to astonish even those sectors of the Canadian mining industry in which excess was a way of life.

The Company's bid was accepted, causing the Company to realise with as much shock as surprise that, as a consequence, it owned an open-pit mining operation in northern Quebec and needed as a matter of some priority to determine how the hell it was going to run the operation properly.

The Company could of course lay its hands on plenty of its own people with all the required academic qualifications for filling key technical and managerial slots. Irrespective of this happy state of affairs, however, few of the candidates were likely to be equipped with the essential experience and toughness of attitude to cope with the challenges involved in the Selbaie operating environment.

The Company's customary procedure after making an acquisition such as Selbaie was borrowed from Uncle Joe's book of standard practices. It involved the Company replacing, as far as was possible, the pre-existing top management with its own people. Those who occupied lower staff echelons were permitted to ride on for the time being. A minimum replacement of the original top management was sure to include the positions of the general manager and the finance manager. With these jobs secured for the Company the key controls were in place. The only obstacles to progress were likely to be posed by those who had been replaced demanding to be bidden farewell with monumental golden handshakes.

AN INCIDENTAL HURDLE that the Company's acquisition of Selbaie threw up was the thorny decision on what to do about the newly current TM and his disciples residing in Adelaide-based opulence in Toronto. Since the days of the Detour development project bid (all of a decade earlier), the person of TM had changed a couple of times in the great cock-up-and-run tradition of three-year assignment cycles. For the sake of continuity it was just as well that through it all the bullshit element went on unchecked. In the midst of change it was also worth recognising that the pressure on Toronto by Uncle Joe's mineral exploration outfit over in Calgary had not in all that time diminished by one jot or tittle.

A replacement general manager for Selbaie was located from within the senior ranks of the Company and his formal appointment was announced. The principal priority assigned to him was to ensure that the Selbaie operations ran successfully. To this end Selbaie was the place of work where his time must perforce be put in. His seniority decreed that he outranked all other Company people, not only in Quebec but also in the whole of Canada, to the extent that all were required to offer obeisance to him. The numbers of the deferential included the then TM and his entire gang luxuriating in the Toronto suite. Sadly enough for these Toronto boys and girls, what the Company's acquisition of Selbaie meant for them was that they were not about to luxuriate in the Toronto suite for much longer.

It went without saying of course that no serious mining company could offer a credible face to the Canadian mining industry if it was not represented in Toronto. Toronto was where the Canadian mining industry pumped its blood. The new Selbaie general manager was therefore compelled to retain a small Company presence in that fair city, even if he himself was mandated to work in less salubrious territory.

TM's day was one of the first to be done. Those of his henchmen whose presences were no more either wanted or prepared to be tolerated in a Toronto set-up of reduced circumstances were given the option of relocating their place of work to Selbaie or hitting Adelaide Street running. Most of them chose, with no small measure of reluctance, the rock-strewn path to relocation, notwithstanding that, as dedicated English speakers to their last breath, they would form the squarest of pegs in settling into the roundest of holes in the French Canadian cultural desert characterising Selbaie.

AMONG THE PERKS of employment provided by Selbaie to its people, family housing in a dedicated town site close to the mine was not included. There was, however, on the mine property an extensive array of single-status bunkhouses and an associated canteen serving regular meals to the residents of those bunkhouses. The nearest thing approaching a Selbaie-inspired town site was the aforementioned village of Joutel. With no mines left in the immediate vicinity to sustain Joutel, Selbaie picked up the whole village for a song. The Selbaie employees who lived in Joutel worked a standard five-day week of eight hours per day, commuting the eighty kilometres up and down to Selbaie on every working day in specially contracted buses.

Other employees lived in towns and locations that were distant enough from Selbaie to preclude a daily commute. Such towns included Val d'Or, La Sarre and Rouyn in Quebec, and Timmins over in the part of Canada they called Ontario. Those who resided thus worked four-day weeks of twelve hours per day, starting on Mondays and finishing on Thursdays. During their four days at Selbaie they were accommodated in the bunkhouses. They drove up to Selbaie from home in their own vehicles late on Sunday evenings and departed again for home at the conclusion of their shifts on Thursdays.

THE FORMER ADELAIDE-SUITE boys who accepted jobs at Selbaie were naturally very keen to continue living in Toronto and fervently wished to commute from Toronto to Selbaie on the basis of the four-day week schedule. They envisaged flying from Toronto up to Val d'Or or Timmins or Noranda and travelling onwards to Selbaie by road on Sundays, and doing it all again in reverse on Thursdays.

The law according to the new general manager was not at all supportive of the Torontophiles. He declared that commuting to Selbaie over distances that could not reasonably be covered in a four-wheeled vehicle alone was not acceptable. The Torontophiles, forced to comply with this edict, mostly went to live in Timmins. Timmins might well be a sticks town by comparison with Toronto, but at least English was spoken there.

The new general manager didn't apply the rules of commuting practice to himself. He flipped as regularly as clockwork through the mine gate on Thursday evenings in his recently washed pickup (recently washed on those occasions when the temperature was somewhere above zero), in either a cloud of dust or a drift of snow, depending on the season. He was bound for Val d'Or airport to catch the last flight of the day to Montreal. The gander was not served up with the same kind of sauce as the goose.

THIS LONG-DISTANCE general managing shuttler was originally Dutch by nationality. He was a dyed-in-the-wool, glued-in-place Company stalwart who might have already reached an age at which any mid-life crisis was behind him. Although the excellent English that he spoke was not necessarily a major asset in Quebec, his very good command of French most definitely was. On that score alone his qualification to generally manage Les Mines Selbaie was impeccable, even though his French was of the Parisian variety, the spoken form of which was to the French Canadian tongue as night was to day.

I knew the new Selbaie general manager on the strength of a nodding relationship forged on the many occasions when we chanced to pass one another in a corridor back at the Company's head office. I saw him often enough to view him as a regular head-office fixture, and on the strength of that I can only imagine that he entertained similar thoughts about me. It was reported that he possessed a university degree in geology, an award that had clearly come to him a long time ago, since he appeared to be totally immersed in the cloudy waters of administration and strategic planning, floating weightlessly either within or in the direction of the ripples of senior management.

His voice was both soft and wheedling. It afflicted the ears of those forced to listen to it with an irritating insistency. When he demanded something from an underling, generally related to an item of impressive triviality, his voice pecked away at the shelly indifference of its target until its target gave up and let him have his way just to get rid of him.

In the best Company traditions of those involved in the field of planning, whether their respective penchants were of the strategic, financial or commodity-price variety, the new Selbaie general manager was highly accomplished in obscuring the big picture by chasing after a maze of details. A slight enough figure, he could be counted on to appear when least expected and was rarely as welcome as the flowers in May when he did.

Consequently, and since he had to have one, I invested him with an informal reference indicator "PA". For the information of the curious, PA formed the initials of the rather more descriptive "Phantom Ass-hole", although it could equally have referred to "Perfect Asshole", since this particular PA (or Peeyay) was a man destined never to suffer from haemorrhoids.

The illustrious title of Phantom Asshole was derived from an old primary school joke about a teacher anxious to find out which member of her class had surreptitiously crapped on the classroom floor alongside her desk. No one in the class was willing to own up to the dastardly deed. She invited the class to accompany her in closing their eyes tight, during which blind interlude the culprit was expected to tiptoe from his or her seat and remove the offending pile of turds in anonymity. The matter would then be considered closed. All eyes were closed tight. There was a short silence followed by a patter of feet, another longer silence, the scratch of chalk on blackboard, the patter of feet once again, then more silence.

The members of the class were bidden by the teacher to open their eyes. There, lying beside the first pile of shit was a second pile of similar material. On the blackboard behind the desk was written the words, "The Phantom Asshole strikes again!"

I HAD AN unexpected encounter with the Peeyay on an occasion not long after the formal announcement of his appointment as Selbaie's new general manager was made. Within a very few weeks from then he was due to head out to Selbaie to take up his general managerial duties full-time.

We met at a one-week course on ore reserve estimation at the Royal School of Mines in London. Neither of us knew that the other would be in attendance, but there was no surprise in that as it was the way Company co-ordination often worked. The record in the left hand not knowing what the right hand was doing book involved six Company delegates sent to a conference on tungsten production and marketing in Stockholm, independently of and unknown to one another.

My presence on the course in London was incongruous enough, as the course's content turned out to be so basic that I learned nothing much that I didn't know already from my working experience. The course additionally embodied very little of the practical realities of justifying ore reserves on a day-to-day basis on operating mines. For all that, the Peeyay's participation in the course was perhaps even more questionable than mine, given his seniority and the requirements of his task at Selbaie. Invoking that great and much beloved Company euphemism, the Peeyay told me he was attending the course to "refresh the memory".

The next time I met the Peeyay was in the month of February in the year 1995 at Selbaie, when he was already in place as general manager. My visit to Selbaie was governed by the Absolutely mandate. I was required to make an independent assessment of Selbaie's remaining ore reserves. I had no means of knowing whether or not the Peeyay supported my visit, but I rather suspected he did not.

IT WAS MY second visit to the locality. The Detour development project had ceded way to Les Mines Selbaie. To get to Selbaie I decided to take a leaf out of the book of the exiled Toronto boys and go in via Timmins. Rob, one of the said Toronto boys living in Timmins and working in the area of financial planning at Selbaie on the four-day shift system, very kindly agreed to give me a lift up to the mine from Timmins on his regular Sunday evening commute.

I took a Sunday afternoon KLM flight from Amsterdam to Toronto International airport, expecting to make an onward connection with Air Ontario to Timmins that same evening. Unfortunately the departure of the outbound flight from Amsterdam was delayed by four hours, as a consequence of which the connecting flight to Timmins had departed without me by the time I finally got to Toronto.

Arrangements were made for me to stay at a hotel inside Toronto airport and to catch a flight to Timmins on the following morning. I phoned Rob who said he would wait for me. I didn't phone the Peeyay so didn't know what his reaction was, not only to my turning up late but to my delaying Rob until Monday as well.

The aircraft for the ninety-minute Air Ontario flight to Timmins was a propeller-driven Dash 8-100 aircraft. There were fourteen passengers on board, one of which was a very large dog. For air travellers who revelled in looking down on endless vistas contained under a thick midwinter snow blanket relieved by an occasional sliver or hint of black, and once in a while by a grey-tinted hollow, there was plenty to enjoy from the aircraft window as the aircraft moved north. We left Toronto basking in a temperature of −14°c. At Timmins they managed to do a lot better than that and double the figure to achieve twenty-eight below.

THE BURGEONING TOWN that was Timmins was laid out in geometrically precise street-bounded blocks. Even the muffling snow couldn't do much to ease the hard angles and the sharp edges that sliced through town and perished abruptly in the all-enveloping wilderness beyond. Well outside the town, sporadic mine head frames thrust up through the ubiquitous snow like sorely frostbitten thumbs, their lone peaks dribbling streams of ice crystals as charged air rose through them from the deep heart of the mines below and suffered the shock of instant condensation.

Rob met me at the Timmins airport terminal in a rented pickup truck in which we were to make the four-hour road trip east to Selbaie. The airport terminal was not large by comparison with the king of its race in Toronto, but it seemed to be a veritable palace when set against the distant memory of its poor cousin over at Matagami.

Rob had some trouble to get the pickup engine started. I supposed this might have constituted a mechanical protest against the powerful cold, although it didn't take a genius to work that out. With the help of a friendly driver of another pickup that did manage to start and the production of a set of linking jump leads by Rob, we managed eventually to hit the road to Selbaie.

THE APPEARANCE OF the road surface suggested a long history of its having been patched and then patched again and extolled the many current virtues of super-cold and compressed snow in holding the conglomeration firmly together. Snow was banked high along the verges, commemorating either the passage of countless snowploughs or the passage of one snowplough countless times. The crests of the snow banks smoked in the crosswind and cast snaking tendrils across the road surface. A clear and present danger was posed by logging trucks as intimidating as they were gigantic, piled so high with the fruits of deforestation that they appeared to be testing to the limits the last-straw principle as applied to a camel's back. These behemoths thundered along the crown of the road followed by swirling clouds of blinding ice crystals, offering no quarter to lesser traffic.

The road ran through the mining district known as the Porcupine trend, which stretched all the way from the vicinity of Timmins up to Rouyn-Noranda in the province of Quebec by way of Kidd Creek. The principal town that we drove through on the way, at which time seeping darkness ahead was already threatening to banish the residual glow of a glorious sunset behind us, was La Sarre, somewhere beyond the Porcupine trend. Rob handled the driving easily and didn't take the ditch once.

We reached the Selbaie mine gate shortly after the descent of full darkness. Wind was gusting strongly. The wind-chill factor, as the gateman who handed me the waiting key to open my on-site accommo-dation told me with some glee when I signed his register, lowered the relative temperature outside his gatehouse to perhaps as low as −60°c. Together with the key I was given a few items of safety equipment, including a hard hat, earplugs and safety glasses. The gateman's offer of a set of protective rubber gloves seemed somewhat redundant in the light of the ambient temperature, let alone when the modification of wind chill was added in.

My accommodation was to be in the "Auberge", otherwise the Selbaie on-site guesthouse. It was a large wood-framed building set up on the fringe of a complex of bunkhouse blocks, adjacent to a track leading four kilometres out past the process-plant tailings dams and the site garbage dump to terminate at the Wawagosic River water supply pumping station.

The interior of the Auberge was very comfortably appointed. Half of its area was devoted to guest sleeping quarters arranged in individual rooms on either side of a dimly illuminated corridor. Each guest room was fitted with its own shower unit. The central heating in the Auberge was as effective as it had to be. Parts of the floor were hot underfoot.

The other half of the Auberge comprised a carpeted communal area adjoined by a large entrance hall in which snow boots and associated garments were required to be removed in order to glorify the longevity of the carpet. In addition there was a smaller chamber fitted with a washing machine and dryer; a kitchen section equipped with a large refrigerator, an even larger cooker and a mighty array of cutlery and crockery; a small bar set in an alcove; and a lounge with a number of strategically placed armchairs focused on a television set. A small pool table stood off on one side. The cue rack was mounted on a pillar that not only supported the roof of the Auberge but also placed an acute constraint on the arc within which strokes could be made from one corner of the pool table.

THE PEEYAY CALLED in to see me at the Auberge shortly after my arrival. He made me feel quite welcome, which in itself came as a minor surprise. Slightly more surprisingly, he did not attempt to disparage the objectives of my visit, at least when using any direct approach. He did suggest that certain stipulations placed by certain persons back at the Company's head office on my making a definitive assessment of the Selbaie ore reserves had afforded him "some amusement". That made it obvious enough, in the context of corporate-speak, that the powers that be must have placed the Peeyay under more than enough pressure over my visit to have substantially pissed him off. He told me, in his inimitably insistent way, that he was not placing me under any pressure at all, which by the same corporate-speak token made it abundantly clear that he was.

The Peeyay said that he wanted a statement of the ore reserves from me – a statement agreed to by both of us, that was – before I left Selbaie for my return trip home. That implied that he required my report to reflect and support whatever gospel he had been hitherto delivering to head office. I told him that as far as I was concerned I would do the best I could. Whatever I did would be entirely objective and as long as I was happy with the result I didn't care if the Peeyay agreed with it or not, although I didn't tell him that.

I had arrived on Monday night and was scheduled to leave Selbaie on the following Friday. The Peeyay would depart for his three-day weekend break in Montreal on Thursday. I had never believed that the original intention of four working days would be enough for the task, let alone the three that remained as a result of my flight delay. At the meeting with the Peeyay in the Auberge I told him I really needed at least an extra week on top of the three days, and he acceded to that, extending the duration of my visit to ten days at a single stroke.

Since the Peeyay was the very person who I understood to have previously determined that four days was more than enough for me, this *volte-face* would have been amazing had it not also been typical of his more mercurial qualities. The extension of the visit left me a little inconvenienced in having to arrange for my return flight schedule to be amended, but that was a small price to pay to get the job done properly.

WITH THE TIMING settled, the Peeyay passed me a sheet of graph paper on which several hand-drawn frequency diagrams were displayed. These purported to bear some kind of relationship to metal price forecasts on the international commodity markets. The objective classification of material in the ground as ore reserves depended on a range of economic and practical factors, one of which was the expected long-term metal price. Metal price structure was complicated at Selbaie by the fact that although the key metallic components of the ore mined were copper and zinc, there were also not insignificant associated quantities of lead, silver and gold, all capable of generating revenue at the smelter. The sales prices forecast for all five of these commodities, once mined, processed, concentrated, transported and recovered, formed an important element of the ore reserve estimation equation.

The Peeyay's frequency diagrams were prepared from considerations of average monthly London Metal Exchange market prices realised for the five commodities over the previous ten years. The Peeyay took the mean value of each of the respective price frequency distributions as the future five-year forecast price for the relevant commodity. He wanted me to use the price figures thus devised in preparing my Selbaie ore reserve estimates.

The Peeyay's figures were all substantially overvalued when compared with then current metal prices and Company forecast trends and, moreover, had been put together on an entirely spurious premise. Metal prices were dependent on the passage and related intrigues of time and were likely to fluctuate up or down on the whim of the unexpected. I offered this observation to the Peeyay and found him disinterested in listening. It was decided (by him) merely that we would speak of it again.

WHEN THE PEEYAY had finished with me, I left the Auberge to go and eat in the canteen. That facility was a vast and clattering hall fitted along one side with a serving counter equipped with structured racks and deep, trough-like trays that owed much to the virtues of stainless steel. In behind the counter lurked a steamy kitchen where the food was prepared. In the main body of the canteen hall stood a host of long refectory tables arrayed along each side with benches for the comfort of diners.

During my ten-day stay at Selbaie I took all meals, breakfast, lunch and dinner alike, in the canteen. The times when meals were served were strictly controlled. The window of opportunity during which meals were available was not wide. Outside formal meal times, however, the hungry might find consolation in a supply of neatly packed sandwiches, cartons of fruit juice, pieces of fruit and loads of cookies that could be extracted from a display cabinet close to the canteen entry hall.

The quality of the food varied from being occasionally not so good to generally not bad and not infrequently very good. The fare could have done with more spicing up but was flavoursome and satisfying for all that. I partook of it for only ten days and so to a certain extent each day brought along something of a novelty. I realised that my feelings on the menu might not have been quite as favourable on the strength of a significantly longer exposure. No one anxious about his long-term popularity ever took on a job as a cook at a mining camp.

The lunches and dinners that I received, and which to a large extent I enjoyed and appreciated, made an interesting litany to contemplate. The congregational response of "Good Lord, deliver us", tended to be only a weekend phenomenon. Those Monday through Friday meals that were on offer, when the real cooks were on shift, involved *inter alia*, chicken and potatoes, cottage pie, chicken and spring rolls, pizza, ground beef pie, *coq au vin*, crab sticks, scampi, gammon with pineapple, fried chicken, and fish and mashed potatoes. At the weekend the B team of cooks was on duty charge, and then emerged hot dogs, hamburgers, hot chicken sandwiches, *rigatoni* and fried baloney, and finally *rigatoni* on its own (one shot at the fried baloney proved to be more than enough for me).

For those who loved desserts there was almost always an abundance of riches begging selection. There were jellies, cakes, fruit pies (inclusive of the blessed blueberry variety), ice cream, and fresh fruit, including bananas, purple and green grapes, and apples that looked as if they had all been individually hand-polished by an expert. Snow White would have been happy to take a bite from any one of them, although where Canadian apples were concerned the taste of the crunchy part rarely matched up to the promise of the gloss.

Breakfast in the canteen contained something for everyone. There were cereals in abundance, potted yoghurts in a kaleidoscope of flavours, a selection of jams, honey, bread, tea, coffee, eggs done to order in any way that could ever be imagined, bacon, sausages, beans, the whole works and more. You name it, there it was. The grand prize at breakfast (Monday to Friday, that was) was an array of fresh muffins – a different type of muffin each day. The muffins that were left over after Friday's breakfast turned up again on Saturday morning. Not a single muffin ever survived to make it through to Sunday's breakfast. Sunday was a muffinless day. Selbaie muffins were of a comfortably handy dimension to enjoy, not at all like those monster gut-busting versions they produced down in Toronto.

As I descended the canteen steps to make a cold-gripped return to the Auberge after breakfast on the second morning of my visit to Selbaie, a flicker of colour caught the corner of one of my eyes. Turning towards the source, I saw a little fox trotting by. It disappeared into the snow-bound walkway between two bunkhouse units.

The fox was long-haired, bearing a russet-red coat pointed in black tips. Its legs were black, contrasting with a bib beneath its chin that was whiter than the well-trampled snow under its feet. The black pointing was most pronounced on the fox's tail, a mightily fluffed-out appendage that was quite as long and almost as thick as the rest of the animal attached to it.

Following the next day's breakfast I looked for the fox again. I didn't see it, but that omission didn't prevent me from depositing a wad of fried bacon strips, surreptitiously extracted from the canteen, on the snow bank by the bunkhouse corner where the animal had moved out of sight on the previous day. When I passed the same spot only a little later on my way to the offices of the Selbaie engineering department, it was interesting to note that the bacon was no longer there.

I placed more stolen bacon in the identical location on the next day and this resulted in a similar disappearing act. A day later, on the third occasion of offering up purloined bacon for vulpine delectation, the fox was sitting a few metres away from the place of deposition. Its poise suggested the anticipation of one genuinely waiting for a handout. I dropped the bacon in the customary place and stepped aside. The fox moved in cautiously, snatched the bacon up in its mouth, and flitted from sight.

This episode established a pattern for the next few days, and as those days progressed, the fox and I enjoyed a developing familiarity. The fox grew confident enough to approach so close to me that I could have reached down and touched it on the head.

At the penultimate breakfast of my ten-day visit, bacon was off when I went to the canteen counter to prise the fox's daily ration away from the greasily woven mat of bacon strips that floored a dedicated stainless steel trough at the canteen serving counter. The absence of bacon dealt a savage blow to my post-breakfast morale. The closest equivalent comestible for the fox that I could find was hot-dog frankfurters, and so I took two of them as a by-no-means very satisfactory alternative.

The fox was again steadfast in wait. I extended the franks towards it. The fox lifted its head, sniffed at the franks, took them delicately in its mouth and strolled off slowly for a place of consumption that only it knew the location of.

That was the last time I was to see the fox. Perhaps hot-dog frankfurters were not to its taste, as it didn't show up on the following morning. I laid some more bacon out for it, since bacon was by then back on the breakfast menu. Not long afterwards I left Selbaie to return to Timmins. The fox and I had parted company in more ways than one.

Feeding a naturally wild creature at an isolated mining camp was not a very sensible thing for me to have done, much though I valued my daily relationship with the little fox. Our meetings did a great deal to ease dark contemplation concerning likely encounters that I might have with the Peeyay at later junctures of the day.

The real problem in encouraging such familiarity in non-domesticated animals was that they didn't know quite where to draw the line on their own enthusiasm for more of the same. The opportunistic feeding of bears attracted to the vicinity of some mining camps through poorly organised disposal of camp garbage, not least after a successful

Steak Night, invariably resulted in an eventual ursine invasion of bunk-houses, as a consequence of which one or more bears would be shot by the unnaturally wild humans for causing a predicament for which the bears bore no responsibility at all.

THE CUMULATIVE DISTANCE between the back door of the Auberge and the entry door to the processing plant and adjoining offices for the processing, engineering and other technical department staff was no more than a couple of hundred metres. The route from one door to the other led through a maze of bunkhouse blocks (in which I regularly lost my sense of direction and had to scout around for bearings), past the canteen on the left and the administrative office building on the right, and finally across a bleakly open mine yard. Although it was not so very far to walk, the journey took on all the significance of an expedition into unknown territory when the snow flew and the wind slashed between the bunkhouses and blistered across the yard.

The declared outside temperature on the Auberge's thermometer on the first morning of my visit to Selbaie was −28°c. During the subsequent ten days of residence so kindly arranged for me by the Peeyay, that was about as cold as it got. On one morning I was greeted by a comparatively balmy −10°c, but otherwise the temperature showed a general reluctance to slip much higher than an enervating twenty below.

THE PROCESSING PLANT and the associated offices unit was a large and rambling collection of starkly rendered structures architecturally designed in apparent homage to the power of vertical lines to impress. The complex was dominated on its mine yard side front by a mighty head frame clad entirely in black-painted metal sheeting. The base of the head frame was slotted into a jumble of somewhat (but only some-what) lesser constructions contrastingly sheeted over in metal painted white. The sole relief provided to this monochrome arrangement was derived from two immense rusty red girders that slanted out from beneath the cap of the head frame where they no doubt lent support to the hoisting sheave. The hoist cable above the two girders made a frail black trace against the smouldering sky.

This head frame graced the collar of a shaft that led down into the B-zone underground mine. Its magisterial appearance placed in a proper poor man's perspective the Detour development project shaft head frame that I had confronted a decade and a half earlier. Since the B-zone had been mined out by the time of my second visit to the property, I wasn't going to get the chance to go down the more recent shaft and see the grown-up version of the underground mine.

The conglomeration of white-sheeted, block-like buildings stretched behind the head frame in an arrangement which suggested that a contumacious committee had played a role in their placement. The blocks were linked by enclosed walkways, also covered in white-painted sheets of metal. From within, the walkways felt as if they were virtual mine tunnels.

Once within the complex, to reach the engineering department offices one had to undertake a walk of half a kilometre or so through a sequence of these walkways, interspersed with flights of steps, left and right transits through building blocks, and a traverse of the processing plant along a gallery running over the top of the concentrate thickeners. Inside the walkways the walls were rimed all over in thick frost. Hard white icicles hung from the roof struts and their fallen relatives gathered in a jumble along the edges of the floor, waiting to be banished by a thaw that was surely coming, but not yet.

I rambled along the frozen route and stumbled into the engineering department offices with some sense of relief. The temperature in the offices was warm but the atmosphere was cool, and my welcome was only just on the guarded side of being chilly. I had expected as much, as in my experience French Canadians were among the most reticent people with whom to build mutually trusting working relationships. A long history of being treated as second-class citizens in their own country of Quebec by Anglo-Canadians from across the border ensured that French Canadians were instinctively xenophobic. I didn't anticipate being fully accepted by them on this visit and thought that the best I could do would be to sow the seeds of eventual acceptance so that on subsequent visits (it took two more for me to achieve what I thought was acceptance) we might all come to feel that we were on the same side.

The engineering department office area consisted of two very big open-plan rooms equipped with a large number of desks and mapping and drawing tables. A smaller walk-through area, which contained not only the departmental photocopying and printing machines but also a fireproof vault for storing original drawings and records, separated the two rooms.

One of the big rooms was dedicated to those serving within the disciplines of mining engineering, surveying and production sampling. The other was the province of the mine geologists, led by a chief geologist who, for administrative purposes, reported to the chief engineer, an arrangement that in my opinion was akin to having a gamekeeper reporting to a poacher. The best way to screw up an ore reserve was to involve a mining engineer in its estimation. Along the front edge of both rooms and facing out onto the extension of the mine yard behind the head frame, was a row of small, partitioned, individual offices allocated to senior departmental personnel.

THE CHIEF ENGINEER sat in one of the little partitioned offices. His door was invariably closed. Any disturbances from without, to the well-practised routine taking place within, were rarely received from within with good grace. He hoarded information in the manner of a hamster, and indeed there were elements of his personality that were quite as furtive as those of that busy rodent. His name was Denis. He was a five-day-per-week man who lived down in Joutel. Denis was in his late thirties but conducted himself as if he were twenty years older. His looks were slickly sombre and intensely Gallic, tailor-made for insertion into a bad French movie, of which genre there were far too many of that particular quality foisted on an unappreciative world.

Within Denis' office the only open space available was on the seat of a chair behind the desk, whenever Denis was not sitting in it. Everywhere else was inundated with documents, reports, files and a scattering of mining-industry trade magazines. This treasure trove contained much information that was critical to the orderly estimation of the ore reserves and the efficient operation of the mine. Denis considered it all to be his personal property and guarded it with the zeal of a high-security prison officer.

Many reports vital to my ore reserve-related deliberations were held by Denis within this welter of paper. That would not have mattered so much had it not been for the fact that their pages had yet to benefit from the reproductive power of a photocopying machine. On the many occasions when I was unable to locate a document that I urgently needed, I took the line of least resistance in going directly to Denis to request it. Denis then waved his hands around, waggled his shoulders and exhibited more than a little reluctance to comply. Although he usually did deliver (eventually, that is), he showed no reticence at all in coming to me to seek the recovery of his precious documentation when he deemed that I had held on to it for long enough.

Denis' deputy was named Marcel, an amiable and wholly engaging character with an openly straightforward approach that made him a most useful counterpoint to his boss. Marcel was a four-day-week type, commuting up to Selbaie from La Sarre. I could rationalise reasonably well how Marcel coped with working for Denis, but couldn't imagine why, as I felt that Denis kept Marcel just about as much in the dark as he kept me.

Marcel was a kind of executive gopher for Denis, the owner of the legs that ran around the AI-zone open-pit and tailings disposal area and managed the production schedule and design of the tailings dams on Denis' behalf. I went on a tour around the dams with Marcel on one of his regular inspections, driving along the snow-bound tracks topping the dam walls. The view was one of snow and yet more snow. There were tailings under there somewhere.

Marcel took me into the open pit with him on a number of occasions, initially to give me an informed overview and then to clarify specific details regarding the geology and the future availability of ore reserves. On the strength of my Detour development project association with the AI-zone, I felt that I had a personal stake in ensuring the open pit's success.

The open pit was an immense basin, ringed around its walls by crumbling benches that dwindled into a grandly frozen maelstrom-like vortex down at the bottom. Snow clung to the benches as it fell, etching out irregularities and highlighting the geological structure in a wintry palette of multitudinous grey shades. The deep cold of the open pit peeled away my pretensions and exposed humility with every stroke of its blade.

On some evenings after dinner Marcel came along to the Auberge from the bunkhouse where he resided when on site, and we walked together along the twisting track down to the Wawagosic River and back. The track lay like a starlit white ribbon slicing through black impenetrable forest. Snow squealed under our boots. Now and then over to the west there might be a curtain of aurora swishing across the stars, but apart from the pair of us trudging the road, there was no other movement in the frozen night.

ONLY ONE MEMBER of Denis' engineering staff complement was of the Anglo persuasion, but even so, he gave the impression of being one too many for Denis. The Anglo-Canadian in question was a mining engineer named Mike, sent up from Toronto as part of the Peeyay's purge of TM's former Torontonian empire. Mike's globular shape probably owed much to the propensity of doughnut consumption to shape physique. I judged him to be a mining engineer with evident ability to achieve very good things in the area of mine planning, and indeed, ensconced as he was in a cubicle surrounded by papers on which he always seemed to be so eternally busy, it was possible that very good things may well have been in the offing.

It was perhaps something of a pity that neither Denis nor Marcel appeared to take a blind bit of notice either of Mike or of what Mike was working on. Marcel told me that no one of any persuasion in the engineering department wanted to work with Mike, not so much owing to language or cultural differences (although that might have offered a good enough reason in itself) but because Mike's manner was rather abrasive and a conviction that he was right and everyone else was wrong was deeply engrained in his attitude to others.

Marcel's opinion of Mike was one that I found myself moved to agree with following a number of foundered attempts to co-operate with Mike, whose stock in trade of mine planning was so essential to my own cause. Face to face I had no insurmountable issues with Mike, but when I was not with him this situation went into reverse gear. Mike seemed to be ever ready to assimilate useful ideas gleaned from other people and act to turn them to his own advantage by subsequently presenting them as his own to third parties, not least the Peeyay. Mike would have made an ideal candidate for transfer to the Company's head offices, where he would have adjusted to the covert knife-in-the-back climate as snugly as a double-socked foot would fit a felt-lined snow boot.

THE PEEYAY'S ANGLOPHOBIC credentials were rarely well disguised, which may or may not have been to his credit. Irrespective of such a jury-out characteristic, the Peeyay was generally willing to make use of back-door intrigues brought to him by people like Mike, even though he made it all too clear that he viewed Mike's usefulness to Selbaie in much the same chocolate teapot-inspired custom that Denis and Marcel evidently did. As far as the Peeyay was concerned in both word and deed, the few remaining Anglo-Canadians on site were regarded as an unnecessary evil inflicted on him. I imagined that the Peeyay believed if the Anglos could be sidelined for long enough they would quit Selbaie voluntarily and thereby ease everyone's headaches, not least their own.

Given that the Peeyay's reactions to any set of circumstances were set firmly on Francophile-oriented rails, it was then somewhat incongruous that he insisted that the formal ore reserves report for Selbaie must be written in English. He declared (not incorrectly) that the formal language of the Company's board of directors and its centralised executive management in head office was English, and so, he went on, that linguistic preference must be directly reflected in stating the ore reserves.

I could fully accept reporting the ore reserves in English but knew only too well that what the Peeyay did not take into account was that Denis and his team of engineers and geologists, who would need to compile and agree the contents of the final ore reserves report (with my assistance), were able to write in French of a quality that was not reflected in their lesser level of skills with written English. Not to put too fine a point on it, our first united attempt at preparing an ore reserves report in English produced a result so idiomatically execrable that the options of laughing or crying about it hung in fine juxtaposition.

I suggested to the Peeyay that Denis and his people might first of all write the ore reserves report in appropriate French. I could then translate the report into decent English, all the while retaining the content and intent of the French version. The Peeyay rejected this suggestion so forcefully that I wondered if I had inadvertently implied that some form of sabotage might be involved. Rather tellingly, the Peeyay was supported by Denis, who claimed that if I wrote an English version of a French ore reserves report, even under circumstances permitting the French version to prevail in any dispute, then the report would be mine and not his, and he couldn't have that.

And so it came to pass that far too many of us, with the notable exception of the Peeyay, sat through crushingly interminable hours in producing English draft after English draft of a Selbaie ore reserve report. Each draft seemed to take a lot longer to correct and otherwise edit than did its predecessor.

The final version of the Selbaie ore reserves report was chimerical, satisfying no one who had contributed to it. The Peeyay was equally dissatisfied, as his castles-in-the-air metal price forecasts were deposited in the round file at an early stage and replaced by something more realistic. Mike, who in an open forum agreed the results of the report, was privately less content and set his best endeavours, laced with habitually clandestine guile, to discredit the final ore reserve figures, although fortunately with a striking lack of success.

A CHIEF GEOLOGIST named Jean-Jacques led Denis' geological group. Jean-Jacques was usually referred to as Jayjay. He was bluff, fat and bristling as much with his own self-importance as with the bushy black beard that he hid behind. In a film of Jayjay's life the casting director could have done no better than select Brian Blessed to take the lead role.

Jayjay sat in a paper-strewn office cubicle, much in the manner of Denis, with whom he had the privilege to travel up and down in the bus each day from Joutel. Jayjay's office door, unlike Denis' counterpart portal, was normally open, although for all that, this apparent concession offered little in the way of encouragement, as Jayjay's accessibility was not an awful lot better than that of his superior. His convention was to declare to those desirous of taking up some of his time that he was extremely busy at the moment but would get back to them later. He managed to convey to all such petitioners an image of a man in the process of being harried by duty towards an early grave.

At the time of my visit Jayjay had two assistant geologists under his command on site. One of the two was Daniel, a dark-complexioned little Frenchman from (of all places) France, and the other was Mehmet, himself somewhat swarthy-featured, a naturalised Canadian who hailed originally from Turkey. Both Daniel and Mehmet were ideas men, and brilliant with it. Daniel was to Jayjay as Marcel was to Denis, providing the feet that covered the pit and additionally the mind that analysed options. I had no doubt that without Daniel to support him, Jayjay's career at Selbaie might have long since been called into question.

Mehmet's geological orientation was of the academic variety. He was a fine conceptual thinker with wonderfully lucid ideas that could, if Jayjay had managed to summon up the motivation to listen to them, have provided a major boost to the longer-term future aspirations of the Selbaie operations, as well as furnishing some key support for the assurance of short-term routine production. As it was, Jayjay appeared to me to view Mehmet's ideas as threats directed against his personal authority. He devoted a fair portion of his personal strategic planning to weaving a web of isolation around Mehmet, behind which Mehmet was barely heard and, for that matter, rarely seen.

I found that Mehmet had so much to offer me that I spent a fair amount of time with him in order to benefit from his knowledge and experience. For his part, Mehmet was almost tearfully grateful to have someone come along and actually be prepared to listen to him. This made Jayjay less than happy with me, although such invective as his displeasure gave rise to was mumbled into his beard in the sanctuary of his office so that none of it hit the fan and flew at me while I was at Selbaie.

However, the keen-edged axe of Jayjay's ire did take a swing at me a week or two after I had departed from Selbaie. It came shortly after I submitted a draft visit report to Denis for review prior to finalisation. Such courtesy submissions were by then standard practice for me. They allowed inadvertent errors to be identified and corrected and misrepresentations to be clarified.

Jayjay's immediate reaction to my draft visit report was to fax me a twelve-page epistle, each page of which was hand-written in English that creaked a little but served the cause of condemnation quite adequately. Jayjay's words cascaded across the twelve pages as if they had been poured from a bucket of liquid manure. Their tone stopped short of being hysterical by no more than the breadth of a slice of fried baloney. Jayjay's paramount bone of contention with me was the fact that I had quoted Mehmet's work in several places in my visit report.

Jayjay demanded that all references to Mehmet in the report should be expunged and replaced by certain of the emissions contained in his twelve-page fax. To do that would be to virtually double the length of the visit report and would have required me to include a number of points from Jayjay that were somewhat less credible than anything I ever heard from Mehmet's lips. I thanked Jayjay and left things to mature on a very polite shove-it-up-yours basis.

Had our ore reserve estimation team been a family, sociologists would have described us as dysfunctional. Between ourselves we were pulling in so many different directions at the same time that reaching agreement on a final ore reserve statement seemed no less remote a possibility than that of *rigatoni* not featuring on the weekend menu in the canteen.

With our allotted cast of characters a tragicomedy of errors played itself out as if Shakespeare had somehow confused Macbeth with Machiavelli.

The Peeyay's starring role had him walking a delicate line between a Richard III sowing a winter of discontent for the rest of the cast and a Shylock intent on obtaining a gory pound of flesh from one or other of us as expeditiously as possible. As Shylock, he was a brick not yet ready to plead, but was however alert to any means of manipulation of the affected parts.

Mike's dagger-wielding virtuosity qualified him to play the part of Cassius in the unfolding drama. He thought too much perhaps, and such men were dangerous. On the other hand he failed dismally in the lean and hungry look department insofar as his appearance was diametrically opposed to emaciation.

Jayjay, a man who sweated to death and larded the lean earth as he walked along, could easily have been cast as Falstaff. In his case he genuinely looked the part. He did, however, exhibit overtones of Cardinal Wolsey that were perhaps more apt to consider. His promises were mighty, as he no doubt once was. His performance was as he now was – nothing.

Marcel and Daniel entered from stage left as Rosencrantz and Guildenstern. It did not matter which was which or who was who. They were courtiers, on site to serve their masters, indifferent children of the earth science, neither being over-happy nor for that matter forming the very button on fortune's cap.

Mehmet might have made a good Othello, but the Prince of Denmark was perhaps a rather more relevant assignment for him. Should he be or should he not be? That was the question. Mehmet was resigned to suffering the slings and arrows of outrageous fortune while lacking the conviction to take arms against his Jayjay-directed sea of troubles and end those troubles by opposing them.

Within and around this den of intrigue French Canadian Capulets stalked Anglo Montagues, two households, not unalike in dignity, breaking to new mutiny from ancient grudge.

Then there was me, and what could I do but see myself as a Chorus setting the scene, providing continuity between the protagonists and pulling the ingredients of the poison'd chalice together while endeavouring neither to drink too deep of the dodgy draught nor to be forced to exit pursued by a bear.

The play was the thing, and at the final curtain we had compiled an ore reserve report that, as far as I was concerned, stood sound on the basis of figures that I could support. I don't think the report quite caught the conscience of the king, but perhaps the Peeyay didn't have much of a conscience to be caught in the first place. "Yes, indeedy", and as Irving Berlin put it so succinctly, there was no business like show business.

As a result of my many frustrated attempts during the ore reserve reporting process to imitate the actions of the tiger, I felt that I could, on its alleged completion, return to Timmins from Selbaie with my life having some smatch of honour left in it and with all thoughts of running upon my sword banished for a while at least.

The Peeyay, a man ever prepared to make one last roll of the dice to do me no obviously direct favours, still had one ace left up his sleeve. He allocated to me transport out of Selbaie as a passenger in the cab of one of the giant trucks that regularly plied the road wending west to the smelter at Kidd Creek mine, bearing heavy cargoes of copper or zinc concentrates from the Selbaie processing plant. Kidd Creek was reasonably, if not comfortably, close to Timmins.

The Peeyay's plan was that I should travel in the concentrate truck to the Kidd Creek mine gatehouse where the Kidd Creek gateman could phone a Timmins dispatcher to order a taxi for me. The taxi would then come out to the Kidd Creek gatehouse to convey me to Timmins airport in time for my rescheduled Air Ontario flight to Toronto.

Mike came along to the Auberge to see me and express outrage at such treatment, describing my consignment to a concentrate truck as a calculated insult by the Peeyay. Mike advised me, in a voice throbbing with passion, to contest it and insist on an alternative means of transport befitting what he referred to as my "station". The intensity of Mike's keenness to have me depart on an acerbic note was almost touching. With some people, I thought, the capacity for conspiracy died hard.

I was only too glad to be the beneficiary of any transport out of Selbaie calculated to place distance between the Peeyay and myself, and apart from that essential consideration, travelling in a concentrate truck shaped up as a great experience in prospect. I was ready to cross the nations over to Timmins by whatever means the Peeyay decreed, and moreover to do it with a smile.

At 6.45 a.m. on the morning of my departure the external temperature registered at the Auberge had risen to a pleasant −14°c. Light snow was falling, a common consequence of sudden elevation in local temperature.

The concentrate truck was waiting outside the Selbaie gatehouse for me to board it. Mike, in it to the bitter end, drove me in a pickup over to the gatehouse from the Auberge. On the way he stopped briefly outside the administration office block for me to go in to say goodbye to the Peeyay. Perhaps I imagined that the Peeyay showed me a less gracious face than he ought to have done under the circumstances, as I felt that he was as glad to get rid of me as I was to see the back of him. He thanked me for the job I had done, and I thanked him for letting me do it. Even the freshly fallen snow was not as white as those two lies.

The Peeyay, in a rare moment of indubitable sincerity, wished me a safe trip to Timmins. He then went on, belatedly I thought, to question the dimensions of my luggage. The space to contain the luggage and myself inside the cab of the concentrate truck was believed by him, he said, to fall a long way short of being ample. I would have liked to have said, "So what?" but had to content myself with thinking it instead.

The concentrate truck was not of recent manufacture. It shook and rattled a lot, and that was just when it was standing still with the engine idling. However, it was warm enough inside the cab where I wedged myself into the seat on the passenger side with a briefcase tight under my legs and my suitcase upright on my lap. My chin cleared the suitcase handle by as much as a couple of centimetres. The arrangement could have been more comfortable, but I wasn't complaining.

The driver was a diminutive French Canadian named Louis, who came from Rouyn. He told me he had driven the truck up from Rouyn a few hours earlier to pick up a load of thirty-three metric tons of

Selbaie copper concentrate for delivery at Kidd Creek. From Kidd Creek he intended to return to Rouyn and his day's work would then be over. He pulled the concentrate truck away from the Selbaie gatehouse at 7.45 a.m.

Louis apologised for the antiquated condition of the truck. He was at great pains to tell me that it was not the truck he customarily drove. A month ago, he said, he was involved in an unfortunate accident with his usual truck. He left the characteristics of the accident veiled in mystery for a while, but later on along the road, as we came to feel easier in one another's company, Louis passed me a grubby, well-handled envelope containing a few photos of the great event. I looked the photos over and decided at once that I would have preferred the mystery of what had taken place to have remained unsolved.

It seemed that the former truck, with Louis at the wheel, came over the crest of a rise along the road between Selbaie and La Sarre to be suddenly confronted by a broken-down logging truck standing at the top of the downgrade in a position more or less designed to promote a collision. Louis frantically tried to swing his truck out to the left of the static logging truck but didn't have either the time or the space to make it all the way around the obstruction. Logs projecting from the back end of the logging truck impaled Louis' truck cabin on the passenger side, eliminating everything in their path. It was a miraculous escape for Louis who was missed by the impacting logs (he told me) by a margin of mere millimetres.

As fate had it, on that special day Louis was not travelling with a passenger. That was the role I was fulfilling when I looked at the horrifying photos of the accident. The suitcase on my lap would not have served as an adequate shield from those logs. I crossed my fingers on the upgrade of every hill we came to subsequently.

As we progressed towards Kidd Creek the rate of snowfall gradually intensified from light to moderate to heavy. It may not have aspired to be a genuine blizzard, but the sheer volume of falling snow made it closely approach a blizzard's near relative. The snow cut visibility, turned all vision to monochrome and lay on the road in an ever-deepening accumulation. The wheels of the concentrate truck punched through the unresisting snow with the aplomb of born victors. I began to revise one of my opinions concerning the Peeyay, who had done me a good turn after all, if inadvertently. A car or a pickup with me as a passenger might not have made such a successful transit as did Louis' concentrate truck from Selbaie along that snow-ridden road to Kidd Creek.

At the point where the truck crossed from Quebec into Ontario Louis told me we were entering Canada. He said it in all seriousness and left me in no doubt as to which side of the border could claim his allegiance. In Canada we made a short halt in a little village named Palmarolle, where Louis had some breakfast at a truckers' diner and I was glad to stretch my limbs and drink some coffee.

Louis pulled up the concentrate truck at the Kidd Creek gatehouse precisely at noon, where I was dropped off in accordance with the Peeyay's master plan. I was most grateful to Louis for his service and his company and was sorry to part from him. I told him that I would be glad to travel with him again.

The snow was falling so thickly at Kidd Creek that not only did the thought of reaching Timmins by taxi call for a leap of imagination but the odds on getting a flight that day out of Timmins to Toronto felt as if they might confidently have been quoted at six figures to one. Taking the few steps from Louis' truck to the Kidd Creek gatehouse door liberally coated both me and my luggage in white. However, I reckoned not with Canadian expertise in all matters relating to coping with snowfall before, during and after the event.

The Kidd Creek gateman, who told me he had worked at Kidd Creek mine in one capacity or another for twenty-seven years, and who was therefore expected to know whatever there was to know about the road into Timmins, phoned for a taxi with a air of great nonchalance. Half an hour later a taxi emerged from the blanket of near-blizzard to conduct me through drift upon drift of snow all the way in to Timmins airport, where we arrived at 1.15 p.m.

At the airport Air Ontario checked me in for the Toronto flight without compunction and presented a steadfast impression that all their systems were go, which of course they weren't. At 2.30 p.m. the said flight was cancelled, allegedly owing to the presence of freezing rain in Toronto. Perhaps Air Ontario's Timmins-based staff just didn't want to give in to the snow.

They then booked me out on a still scheduled evening flight to Toronto. I waited, and the snow continued to descend on the airport in wild profusion. At 4.30 p.m. it was the turn of the evening flight to be cancelled, and finally, half an hour later, the airport authorities were forced to concede defeat and close the airport for the day. Interestingly, at that very time the snowfall seemed as if it was commencing entry to a waning phase.

I was awarded a 12.45 p.m. flight to Toronto for the following day and left the airport with the help of another stranded passenger intent on battling into Timmins in a rented car. We both took rooms at the Riverside Inn, a decent motel-styled establishment on the outskirts of the town. I had chicken parmesan for dinner at the inn. Was it good? Well, no it wasn't.

ON THE FOLLOWING morning the sky was blue and cloudless. Timmins sparkled under a new half metre accumulation of snow. The snow-ploughs had done their work and roads and airport runways were all clear, clean and ready for action. That morning's local newspaper advised in a glaring front-page headline, "Timmins lashed by a snow-storm". In the sunlight it was hard to credit that for once a headline spoke the truth.

Prior to leaving Timmins I gave Selbaie a phone call to let someone know, assuming anyone was interested, about my movements and delays, and was put through to Mike, who was presumably the only one available or willing to take the call. I learned from him that further discussions aimed at amending the ore reserve estimation criteria were already taking place at Selbaie, only a scant day after my departure.

It seemed that the Peeyay was in a mood to strike again.

– 6 –

Vasty Fields of the Cockpit

Red charcoal's heart glows on the wall,
  The old rass tending chews his nail.
A tin of jerk sauce in his stall
  Next chopped-up chickens in a pail.
The grill bars hiss 'neath fiery fowl
That rightly maketh stomach growl.
              For who?
For what? For you, a Marley note,
While pickney John doth scour the pot.

Scotch bonnets cap the crisping show,
  With luscious yam and breadfruit slabs,
Corn kernels crinkling, sweet and slow,
  Some black as night, some brown as crabs.
A weed filled pipe crafts fragrant bowl
That daily saves the dreadlocked soul.
              For who?
For what? For you, an irie note,
While pickney John doth scour the pot.

With apologies to Mr William Shakespeare

In a souvenir shop in Kingston, located directly across the road from the Wyndham Hotel where I was staying, I bought a satellite photograph of the entire island of Jamaica. It was a long photograph, rolled up for convenience, the roll held tightly closed by an elastic band. The head of the shop attendant who sold me the photograph was festooned in Medusa-like dreadlocks that swung in costly abandon with all the diminished flexibility of old ropes soaked in tar a few years ago.

The shop attendant's eyes, when they were not engulfed by the dreadlock forest, were observed to be coloured puce yellow with red highlights – this, together with the fact that the movements of the said shop attendant seemed to have been directed by a slow-motion choreographer and to be taking place underwater, suggested that an association with "the weed", as Barney from the Jamaican Bauxite Institute put it, played a not insignificant role in his life. The suggestion was strengthened in my mind by an odour related to a gauzy haze that hung in suspension around the shop counter (once someone had advised me what the odour signified).

My newly acquired satellite photograph depicted a Jamaica dotted by only a few clouds, almost exclusively collected in the region of the Blue Mountains to the east of Kingston. These clouds, unlike their counterparts in the souvenir shop, were no doubt legally constituted with all due rights to be where they were.

The coast-formed outline of Jamaica on the photograph was like that of a hawk hunched on a perch, poised for a flight to Yucatan in order to escape the great grasping jaws of Hispaniola opening behind it. The Blue Mountains added bulk to the hawk's tail. Its beak was out at South Negril Point. Montego Bay squatted like a fly in the nape of the neck. The fiercely gripping talons reached into Portland Point. In related anatomical terms Kingston was then located just about where the hawk's asshole ought to have been. In all probability there were not many who might have been unwilling to deny Kingston that anatomical role.

CROSSING THE ROAD from the Wyndham Hotel to the souvenir shop might not have constituted the maximum extent of my expedition into Kingston as a pedestrian, although I didn't choose to go much further than that. Kingston seemed to me to possess an atmosphere charged with calculated menace. I couldn't escape the feeling that on the open streets of the city I was being constantly and actively sized up as a mark by rather too many of its residents.

Kingston was a magnet for the disillusioned and the disgruntled members of society's fringe from all over Jamaica, to the extent that much of the city appeared to have become a great festering ghetto chewing away at a few residual fortresses of privilege, in one of which the proud tower of the Wyndham Hotel looked gigantically down, for the time being at any rate. The steel-drum bonging orchestra on the hotel terrace at the poolside in the evening tried its best to drown out the drifting whine of police sirens occasionally punctuated by the crack of what might have been a car backfiring (and then again might not) but never quite came to succeed.

The amphitheatre of hills sweeping around the north flank of Kingston was studded with the grand houses of those who were keen, in more ways than one, to raise themselves above the squalor spreading from the foothills below right through the downtown area and on out to the port area on the sea front. These hills, and certain of the more fragrant uplands of the interior, were favoured for the construction of residences by "cumbackies", who I understood to be certain people of Caribbean origin who had made it big in the UK and had come back to lord it over their contemporaries in Jamaica. Cumbackies were a lot less popular with the downtown gun-toting and weed-smoking masses than they would have wished to be.

Since the congregation of so many of the less desirable elements of Jamaican society in various sectors of the capital offered the assurance that most other places in the country were relatively depleted in terms of the criminal underclass, these demographics were much to the benefit of everyone who lived anywhere other than in Kingston. Another significant advantage accruing to those who lived outside Kingston was that going to Kingston was a matter of choice and not of necessity.

For administrative purposes Kingston was constrained within an urban area of the same name, charmingly referred to as a "parish". It was one of fourteen such parishes into which Jamaica was subdivided, in most other cases with consistency retained by the rural sentiments implicit in the title of parish. Six parishes covered the northern half of the island and were named, from west to east, Hanover, St James, Trelawny, St Ann, St Mary and Portland. The southern half of the island featured the eight parishes, again from west to east, of Westmoreland, St Elizabeth, Manchester (demonstrating that when it came to naming you couldn't win them all), Clarendon, St Catherine, St Andrew, Kingston and St Thomas. Whether or not it was real or imagined, there was a great deal of comfort to be drawn from the litany of names, once Kingston was excised.

Jamaica was, in principle, a simple enough country to get around in. The accent was literally on getting around, as the fairly well maintained road that either followed the coast or ran within spitting distance of it all the way around the island was the key national artery. That was the good news.

Jamaica was only about seventy-five kilometres wide from north to south and a couple of hundred kilometres broad from east to west. It was not so very difficult to drive through the full circuit in a day in a good car. The less good news, however, was that Jamaica's road network was constructed at a time long ago when a more genteel forecast of future traffic volume was accepted by the planners. Even on a good day, far too many roads tended to be steadily choked by a host of vehicles held together by rust and prayers and driven by a cast of characters to whom road rage was a virtue and overtaking a mandate to be obeyed at all costs. A situation in which vehicles with the steering column set on the right-hand side were just about matched in number by those with the steering column on the other side gave a whole new meaning to the art of blind overtaking, especially where the alarm of front seat passengers was concerned.

The road circling the coast bordered the Jamaican uplands on its inner edge. The Blue Mountains, rising to an impressive 2,256 metres above sea level, filled in the circuit out to the east of Kingston. To the west of Kingston most of Jamaica was covered by the central uplands, sometimes known as the Manchester plateau, the highest point of which was around 1,000 metres above sea level.

The central uplands were underlain by a formation of soft white limestone that became eroded over a grand scale of geological time into a classically karsted land of fantastic character. It featured deeply precipitate gorges, rolling feathery hills and steep bluffs, sink holes, caverns, and the uniquely distinctive "cockpit" country of a myriad of densely forested little domed and rounded hills set one alongside the other in an endless maze that defied anyone bold enough and foolish enough to enter it, take it on and come out again in one piece.

The greater part of the cockpit country was a trackless mystery. It commenced not much more than a few minutes drive from where great cruise ships docked to inflict their passengers for a while on a Jamaican coastal infrastructure primed to greet them and deprive them of as many yankee dollars as possible before they re-boarded.

The typical "cockpit country" commenced only just back from the section of north coast road linking the tourist resorts of Montego Bay and Ocho Rios, where its front rose in an escarpment behind a rustling sea of rum-destined sugar cane that bristled through the flats of the parishes of St James, Trelawny and St Ann. Between the domed hills of the cockpit squirmed convoluted threads of open grassland, appearing to be the virgin layout for an endless golf course from which there would be no escape.

The interesting thing about the highly fertile and interconnected strips of grassland tangled around the cockpit hills was that the soil consisted of no more or no less than the humus-enriched surface of strung-out deposits and pockets of chocolate-brown bauxite that filled and fingered down into the karsted gullies and pinnacles of the limestone bedrock beneath.

Although in a very local sense the individual occurrences of cockpit bauxite deposits took on a rather small scale, the whole mighty cumulative jumble of the occurrences from one end of the cockpit country to the other turned them into a natural bauxite resource on a world scale. It was indeed a bauxite resource fit to be numbered among the truly great and to be exploited by the great (not to mention the good as the great were not necessarily good and vice versa) aluminium industry companies of the world.

Established bauxite mines nibbled away at the fringes and ate into the cockpit country in St Ann and Manchester parishes. The associated alumina refineries fumed away actively on the adjacent flats. A number of dedicated alumina and bauxite shipping ports disfigured the Jamaican coast and discoloured the limpid waters of the Caribbean.

The Jamaican subsidiaries of major international aluminium industry companies operated what, in their view, were well-integrated mining and refining activities. Their proudest boast was that they mined bauxite, healed and rehabilitated the scarred ground, restored the said ground to a kind of grassland that it never was in the first place, raised dairy cattle on the newly grown grass and marketed fresh milk from the dairy cattle to those members of the general populace who could afford to buy the beverage. In proof of the foregoing, they offered tours for visitors through the entire process, commencing with the visiting feet treading on the raw bauxite and ending up with a stroll over grassy fields in which the more careless of those feet stepped in bullshit a lot more genuine than the variety they had heard from their guides along the way. As a grand finale, a cold glass of milk was placed straight into the hands of each of the visitors in a spotless dairy parlour. All in all, it was highly commendable.

IN THE COMMISSION of their operations these companies (let's call them "the mining companies" to suit the local context) seemed to behave as if they were neo-colonial feudal lords. No matter how much the government of the day might have resented it, the power of the mining companies and the tenacity of their individual and joint grip on the throat of the Jamaican economy was so intense that any changes in their *modus operandi* occurred slowly enough to give a good impression of the situation being static.

Pressure on the mining companies from the state authorities, the latter seeking enhanced involvement in the exploitation of what after all was Jamaica's own natural bauxite resources, provoked much discussion, an endless string of meetings and negotiations, a fair amount of complaining and a lot of screaming from both sides. For all the satisfaction it appeared to get, the state might have been enrolled as a one-legged man in an ass-kicking contest. The mining companies yielded to pressure when it suited them to do so and not otherwise.

Between them, the mining companies' land concessions formed an area covering most of Jamaica's more accessible bauxite resources, and held on to a great deal of the less accessible extensions of the same within the impenetrable cockpit country, firmly sewn up under exploration rights. Third parties desirous of acquiring a position in Jamaican bauxite mining, the Company being one such, inevitably found themselves faced by a closed shop door with the cold and hostile shoulders of the mining companies firmly pushed against the back of it. Individually the mining companies may have had very little time for one another, but as a group they had no time at all for would-be newcomers.

IT WAS PARTLY to monitor and co-ordinate the activities involved in the mining companies' dominance of the exploitation of Jamaica's bauxite resources that the Jamaican Bauxite Institute, otherwise known as the JBI, was founded as a state-owned enterprise. The JBI, working from headquarters in Kingston, was graced with a politicised civil servant as its president and was directed in its operations by an executive vice-president responsible for a substantial staff of self-confessed experts in a range of technical disciplines specific to bauxite exploration, mining and refining.

The JBI was assiduous in its dealings with the statutory information and intelligence supplied to it by the mining companies. With the aid of the information provided, the JBI knew as much as and no more than the mining companies were prepared to let it know, and frankly that was not much and less than current, not least when it was related to land concessions that the mining companies were interested in holding on to.

On the other hand the JBI knew a lot more about land containing bauxite resources that the mining companies weren't interested in. Lack of interest by the mining companies as often as not implied a lack of bauxite quality. If the bauxite potential looked good, the mining companies would have had their controlling hands on it already. The mining companies had had enough long-term experience of working in Jamaica to leave nothing to chance.

The mining companies were engaged in the kind of competition with one another that stopped only a few shades shy of open warfare. It would be fair to say that not one of them knew with absolute certainty what the others were doing in the operational field, and it seemed that each placed vast amounts of effort and energy into sustaining this status quo. When it came to persuading the JBI that the JBI was in charge, and to keeping would-be new entrants into Jamaican bauxite mining out of Jamaica where they belonged, the mining companies acted in accordance with the motto of the Three Musketeers in being all for one, although they were still far too suspicious of each other's motives to be one for all.

I WAS SENT out to Jamaica as one half of a two-man Flying Circus team. The other half, a business analyst by profession, was the team leader for the Company's newly conceived Jamaican bauxite project. The project objective was to obtain an entry for the Company into the Jamaican bauxite industry, initially through the low-key acquisition of an exploration concession over some prospective ground. The team leader's agenda involved meetings, at various stages during a couple of days in Kingston, with the JBI president and his executive vice-president to examine possible options for achieving the objective. I was delegated to spend a few more days beyond that in the field, together with a couple of the JBI's technical staff, with the purpose of examining any identified bauxite opportunities at first hand.

On our first evening at the Wyndham hotel we dined on "jerk" pork at the poolside terrace restaurant, to the background accompaniment of the unique rhythms of the steel orchestra (there were too many musicians involved to call it a band) inducing melodies from shiny instruments that Uncle Joe would have recognised at a glance, even if Uncle Joe's agent from whom the basis of the instruments had been purloined was probably not looking for them any more.

Jerking was a traditional Jamaican process of marinating meat and fish prior to barbecuing the succulent delicacies. Jerk seasoning contained a range of spices and herbs supported by a key infusion of incendiary scotch bonnet peppers. The blend of jerk ingredients managed to retain the full flavour of the subject of the marinade while imbuing it with a blistering resonance of heat that took no prisoners and offered a true Jamaican gift to the world that was right up there with steel bands, calypso, reggae, victorious cricket teams and Mr Bob Marley.

On the following morning we had breakfast of a rather more bland nature, since I judged that the traditional local combination of salt fish and ackee on offer was best avoided and left to find its appropriate level of popularity with more practised tastes than mine.

We waited subsequently for a promised call from the executive vice-president of the JBI, a charming Jamaican gentleman named Parris. The call came in good time, bearing with it the less than cheering message that our schedule of meetings at the JBI would only commence tomorrow. However, Parris advised that we should not worry, as he would personally come along to the Wyndham hotel that very afternoon to conduct the team leader and myself along to the JBI for an informal visit during which we could "look around", and talk about our visit programme.

Parris was true to his word, as in fairness he usually was when he gave it, and he arrived at the Wyndham hotel at precisely 1.30 p.m. The JBI office building that he drove us to was located in its own grounds in a leafy street, where it formed part of an adjoining complex containing other offices in which large numbers of civil servants sat and whiled away the hours.

Parris was the personification of Caribbean affability at its very best. His heart was young and gay (by pre-war definition) the last time I saw him. He welcomed all due deference for his elevated position in Jamaican business and social life and was more than content to receive flattery in large measure. Everyone in Jamaica knew everyone who was anyone in Jamaica, it seemed, and there wasn't much that could be done by anyone and not recognised and more importantly got away with – not that that was any deterrent to trying. Parris bore himself with style and informality, a trim figure, tending towards baldness (but who cared?), clad in a neat short-sleeved white shirt, modestly highlighted with greyish stripes, and black trousers with ironed-in creases as sharp as his undoubted acumen.

He stood foursquare on a figurative bridge in the manner of Horatius, warding off the ire directed against the political masters at his back by both the mining companies and the public alike. There was no doubt that his sympathies lay with the politicians, to the extent that he had long since clearly thrown in his lot with them. No entreaty addressed to the JBI was so pressing that Parris was not able to put off dealing with it on the grounds that he had a meeting to attend to at one ministry or another.

Downward delegation of executive responsibility at the JBI appeared to be an unknown clause in Parris' charter. When Parris was out of the office (which was often) or out of town (a no less frequent occurrence), obtaining a decision on matters pertaining to the in-tray was not possible. No international conference, symposium, gathering, wheel-reinventing seminar, colloquium or what have you with even a hint of bauxite in its proceedings was ever too obscure in focus or too far flung in location not to be able to count on Parris' willingness to participate. It was only when Parris was in town (town being Kingston) and sitting squarely in his office at the JBI that eager petitioners could be sent on their way by being told by Parris what they wanted to hear, which was by no means the same thing as what they needed to know.

Under Parris' direction, the level of general effort expended throughout the JBI in the pursuit of a reigning atmosphere of intense industriousness eclipsed actual productivity by a long margin. Parris wanted to be the captain of a happy ship, and he was all of that. His entire crew were devoted to his command and there was not one of them who did not rejoice in believing that he or she was an essential part of a hive of intense activity. That was leadership!

With Parris on the bridge, the JBI squeezed whatever pearls of information it could out of the carefully selected dribs and drabs released to it by the mining companies and went on to pursue its chosen course while the mining companies equally pursued theirs.

In the light of such machinations, I imagined that whatever the JBI might be prepared (or able) to place on the table in terms of currently available bauxite deposits for the attention of the Company, it would feature the said deposits as being either of low quality or otherwise located somewhere deep in the heart of the cockpit country where few legitimate feet had ever trodden.

Setting lack of quality aside for the moment, I had no concerns that remote country was anything other than manageable, as, in nine cases out of ten, remoteness of location was an occupational expectation anywhere in the world in the hunt for good projects. The great imponderable facing us was what the mining companies' reaction to the Company's interest in taking a position in Jamaican bauxite would be. Whether or not the likely obstacle that this would throw up could be overcome was another pressing question. Probably not, I thought: the mining companies no doubt already held an action plan for our exclusion.

THE FIRST ORDER of the day on the arrival of the Flying Circus team leader and myself at the JBI was to take a cup of coffee with Parris. I sipped at the coffee from a bone china cup containing the brew. If I could have gained access to the roof of the JBI and once up there have looked over to the east, craning my neck as sharply as I could, it should have been possible for me to revel in a view of the Blue Mountains. Up on those azure heights the benign climate ensured that one variety numbered among the ranks of the world's best-quality coffee beans was grown. The Blue Mountain coffee plantations were not so very far away from the JBI as the crow flew. Given this proximity to such excellence I wondered how the coffee served at the JBI could be so appallingly bad. It was yet another of life's great mysteries.

With the coffee at my elbow, cooling in bone china down to a temperature at which I could swallow it in a couple of gulps and so minimise any taste-borne risk to life and limb, Parris launched into a two-part presentation, the first part of which dealt with our visit programme. The programme actually sounded not all that bad.

The next day the team leader and I were to meet with a number of dignitaries, not least among whom were to be the JBI president, the Jamaican mining commissioner and the director of the Jamaican Water Authority. Parris was well connected. Such august encounters offered me the opportunity to take a rare step across the political divide.

Thereafter I was scheduled to undertake three days of field trips, accompanied by two of Parris' key field operatives, one being the afore-mentioned Barney and the other named Basil B (in order to distinguish him from the as yet unmet director of the Jamaican Water Authority, a certain Basil F).

At the end I would need to put in a final day with Parris at the JBI offices for a round-up and debriefing on my field trip and an assessment of perceived future options. It really did seem that the JBI was taking the Company seriously in spite of what the mining companies might or might not be thinking.

The field visits were intended to obtain a conspectus of current bauxite mining and exploration activity and examine as yet unallocated (unallocated to the mining companies, that is) bauxite deposits in the cockpit country of the parishes of St Ann and Trelawny. I liked the sound of Trelawny parish, inspiring and romantic at the same time, a region to be entered with a good sword and a trusty hand, a merry heart and true.

Parris then struck into the second part of his presentation, providing us with an overview of the existing status of the Jamaican bauxite/alumina industry. It was the gospel according to the JBI. Barney, together with a JBI colleague named Lascelles, who preferred being called Las, brought in a few reference maps for us to examine. The maps were reputedly extracted from a substantial database that provided a comprehensive record of the location and status of all known bauxite occurrences in Jamaica, those pertaining to the mining companies notwithstanding.

My reading-between-the-lines sentiment was not only that the maps were perhaps a little scrappy in the way they were drawn up but also that they could be presumed to represent just about all of their kind that the reputedly substantial JBI database contained. To my chagrin, these thoughts were less than generous, although nothing I subsequently saw — or rather didn't see, as not too much more in the way of maps came forward either then or on the following day — did anything to dispel the presumption. Nevertheless those who toiled at the technical prow of the JBI believed that they were situated right up there at the cutting edge of information technology, and I could only admire the ability of those involved to have faith in so little being representative of so much. Such faith could have fed the five thousand on a barley loaf and a fish and gone on to turn water into Red Stripe beer for an encore.

We were taken to visit the facilities of the JBI's analytical laboratory and bauxite processing pilot plant adjacent to the office block. On the far side of a ditch behind the pilot plant a tight line of mango trees was swinging heavy fruit. The pilot plant set-up was not quite as well maintained as it might have been and managed to look tired out, even though little of the machinery on view seemed to have seen any recent action.

WHEN THE NEXT morning dawned it was hot and hazy. Las came along to the Wyndham hotel at 9.30 a.m. in a JBI vehicle to collect and take the team leader and me to the JBI offices to meet the elite in accordance with Parris' schedule. The principal topic of Las's conversation in the confines of his vehicle on the way to the JBI dealt with Kingston's existing water shortage. Las was concerned that the beginning of May had recently come and gone and the wet season had yet to commence. The fact that the wet season was pending was exercising many minds other than Las's, not least that of the celebrated Basil F.

It was therefore something of a happy coincidence that the first of our arranged meetings that morning was with that self-same Basil F. We met with him in a set of offices located in a block only a short walk away from the JBI building. Basil F's appearance was appropriate for a man born to command broad waters, although command from the poop deck of a pirate ship under full sail seemed more relevant than direction from an office in Kingston. He seemed totally in control of his demesne, well able to undertake the trickier aspects of allocating precious water resources to public utility service and industrial use alike. It wouldn't have mattered that the climatic conditions that Basil F was saddled with permitted him only to count on a small net surplus of rainfall over evaporation had it not been for the fact that much of the precipitation run-off disappeared down into the depths of the karst of the central limestone plateau.

A dry season of even a limited duration couldn't end soon enough for Basil F. We came upon him pondering the features of a large-scale map of Jamaica that took up the best part of one wall of his office. The map was covered with an acetate sheet on which the most recent felt marker notations had probably been made when Mr Bob Marley was still alive.

Our subsequent meeting was with the Jamaican mining commissioner. His first name was Coy, and in the time we were with him he did his best to live up to it. Coy informed us that among his key responsibilities were not only the co-ordination and issue of mining and exploration licences and concessions but also safety inspections at operating mines. He was an amiable man whose sense of reality seemed to be not exactly on the ball. The mining companies would almost certainly not have seen Coy as a threat to their Jamaican hegemony. Coy exuded the impression of a man who believed implicitly in the principle of letting sleeping dogs slumber on.

Next, we met with Carlton, the president of the JBI. Prior to the meeting Parris advised us that Carlton was not only the JBI's president but also its founder. Carlton's place in history seemed assured. Parris ushered us into Carlton's presence with all the aplomb of a serious sinner approaching the Judgement Seat.

Carlton was additionally the author of a statutory levy on bauxite production that the mining companies hated with great vigour but hadn't yet been able to do anything about. He had to be greatly admired as much for his intellect as for his success, although if Carlton wasn't aware that the mining companies must be actively seeking diverse ways and means of avoiding paying their respective levies he would have been deluding himself. The levy was designed to extract state revenue from the mining companies, since the more conventional forms of taxation had tended, it was rumoured, to be fallen victims to creative accounting.

Carlton's style of conversation seemed to me to ramble circuitously towards a destination that never quite managed to be reached. However, within the rocky soil of his labyrinthine discourse there formed the tendrils of a suggestion that the JBI might welcome the Company's involvement in a new bauxite project, especially if it implied that the Company would work with the JBI in a more co-operative and less imperious manner than that exhibited by the mining companies.

WE BOWED OURSELVES out of Carlton's illustrious presence and repaired to a boardroom at the JBI where two ultra-friendly ladies, exposing a Christian-dominated lifestyle on their much more than ample bosoms and being much less than reticent to tell us about it, had set out a lunch of such proportions that the prospect of leftovers for someone or other to bear away and take advantage of was a sure-fire guarantee. Two dishes were on offer – namely chicken stewed together with prunes and sweet corn, and a good old Jamaican classic of rice and peas in which the rice really was rice but the peas were actually large brown beans and all the more acceptable for it.

After lunch the team leader and I accompanied Las to the specific section that he habitually occupied in a large open-plan office area and where, on a broad, flat drawing table, he had set out a few (no more, no less) additional maps displaying the geographical location of bauxite deposits and related exploration results for our review. The most comprehensive of the maps had been prepared by an international firm of environmental consultants in support of a preliminary environmental impact statement dealing with the exploitation of unallocated bauxite resources in the cockpit country up in Trelawny parish.

We were only permitted to look at a preliminary draft of the accompanying EIS report, together with the mining prefeasibility study of which it was a part, in Parris's presence. Parris led us to believe that by showing us the information he was doing us a big favour. Qualifying the documents as preliminary suggested that nothing substantive had yet taken place with respect to their recommendations. If the objective of the mining prefeasibility study was to create third-party interest without giving much away, then it was a success, although it was impossible to escape the impression that a huge amount of extra work would be essential if the mining prefeasibility study were to be moved towards a status of genuine feasibility.

Las's colleagues in the open-plan office did sterling work in demonstrating a hive of bustling application to duties for most of the time we were among them, and to their credit it was only on rare occasions that the front slipped to allow any drone-like apathy to crawl through.

THAT EVENING THE team leader and I enjoyed a dinner of jerk chicken, rice and baked tomatoes at the poolside terrace restaurant of the Wyndham hotel. After dinner the team leader left for Kingston International airport to depart on an overnight flight to London during which he would have plenty of time to reflect on how little we had achieved so far. On the other hand we did meet with Parris, Basil F, Coy and Carlton, so it wasn't all bad news. Also, there was always tomorrow, I supposed.

Kingston International airport was located out at the end of a long sand spit thrusting out into the sea at the far east side of Kingston harbour. A two-lane access road ran along the crest of the spit, separated from the sea on one side and the harbour waters on the other by no more than fringing strips of brush. This lifeline to the airport appeared to me to be surprisingly vulnerable to the attentions of the kind of antisocial elements of Jamaican society with which Kingston was all too well endowed.

THE NEXT MORNING came up bright and hot. Clouds were a customary feature of the afternoon, always awaited with eagerness for their portent by Basil F. At 8.00 a.m. Barney arrived outside the Wyndham hotel in a JBI pickup truck to collect and guide me through our first allotted day in the field. He drove us out to the west through the northern suburbs of Kingston where we picked up our companion Basil B in front of his house.

Barney looked to be aged about thirty. He was tall, slim and blessed with a cynical sense of humour that stopped only just short of being truly sardonic. He had a strong jaw fitted with a broad mouth devoted to grinning. He saw things as they were, and that gave him something of a unique talent in the context of the JBI.

Basil B's age was substantially beyond being double that of Barney. He had moved well past the generally recognised age of retirement and gave every indication that the only way he was going to leave the JBI would be if he were carried out feet first. He was a small grey man, a gentleman in every sense of the word, as precise in his manner and the sobriety of his way of life as he was in his appearance.

If there was a problem in the offing with Basil B, it was that he knew too much. His knowledge of all matters related to the location, dimensions, quality and the nature of work carried out on pretty much each and every occurrence of bauxite in Jamaica was both intimate and encyclopaedic. Unfortunately, virtually all the knowledge was held in his greying head and had not yet been committed to the security of a formally written record. The implications for the JBI of Basil B suddenly dropping in his tracks (perish the thought) were profound enough to shape up as representing an intellectual property loss of disastrous proportions. Parris seemed to think that Basil B would live for ever, and of course Basil B wasn't going to do that, even with the best intentions in the world.

Barney had been assigned to Basil B as a quasi-understudy, as the blotting paper mandated to soak up the good ink of all that Basil B could impart to him while there was still time. Barney might eventually be motivated to put all of what he learned from Basil B down on paper, but I wouldn't have bet on that.

Once we had joined up with Basil B, Barney drove us all off in the direction of Spanish Town, due west from Kingston. Shortly before we reached Spanish Town he turned right on to a road leading up to the north coast by way of the Rio Cobre gorge. The gorge was a towering cleft, seemingly so deep as to invoke an impression of cold gloom and to make the thread of road, which hugged one side and then crossed a rather rustic-looking bridge to cling to the other side while the Rio Cobre foamed over its bouldered bed below, look impossibly narrow.

The Rio Cobre gorge sliced into the rim of the central limestone plateau. Up from the direction of Spanish Town the road made a gradual and wriggling descent into the gorge's inner depths. To the north of the ultimate pit of the gorge the road, long and straight, climbed slowly back up into sunshine again, where a multitude of vendors of local fruit and prolific mounds of cold jelly lined their stalls up on the verge to tempt and refresh travellers. The jelly on offer didn't wobble quite as much as did many of the more clapped out vehicles that passed them by. A portion of jelly was the liquid contents of a green coconut. Once the cap of the coconut was lopped off clean with a machete, its contents, slightly sour to the taste but always welcome, could be sucked out by the buyer through a straw inserted by the vendor.

Up at the far north end of the Rio Cobre gorge a disused railway track drifted along an excitingly high ledge and vanished into the maw of a tunnel in order to proceed nowhere much any more. The railway once served the needs of bauxite mine and refinery operations located up on the top of the plateau, at the offices of one of which, near the town of Ewarton, the JBI had arranged for us to call in for a visit.

Obtaining that visit made it clear that the JBI was still able to pull a few strings with the mining companies. Our mining company hosts for the short visit took us to see a disposal dam for the red mud tailings derived from the bauxite refining process. An innovative process of "dry stacking" was being tried out, mildly interesting but perhaps not as relevant to exploration opportunities as would have been desirable. For all that, it was pretty obvious that the mining company was making a genuinely sincere effort to tackle a serious environmental problem. Their pressing concern was not only to conserve water (and incidentally keep Basil F in his job) but also to prevent the waste water from the operations escaping from the tailings dam and finding its way into the intricate karst plumbing system. If unclean water got down into the karst there was no knowing where it might eventually emerge. The consequent avoidance of a bad press went without saying.

An earlier red mud disposal dam had accumulated and evolved over an extended period of time to present a dam wall so high that it had moved beyond looking merely frightening and had entered the realms of being quite terrifying. This mighty construction fronted a gulf-like re-entrant in the face of the limestone escarpment to the north of the Ewarton refinery at a location not inappropriately known as Mount Rosso. From the vantage point of hairpin bends along the north coast-destined road winding up the escarpment, glimpses of the flooded surface of the dam flickered far below through the trees, looking to me like the sort of mess a Canadian miner would have described as a "jackpot". It was impossible to imagine a less appropriate or more potentially damaging location to pen such a threatening monster up in.

At the crest of the escarpment, beyond which the plateau of the central uplands rolled away from us into the northern distance, we came upon an entry gate to a bauxite mining area on the right-hand side. Although we had no authorisation to enter, Barney pulled the pickup in at the gate with the intention of asking the gateman if we might take a brief look at one of the bauxite excavation areas. We had no expectation of obtaining permission, but, much to our surprise, the gateman waved us in through the gate without a single word being exchanged. The gateman must have held the JBI in a lot more esteem than did his employers. For him, the JBI logo on the pickup was identity enough to speak for itself.

We swept through the gate onto the mine property and roared off along the nearest haulage road, trying to retain the illusion that we were important people on site but, as usual, not succeeding. Be that as it may, we were able to undertake a rather comprehensive tour, fortunately encountering no heavy haulage vehicles or, for that matter, light vehicles containing irate members of mine management at any juncture.

The haul roads were excellent, smooth-surfaced and broad, swirling on precise grades like royal highways, coursing through thunderously deep cuttings and across impressively airy embankments. The monumental scale of this infrastructure seemed to be out of all proportion to the myriad minuscule occurrences of limestone-ribbed bauxite deposits interstitial to the maze of timbered cockpit country hills that we observed in passing. Justifying the construction of such roads, which were incidentally the best and broadest I had been driven on in Jamaica thus far, must have been exercising the linked minds of more than a few of the engineers who designed them.

Of the bauxite pits we drove by, some had been mined out long ago and others appeared to have been more recently attended to by machinery that must have included a bulldozer, to judge by the fresh track marks in evidence. Mining activity actually in progress, however, was just about as easy to come across as munching diners would have been on the good ship *Marie Céleste*.

We finally sighted a lonely-looking loading shovel in the company of two trucks down in a distant hollow. The shovel was attempting to load one of the trucks with bauxite lifted from a bulldozed stockpile. Satisfied that some form of mining activity was happening, and reinforced in the knowledge, we made our rapid way back to the road up from Spanish Town to continue with our journey north.

BARNEY DROVE ON as far as Moneague, then forked to the left in the direction of Golden Grove, where we were due to have a brief look at some features of the Lydford bauxite mine. The advice from the JBI was that the estimated reserves for the Lydford bauxite were as much as ninety per cent exhausted, an estimate that, to judge from the derelict appearance of the property, was not lacking in optimism I thought.

During its days as an operating mine, Lydford transported its bauxite production to a north coast shipping port near Ocho Rios via an overland conveyor belt. The concrete-boxed conveyor structure was still in place, but the belt was long gone, given up to both salvage and the soles of a multitude of flip-flop sandals no doubt. The cut-line for the conveyor track hugged the curves and declivities of the hills and, from where we stood on a sun-baked crest, dwindled off into a point of northern infinity thrusting at the ocean.

Some of the original Lydford mine buildings appeared to be in reasonable repair. These were offices and workshop facilities being utilised by the Jamaican Mining Institute (the JMI), a state enterprise allegedly responsible for the care and maintenance of the property as a whole. Interestingly enough, I learned that the director of the JMI was none other than Carlton of the JBI's good lady wife. Around the fringes of the Jamaican bauxite industry, keeping it in the family seemed to be a not unfavoured principle.

WE DEBATED CONTINUING on to Ocho Rios directly from Lydford, but since it was getting appreciably late in the day for travelling onwards much further, Barney decided to reserve a visit to Ocho Rios for one of the subsequent excursions. What we did was to return to Moneague to visit Faith's Pen, a roadside lay-by complex containing more stalls dedicated to jerk barbecuing than could be taken in at a single glance, even with the advantage of a panoramic overview. Chicken pieces sizzled and whole fish crisped, smoked and took on parallel scoring all up and down the regiment of charcoal-fired grills fronting the array of stalls.

We were spoiled for choice, deluged by the entreaties of hawkers to plump for the stalls they respectively represented. To the severe disappointment of far too many of them we elected to offer our custom to "Sharon's Breakfast Stop". A plywood placard nailed above the stall bore this grand title on its left-hand side and, separated from it by a large centralised Heineken logo, an exhortation on the right-hand side, "Share the good feeling", bid us welcome.

Stopping for breakfast was no longer appropriate, of course, given the hour of the day, and for that matter neither was Sharon, who was taking the day off. Sharon's stall was being run during her absence by her brother Everton, who was a splendidly angular gentleman swathed to the point of being almost interred in a voluminous red, white and black striped shirt, a pair of supremely baggy jeans and a big-tongued pair of unlaced Nike trainers. Half of an Uncle Joe oil drum, cut longitudinally and mounted on a waist-high stand, formed the fundament for Sharon's barbecue. Vestiges of Uncle Joe's distinctive twin colours blinked from the half drum in defiance of an internal trial by fire and an external assault by grease. The other half of the drum presumably performed a similar culinary function somewhere further down along the great line of jerk stalls gracing Faith's Pen.

Everton's capable hands delivered to me a quarter portion of jerk chicken dissembled into bite-sized portions of meat and innumerable bone splinters by virtue of a few flourishes of a Chinese cleaver. On the side lay an ear of boiled corn and what just might have been a sort of fried bread roll. On a critical review my respective judgements on the three ingredients of the fare were: not bad, too hard to bite, and greasy enough to lead me to believe that I wasn't quite that hungry. The repast was washed down and hopefully held down with coconut jelly.

Sharon's Breakfast Stop made a fitting end to the initial day of my JBI excursion programme, although it took the delight of dinner at the poolside terrace restaurant of the Wyndham Hotel to provide the effective end to the day as a whole. Always a glutton for punishment I dined on jerk chicken accompanied by red snapper fillets in a light tomato sauce. It did not take me long to conclude that Everton had not had a hand in the concoction.

AT HALF PAST five in the morning of the following day I watched a bank of thin cloud changing colour over the summits of the Blue Mountains as the sun crept up behind them. It was a good starting point for the second day of excursions. Barney came along to the Wyndham hotel an hour and a half later in the JBI pickup, we collected Basil B once more, and we retraced our route of the previous day to Spanish Town and on through the Rio Cobre gorge and Ewarton to Claremont and Golden Grove. The temptation to drop in at Faith's Pen and see if Everton had or had not yet fired up his half of an Uncle Joe oil drum was difficult to resist but was resisted nevertheless.

Our journey north was only marred to some extent by the fact that the JBI pickup's air-conditioning unit was not working. I could put up with that easily enough, but it was rather more difficult to adjust to the vehicle's radio system being in contrastingly tip-top order as evidenced by the mind-shattering volume at which it belted out musical offerings. Both the volume and the supporting musical genre were very much to Barney's taste, but unfortunately for me they weren't to mine. Such music was not the food of love, although it did play on for the couple of hours that it took me to become desperate enough to beg Barney to turn it down a little. Turning it off would have been even better, although given that we were faced by a long day of driving for Barney I could not but respect that he deserved some kind of on-the-road distraction.

We made a brief stop a short distance to the west of Lydford to obtain a general view of an area allegedly underlain by bauxite resources that were hitherto unallocated to any of the mining companies and therefore deemed by Basil B to be available for the Company's consideration. Looking at this opportunity, which was located peripherally to the east flank of a large current mining operation, convinced me more than ever that any bauxite resources that the mining companies didn't already have title to in Jamaica could be safely assumed to be of second-rate quality.

Barney drove along a narrow, nicely surfaced road that switchbacked along the north rim of the said mining property between Green Park and Brownstown. On the way we slipped gently through the villages of Bamboo and Philadelphia, odd little places composed of a mixture of hill-hugging bungalows and shacks, the former reflecting the likely presence of cumbackies, the latter displaying dilapidation and long-term resident poverty in all its imaginable stages.

We were by then in solid cockpit country, one hummocky limestone hill succeeding another in an arrangement that seemed both random and endless at the same time. The road jumped up and down from hill to hill, allowing us to peer down on bauxite-filled hollows and flats given over, for the time being, to the cultivation of vegetable and cereal staple crops. It was an impressively rural setting in which both the human and the natural environments seemed to have achieved an enduring equilibrium.

I knew of, course, from what I had been told by Parris at the JBI, that the eternal permanence of the appearance of these little villages and their supporting agricultural endeavours was somehow ephemeral. Official government policy, a masterpiece of glibness in its own special way, designated any and all Jamaican bauxite deposits for eventual development for mining usage. As a result, those who worked the soil covering the bauxite for purposes other than mining, subsistence living being the prime such purpose, were allowed to do so only under sufferance. I was given to understand that all bauxite deposits were the property of the state and that those who lived around them and grew things on them were therefore officially regarded as being no more than lessees of the ground that they worked.

The action plan following a decision on mine development, as it was explained to me, envisaged giving local residents of the area in question six months' notice to quit their homes for resettlement elsewhere without the right to compensation. If they weren't prepared to leave willingly (so I was told) they could be removed by more coercive means.

Then, once the soil had been stripped, the bauxite dug out and the mined-out areas rehabilitated and restored, the former residents would be free to move back again from wherever else they had been displaced to. The mining companies seemed to find the procedures acceptable, but I wasn't a mining company and I found the thought of it all rather disturbing. If acceptance of such a statutory policy was the price of mining in Jamaica, and if the law supposed that it was, then to borrow the words of Mr Bumble, the law was "a ass – a idiot".

My opinion, following observation of the results of rehabilitation of numerous areas of mined-out ground, was that in the instances where the rehabilitation was carried out in a manner that was not quite obviously token and which was elevated above being purely perfunctory, the only crop that was ever going to grow again successfully on the depleted land was thin grass. Grass might suit the expensive dairy farming showcases for the mining companies, but no rural resident of the cockpit country was ever going to be able to survive on it.

FROM BROWNSTOWN, WHICH was incidentally Barney's birthplace, our expedition diverted to the southwest, tracking through the operating mining concession down to a village named Gibraltar, perched around the sides and on the summits of a couple of conical cockpit hills. The quality of rehabilitation of the mined-out pits that we passed on the way did nothing to alter my growing view that mining as practised in the cockpit country was a net destructive process.

We continued on from Gibraltar to make a circuit of the western sector of St Ann parish, where I had to admit that the unallocated bauxite resources pointed out by Basil B looked to be rather prolific. This was an eerily remote region of deep declivities, yawning crevices, sheer bluffs, death-like sink holes, dark valleys and a bewildering array of hills lying under the thickest of forest cover, all combining to present a natural spectacle on a grand scale. The roads and tracks were like a cat's cradle of tangled threads defying anyone entering the cockpit country without a competent guide ever to find his way out. We were blessed on that day with the company of the ever-knowledgeable Basil B, but even he seemed uncertain from time to time as to which way Barney should be instructed to turn.

It was not difficult to imagine that the cockpit country was a place rife with terrible secrets, in which anything could happen, all of it right out of *Deliverance*. I suspected that there were people in the deep heart of the country who might never have seen a white man, unaware of how fortunate they were in that particular missed opportunity. Not far to the north of where we drove, great cruise ships were calling in at Montego Bay and Ocho Rios in quite another world.

WE EASED OUR way out of the cockpit country under Basil B's benevolent guidance and headed into the dusty town of Alexandria, located within the mining companies' concession, to obtain some lunch. Barney treated us to lunch, but there wasn't much on offer to tax his expense account. I got a small carton of orange juice and a slice of what was labelled raisin cake and which may indeed have contained one raisin, although I wouldn't swear to it. Perhaps more raisins were hidden in some of the other slices of cake on offer and I chose my piece unwisely.

From Alexandria we moved back in the direction of Claremont through an area of deep cockpit country hills hemming in narrow floors beneath which the bauxite deposits appeared to be of little consequence. Small wonder that they were also reported by Basil B to be unallocated. Once the floors broadened, hey, said Basil B, they were allocated again to one of the mining companies. This offered scant encouragement to an eager newcomer.

WE ARRIVED AT Nine Mile, a somnolent village sitting on an open hill. Nine Mile would have been entirely unmemorable had it not been the birthplace of Mr Bob Marley, the reggae king. In commemoration of Bob, a foundation complex was constructed towards the top of the Nine Mile hill on the left-hand side. Enclosed behind a mighty fence of steel, the Bob Marley Foundation not only impounded the cottage in which Bob was born but also incorporated an ornate mausoleum containing Bob's remains, a souvenir shop and various other items of solid memorabilia among which an uncomfortable-looking rounded piece of rock on which Bob allegedly laid his head was prominent.

Along the outer side of the steel fence an assortment of gentlemen of the Rastafarian persuasion stood, sat or draped themselves in various states of repose, each vying with the other as to whose universal dreadlocks were the longest, wildest or most matted. It made a frightening scene for an uninitiated visitor to chance upon. The individual states of Rasta man repose may not have been unrelated to varying degrees of intimate association with the weed. Whatever each one of them on show was so intent on smoking, it wasn't tobacco. The atmosphere in the Foundation's souvenir shop was a hymn in praise of ganja's odour to linger. The hidden vastnesses of the cockpit country were a gift to the cultivators of weed on any scale.

We stopped to tour the Foundation's facilities. A member of the dreadlock brigade, who told me his name was Donovan, offered his services as a guide. It seemed unwise to refuse him. I paid the entry fees for Barney and myself, Basil B having declined the offer, and Donovan opened a sliding gate and took us in through the steel fence.

There seemed to be not a great deal to look at really, since Donovan first of all declared that the interior of Bob's mausoleum was off limits. Bob's one-room cottage of birth was quickly disposed of, and once Barney and I had touched the rock on which Bob had laid his head the tour's highlights were exhausted. Donovan, who, notwithstanding the more ferocious aspects of his visage, was a kindly man, then broke with regulations to the extent that he allowed me to stick my head in through the mausoleum door where I was greeted by a portrait of the emperor Haile Selassie. Donovan regaled us by quoting great swatches from certain of Bob's lyrical compositions in the manner of an evangelist engaged in a reprise of the Sermon on the Mount, while all the time a portion of weed rolled in some kind of paper smouldered in his fingers like a censer.

SHORTLY AFTER OUR departure from Nine Mile, heavy rain, torrential at times, hit the cockpit country. We were forced to stop in the midst of the downpour on a right-angled corner of the road to avoid running into a scattering of large stones, all of which were strategically placed.

A group of six men, similarly selected for their intimidating size, appeared at once out of the deluge and offered to remove the stones on the understanding that we would first of all pay them to do so at a fixed price per stone. Their posture suggested that the consequences of non-payment for such services rendered might be serious for either the JBI pickup or its passengers – or, even more likely, serious for both of them.

Barney wished to debate alternative options, but I sensed that the six would-be road clearers were not gentlemen blessed with the depth of intellect to relish a rational discussion on their motives. If there was ever a moment when discretion was the better part of valour, this was it in my view. I paid up and they removed a sufficient number of the stones to make a way through for us to move on. I looked back through the wake of spray as we sped away to see them replacing the stones in preparation for their next encounter.

The rain held a firm grip on us all the way back to Kingston. It was the first significant rain of the season, more than sufficient to create currents capable of coursing and swishing much of the dry season's accumulation of garbage out of the city's drainage conduits.

The way through the Rio Cobre gorge was closed for repairs that were unlikely to be expedited by the inundation. We were required to make our return to Kingston by detouring from Bog Walk at the north end of the gorge over the hills through Sligoville and Rock Hall on streaming roads of indifferent quality.

The rain eased off in the evening, fortuitously permitting the pool-side terrace restaurant at the Wyndham Hotel to open its facilities to customers. I dined on roast chicken pieces (jerk-free) with steamed vegetables.

That night, Basil F appeared on a national television news bulletin to offer his comments regarding the onset of rain to a grateful nation and thereby associate himself with the cool runnings of precipitation. The rain was a political force worth exploiting to the full.

CRITICAL THOUGH THE rain may have been to national aspirations and Basil F's job security, it stopped altogether overnight. The third and final day of JBI excursions dawned under clear skies. The by-now familiar process of Barney picking me up from the Wyndham Hotel, collecting Basil B and taking the road out to the north through the Rio Cobre gorge reprised itself. The gorge was open again to traffic, but the road through it was restricted to one lane for a considerable stretch and the traffic moved in painfully slow surges when it moved at all. It took three hours for us to retrace our route to Brownstown, taking care on the way to avoid the Nine Mile area and its potential for impromptu road blocks. I couldn't help thinking that it might have been more efficient for excursion purposes for us to have accommodated ourselves at either Montego Bay or Ocho Rios.

From a purely incidental starting point of Brownstown that day, Barney drove west to Stewartstown in Trelawny parish and diverted along a track to allow us to examine an area of the cockpit country underlain by more allegedly unallocated bauxite deposits. Basil B described that bauxite as being of poor quality. As a result, he said, the area had come to be designated for the resettlement of subsistence farmers removed by the mining companies from land overlying better-quality bauxite.

It was an area of cupped hollows and neat conical hills crossed by scattered terraces of dwellings. The aspect was relatively tame compared with that which we saw on the previous day. The bottom flats were under intensive cultivation, sugar cane being of prime importance although with great ranks of yams on sticks hard on its heels. The yams as such grew in mounded-up ground while their vines climbed green and high along sticks or staves cut wholesale from the forested hills.

My disquiet on the morality of the human relocation issue continued to increase. There ought to be some kind of counterbalance to justify what I saw as this high-handed practice, and if there wasn't, well, I didn't want to have any part in recommendations that could lead to mining operations in Jamaica. As if to dismiss such thoughts as irrelevant, two local characters approached us at one stage, both clad in a collection of holes held together by threads of cloth, to ask Barney and Basil B when mining was going to start in the area where they lived as they were anxiously looking for jobs.

We went south through the hills of Trelawny parish to Ulster Spring and from there tracked back to the north to leave the cockpit country at Jackson Town and take a decent paved road west from Jackson Town to Clarkstown. The business of the region between these two equally dust-enveloped settlements seemed to be sugar cane and not much else. Vast cane fields rippled and rustled along the south flank of the road like a lake of green, contained only in the far-off distance by a steep limestone bluff. For the sake of Jamaican rum lovers everywhere it seemed to be of critical importance that the cane fields were growing on soil underlain by no vestige of anything that a bauxite mining company might want to rip out.

BARNEY TOOK US to the Genus Café in Clarkstown where, undaunted by the absence of a lunchtime rush, we each obtained a patty to chase away the pangs of hunger. Patties, Barney said, were a celebrated Jamaican convenience food, composed of a finely ground-up mixture of something which may have had a passing association with meat enclosed in a thin sheet of flaking pastry. In shape, size, form and intent, a patty looked like a cross between a Cornish pasty and a Chilean *empanada*. The Clarkstown version of patty pastry bore a red tinge. I didn't really want to know why, as the colour might well be related to whatever lay within, but it tasted good, and that was more than enough for me to be going on with.

After our sampling of this culinary delight Barney drove us south again, back into the cockpit country. From the precariously sagging catenaries of a power line that clung to the verge of the road as if it were terrified to part company with the latter, it was uncertain whether the rickety wooden poles were supporting the cables, or if the cables were preventing the poles from keeling over in defeat, or if the orchids hanging rooted into the cables were the essential elements in maintaining the cables' integrity.

Basil B guided us alongside monumental limestone cliffs and on through deep woods and scattered coffee plantations. He had intended to take us to have a look at a natural phenomenon known as the Windsor caves, but locating the exact access road in the rabbit warren of tracks on offer placed a sore test on even Basil B's encyclopaedic knowledge of the cockpit. The time available for Basil B's infallibility to assert itself ran out. He gave up, his head bloody but unbowed.

We beat our retreat back to the north through Duanevale, from where the road to the coast drew down adjacent to the Falmouth River, broad and sluggish under bilious green water. Rafting on the verdant surface appeared to be an option for interested tourists. The river slipped into the sea by the village of Falmouth on the north coast, at which happy spot we turned right along the coast road heading for Ocho Rios.

For much of the way to Ocho Rios I would not have wanted to

describe our view from the coast road as being particularly inspiring. Fleeting glimpses of ocean water ranging in colour from deep green to a much deeper indigo could only be caught on the occasions when the fringing mangroves thinned out sufficiently to permit it.

The bauxite mining industry, as if trapped within the compass of its depredations on the rural society of the interior cockpit country, found a form of escape in a series of north coast shipping ports that did little either individually or collectively to improve the local aesthetics. These decrepit and rusting monstrosities were established at Rio Bueno, Discovery Bay and Ocho Rios.

A saving grace for the Ocho Rios bauxite shipping port was that its deep-water wharf was ideal for tying up visiting cruise ships. In this capacity the port was in reasonably close proximity to the Dunn's River falls, a long watery cascade down a precipitous slope coated with smoothly rounded concretions of travertine, offering a popular attraction to scantily clad tourists keen on working the slippery way up from bottom to top. However, the Ocho Rios bauxite shipping facilities' chief claim to enduring fame lay in their earlier engagement to serve as the headquarters for Dr No in the celebrated James Bond film of the same name.

As IF PROVIDING a full supporting cast to the leading role of Dunn's River falls, the north coast road from Falmouth to Ocho Rios featured a widespread scatter of small hotels, guesthouses and restaurants, among which the fertile ground of jerk centres was certain to gladden the heart of any truly discerning visiting gourmet.

There was also Fern Gully to have a look at. Fern Gully was a fragment of primeval rain forest located just to the west of Ocho Rios. The road through Fern Gully, which Barney took us along on our return to the south, was a darkly shrouded cathedral-like tunnel, framed by towering trees, presided over by a cool canopy and suffused with a funereal hush – once we had managed to fight our way in through the clamouring gauntlet of souvenir stalls at the entrance.

We emerged into welcome sunlight at the top end of Fern Gully and continued on to Moneague, from where we threaded our way back to Bog Walk. Sad to say, not only did we give Sharon and Everton a miss once more but also the Rio Cobre gorge was yet again closed to us.

The closure of the gorge led Basil B to suggest to Barney that he might take the west road circuit around the gorge to return to Kingston through Barry and Kitson Town to Spanish Town. He claimed that this would make a shorter route than the hill road detour through Sligoville that we took on the previous day. Looking back on it, however, Basil B's shorter cut assertion just might not have stood up under questioning in a court of law, as the west road was nothing if not winding and seemed to run hither and thither in an extended attempt to work its way through the seemingly limitless orange groves that flanked the hillside approaches.

Kingston had enjoyed a little more rain in our absence – some precipitation for sure, but probably not enough to motivate Basil F to phone up a television station in order to take credit for it. I was glad we had not been rained on at all during our travels that day, although rain had threatened us now and then and the sound of thunder had rumbled over parts of the cockpit where it wouldn't have bothered anyone engaged in lawful pursuits. The JBI had treated me wonderfully well, but I was not unhappy that the three days of bauxite-hunting field trips were now over. I ended the day with a tasteful visit to the seafood buffet at the poolside terrace restaurant of the Wyndham Hotel.

ON THE FOLLOWING morning the only clouds in the sky were adhering to their customarily assigned location over the Blue Mountains. However, a few figurative clouds lay over Kingston, as the broadcast news of the day was dominated by reports of a rather substantial downtown shootout in the Tivoli Gardens district of the city, featuring, according to reports, the Jamaican police versus a virtual army of Kingston's alleged criminal fraternity. The early morning radio news broadcasts spoke of "hundreds of rounds fired from automatic weapons" on the streets of Kingston. Later bulletins upgraded the expended ammunition to "thousands of rounds".

The catalyst for this rapidly burgeoning incident was the shooting by the police of an alleged criminal sometime during the preceding week at Spanish Town. This, it appeared, had caused much umbrage on the part of very many of the alleged criminal's alleged partners in alleged crime.

The impression gained from a succession of news bulletins was of a situation fast spiralling out of control, threatening to engulf the whole city of Kingston in violence. I could not avoid entertaining a sense of rising alarm. The style of reporting employed by Jamaican radio news correspondents came over as being very much longer on emotion than it was on facts. Reporters spoke of children being shot down indiscriminately, the national army (by then firmly in the frame) running amok in the streets, the police losing authority (as if there was anything new in that) and military helicopters circling and shooting with random abandon into the streets of Tivoli Gardens.

From the window of my room at the Wyndham I could see one wasp-like helicopter making tight circles over an area of Kingston, assumed to be Tivoli Gardens, set out towards the sea front. The helicopter broke away twice and made a more open circuit that took it over the vicinity of the Wyndham hotel. No shots were fired that I could determine when the helicopter was in my line of sight; not that that meant much.

A radio phone-in programme, "Sinclair On Line", came on the air. Its presenter was named Motty Sinclair. Later on, Las and Barney described Motty to me as something of a national broadcasting institution. Motty began his show by predicting doom for Jamaica and declaring that the government was on the brink of bringing in "Idi Amin"-styled laws. In almost the same breath he linked this observation with the likelihood of a military coup and the possibility of civil war. It was strong stuff to listen to.

When Las came along to the Wyndham to collect me to go to the JBI at the allotted hour of 1.00 p.m., a phone-in caller was yelling at Motty that the downtrodden and disadvantaged residents of Tivoli Gardens should get out into the streets of Kingston and start burning. It didn't matter what they burned: anything would do. On that happy note I went along to meet up with Parris again – he had phoned me earlier on to arrange an afternoon meeting as he wished to spend the morning working on yet another presentation for a JBI board meeting on the following day.

I THANKED PARRIS profusely for what the JBI had done for me by providing such well-informed and friendly guides to take me so far around and through the cockpit country as well as for giving me the opportunity to see so much during those three days of field visits. I thought that I (or rather the Company) should recompense the JBI for the incidental costs of the trip. I was ever generous in shelling out Company money in return for services rendered. The Company's reputation for parsimony was always kept at bay by my hands. I felt obliged to make the offer, but Parris would have none of it. He said he had obtained a good feel for the Company's intentions and the warmth of its approach through me. As Parris hadn't yet heard my report I thought I had better not shelve my offer for the time being.

I then gave Parris an outline description of the field trips that I had undertaken. The reputedly unallocated bauxite resources that I saw were really substantial, and I thought that the best of them were located in the western sector of the cockpit country (St Ann and Trelawny parishes). I expressed my concerns about what I understood to be the official resettlement policy for local residents. Parris dismissed the issue, if such it was, as being "manageable", a word containing a wealth of meaning.

I told Parris that I would be reporting back to the Company and expected that the Company would get back in touch with him within a few months regarding the follow-up process. A few months sounded like an immensely long time for Parris to have to wait for a decision, but he didn't know the Company as well as I did.

Parris drove me back to the Wyndham Hotel, where we parted on the best of terms. The visit was over. He said he had arranged for Barney to take me on the next day to the small Tinson airport in downtown Kingston from where I was to take a light commuter aircraft flight up to the international airport at Montego Bay to connect with a scheduled flight of the Martinair airline to Amsterdam. The original intention had been for me to be driven up to Montego Bay to catch the Martinair flight, but I had by then seen enough of the road north and the commuter flight from Kingston emerged as a better option.

I then found it more than a little disconcerting, to judge from a glance at a city map, that Tinson airport might not be all that far removed from Tivoli Gardens. The battle of Tivoli Gardens was still continuing in full spate that evening, although the saga, as it was being reported, sounded to be more than a little confused. There was no end of conflicting accusations and counter-accusations emerging: shots were or were not being fired, the involvement of the military was great or small, and all of it depended entirely on the inclination of who was being interviewed at the time.

There was no question but that the situation "remained tense". A six-year-old child, it was reported, had been shot and killed. Confirmation of this tragedy would be forthcoming when or if the body, currently missing, was located. Otherwise there were at least five people claiming to have gunshot wounds. Given the circumstances this sounded like a ludicrously light casualty count.

The next day's early morning news report, on the second day of the great downtown battle of Tivoli Gardens, spoke of an "uneasy calm". Casualties, in spite of the ingrained propensity for exaggeration, remained surprisingly few. It was starting to appear to me that in the prevailing social culture, at Tivoli Gardens the game was more important than the result. The serious intent on both sides of the conflict might not have contained all that much intent, and for that matter might not have been all that serious. I was getting a little more acclimatised to the situation, my personal feelings of tension receding a little. Credible information was about as difficult to come by as were high-quality unallocated bauxite resources in the Trelawny parish cockpit country.

An ominous manifestation of the ripple effect of the battle was the overnight presence of a large number of armed troops clad in camouflage gear lurking on corners of the Wyndham hotel grounds and rustling around under cover in the ornamental bushes of the same. Possibly the soldiers were hunting an early breakfast, as they faded from sight once the sun cleared the Blue Mountains.

As if to draw my attention back to the real world a provisional hotel bill was pushed under the door of my room at an all too small hour of the morning, delivering a sharp reminder that either I would be checking out of the establishment in the normal manner or I would be driven out of it, maybe even at gunpoint, later on. The general atmosphere in and around Kingston was nothing if not fluid.

Basil F, a gentleman it seemed impossible for me to evade, cropped up yet again in a morning news bulletin on the radio to expound his views on water conservation and the contamination of aquifers by the mining companies. Although he didn't exactly refer to the mining companies as multinational predators, it seemed to me that the implication was clear enough in his remarks. On the other hand I may have been looking for any excuse to pick out such an implication to support what I was increasingly drawn to believe about the baser elements of the world of Jamaican bauxite mining practice.

Motty Sinclair led off his morning show with a full flight of personal invective directed at the role of the government as related to the ongoing battle of Tivoli Gardens. He likened the existing situation to a "rough beast, its hour come at last", quoting Mr W. B. Yeats to make his point. However, Motty's general tone sounded a good deal less hysterical than it had appeared on the previous day. His principal line of attack was vested in accusing the Jamaican government of abuses of justice spread over decades. I had to take Motty's word for that.

I ATTEMPTED TO do some work on a visit report, but my mind was not entirely on it.

My experiences on the visit drew me to define the working relationships between the mining companies and the JBI as being neither quite as cosy nor as starkly black and white (in more ways than one) as they were originally presented to me as being. The JBI was able to exercise just as much authority over the mining companies as the mining companies allowed it to. The means by which the JBI exercised its authority were akin to pushing loose cow shit up a hill with a thin stick. And then, whatever any of these great protagonists should decide with respect to the allocation and exploitation of bauxite resources, it was certain that the interests of rural Jamaica were always going to be relegated to second place.

I had the feeling that I was tending to lose my objectivity. I gave up thinking about the visit report.

As ARRANGED BY Parris, Barney came along to the Wyndham hotel at 11.30 a.m. to drive me to the Tinson downtown airport. He put me slightly at ease by telling me that Tinson was separated from Tivoli Gardens by a good three kilometres or more. I was destined not to find out how the battle was resolving itself – or, for that matter, which seemed more likely, if it ever did.

Mindful of my having politely extolled the virtues of the Genus Café patties at Clarkstown, Barney drew up outside a fast-food joint named Tastee, not far away from the Wyndham hotel, to buy two patties for me. He said that Tastee patties were the best in Jamaica. I didn't know about that, but they were a great deal better in quality than their Clarkstown cousins, even if the Clarkstown version of the patty was not at all bad in its own right.

We reached Tinson airport without incident. Not a shot was fired at us by either man or helicopter. I was almost, but not quite, disappointed. I checked in for my Montego Bay flight, and Barney departed thereafter to return from downtown Kingston to the JBI offices – from one potential war zone to another, perhaps.

Before he left me, he asked when we would see each other again. I said I genuinely didn't know and imagined it would be some time after a decision by the Company. Barney, not without perception, said that I must really know already what that decision was likely to be. I only knew at the time what I was likely to recommend. I told Barney that I was happy enough that there was plenty of unallocated bauxite kicking around the cockpit country, but I was rather less enamoured with certain of the social aspects of mining it.

THE 35-MINUTE flight to Montego Bay, in a twin-engine, square-bodied Dornier aircraft, departed on schedule. The plane climbed to a cruising altitude of 4,000 feet and stuck at that all the way along its diagonal flight path over the island. It beat going to Montego Bay by road into a cocked hat. Following take-off, the captain incorrectly predicted a turbulent flight, which was much better than if he had done it the other way around.

As the aircraft rose out of Kingston I looked for signs of smoke rising from where I thought Tivoli Gardens ought to be located. I saw nothing and felt cheated. The consolation was that I was probably looking at the wrong place. Whatever the event, I wasn't so very sorry to be leaving Kingston.

Through the window of the aircraft there were good views of virgin cockpit country, hills as round-topped as eggs stacked together in a box and as plush as velvet. The in-between areas of the cockpit affected by mining stood out in stark contrast, red-brown scars and limey-white seamed pit floors looking like bleeding gums and turning the hills they surrounded into savage green teeth. The view added weight to my impression that the successful rehabilitation of mining areas was as cosmetic in its intention as it was deceptive in the illusion it attempted to create.

We crossed the north coast at the blot of Discovery Bay under a clear sky and turned west to follow the coast along to Montego Bay. The water below was sparkling blue and green, flecked by white horses looking like flickering reefs of limestone. The aircraft made a wide bank in order to touch down at Montego Bay airport from the west. Beaches over on the right of our descent were littered with sun worshippers. I wondered if any of them were thinking about the cockpit country at the time, and decided, probably not.

My arrival was too early for me to check my luggage in with Martin-air for the flight to Amsterdam, so I left the bags in a supposedly secure place and went out of the airport terminal to have some lunch at a nearby restaurant named The Pelican. I had red pea soup to start with and jerk chicken (what else?) to follow up. Both were excellent. The peas in the red pea soup were the standard red beans by Jamaican convention, which, a rose by any other name, was still all to the good.

I returned to the airport to check in for my flight at 3.20 p.m. Having saved a Jamaican five-hundred dollar bill to pay my statutory airport tax, I was disconcerted to be unable to find it in any of my pockets. I then realised that I must have given it to a porter who assisted me, having mistaken it for a bill of rather lower denomination. Good luck to him! I didn't begrudge him that stroke of luck, and for me the mis-placed tip placed a pretty satisfying seal on the whole visit.

– 7 –

No Enemy but Time

I was a stranger in that antique land,
  Where stands a vast and blocky dump of chrome
Ore, stacked on the dock at Durres. Near it, by the strand
  Half sunken, rusted hulks lie, rimmed with foam.
There on a dockside wall stark words appear,
  Port workers shuffle by, averting eyes,
"Look on my works ye minions, and be clear
  My name is Hoxha, Lord of the earth and skies!"
Nothing of worth remains. Round the decay
  Of that benighted port of shattered hope
The Adriatic sands stretch far away.

With apologies to Mr P. B. Shelley

THE BOEING 737, property of Olympic Airways, flight number OA 115 for the benefit of those who like to know these things, had taken off from Ioannina airport in northern Greece no more than an hour earlier. I was a passenger on the flight.

At the time of our departure from Ioannina the Greek sun was a force to be reckoned with. Its light was as white and as hard as a sea-sculpted quartz pebble. Its rays cast shadows with edges sharp enough to slice a block of feta cheese with.

After an hour or so of flying north of Ioannina, both the status of the sun and the part of the world down there on the ground were very different entities from those we had left behind. Swollen rain clouds pummelled at one another for space and lay over the land like dull bruises. The aircraft made a lumpy and erratic descent through them. Its destination was Rinas airport near Tirana, the capital of the People's Republic of Albania, best abbreviated to PRA for the sake of convenience.

As the aircraft dropped through the base of the cloud ceiling a great patchwork of fields sprang into focus below, spread out like a quilt that looked hand made from odds and ends. Some of the patches were startlingly green, some bore a reddish tint, and others were white or ripely yellow. None of them appeared to lack cultivation. Rain was falling. In spite of it, little knots of people could be seen scurrying about their presumed toil in a manner suggestive of there being no tomorrow, which, I thought, there probably wasn't as far as their future aspirations were concerned.

The Olympic aircraft made an approach to Rinas airport from the south, although it was to be not so much a final approach as an intended final approach aborted into a low pass. Far too close to the ground for my liking, both engines suddenly, and rather too alarmingly, increased power. The aircraft banked sharply to the east and regained altitude. The single runway, of which Rinas airport could presumably boast if it wanted to and on which we had yet to land, fell away behind us. The runway was paved with huge hexagonally interlocking forms of concrete that added to the patchwork impression conveyed by the surrounding fields.

At the north end of the runway, evidently as oblivious to the inclement weather as were the agricultural hands, a squad of arms-porting military personnel stared up at the belly of the aircraft. What they were thinking, only they knew for sure. Probably they weren't thinking at all. Off to one side of the squad, four forlorn looking antique flying machines that had the appearance of internally cannibalised DC 6s, were parked in a row beside a khaki-coloured jet fighter that, given the context, was probably some kind of Russian MiG. There was an air of tired immobility about this assembled fleet, which, as far as I was aware, almost certainly constituted the full might of the air force of the PRA. The cockpit canopy of the MiG was raised, letting in the rain. Perhaps it couldn't be closed. The MiG wasn't going anywhere in any case.

FLIGHT SCHEDULES IN which Rinas featured as an airport of call, if not of choice, were not characterised by frequency. In fact, as I learned a little later, there were usually only four commercial flights a week into (and, much more importantly for me, out of) Rinas airport. My Olympic flight up from Ioannina comprised one whole quarter of this set of rare occurrences.

A bet that any one of these four departing flights would contain a few empty seats might be a reasonably sure thing, although first of all it would be necessary to find someone willing to cover the bet, as it seemed that no one ever really knew where they were for certain in the murky world of Albanian aviation schedules. A failure by a ticket-holding passenger to reconfirm a seat for departure was all too likely to guarantee that the seat would be lost. The process of reconfirmation of seats was complicated by the mountainous challenge of confirming or reconfirming anything or getting a decision on anything else other than the time of day in Tirana, where the only thing that anyone knew with any degree of confidence was the immediate state of the weather in the street outside.

An option served up without relish for those unfortunate enough to miss departure flights from Rinas airport – either through their own fault or because of the pervading local lack of official diligence (or a combination of the two) – was that of spending just a little more time in Tirana. The degree of comfort of the accommodation to be either enjoyed or endured by a delayed passenger would be entirely dependent on the amount of time remaining on the elaborate entry visa stamped into the passenger's passport prior to its becoming invalid.

An alternative possibility for departure was perhaps especially appealing under circumstances in which a delayed passenger's visa might be on the point of expiry and the said passenger was unwilling to share a similar fate. Put to me in all seriousness, it involved engaging a taxi – no mean feat in itself in Tirana – with a driver willing to make a run of three hundred kilometres north to the Yugoslavian border to reach a destination graced with the charming name of Hanni Hottit. At the Yugoslavian border it might, unless it might not, be possible to cross over and transfer to another taxi to proceed onwards to Titograd. From Titograd a flight connection to Belgrade was achievable. Eric Ambler could not have conceived a more thrilling itinerary, although in the PRA such things, it seemed, were pretty routine.

THE YELLOW, WAND-LIKE Rinas airport control tower slipped behind us as the Olympic flight soared up from its aborted touch-down and made a long, curving sweep towards the coastline out to the west. Conical hills punched up through the fields in the manner of rogue teeth. The hills, neatly terraced from base to summit, looked as if they had been constructed from Lego blocks. The terraces bristled with what might have been vineyards and orchards.

At the foot of one hill a large number of field workers milled around like a disturbed nest of ants, the rain perhaps having finally taken its toll on them. The aircraft was flying low enough for me to observe that their company was laced through with individuals in uniform. The PRA was devoted to placing as many of its people as it could in uniform, and lo and behold, there some of them were.

Crossing the fields and dotting up and over the hillsides, regular necklace-like trains of tiny concrete constructions tripped through in deadly diagonals, occasionally coming together in small clusters as if yet another moment of indecision had intervened in their designed layout. These were pillboxes, established as a first line of national defence. Each pillbox was a dome-capped cylinder enabled to hold a single armed defender. The pillbox entry ports faced inland and the slits through which gun barrels could be poked, when the right time came along, always looked towards the sea.

The anticipated direction of the next expected invasion was thereby absolutely defined. This being so, it was equally clear that in the event of an attack from any other direction the defenders in the pillboxes were likely to find themselves in a spot of trouble. On the other hand, I thought, it really didn't matter, as it was barely credible that anyone could actually be crazy enough to want to attack this particular country.

The chains of pillboxes maintained an ominously relentless presence on the ground. They were there and they were ready. When I got to see them in close up they did not appear to be all in especially good repair. Some were still under construction. Although my field of inspection was confined to the region between Tirana and the coast, I had no reason to believe that the pillboxes were similarly restricted in their distribution. The PRA must have contained hundreds of thousands of these tributes to the misuse of concrete. Their manufacture may have been a key industry of the state. Their ubiquity conveyed a creed of trench warfare, endorsed by state-inspired paranoia.

In their depressing way, the pillboxes offered a snapshot of the PRA in microcosm. The PRA was a nation lagging fifty years behind an average European country's level of post-war progress, and its government was introspective to a degree that verged on being mediaeval. Our incoming aircraft was a virtual time machine. The overpowering siege mentality was sustained by a totalitarian regime burdened with an ideology that reached beyond overkill in many more ways than one. The reputation held by the PRA as the world's most politically isolated country might not have been unjustified.

SWEEPING BACK TO Rinas airport from the west, our aircraft finally made a successful touch-down. The aircraft flung an obscuring wake of spray from the rain-running hard hexagons beneath its wheels. It slowed, taxied up to a walkway leading to a modestly unappealing airport terminal building, and stopped. The walkway was lined on either side with what appeared to be a thin grove of temperate-climate palm trees or tree ferns. The front door of the aircraft was opened, a ramp was wheeled up to it, and the dozen or so disembarking passengers in whose company I was included trooped out and down into a wet day in the PRA.

About half of the passengers were businessmen, and the rest were Greek citizens intent on visiting relatives resident in the southern part of the country, where a strong Greek influence was contained and isolated by the impenetrable national border.

At the bottom of the ramp my feet touched the concrete-covered soil of the PRA for the very first time. The date was the seventh of June 1983. An official dressed in a deep brown uniform approached the disembarked passengers. He wore a tight cap in a matching colour, fitted with a floppy peak. A red enamelled metal star was set in the centre front of the cap. He demanded passports from all of us. The passports were handed over with reluctance and received by him with equanimity. With the passports in his hands he led us along the walkway to the entrance to the terminal and so on into the building itself.

THE RAIN MADE a grey feature of the immediate prospect. There were no flowers growing along the verge of the walkway to provide any relief to the sombre scene. Horticulture did not shape up as featuring prominently in local civic planning. It seemed that crops that could be eaten took precedence over blooms that might merely serve to release a dangerous touch of brightness into the unremitting sameness of everyday Albanian life.

Flowers did appear at Rinas airport three days later, however, when I was about to depart for other climes, this time in a Tupolev 134 aircraft, flight number MA 431, with destination Belgrade. The Tupolev was incidentally, not to say rather unnervingly, equipped with a transparent panel set into the floor immediately adjacent to the single pair of up-front seats reserved for business-class passengers. It was not a facility that most passengers, not least myself, wished to place their feet in the vicinity of.

Prior to the first call for passengers to board that hair-raising machine of Tupolev manufacture, a thin man in a poorly fitting grey suit, who had no doubt only recently stepped out of an equally poorly fitting drab uniform, shepherded two little girls through the departure area.

The girls were dressed in long white socks, navy-blue skirts and blouses that, had the time and place not been what they were, could have been recently washed in Persil. Knotted scarves made a scarlet splash of clean colour at their necks. Their hair was black and cut straight. Their faces were proud and their eyes shining. Each little girl carried a bouquet of blood-red flowers that they were induced to hand to a departing female dignitary. At first I assumed (somewhat unkindly) that the lady in question was a party hack. It was an opinion that I was later glad to revise when it emerged that she was a delegate, albeit from an unspecified country, to an international women's conference that had just ended in Tirana. The little girls were brighter by far than both the flowers they bore and the cause they served.

ON MY INITIAL arrival at Rinas airport, the flurry of red that spread across a great rank of lettered slogans suspended over the walkway leading up to the terminal building might have been intended to make up for the absence of a floral-bounded approach. The slogans were cast in eye-catching Albanian. The letters on them were as large as they were stark. An interested student of the slogans, on the grounds that he could either read Albanian or, as in my case, be the beneficiary of a helpful interpretation, would find himself exhorted to praise and glorify an endless range of aspects of the state and party apparatus. Presumably the specific party referred to would need to be qualified as Marxist–Leninist rather than to imply any capacity for association with a celebration.

Typical of the slogan-mandated essentials were the proclamation of the Liberation (yet to come, in the opinion of many), the worship of Marxism–Leninism, preparation to fight the invader and, most importantly, hailing the First Secretary of the PRA and self-styled Father of the Nation as a god among gods.

Such slogans, some exceedingly huge and thereby enabled to be as garish as could ever be imagined, even in a country where imagination ran at low ebb, were constant swathes mounted on the majority of the state and public buildings in Tirana. Any buildings with any other function were also fair game for the capacity of slogans to assault. It was therefore interesting to realise that after I had spent two days in their implacable presence the universal slogans began to recede into the gloominess of their surroundings. The slogans were still present as an integral part of the scene, but no more so in terms of their impact on the senses than was the door of a house, or a lamp-post in a street, or an open window.

It was as if the healing process of lapsed time ensured that the red-bile onslaught of the slogans no longer existed in a form in which it could dim reason, provoke outrage or make a direct attack on the tranquillity of a careless observer. Perhaps this effect represented no more than a small victory for an individual, but in the PRA any form of personal victory, no matter how minute, was worth embracing.

THE FIRST SECRETARY of the PRA was most assuredly a gentleman on his own cognisance. He delivered the strength of his personality to a cosy clique of cohorts with stunning success, and they, in their turn, had with consummate assiduity transformed that said personality into a national cult. The First Secretary was named Enver Hoxha. His given name, Hoxha, was pronounced as if it rhymed (not inappropriately) with "dodger".

Giant portraits of Hoxha (the dodger) in ferociously contrived postures of heroic mien, were not least among the unabashed accessories, slogans included, that characterised both the exterior and the interior of any building in the PRA claiming the least functional association with the state at large. Hoxha was all too often portrayed in the midst of a crowd of apparently admiring children. In such dubious set-ups, Hoxha not only endeavoured to look like an avuncular Santa Claus but also, in a touch of stupendous irony, generally managed to pull it off.

Hoxha, I was told, came to power in 1944. As far as I could judge, he was not only the PRA's maximum leader, holding the power, dominion and threat or promise of life (and death) over all, but also the sustaining embodiment of the national persecution complex. Ludicrous though it seemed, Hoxha could probably bank on the willingness of most of the citizens of his PRA to defend the land to the very last drop of blood they possessed. That was the idea at any rate. Visitors, like me, delicately skirting the surreal and shadowy world in which Hoxha moved with the aid of smoke and mirrors, were warned not to doubt Hoxha's resolve. If you didn't like him it might be possible to get away with thinking about it, but even that was a risk.

A centimetre outside the border of the PRA, Hoxha's resolve was worth as much as a cup of warm spit, although with a shuffle of two centimetres back in the other direction it was quite another matter. His tolerance to open criticism was equipped with the staying power of a snowball in Hades, a locality Hoxha was no doubt destined to become an eventual resident of.

Hoxha, and through him the PRA he controlled, was able to claim no other national government anywhere in the whole wide world as a friend, let alone as a suspicious ally. He had courted the leadership of Russia and China on separate occasions and had distinguished himself by falling out and breaking relationships with both parties owing to what was described as irreconcilable ideological differences. That achievement took rare talent!

The government under Hoxha's dictatorship was the only truly inflamed pustule of allegedly practising Marxism–Leninism on the face of the earth. In Tirana, a statue of Stalin glared across a boulevard at a statue of Lenin, neither effigy prepared to give way to the other. A famous mural in full view in the central square of Tirana depicted no one less than Nikita Khrushchev quailing under Hoxha the dodger's imperious hand.

Hoxha may very well have been seen as some kind of god by far too many of the fellow countrymen whose lives he dominated so totally. Under his special brand of excessive despotism the practice of any flavour of religion not involving the worship of his own self was banned. The PRA was an officially Atheistic state in all respects other than those specifically adjusted to promote the worship of Hoxha.

When, a day or so after my arrival at Rinas airport, I complimented one of my Albanian associates on his ability to speak not only excellent English but also good German, my host commented, "Acquiring a new language is like acquiring a new soul." It was a stimulating rejoinder, as the concept of soul was not supposed to exist in the irreligious morass muddied up by Hoxha. I asked my associate what he meant by "soul". He said nothing more, but he smote his chest with a clenched fist. Whatever it was that he meant, Hoxha wasn't going to be privy to it.

Prior to the proscription of the practice of religion, some seventy per cent of Albanians were reported to have been followers of the Muslim faith. Their empty mosques, gates locked and chained, sat intact but unhallowed in Tirana beneath impotently pointed muezzin-deprived towers.

HOXHA WAS A real live Antichrist who was liable to appear all too frequently to his people in order to direct their every thought and action towards his glorification. His written works, of which there appeared to be a stultifyingly large number available for consultation, unfortunately more often than not within easy reach, constituted the genuine opium of the people.

The cumulative library of Hoxha's writing formed an effective bible manipulating both the thought processes of its readers and also their philosophy of life, or of whatever passed for life in Hoxha's PRA. The number of volumes of Hoxha's output might only have been rivalled in quantity by the multitude of defensive concrete pillboxes in his fields and on his hills, and even that assertion could have been open to challenge in favour of Hoxha's works.

Books of turgid prose by Hoxha, in Albanian and numerous foreign-language translations, were ever ready to be picked up at the designated outlets in Tirana that were open to access by foreign visitors. In fact, apart from a rogue tome from the pen of Marx and Engels thrown in to relieve the monotony, books authored by Hoxha were really all that were available to green the barren soil of the local literary field. The term "literary" applied to Hoxha's prolific output should be understood to be used only in its broadest sense, of course.

A perusal of two or three of those weighty tracts could do none other than lead the reader to make a rapid conclusion that any one of them was derived from a simple rearrangement of the pages of any other of them. From the awful sameness of their contents and the soporific cant that they presented it was all too easy to imagine the mind-numbing impact that a constant diet of Hoxha would impose on captive readers.

As ONE WHO was fortunately enabled to observe this dismal scene from without, I was the exception proving the rule of Lyndon Johnson's assertion that it was better to be on the inside pissing out than on the outside pissing in. I concluded, not without misgivings, that Hoxha's control of his people in thought, word and deed was unshakeable as it stood. No one subject to Hoxha would ever express displeasure more than once. One shot at dissent was all anyone was going to get, prior to an inevitable bundling away by uniformed individuals who were not unlikely to subsequently take a more telling shot at him.

At the same time, it seemed to me that Hoxha was very much living on borrowed time. The PRA would only continue to exist in a climate of fear-spangled stability for as long as the country could remain politically and geographically isolated from the rest of the world while retaining self-sufficiency in feeding its people. Only in an introspective PRA, hoodwinked by Hoxha, could the nervously bland norm of established life drag on. When the lid came off the stew, the pot would certainly boil over. Hoxha would then be lucky if he merely disappeared from sight behind a gush of steam.

ONCE WE WERE in the terminal building at Rinas airport, our group of newly arrived passengers from Greece were shepherded, by a burgeoning pack of variously uniformed officials, through a large glass door and into a small holding room. There we were individually instructed to select and occupy a position on one or another of a number of overstuffed, leather-covered chairs that were lined up around the walls. The worn leather was a lot more comfortable to sit on than it looked to be at first sight. The atmosphere in the room was cloying and close. The air was hazy with the memory of a multitudinous succession of cigarettes, each smoked down to its very last shred.

It was immediately clear that if an anti-smoking movement had ever existed in the PRA, it had been met and destroyed head-on by those opposing it applying an equivalent level of determination to that wielded by Hoxha in furthering the science of eliminating political dissent. Most probably, I suspected, a campaign against smoking had never been contemplated, since adherence to reducing cigarettes to ash by way of mouth was all too obviously a national institution, practised with impressive commitment by just about every male adult worth his salt. Wherever Albanian men gathered, for whatever reason, a dense fog of cigarette smoke soon drew thickly around them.

SEATED IN THE holding room, all the disembarked passengers were provided with customs declaration forms by yet another uniformed character, whose personal attitude, as with that of his associates, was guardedly courteous, if a little less elastic than was desirable. If this official did not altogether make us appear welcome to the base realm of Hoxha the dodger, neither did he make us feel unwelcome. We were there, we merited no favours, and that was it as far as he was concerned.

The customs declaration form incorporated a bite in its requirements. After demanding the essential details of my passport and visa, the form proceeded to insist on an itemised inventory of all the personal effects brought by me into the PRA. The list of the type of items to be declared included books, magazines, articles of clothing, cameras, electrical and electronic items, all foreign cheques and currency (coins as well as notes) and, rather ominously, drugs and explosives.

I could only marvel at the inclusion of drugs and explosives on the list and assumed that they were there in the spirit of what might have passed for a joke. After all, it was a well-known fact that cinema films starring Mr Norman Wisdom were revered as an art form in the PRA. (For which, may heaven preserve us all.)

As to whether or not anyone bringing in a personal supply of drugs and explosives would be motivated to make a formal declaration of the said commodities, and even to imagine that the authorities would think that they might, well, that would make an even better joke than asking for the declaration in the first place.

Any failure by me to list on the customs declaration form any item that came to be subsequently discovered in my possession would, the form advised, be regarded as smuggling, and would be "punished by the full weight of the law". As a threat this seemed all too dreadfully sincere and, unfortunately for any would-be transgressor, only too believable.

When I departed from the PRA through Rinas airport, I was required to prepare a comparative exit inventory of my personal effects. This second list needed to duplicate its original counterpart in every detail, with due allowance made for currency spent or personal effects left behind. Whether the latter were lost, stolen, mislaid or given away appeared to be immaterial to the cause of keeping me on my toes.

The customs authorities were, by reputation, not happy when items of substance brought into the PRA by visitors were not taken out again at the conclusion of their visit. Yet for all that, there appeared to be no special restriction on bringing in a reasonable range of personal effects. Cameras were not prohibited, although the range of legally condoned photographic opportunities was constrained enough to render a camera a much less than useful implement.

High-technology items such as calculators were additionally permitted to enter the PRA under the heading of personal effects. I had one such calculator, an HP 34C model, that I declared on my entry list. Apart from that particular one, I never came across another calculator anywhere I went – hotels, banks, a post office, and technical and administrative offices alike. For all that I knew, the calculator that I carried during my visit was the most advanced piece of electronic technology within the whole PRA at the time.

I COMPLETED MY customs declaration form with the meticulous care that I always applied to such formalities. The petty officials who dealt with the public throughout the world embodied the power to make life rather difficult for those who stood before them. Such officials needed to be co-operated with by virtue of supplicants employing a manner of obsequious correctness. The customs search of my luggage on my arrival at Rinas airport was limited at best, coming, after the heavy-handedness of the declaration form, as something of a surprise. On my eventual departure there was no customs examination at all. So much then, I thought, for the implied threat of the twin declaration forms.

Even if the airport formalities were not desperately thorough where they mattered, they were certainly slow enough. My passport was returned after an oppressive near-hour of sequestration in the ever-thickening uniformed official-generated smoke haze of the holding room. Myriad faces of PRA residents pressed hard up against the smeared exterior glass of the room's entry door and held all of us within under a scrutiny as perceptive as that provided by the portentous glare of Hoxha from a portrait hanging on a wall.

THE AIRPORT ARRIVALS process had to come to an end some time, and so it did. I collected my luggage and got out of the terminal as quickly as I could, leaving the mandatory passive-smoking imposition behind me. For this relief, much thanks. Rain was still falling. The stage seemed perfectly set for grey people to act out dull lives against an austere backcloth.

I was met outside the airport terminal building by a technician from the state Minerals Department, the organisation that I had come to consult with and which was incidentally sponsoring my presence in the PRA. The technician was dressed in a short-sleeved shirt as if to give the impression that he was immune to rain even if the shirt wasn't. He was an imposing character equipped with a shock of rain-plastered dark hair drooped over lively eyes. He spoke good English, and his sense of humour felt as warm as his welcome.

I accompanied him to a black Fiat car of Polish manufacture, parked nearby, in which we were destined to journey together to Tirana, twenty-five kilometres away. As a model, the car was basic to a fault. No hint of luxury was in evidence, although in the PRA the car itself was a luxury in its own right. Those, like us, who travelled in cars, were ranked among the privileged.

I took a place in the back seat of the Fiat. A certain individual was already sitting with a well-practised solidity in the front passenger seat. He looked to be of Albanian extraction but made a point of not identifying himself to me. Nor did my technician host make any introduction. During the entire journey to Tirana the front-seat passenger showed signs of life only when extracting cigarettes from a packet in chain-like succession, the one lit from the other with a well-practised flourish.

The PRA was a country that contained exceedingly few motorised vehicles. I understood that not one of the few was privately owned. All such were the property of a state outfit of one kind or another, designated for the use of the political hierarchy, party worthies, and their favoured cronies. The rewards for achieving the status of favoured crony were many. The great drawback to this status was that it was only as good as the quo that held it together. However good it might be today, tomorrow it could be quite another matter, and all too often it was.

The traffic on the road to Tirana was therefore light enough for the roads to look just about deserted. Perhaps as a result of this, as far as I could tell there was no obvious national code of driving practice to speak of. Traffic moved nominally on the right-hand side of the road, although since there were two sides to every road, such drivers as were out gratefully accepted the rare element of choice applied to journeying along either one of them. They were masters of a head-on seizure of the moment technique, adapting their eager hands in an instant to the circumstances of the moment.

Within the mighty expanses of the less urbanised areas of the PRA, horse-drawn transportation formed the most common means by which Hoxha's subjects got around. In the towns and cities as well, horse and cart combinations were far from being unfamiliar sights. Horses, harnessed to one kind of contrivance or another, plodded along roads and tracks at their own pace and did all they could, inadvertently or not, to impede the passage of motorised vehicles.

The cited motorised vehicles not only consisted of occasional cars bearing friends of the state hither and thither but also incorporated a scattering of erratically scheduled buses, long in length and blue in colour, articulated at the midriff with rubberised concertina-like connections that seemed as perished as hope. The buses were jammed with passengers to an extent that had declared total war on the limits of design. Their exhaust pipes smoked as avidly as any Albanian male as the buses bore down with magnificent unconcern on the crawling seethe of pedestrians, every footloose member of which regarded an open road as a territory to be invaded.

Pedestrianism seemed to provide the unique right of passage for the overwhelming majority of the people. If they wanted to go somewhere, they went on foot. If they did anything, they did it by hand. The PRA was not short of people, that was clear. The un-uniformed among them were compelled by the uniformed to desist from falling short on expenditure of effort in the daily grind, and in this manner of co-operation by coercion, the PRA trickled along.

The racing dribble of blue buses was accompanied by a set of dull green-hued trucks with a military redolence about them, each a museum piece in its own right. Most of these trucks were made in China and supplied to the PRA by the Chinese government at a time long ago before the Chinese fell out of favour with Hoxha and thereby became indisposed to bestow on him any more such gifts. The trucks were grapes of wrath, all more than able to load up with a few sticks of furniture and a chicken coop, so to bear the Joad family off to California.

As the Fiat proceeded along the road to Tirana, the rainfall intensified. The downpour threatened to overwhelm the car's noisily valiant windscreen wipers. The interior filled with cigarette smoke as the anonymous front-seat passenger, closely followed by the technician, indulged in the PRA's standard vice. It was, I thought, probably the only vice available for either of them to practise openly.

In impeccable English the technician observed for my benefit, "This is what you call 'raining cats and dogs'! The rain really came from nowhere. Before your plane arrived, the sun was shining." The inference was that I had brought rain to at least a part of the PRA.

Whether or not the rain was a welcome gift was a moot point that could easily have been opened for debate. We passed gangs of agricultural workers now dashing from fields to huddle in clumps under trees, or to press their backs against barn and cottage walls in the faint hope of receiving scant shelter from the hanging-tiled eaves above. A few of them made a practical use of the defensive pillboxes to protect themselves against the pouring natural elements of a relatively benign kind.

The heavy rain was a universal levelling agent. It soaked everyone, whether they wore uniforms or not. Women in white scarves ran alongside children whose knees were freshly earth-stained from pulling weeds. However, none of them seemed to be bothered too much. It was as if the rain had brought them a respite from their daily toil, placing a small touch of variety in lives that were otherwise much too regulated and predictable. Time for them was measured by the season of the year. The passage of days was signposted by tilling the soil, and by planting, growing and harvesting the crops.

I learned that there was no formal schedule of work for those employed on the land, although agricultural work did fit more or less into an Albanian six-day week working standard. For two of those six days the official working hours extended from seven o'clock in the morning to two o'clock in the afternoon, and then, following a three-hour interval during which a few pages out of one or other of Hoxha's books might or might not be read, from five o'clock in the afternoon to eight o'clock in the evening. For the other four of the six working days, only the 7 a.m. to 2 p.m. requirement was *de rigueur*.

It seemed rather ironic that the allotted day of rest was Sunday. God may have spoken to Hoxha, or vice versa. An opportunity for Hoxha to have shown a touch of originality and turned Tuesday into the day off was unfortunately lost, probably by an oversight.

I was told that everyone of any age who was able to work went out and worked, whether they wanted to or not, right down to the last woman and able-bodied child. It was unknown for women to remain at home to look after their children. Crèches took care of that inconvenience to sustaining the full body of the workforce.

Individuals were, in principle, assigned by the state to work at the job that they were assessed as being most qualified to do. The workers themselves had no say in the matter. Any arrangement of labour was allegedly made for the good of the state. If in practice an assignment was not to the liking of an assignee, the type of luck the assignee received could only be characterised as tough. The limited technological resources of the PRA meant that all available hands were needed to keep the wheels of state turning, to hold industry on its hesitant track and to ensure the all-important ability of the PRA to feed and continue to feed its people. In the PRA many hands made trite work.

I asked a geologist at the state Minerals Department about the options workers might have to switch from job to job, whether voluntarily or not. The geologist was suitably vague in his reply to me, as anyone accustomed to working in a walls-have-ears environment would be. Reading between the lines of what he told me, I gathered that a job once assigned, however loosely based on educational achievements, formed an assignment in perpetuity. Individuals did not decide to quit or resign on a personal initiative in order to make a change; the decision could easily be made for them, however.

Promotion was possible, although any opportunity for advancement was based not so much on what was known (or even done) as on who was known. The closer anyone was to Hoxha, the better the chances were likely to be in this context. On the other hand, closeness to Hoxha could be something of a two-edged sword. One side of the blade might well provide largesse. The backstroke offered a much less desirable prospect for filling (or perhaps providing) dead men's shoes.

Although an agricultural worker could always entertain the hope of shaking off the soil to rise to a position of desk-bound prominence, what was more likely was that someone in a position of desk-bound prominence could quickly find himself slaving on the land if he fell out with his backers or if he failed to deliver what his assigned position demanded.

The ultimate consequence of this densely stratified hierarchical system was a tendency to self-defeat. The primary concern of those who occupied the top stratum was devoted to protecting and covering their all-too vulnerable asses. The higher they rose in the hierarchy, the less decisive they chose to become. Decisions delivered the ammunition that was used to shoot down their makers by those circling like helicopter gun ships in the realms above, around and below. The final outcome was a form of persistent stagnation. Competition was invested much less in generating progress than in ensuring survival. I didn't like to think about where I had observed that before.

Since I knew how hugely imprecise the Company's analysts were in the art of forecasting commodity prices and production figures, I was totally unsurprised to learn that similar self-confessed experts who practised in Albania were just as good at the game. Forecasting trends and outputs in the PRA had by definition to present a picture of boundless optimism so as not to reflect detrimentally on those who devised the forecasts. The five-year plans that were so beloved of controlled economies were only acceptable when they indicated a gloriously banner-waving march forward in a climate of ever-increasing productivity.

Reality counted for nothing. The five-year spread was designed to be just long enough for the enthusiastic aspirations layered on the plan at its commencement to be forgotten by the time the plan concluded, since minds would by then be totally exercised on how to disperse the looming thunderclouds of the next five-year plan. I was on familiar ground.

The condition of paved road surfaces in the PRA could be typified as good to fair with respect to bearing up to the light traffic that travelled over them. Whether the surfaces would have been able to stand up to a significant increase in traffic flow was much less certain and, moreover, still to be tested.

The winding road from Rinas airport to Tirana was very smooth. It was an extended avenue, bordered by thick-boled trees that might have been oak. I didn't know what kind of trees they were and I didn't get to find out. For a metre or so above the ground the boles of the trees were neatly whitewashed, making an ironically effective natural safety marker that was additionally quite aesthetically pleasing.

Beyond the trees flicking by on either side of the road, open fields stretched out their rain-soaked bounty to view. The fields were without hedges, although neatly partitioned into distinctive components. Most of the bigger fields seemed to be given over to cereal crops, including wheat and maize, and to hay. The smaller subdivisions contained tomatoes, potatoes, beans and onions, all of which I assumed were key staples of local diet. There were tiny greenhouses standing here and there, seeming somehow to be not very relevant.

A green vine stretched itself across a trellis on the front of one cottage and thrust a few tendrils up on to a red-tiled roof. A few of the terraces on a nearby hillside were also planted with vines. The PRA's tiny wine industry was not internationally noted but must have satisfied certain internal consumption needs, most probably those of the Hoxha faithful. Grapes were used to make a distinctive, acquired-taste jam offered for spreading on the rather coarse and dry bread that either suited local tastes or fulfilled the requirements of Hobson's (if not Hoxha's) choice for consumers.

The hay fields were an intriguing prospect. There were quite a lot of them, but such a range of creatures as might have been inclined to chew so much hay were made conspicuous by their absence. There was no small number of horses to be seen, as well as a few oxen used as associate beasts of burden, but conventional farm livestock such as cattle, sheep or goats were, if they existed, somewhere other than in any fields in the PRA that I passed by.

I saw some chickens – not many, but enough to count for something or other, scratching at the wet ground with free-range nonchalance. I looked with delight on a concrete pillbox adapted to serve as a chicken coop. It represented for me the conquest of truth over illusion.

WHETHER OR NOT the beaks of the hens among the chicken population of the PRA were equipped with teeth was a mystery that remained unsolved during my visit. The hens' teeth were almost certainly no less rare in the PRA than was evidence of shops selling to the general public the balance of the hens' parts – or, for that matter, any other meat products.

Meat, as served up in the meals I partook of, arrived in small pieces of the anonymous variety that was usually deemed suitable for presentation in dishes like stews and kebabs. Dairy produce was additionally in short supply. I failed to come across milk in any guise, and all enquiries that I made regarding milk's availability was met by whomsoever I addressed them to with a look of incredulity that milk should be even thought about, let alone asked for.

I did locate a piece of hard white cheese bearing a suggestion that milk had played a part somewhere far back in its production train. The flavour of the cheese was so sharp that it required smothering with tomato slices, of which there was a genuine abundance fit for purpose, so as to render it palatable. A small portion of butter once appeared on a table that I sat at in the Hotel Tirana, probably by mistake, as that single appearance was not repeated at subsequent sittings.

Although the apparent absence of farmyard animals did not necessarily mean that the PRA could claim no association with animal husbandry, it probably implied that the local scope of animal husbandry was restricted at best. The priority land use was for crops destined to feed people, permitting reduced options for feeding ruminants. I was prepared to bet, however, that Hoxha was not short of a drop of milk to put in his tea, on the assumption that Hoxha had access to tea as well.

Equally, although liquid cats and dogs may well have dropped from the clouds over the road linking Rinas to Tirana, the presence of felines and canines in the PRA in more solid manifestations was less obvious. During my visit, I saw only one dog, a small black creature, trotting behind a horse-drawn cart.

In all the labyrinthine wanderings of pedestrians in the streets and squares of Tirana, no accompanying dogs appeared. No cats slunk along roofs or sunned themselves on windowsills. Presumably, in a survival of the fittest competition for food, domestic animals had offended the law of natural selection and so fallen foul of their human counterparts.

No flowers; no pets. Who would have been able to find the time outside work to tend the former or look after the latter in any case?

I was reminded of an old song, "Life gets tedious, don't it?" I thought of a verse in the song concerning a mouse chewing on a pantry door. The mouse had been at that task for a month or more. When the mouse got through he was sure going to be sore, because there wasn't a durn thing in there.

THE POPULATION OF the city of Tirana at the time of my visit numbered around 300,000. The city in which they all lived contained little in the way of architectural gems, consisting primarily of a mass of moderately shabby and definitely peeling yellow-plastered buildings, red-tiled roofs and narrow streets, all gathered around the social focus of a broad central square. Saw-toothed hills occupied the backdrop out to the north and west. When the rain eased and the sun broke through and warmed the ground, the hills shimmered and faded into a limitless blue haze.

The central square was fitted with a roundabout-styled circle at its midpoint, raised sufficiently, but no more than that, to make a feature of relief. The traffic might have circulated around the roundabout in an orderly manner if there had been any observable rules to direct the flow. It would also have helped if there had been more traffic to flow in the first place.

The city roofs offered a pleasingly jumbled conglomeration, within which the only real notes of discord were caused by the insertion of party slogans. Apart from the tall buildings framing much of the central square, however, the majority of buildings in Tirana seemed to be at most three storeys high and generally less than that. The quality of workmanship and finishing put into the buildings was, to my eyes, so much less than good that I thought it likely that Western European tradesmen had carried out some of the construction.

The tall, flat-faced buildings on the north and south sides of the central square contained a number of government and state departments as well as hotels, banks, museums and certain other institutions devoted to the oppression of the general public. An all-too grandiose portrait of Hoxha made the grim façade of the Bank of Tirana building look even grimmer. As it was, every building around the central square of Tirana rejoicing in a quest for grandeur was capped by either a party slogan or a Hoxha exhortation in stark red letters.

Some buildings were faced in cut marble, which managed to look just as crude and out of place as the square-pillared porticoes at ground level. The pillars were insubstantial and thereby, in a few instances, probably not a little insecure. The saving grace of supporting cement and concrete was no doubt reserved for constructing pillbox emplacements rather than glorifying the central square.

The east side of the central square was dominated by the enormous bulk of the Palace of Culture plus the rather more slender counterpoint of the Hotel Tirana. A vast mosaic decorated one wall of the Palace of Culture: it depicted the PRA's historic struggle for liberation from one forgotten foe or another, culminating in the arrival of Hoxha on the scene.

Early in the morning of my second day in the PRA, under the influence of the rising sun, there was a peaceful sense of old-world tranquillity about Tirana that was almost serene. Then the people hit the streets, and that, as they say, was that.

THE NORTH AND south sides of the central square angled gently together towards the west to give the impression of an open funnel leading into the spout of a wide, conifer-fringed boulevard that stretched a kilometre or so up towards a white tower signing the location of the University of Tirana buildings.

At the entry to the boulevard, set directly across the square from the front of the Hotel Tirana, was erected the imposing statue of a man seated on a horse. This man of bronze looked fiercely proud in close-up. His given name was Scanderberg, the Albanian national hero. Bearded, with a winged, Viking-like helmet on his head and a massive broadsword in his hand, he was gigantic in stature and his horse was majestic. The poet Byron had written about him, and in that part of the world an endorsement by Byron offered nothing less than a supreme accolade. Scanderberg could well have been a mediaeval version of Hoxha for all I knew, but it seemed that time had been kind enough to erase that suspicion from rearing its ugly head.

The rear end of Scanderberg's eternal horse pointed at the effigies of Stalin and Lenin, to the extent that these two architects of ultimate failure stood in their bronze-cast perpetuity behind the horse, on opposite sides of the boulevard. The symbolism of those two figurative horse's asses squaring up to an even bigger and more literal version of the same should not be allowed to go un-noted.

The PRA had come to be so dissected, chopped up, invaded and isolated throughout its turbulent history that the authentic origins of its heroes were as well-nigh impossible to determine as was any objective opinion on pre-Hoxha history. Everything that existed in the PRA, I was told on good authority, was in any case Albanian and was built or otherwise manufactured by Albanians. As examples of this truth there were Albanian Ottoman-type castles and mosques and Albanian Greek-like ruins to point out. The Albanians were indeed a most versatile people.

The name for the PRA in the Albanian language was Squiperia, which, according to my informants, meant "Land of eagles". Scanderberg was perhaps to be numbered among "the first of the eagles". The Albanians who gave the land its evocative name had come from the hills and no doubt swooped towards the coast to repel invaders with the tenacity of such raptors. None of the said invaders survived their respectively monumental errors of judgement in invading Albanian territory in the first place, although the eagles still made an enduring presence in the stylised two-headed black emblem on the national coat of arms. The eagles flew wherever the flag of the PRA was hoisted and a friendly breeze obliged.

Visitors to Tirana from the outside world would almost certainly be required to stay in a so-called "tourist" hotel. The tourist hotels existed for the joint benefit of the visitors and the authorities. By accommodating visitors in such specified hostelries, the authorities would know who the visitors were, where they were, where they went, what they did, and as far as was rumoured, what they said as well. Bugs inside tourist hotel rooms in the PRA were probably not all of the type that crawled on the floor or bit in the beds.

Two of the principal tourist hotels in Tirana stood on the central square. One was named the Hotel Dashti and the other was the Hotel Tirana. I was accommodated in the latter, on the east side of the square. It was a prominent fourteen-storey block of fairly recent construction. The well established Hotel Dashti, which was older and more austere, was located on the far side of the central square, set slightly, but only just, into the boulevard leading from the central square towards the University of Tirana complex.

In spite of its relative modernity, the interior of the Hotel Tirana managed to retain much of the sense and atmosphere of an age long receded. This must have been by design. The ceilings were high, the doors were substantially wide and ornately glassed, the walls were stiff with wooden panelling, the mezzanine was framed by a balcony, and in the lobby, high-backed chairs were grouped around thick pillars and secreted away in shadowy corners.

VISITORS WERE BOTH accommodated and fed in such tourist hotels. They could obtain their foreign exchange at the reception desk, preference being given to serving those who could flash the green of US dollars. All hotel accounts were payable, however, with the local currency, known as the "lek", a sufficient supply of which needed to be obtained for the purpose at an officially designated foreign exchange outlet.

Changing dollars for leks in a tourist hotel was a relatively painless process, provided that the exchange facility was actually open to receive customers, since the availability of the exchange facility to suit the convenience of tourist hotel guests was a moveable feast. A guest checking out of a tourist hotel at an appreciably early hour of the morning could find himself embarrassingly short of the vital supply of leks with no means of getting hold of them. The art of foreign exchange was to obtain, as early on as possible in the visit, only as many leks (and no more) as were needed to precisely cover local expenses.

Unused leks at the end of a visit made good souvenirs, but that was about the limit of their usefulness. I held on to some leks for souvenir purposes, only to find them precipitately removed from me by the imposition of an unexpected departure tax at Rinas airport.

The banks in Tirana were more accessible than were tourist hotels for foreign exchange transactions as they opened for business at 7 a.m. For as long as the bank doors were open (or even ajar), the transactions could be made. Thus it was that I attended the Bank of Tirana located on the central square to get hold of my personal wad of leks for the duration of my visit.

The interior of the bank was occupied by a small army of clerical staff, none of whom, as far as I could judge, was clad in a uniform of any kind. That was so far, so good. If sheer manpower was able to successfully oil the wheels of finance in the PRA, then it was obvious from the scene in the bank that that battle was as good as won.

The clerks were all evidently addicted to conducting transactions first of all by writing in longhand and then by completing all essential formalities in as piecemeal a manner as could be got away with. As many as five clerks could be counted on to do their level best to get in each other's way in carrying out a single task. The clerks in charge of handling passports operated on the principle that the last passport received went to the top of the pile for attention. It obviously did not pay to come along too early.

At the reception desk of the Hotel Tirana, postcards carrying muted-hued views of the city outside were on sale. Albanian postage stamps to place on them could also be purchased. Some of the postage stamps were large enough to cover half a postcard. I was reminded of a couple of rules that I once saw in an old copy of *Punch* – namely, (a) that the international standing of a country was in direct proportion to the simplicity of design in its postage stamps, and (b) that the garishness of colour on the same stamps was in direct proportion to the corruptness of the country's government.

Souvenirs of the PRA were also on offer, including filigree bronzes, somewhat crudely executed wooden carvings, a few furry products and certain of the written works of Hoxha. The latter were obtainable in English translation. It undoubtedly made about as much sense to read a Hoxha-authored book in English as it did in Albanian, whatever the nationality or language skills of the reader might be.

The crowning prizes among the local artefacts on offer were carpets, the alleged quality of which approached that of some perhaps better-known middle-eastern varieties. The carpets, with floral and baroque patterns predominating, were expensive, but their cost was quite commensurate with the expert workmanship that went into them.

The guest rooms in the Hotel Tirana were not individually equipped with television sets, yet for those guests with a penchant for watching television all was not lost, as there was a chamber somewhere on the premises dedicated to communal television viewing.

The main thrust of the PRA's television programming appeared to be vested in promoting the thoughts, works and actions of Hoxha, to the exclusion of virtually anything else. At the commencement of each evening television news bulletin it was alleged that an obsequious newsreader opened the proceedings with "Good evening, Mr Hoxha", since Hoxha and his cronies may very well have been the only viewers of the pretentiously fustian and wholly predictable offering.

Such television sets as did exist in the PRA were mostly installed either in the homes of the party faithful or in the homes of those otherwise favoured by the party faithful. One among the ranks of the thereby favoured, who incidentally worked for the Minerals Department, told me that it was possible for him to receive television transmissions from both Yugoslavia and Italy at his home. He professed, however, that the Yugoslavian programmes were "too shocking" to watch. He didn't say what he thought of Italian television (just as well maybe, given his opinion on the Yugoslavian offerings), although it did seem that he cut himself short of any further comment in the sudden realisation that he might have told me something that he really shouldn't have done.

DURING MY SHORT stay at the Hotel Tirana, the Austrian national football team joined me as fellow guests for one night. I saw the team members only from afar, but they were there for all that. The Austrian team played a football match against an Albanian national team. The game was shown live in glorious black and white on the PRA television service. From the window of my room on the eleventh floor of the Hotel Tirana, looking across the central square, I could easily see the crowds streaming first to and afterwards from the game along the great boulevard. The match was won by Austria by a score of two goals to one.

Following the event, no football fans ran amok, no windows were smashed, and no elderly people or other innocent bystanders were assaulted. Nor, given their absence from the scene, were any parked cars vandalised. It appeared that football fans in the PRA still had much to learn from their Western European counterparts about post-match protocols. Large crowds stood about for hours in and around the central square after the game was over, presumably engaged in post-match analysis. Irrespective of the actual result, the football match must have made an extraordinarily welcome intervention to their otherwise largely joyless lives.

The sport of football was a genuine boon to morale in the PRA. This was on the assumption that it was right and proper, and not oxymoronic, to link the word "morale" with "PRA" in the same sentence. I remembered reading somewhere that whenever any reference to the state of morale was made it implied a situation of deep trouble. If spirits were high, questions of morale never entered the equation.

Football in any case was the PRA's national sport. Albanians loved to talk about it, much in the manner in which the state of the weather might be discussed in other countries. In memory of its long gone and probably never to be repeated days of glory, the England football team retained an immense popularity in PRA sporting circles. I was asked on several occasions during my visit how Bobby Charlton was doing. Had Bobby turned up in Tirana he could have ousted Hoxha from the popular consciousness at a stroke.

Albanians were also keen to the point of inquisitiveness in enquiring after the level of sporting prowess, or lack of the same, possessed by visitors to their unfair land. From that needlepoint of curiosity they moved on to ultimately extract and dissect the visitor's entire family history. This talent for digging and delving was only matched by their own propensity to give so little of themselves away.

THE AUSTRIAN NATIONAL football team moved about in an unsurprisingly well-marshalled squad. They brought their team chef along with them. The chef was blessed with a tall chef's hat in confirmation of his office, and it was clear that he prepared all the team's meals with ingredients specially imported for the purpose. My informant at the state Minerals Department told me that such practice was common for many extended groups of professional visitors of this type. "They all think there is no food in Albania," he said.

Well, if that was what they thought, then the thought was not quite justified. There was food, and it was enough to be filling, even if it was rather plain and lacking in any real variety. On the other hand, the tourist hotels in which my experience of food was gained almost certainly showed the positive side of the PRA's culinary face, to the extent that my passing judgement on the general availability and quality of food in the PRA on that basis might not exactly be objective.

My first repast at the Hotel Tirana, which as it turned out was not atypical of other plates of fare that I came to sit behind, both in that hotel and elsewhere, commenced with an introductory salad of delicately sliced tomatoes, with a little onion and cucumber included, all making a gang of bold associates to support a slightly more meagre sliver of that powerfully flavoured hard cheese. There followed a small piece of fried fish, which might have been excised from a large tuna in a former life, accompanied by a light decking of thinly pared and over-fried pieces of potato, *rösti* in all but name. Whereupon appeared a few lightly peppered pieces of meat of an uncertain origin, their anonymity only enhanced by spicing. The meal ended with an ultra-sweet piece of heavy pastry, coffee that was so strong, black and rough with grounds that it merited the "Shaft" theme to be played in its honour, and a seemingly unlimited supply of raki, an incendiary beverage of a proof that might have been registered in a minimum of three figures.

Table hygiene standards at the Hotel Tirana could reasonably have been described as fair, but it would have stretched the imagination to characterise them as good. The standards were modest endeavours with unfinished edges. A certain amount of excavation of the salt dish and the sugar bowl was advisable prior to selecting for consumption any of the respective contents sitting under grey crusts in which cigarette ash played a minor role. A perusal of the tablecloth set out an immediate inventory of the contents of many of the plates placed on it over the previous few days.

I took the hotel lift to return to my eleventh-floor room. The lift clanked its way up at a rate of about a metre per second. A single trip within its ponderous seclusion was enough to provide an aspiring writer with the time to pen the outline of a short story.

The reception desk clerk who directed me to the lift was a young man clad in an ill-fitting suit, under which he wore a large-collared, open-necked shirt. If there was a suit anywhere in the PRA that actually fitted its wearer in places other than where it touched, I never came to see it, not that that disappointed me all that much. The mythical law of averages demanded that someone, somewhere in the country, must have been wearing a made-to-measure suit or have managed to buy, beg, borrow or steal a suit that matched his frame, but who and where was a mystery to be pondered. It seemed that Albanian suits were all tailored with illness of fit in mind.

My hotel room was comfortable enough. It incorporated a shared bathroom cubicle – shared, that is, with an unspecified number of cockroaches. Those bugs were, at least, known quantities in my room. The sheer enterprise of such insects ensured that they had lost very little time in establishing a post-construction presence in the hotel.

The mattress on my hotel-room bed sagged dramatically in the middle, although I was advised that sagging was a common feature of mattresses in the PRA, as if back-bending curves were an essential element of the manufacturer's original design. The mattresses might equally have been adapted for the use of men intent on sleeping in their suits in order to add a fashionable crumpled look to illness of fit.

I had brought a small short-wave radio with me, and I discovered on tuning it in that I could receive the BBC World Service with clarity. I felt very uneasy about listening to the BBC World Service news in my room, wondering who else might be listening in and monitoring my taste in broadcasting with the aid of the kind of bug that wasn't watching me from the bathroom floor.

THE APPROPRIATENESS OF the relative quality of suiting notwithstanding, the everyday garb of the residents of Tirana was characterised by neither fashion nor elegance. Clothes were of a type that was entirely proper but not cut from wonderful textiles. The general style of men's wear could adequately be described as "post-war reconstruction". Very little colour marred the kind of drabness that would have triggered instant recognition in any displaced person worthy of the title. Men's shirts were either white or grey, presumably depending on how often they were washed. Trousers were grey or black, depending on how often they weren't washed. Shoes were as synthetic as Hoxha's benevolence.

Ladies' wear offered a little more in the way of colour tones but certainly conceded no more than their male counterparts did in terms of dampening out-of-date impressions.

T-shirts, jeans and trainers as accessories for both boys and men were as unknown in Tirana as was the not necessarily unrelated incidence of hair worn long. It was rumoured that there was a resident barber at Rinas airport empowered to deal in a summary manner with incoming foreign males whose hair length offended Hoxha-inspired susceptibilities. As with all good rumours, there was a reasonable deal of truth in it somewhere.

I thought that many of the people that I saw around me in Tirana might not look too out of place if they were suddenly plonked down in the streets of a Western European capital. For many of them, I was sure that an extraction of that kind was an aspiration devoutly to be wished. On the other hand, when I was among them in Tirana, there was not one who did not sneak a sideways glance at me. That was all it was, really – just a fleeting peep, quite enough to let me know that I stood out in the crowd as being different. Some of the glances carried a hint of pity as well as of curiosity. After all, I was a long way from being as Albanian as a Greek ruin.

I walked through the streets of Tirana around and about the central square and all along the boulevard up towards the University, sensing no obvious restriction on my movements. There was no kind of surveillance that I was able to detect, even though I knew that there were people not so very far distant who were well aware of me and probably monitoring all my movements at the precise time that I was making them. For all of that, to all intents and purposes it seemed that I was free to come and go from the Hotel Tirana at will, as long as I remained reasonably close to the central square.

TIRANA WAS GRACED with a few small parks, in which trees were the lead players, with flowers yet to make the list of extras. An ample number of benches for sitting on were set alongside tree-shaded walks. Many of the streets were also tree-lined. There seemed to be a genuine civic pride in the maintenance of such an integrally sylvan arrangement.

Tirana impressed itself on me as representing the epitome of a safe city. I felt no sense of insecurity in its streets. The nearest would-be mugger was probably located somewhere in Greece, just across the border, if that country was to be judged correctly. Street crime did not appear to be an issue in Tirana.

Within the PRA's controlled society in which all property was allegedly communal, theft was pointless, especially theft from foreign visitors. There was no hint of a black market in foreign currency, although it would have constituted a truly atheistic miracle if there hadn't been one behind the scenes.

The formal procedures for obtaining foreign exchange were, as I had found out, so convoluted that no self-respecting Albanian citizen would ever have dared to try and crack them. Summary justice at the hands of uniformed types was always only a heartbeat away.

One evening, just as I emerged into the central square through the entrance of the Hotel Tirana, a for-once straggling member of the Austrian football team was approached on the hotel steps by a local non-resident made voluble by a likely surfeit of raki. Maybe the spirited indulgence of the latter had ignited his interest in obtaining an autograph, although the opportunity for him to make an appropriate request failed to arise, as a running phalanx of uniformed types appeared as if from the ground to envelop him as completely as though he were a stone sinking into a pool. The unfortunate would-be celebrity hunter was borne away by his captors to parts unknown, where he may well still be.

As I WALKED around, I edged out of the passing parade, now and then to call into a number of establishments that, as far as Tirana was concerned, purported to be shops. These vending outlets were typically hollow-fronted and almost uniformly sparsely stocked. Only the vegetable market appeared well provisioned, offering to its customers an abundance of fresh produce including tomatoes, fine white onions, cucumbers, beans, small new potatoes and some rather battered-looking apples. The produce was probably untouched by the cold hand of refrigeration as there was no such bunch of refrigerated digits to touch it that I could see.

As judged by the internal appearance of the said shops, display and presentation skills did not form evident priorities for shopkeepers. The few goods that were actually on display were, however, inexpensive (in lek equivalent terms) by any pricing standards that I was familiar with. There was in any case no sense of competition between establishments for sales.

The art of packaging had yet to reach Tirana's commercial circles. That shortfall may have been the principal reason why the city streets were so impeccably litter-free. It might also not yet have occurred to local residents that throwing litter in the streets was something they were going to need to learn if they were ever going to entertain a Western-styled democracy in their country.

The daubing of graffiti on the walls and cherished monuments in public places was another vital facet of Western life that Tirana was a stranger to. On the other hand, there were always the Hoxha slogans scattered around in profusion to fill the gap. The slogans made it clear enough that Tirana had a foot on the ladder of graffiti art, the unavailability of cans of spray paint in the city notwithstanding.

THE STREETS OF Tirana were always thronged with people when I set foot in them. Elderly men sipping at strong coffee clustered around small tables set up on corners, playing a board game that looked like draughts but probably wasn't. Two flimsy wooden kiosks, one vending ice cream and the other selling popcorn, were under siege while the products lasted, which wasn't for very long.

The availability of luxuries as specific as ice cream and popcorn was ephemeral. In the shops I saw nothing of these or of any related sweet-tasting items, or toys, or books, or games oriented towards children's tastes. It was becoming increasingly obvious that childhood ended early in the PRA, if it was ever a reality as a formative stage of life in the first place. A child's hands were seen as implements destined to wield a hoe, and as soon as a few hours of such toil a day could be guaranteed, childhood was over.

OF COURSE, THE purpose of my visit to the PRA was not exclusively related to sampling the rare delights of the Hotel Tirana or to wandering the streets of Tirana like a foreign spectre in search of a suitable place for manifestation. The real objective of the visit had a much more mundane basis than that.

Uncle Joe had, for some considerable time, supplied certain state-related agencies of the PRA with quantities of various of his oil-related products. The passage of such considerable time ensured that the cumulative quantity of the commodities so delivered by Uncle Joe was rather large. It was then a matter of some concern to Uncle Joe that his invoices for the same remained to a very large extent unpaid, and beyond that were as likely to be honoured as it was likely that Hoxha might join a flight of pigs over a line of pillboxes. The dilemma for Uncle Joe was whether he should cut his losses and pull the plug on the PRA or recognise that he was so far in that all he could do was hang tough, travelling hopefully.

Uncle Joe hadn't forged his hard-won reputation all around the world by ever taking the easy way out.

It was a fact that the consumers of Uncle Joe's products in the PRA, state agencies all, owed so much to Uncle Joe in terms of unpaid bills and gratitude for Uncle Joe's goodwill that they were effectively calling the shots on future deliveries. Cutting his losses was not an option. Besides, if Uncle Joe pulled out, there were Big Oil rivals eagerly waiting in the wings, ever alert for a sniff of opportunity. There would be no chance of any of them being paid either, but they would be fresher to the game and thereby able to entertain faint hopes of success.

At a given moment, the offending state agencies that were, to borrow an expression from my old friend the General Manager of the Avoca Mines, "broke as flat as piss on a plate", dreamed up a scheme affording a possible (and partial) solution to their self-created non-payment problem. In the interior of the PRA were located numerous deposits of the mineral chromite, some of them under active mining exploitation for chrome ore. The state agencies suggested to Uncle Joe that a direct swap of mined chrome ore for oil products could be arranged. Uncle Joe had no choice but to instruct the Company to take an interest in this scheme by first of all establishing to the Company's own satisfaction that sufficient reserves of chrome ore actually existed, in or out of the ground, to properly justify the swap.

I WAS SENT by the Company to the PRA in order to get hold of a reliable estimate of available chrome ore reserves, in the course of which, under the auspices of the Minerals Department in Tirana, I would need to visit a selected number of the mining operations hosting the said reserves. As a first principle I considered it essential that ore reserves should be verified objectively by sight and touch, and by subjective intuition beyond that when the facts were on the table.

I quickly discovered that the great hurdle to be surmounted was that although there was certainly an appropriate table in Tirana to place the facts on, there were precious few facts so far volunteered to place on it. Indeed, following no more than five minutes of closeted association with a group of five officials of the Minerals Department in Tirana, (inclusive of time spent effecting translations from spoken Albanian to English and vice versa), it was as clear to me as an empty glass of raki that whatever my own expectations were for the visit itinerary, such expectations were not shared by those five officials.

Over a couple of days I attended a progression of meetings at the Minerals Department building in the course of which I repeatedly asked, in my most diplomatic manner, for a decision on when and how I could visit the mines involved in the chrome reserves swap for Uncle Joe's products. The Minerals Department five answered the requests by employing well rehearsed and altogether more accomplished forms of flowery diplomatic skill that gave away absolutely zilch.

THESE MEETINGS ALL took place in a room that must have been specifically designated for the purpose. The room featured no windows. When the door was closed, all of us present for a meeting were enveloped in a comprehensive gloaming. We sat in hard-backed chairs grouped around a long, narrow table covered with what might well have been green baize. The five smooth-tongued representatives of the Minerals Department occupied one side of the table, and I, as a disillusioned representative of both the Company and Uncle Joe, sat on the other side. The face-to-face closeness of our respective parties ensured not only that flying drops of spit could easily be caught by me during the peaks of debate but also that a staged assault of cigarette smoke could claw its way across the green baize-covered table and grab me in an instant.

At the meetings the Minerals Department five could bask comfortably in a considerable superiority in numbers. To a man, they smoked incessantly. The cigarette smoke spread and intensified, mushrooming over the table, thickening the atmosphere inside the tightly contained meeting room and providing an effective partnership to the bewildering fug of discussion.

Our meetings seemed to have no given agendas, no sense of order and no clear objectives. Proceedings rarely began on time but invariably ended abruptly. Each day, at the death knell of formal working hours the meetings stopped, irrespective of the point that had been reached, whether crucial or not, whether in mid-question or mid-answer – it made no difference to the five.

Exactly who was chairing the meetings was anyone's guess. I didn't have a clue. Any one of the five could have been chairman at a given instant, or (for that matter) all of them might have been assuming the chair function at the same time. No one spoke with an air of authority. If anyone was in responsible charge it failed to show. Sub-meetings broke out up and down on the Minerals Department side of the green baize-covered table and ended only when their course was fully run.

The character of our discussions was baroque in design and Byzantine in intent. It rambled everywhere and got nowhere. It turned obliquity into an art form. A sense of direction was a lost cause. There seemed to be no Albanian language equivalent for the word "yes", although as we proceeded it seemed that there were more ways to imply "no" in Albanian than there were for Eskimos to describe snow.

A suspicion I held that our meetings were bugged might not have been entirely unjustified. None of my five opponents gave voice to any comment or observation that could conceivably be judged as a decision or even to imply a near decision. Decisions in the PRA were creatures that could come back to haunt those who made them.

At about twenty-minute intervals during the mind-numbingly tangled course of these meetings, a stocky girl entered the room bearing a large tray and fought her way through the smokescreen to the side of the green baize-covered table. Little cups of seriously sweetened black coffee, accompanied by small glasses charged to overflowing with raki, were set out on the tray. Suitably provided with both cup and glass, all present at the meeting knocked back the raki in one fell concerted gulp and sipped at the coffee, eking its savour out until the bell sounded for the routine appearance of the stocky girl with the next round.

Between servings, in order to offset the awful prospect that the subsequent delivery of raki and coffee-flavoured sugar could be delayed by a long count of a few seconds (and perish the thought that such delay might extend to as much as a few minutes), a visitor from foreign parts, like me, was traditionally required to arise and walk around the green baize-covered table to replenish the emptied raki glasses with the contents of a more than welcome bottle of amber liquid, produce of Scotland, as purchased by the said visitor at a duty free outlet in an airport other than Rinas.

By the conclusion of such meetings the haze inside the heads of most participants was likely to be as all-encompassing as the by-then virtual miasma of tobacco smoke that characterised the immediate ambience.

THROUGH ALL THE meetings I kept right on asking when I might visit the chrome mines and the five representatives of the Minerals Department kept right on displaying an endless facility in the art of skilled evasion (a skill that might also have justified being described as breathtaking had not the cigarette smoke usurped that particular qualification). No satisfactory conclusion was produced.

Emerging once from the meeting room into the glory of fresh air, I shook my head. A Minerals Department technician shrugged his shoulders and appeared to be sympathetic. There were obviously no bugs in the vicinity. "The ball is round," he said to me, "and who knows which way it will bounce?" That didn't really help much, but it was a philosophical statement that was probably not entirely devoid of a wry Cantonaesque humour. The ball bounced this way today and could well bounce another way tomorrow. What I had been given by the five was a balls-up, whereas what I really needed was a ball in the back of the net. The lamented absence of Bobby Charlton took on a new significance.

A VISIT BY me to any of the chrome mines of the interior had yet to be ruled out, but I knew it was a totally lost cause. However, as if some kind of ball really had bounced unexpectedly, a consolation prize was suddenly thrown into the smoke-ridden arena. From out of the scheming depths of the Minerals Department came the word that a large stockpile of chrome ore, allegedly ready for immediate shipping to market, was lying somewhere on the docks at Durres, the principal port of the PRA, located over on the Adriatic coast to the west of Tirana.

This chrome ore stockpile, I was advised by the five, was there for me to inspect and assess. I agreed, not without alacrity, to go across to Durres to take a look at it. The stockpile was the best thing – the only thing really – that I was ever going to get from the state Minerals Department. Anything was preferable to another soul-destroying meeting – my soul, that was, not the Minerals Department representatives' five souls, as Hoxha had decreed that they weren't supposed to have such attributes.

It was pretty clear in any case that the chrome ore stockpile was all that they had ever intended to let me see all along.

I WAS DRIVEN from Tirana to Durres along a road that ran for a while between a succession of sharp hills. Once we were out of the hills, the tree-fringed road wound on through extensive areas of cultivated crops. We passed a long line of men scything their way across a hayfield. As the hay fell to the hissing scythes, a second file of men followed behind the scything front, pitch-forking the cut hay up into deep carts drawn by horses. In another field, wheat was being manually harvested, cut by men with sickles and bound into shocks that were placed in standing groups of three or four shocks for their final period of ripening. Weeding and hoeing in vegetable plots appeared to be the sole province of women and children.

Our car overtook a convoy of three large mechanised hay-cutting units. These not only appeared to be of relatively recent manufacture but also represented a surprising local concession to mechanisation, assuming that a skeletal, rusting bulldozer out at the end of an erratically bladed swathe across one field was discounted. The bulldozer was tilted sideways, silent and apathetic. Perhaps it would never move again.

The car rounded a bend in the road crossing the crest of a low rise, and a field of ripe-headed sunflowers set the land aglow in a moment of time. Beyond the golden sward was a wide and flat-bottomed valley through which a river meandered between sharply incised banks, flanked on either side by a sea of wheat stretching as far on as the eye could see. The slotted caps of defensive pillboxes rose ominously above the heads of grain.

I had a vision of waves of invaders cresting the riverbank and falling to a withering fire from pillbox-protected defenders, dropping much as the hay had done before the advance of keen-edged scythes further back towards Tirana.

Not far from there, a group of women were seated in a circle in the shade of a broadly spreading tree on the edge of a long tomato plot. Some of the women were gazing vacantly into the distance, others sat with their heads downcast. None of them appeared to be paying any attention to the white-shirted man who stood at the centre of their ring, one of his hands gesticulating with Italianate passion, the other gripping a sheet of paper from which he may have been reading. Perhaps he was delivering that day's, or for that matter tomorrow's, order of work. He might have been a local ideologue recounting the latest serialised segment of the works of Hoxha the dodger. The women didn't seem to care one way or the other. They seemed to have retreated into places of the mind where a ranting man in a white shirt couldn't reach them.

THE CITY OF Durres had the appearance of a somewhat smaller and significantly more run down version of Tirana, insofar as it was possible for some parts of Tirana to be run down any further than they were already. The people of Durres were ill-clad, shuffling with an apparent aimlessness along mean and sombre streets. Against such a background the prevalence of the red-lettered slogans seemed to be more menacing than intrusive.

The clutter of Durres was heaped around the city's substantial dock and port facilities. A skeletal tracery of derrick cranes marked the outer rim of the docks. I counted around twenty ships in port, something like half of them tied hard up against the quays. I didn't know if oil products formed part of any of their respective cargoes, as I was not authorised to enter the inner sanctum of the dock area to have a look.

The celebrated stockpile of chrome ore covered a disproportionately large area in the outer precincts of the docks, and in its case I was able to get a guided tour of the principal features. It was instantly obvious that the stockpile was a venerable resident. It had been in that place for more years under the rule of Hoxha than it might like to admit.

The surface of the stockpile was abraded into badlands-like channels by far too many seasons of rainfall and was otherwise studded with a range of exotic items including the uppers of a couple of boots (possibly a pair), pieces of wood, chunks of rock bearing a dubiously remote geological association with chrome ore, and at least one rusting oil drum. This was a stockpile that was going to remain a feature of the outer Durres docks, I thought, until the rain could wash it all away into the oblivion that it merited.

This encounter, in effect, made both the beginning and the end of my hands-on association with the chrome ore reserves of the PRA. Still, there was always the prospect of lunch in Durres to compensate.

FOR LUNCH WE moved on from the long-suffering chrome ore stockpile to the Hotel Adriatic, a beachfront tourist hotel located a short distance to the south of the port. The Hotel Adriatic came as a startlingly contrasting revelation when set against the imposing dinginess of the nearby Durres. The hotel was an art deco-styled architectural gem set on a shining beach lapped by an azure sea. Beyond the hotel, the pure sands of the Adriatic littoral stretched away to infinity or to Greece, whichever was closer, a beach of consummate length and quality with not a soul in sight to mar its perfection.

The early afternoon was hot and sunny. A number of tourists were sunbathing on a glaringly white open terrace in front of the hotel adjacent to the beach. Other tourists were laying siege to the reception desk, seemingly intent on buying up each and every Albanian postage stamp that the patently harassed desk clerk was able or willing to lay his hands on.

The respective tourists were mostly middle-aged people, appearing to be prosperous, well fed, plump and supremely confident in manner. They were clearly not citizens of the PRA. I discovered in talking to them that they were Germans, or rather East Germans. That explained their attitude. People of their nationality were not unaccustomed in their own land to effigies of Lenin and exhortative slogans mounted in public places.

Lunch was taken in the cool interior lounge of the Hotel Adriatic, at an ornate table set under a high, chandelier-infested ceiling. I believed that if I blinked I might see Noel Coward step through the winged doors leading out to the sea front, clad in a long silk dressing gown, its hem gliding a millimetre above the floor, his cigarette trailing strings of smoke at the end of a long ivory cigarette holder held in one effete hand. The feeling of transposition of time might have seemed surreal had it not taken place in the PRA, where time was at best a reluctant traveller and where it seemed that even East Germans looked good by comparison with the local population.

THAT EVENING IN Tirana was my last in the PRA. The sunset threw up a deep crimson screen behind the hills out to the west. The hills cut crisp, black silhouettes against the glow, looking like the bent backs of an army marching to glory, their crests streaming rays of red and gold in a heavenly spectacle that might well have been orchestrated by Hoxha.

All it lacked to make it complete was a slogan in the sky, fading into the creeping dusk.

In the Elevated Interior of the Pearl of the North

My head aches, and its drumming hammer pains
My soul, as though of chicha I had drunk.
Flames rim my eyes, my inner being strains
To plead surcease for muscles deeply sunk
Beneath the twisting knives of my unhappy lot,
Lost life then fair, now swamped by savage chill,
For thou, horn handed menace of the height,
Insane full odious plot
Of air starved waste, hath visited me ill,
Fearful the light of day, dreadful the gloom of night.

Thou wast born for death, thy cards are dealt,
No player bold enough to draw thee down.
Thy touch on me these passing days was felt
In other times by Inca prince and clown.
Perhaps the self-same hand that swept a scythe
Through ranks who chose to venture far from home
In search of wealth amidst a landscape lunar,
Ascents begun with spirits blithe,
O'er rocky casements, nitrate crusted loam,
On perilous peaks, in weary lands of Puna.

With apologies to Mr John Keats

G IVE A LITTLE take a little, the more insidious side of the personality of high altitude made itself known at a topographic elevation of around 3,000 metres above sea level. At least, that was how it was as far as I was concerned. I couldn't speak for others. Below that fabled level I felt good. Above it I got to experience certain symptoms of the composite malaise known as "altitude sickness".

The higher I went above 3,000 metres, the worse those symptoms were. That was logical! I once attempted to drive up a precipitous zigzag track to reach the famed property of a sulphur mine located on the 6,000 metres high summit of an extinct volcano in northern Chile named Auchanquilcha. At the 5,500 metres mark it was something of a toss-up as to which was going to expire first, the vehicle or me. Altitude sickness beat the both of us into painfully disoriented submission and forced us into an inglorious retreat.

No mining operation anywhere else in the world operated at a higher altitude than did that one at the top of Auchanquilcha. The men who chopped out the volcanic sulphur were specially brought in from Bolivia. Chilean miners couldn't hack anything of any kind up there. Although short in stature, the Bolivians were giants among miners about whom ballads were sung.

Down below the cited 3,000 metres, altitude sickness couldn't and didn't exist. I suffered mightily in the realms above it, and then, when I descended beneath, the relief was so rapid and so utterly complete that it seemed reasonable to doubt that I had only just recently been affected by altitude sickness at all. But that was a dangerous illusion. Altitude sickness really had cut me down to size when I was up there, where, as Frank Sinatra sang in an invitation to come fly with him, the air was rarefied.

At high altitude the symptoms of altitude sickness were all too real. They left no room for uncertainty. They were unpredictable, as much in the when and how of their occurrence as in whom they occurred to. Without warning, they were as ready to strike at the apparently healthy as they were to ignore the more than obviously unfit. Altitude sickness attacked the mind as effectively as it sapped the body.

IN THE HIGH cordillera that formed the Andean spine of much of Chile in South America, the collected symptoms of altitude sickness were more evocatively referred to as "Puna". This was a deceptively attractive name for such a stealthily rapacious hunter. That Puna would seek out and find the Achilles heel of any visitor to its unforgiving demesne was a cast iron guarantee.

Puna defined the ability, on an entirely individual basis of selection, of workers to perform adequately in an environment for which the majority of them were physiologically unsuited. Unfortunately there wasn't a single one of the five conventional senses that could be used to address the substance of Puna. At high altitude Puna was there, always there, posing as great a threat to kings as to commoners.

Apart from a precious few who were born to and lived their lives out in the cordillera, such elevated terrain tended in the main to be the casual province of sportsmen, nomads and certain characters at odds with the law, or whatever passed for the law on the day in question in the general run of countries that had the Andes in common. Such audacious adventurers might all have been strong in heart, but not one of them was ever more than weak in flesh in Puna country, no matter how well they prepared themselves for it.

Accidents that befell them and incidents they inspired were usually regarded as issues of short-term interest and were soon forgotten, as much by those who reported them as by those who read about them. The name of Puna rarely entered the equation. The usual suspects for an occasional death through miscalculation or tragedy on a snowy peak here and there were generally alleged to be thin air and exposure.

I thought that accusations levelled against thin air didn't quite hit the mark. In my understanding, air floating around at high altitude contained the very same proportions of oxygen, carbon dioxide, nitrogen (and whatever else could be remembered from chemistry lessons at school) as did air sitting down at sea level. If the former was thin then the latter must have been thick, which it wasn't. Although, come to think of it, anyone who strayed into the vicinity of the fish-meal processing plant at the coastal port (and incidental gateway to the cordillera) of Iquique in Northern Chile could be forgiven for thinking that it was.

With increasing altitude, atmospheric pressure decreased sympathetically. The relative rate of atmospheric pressure diminution was quite gradual up to 3,000 metres, to the extent that physiological adjustment to the change was unremarkable. Above 3,000 metres, however, the pressure reduction picked up pace in an accelerating progression as further height was gained. Problems of exposure, chiefly involving solar radiation and diminished temperatures exacerbated by wind chill, kicked in concurrently. As a result, omens for the physical comfort of travellers ascending into especially high mountainous regions were rather unpropitious.

WHAT PUNA WISHED on me was, in a word, hypoxia. In two words it would have been oxygen deprivation. It was a shame, but reduced atmospheric pressure didn't allow my blood to absorb oxygen very efficiently. If the consequence had merely been to slow me down, I wouldn't have minded too much. That would have been all right. A valid excuse for being sluggish would have placed a kind of trump card in my hand, to be produced whenever the occasion demanded it.

Unfortunately, Puna provided me with a range of physiological and psychological effects to contest. None of them was very nice. Some of them were not very nice at all.

Once I accepted that when I was at high altitude the need to cope with Puna was unavoidable, I was faced with two options. The first of these was to get the hell out of there and never (ever) come back again under any circumstances. Although that made an unduly attractive prospect, I could only see it as taking the easy way out, running away from something that had to be tackled directly if I was going to come to terms with it.

That left the second option, which was to co-exist alongside Puna by doing whatever I could to stare it down and carry on regardless without (hopefully) compromising either my health or my safety. I didn't doubt that Puna gave me a significant disadvantage, but I thought that I could work on that and handle it, as it evolved, to the extent that I was able. I couldn't beat Puna in a straight fight, but perhaps I could live with it under a tattered flag of truce.

RICH NATURAL MINERAL resources, some of breathtakingly vast dimensions (in more senses than one), were waiting to be discovered in seismically active high-altitude regions of a number of countries, among which Chile was by no means the least. The exploitation of such resources demanded major construction activity involving large numbers of dedicated personnel, most of whom would, on the day they were hired, have been accustomed to living their lives at much lower altitudes than those occupied by the resources.

The march of industrial progress up to and across the high-altitude frontier could be reckoned as being highly positive were it not for the fact that adequately informed planning for the health, welfare and safety of those engaged to undertake employment on the top side of the frontier tended to be the exception rather than the rule.

My experience of working alongside Puna took place in the late 1980s during a period of four and a half years spent on a Company assignment to a high-altitude development project in the so-called "interior" of Iquique in northern Chile. It was an exploration and development project, named Collahuasi in accordance with the Inca name for the immediate locality.

I saw many people come and go from this and other high-altitude projects. Many went sooner rather than later. According to my observations, some general workforce statistics were as follows. In every hundred employees newly brought up to such projects, at least one-third of their number were sure to be eliminated by Puna within the first few days. These victims to Puna would then need to be expeditiously evacuated to the lower altitudes whence they originated. Between five and ten of them would exhibit serious Puna symptoms, and two or three of the same would be stretcher cases, one likely to be in a life-threatening condition.

A significant proportion of the remaining sixty or so out of the hundred recruited would succumb to Puna at some juncture during the first few weeks and would also have to leave the project. Disaffection and natural turnover, those twin delights of the working man's condition, would cause an additional depletion of the establishment. Only the strong survived, and there weren't many of them.

If equivalent drop-out figures were a feature of recruitment for a manufacturing plant or a mining operation situated down below the reach of Puna, they would be considered so unacceptable as to be even unthinkable in terms of the implications for occupational health risk. On a high-altitude project these statistics did no more than reflect the deadly reality of Puna's ability to wither flowers in gardens of hope.

I believed that the most important challenge facing the management of high-altitude projects was to take control of Puna through the intensive medical screening of recruits so as to identify and eliminate anyone at obvious risk at the earliest possible stage. Those who passed this first test would then need to have the further benefits of positive monitoring, training and instruction protocols, thereby ensuring that their health and safety in employment would be properly cared for at all times.

THE ALTITUDE OF the area of the cordillera covered by the Collahuasi project ranged from 4,700 to 4,930 metres above sea level. It might have been a matter of regret that it didn't quite make 5,000 metres, although fortunately it wasn't. The personnel camp for the project, where I was accommodated together with the rest of the work crew, was situated at 4,200 metres, on a bluff above a shallow but jagged canyon named Quebrada Blanca. This camp, which was about fifteen kilometres distant from the project area, was always referred to as "QB" for convenience.

When we went up, we went "up to QB".

I spent the greater part of the initial three years or so of my assignment to the Collahuasi project up at QB, conducting a steady physiological contest against Puna. Sometimes it seemed that most of my effort went into the contest. By the end of the third year the psychological effects of Puna became too much for me to cope with. For the final year and a half of my assignment I worked in Santiago, the capital city of Chile, set in a smog-choked basin at an altitude of a negligible 750 metres.

THE SETTING OF the Collahuasi project was a region of the cordillera known as the *altiplano* (the high plain). The *altiplano* was an undulating landscape of surreal beauty on a heroic scale. It contained salt-crusted lakes, painted around the edges with a colour wash of pink flamingos. The lakes, called salars, glittered at the feet of brick-red volcanoes capped with snow. Yellow flowers of crystalline sulphur blossomed around smoking fumaroles on the crumpled peaks of the volcanoes. Brown hills smudged with scant and brittle vegetation seemed to roll away for ever in air so pure that details fifty kilometres distant could be made out with razor clarity. The sky was a great encompassing dome that was more violet than blue. The sun shone without heat yet burned exposed skin at will.

There were very few nights up at QB when the ambient temperature didn't drop into double figures below zero degrees Celsius. The maximum daytime summer temperature was seldom much greater than six to eight degrees Celsius above zero. Constant wind whined and moaned to such an extent and with such monotony that it could be almost surmised to have originated in the Company's head office.

The wind formed a fittingly orchestral-like accompaniment to the infrequent visits to QB of members of the project management committee (the PMC), all of whom seemed to believe that facts were much lesser objectives for them to find than faults. If they couldn't discover enough to complain about during their visits they were quite adept at making up the shortfall by complaining about one another.

The Collahuasi project was a joint venture of three great company players on the international stage: two in big oil (Chilly Joe and Stripes) and one in mining (Hawkspan). They were three disparate outfits united not only by an interest in the project but also by the intensity of their mutual dislike for each other.

Since the direct venting of their spleen on one another was undesirable for the sake of appearances, they tended to use those who worked for the joint venture as proxies for the reception of their bile.

The PMC representatives of Stripes and Hawkspan were never slow to allege that my salary was too expensive a luxury for the joint venture to have to bear. They needled me to my face and sniped and snipped at me behind my back. I heard, on reliable authority, that Stripes' lead man on the PMC, a certain Diamond Jim, was keen to see me gone in order to "save a few bucks". None of this was calculated to fill me with self-esteem.

A YEAR ON the *altiplano* offered two winters to those who were there for the duration. One of the winters was perverse enough to take place during the so-called summer months. It was characterised by storms laden with hail, snow, solid cascades of cold rain and apocalyptic lightning bolts that lanced the ground like ragged pillars of fire. It came out of Bolivia and so was known as the "Bolivian winter". Cloudburst deluges were frequent Bolivian winter attributes and, depending on where they fell, caused tumultuous mudslides that wiped out access roads and tracks in an instant.

The second winter came along at the more conventional and similarly named season of the year and was replete with an exceedingly bitter spell of dry, searing cold punctuated by occasional snowstorms. The accompanying wind-chill factor was a living creature. Although no great volume of snow ever fell during this real winter, such snow as did descend was so dispersed and so held aloft in the grip of the ubiquitous wind that on some days it seemed to be snowing steadily when it really wasn't.

PRIOR TO ARRIVING for the first time up at QB, the sum total of my high-altitude experience was limited to a mere three days spent at a mining property in southern Peru at an altitude of no more than 3,600 metres.

Other than a pronounced breathlessness accompanied by a rapid heartbeat when making any steep ascents during that short sojourn, I encountered no additional distress in Peru that might reasonably have alerted me to the existence of Scoroche, the Peruvian equivalent of Puna. But, as Shakespeare queried, what's in a name?

Although a good deal of the three days in Peru was spent in the field, moving around was achieved largely by pickup truck, and that meant that my being put to the test by walking was fairly well constrained.

The experience taught me that high altitude could cause physical discomfort, but, as with so many others conditioned to living in the near vicinity of sea level, I wasn't equipped with any personal yardstick by which I could judge the relevance of the Puna (or Scoroche) symptoms that I felt in Peru. That understanding came later, and three days in southern Peru did not prepare me to walk in the valley of the shadow in any way.

THE TERMS OF MY assignment to the Collahuasi project required me to be based at QB. My regular schedule of work, or "tour of duty", involved my spending fourteen full working days up there, followed by seven consecutive days, inclusive of travelling time, at home in Santiago. The latter period of seven days was officially designated as "descanso" (or rest days).

Tours of duty commenced on a Wednesday morning and concluded on the Wednesday morning two weeks later.

AT THE OUTSET, I travelled for a tour of duty between Santiago and QB in two stages. The first stage comprised a scheduled flight on the Chilean domestic airline Ladeco, north from Santiago to either of the coastal airports of Antofagasta or Iquique. The second and subsequent stage was undertaken in a light aircraft out of Antofagasta or by road transport in the case of Iquique.

The flight from Antofagasta to a two kilometres long dirt-floored landing strip (elevation 4,400 metres) near the QB camp was uphill all the way and was endured for approximately one hour and twenty minutes. The reciprocal return journey was one of continuous descent and lasted in the order of an hour. The drive from Iquique to QB by road took anywhere between four and five hours to accomplish, depending on the condition of the road (or track would be more appropriate) up through the face of the cordillera.

When I got my Chilean assignment, the health hazards of working at high altitude only entered my thinking in a peripheral manner. Without any real personal experience to draw on, considerations of that sort more or less dropped out by default.

The Company was probably equally naive insofar as appreciating the symptoms of Puna went. The Company, and for that matter Uncle Joe's Chilean-based outfit (Chilly Joe) as well, appeared to have no recognisable policy within its huge library of meticulously detailed standard procedure manuals that could offer instructions on how to deal with high-altitude occupational health risks.

My pre-project assignment medical examination was carried out at the well-appointed facilities of Uncle Joe's excellent medical establishment in The Hague. Let it be said, for those who don't know, that the country graced by the presence of that fair city was not noted for its mountainous terrain. An otherwise comprehensive medical examination didn't ponder on my suitability for high-altitude employment. No formal guidelines relating to occupational health at the working environment of the Collahuasi project were offered to me, perhaps because there weren't any to be offered.

ON THE OTHER hand I was, prior to going out to Chile, given a wide-ranging and advantageous briefing on lower-altitude aspects of the culture and society of my country of destination at, of all places, the Centre for International Briefing at Farnborough Castle in the UK. Uncle Joe really knew his stuff in arranging things like that for Company assignees.

I additionally participated in detailed technical discussions related to my intended role on the Collahuasi project and went through an intensive three-week course in the basics of the Spanish language. At the end of the first week of the Spanish course I was amazed by how much I had learned. By the end of the third and final week I was shocked by how little I seemed to know.

From all of this instruction, study and debate, it seemed that I was reasonably well prepared for many eventualities, even if health and safety at high altitude were not numbered among them.

With the benefit of hindsight, this perceived lack of attention to high-altitude occupational health risks was quite understandable in the context of its time. Since the effects of longer-term exposure to the working environment of high-altitude projects were relatively untested in practice and seldom reported on in detail, there were no documented case histories available to assist newcomers to the game in making plans. Consequently, lessons had to be learned the hard way.

Up at QB I was part of a work crew about twenty strong. I was an incidental supervisor as well, a clear case of the blind staggering in to lead the fully sighted. The rest of the crew was well established and fully adapted to working at high altitude. They knew what they were doing and I didn't, so I decided to take my lead from them until I did.

The conditions of employment which the crew enjoyed (or perhaps more or less accepted as their due would be a better way of putting it), in terms of provision of food, camp accommodation, salaries, travel allowances, fringe benefits and so on and so forth, were rather better than was normal in Chile under such circumstances. As a result there was virtually no crew turnover on the Collahuasi project and they all did their work with diligence.

Darwinian-styled natural selection formed the crew. Through a rigorous process of pruning out dead wood (from which, come to think of it, the Company's head office could have picked up a few tips), there survived within the crew's cadre only those who were physically and psychologically fit to resist the twin evils of both Puna and isolation. The hard-earned ability of the crew to live and work at high altitude was the benchmark against which my performance was measured and judged, not always fairly.

The fit-for-purpose air transport links from Santiago up to QB, considered in conjunction with the location of the Collahuasi project's administrative offices in one of the more pleasant uptown *barrios* of Santiago, provided the essential assurance to all members of the PMC that their presence at the project site, when it became inescapable, only needed to be a casual affair of blessedly short duration. The sybaritic delights of the Santiago Sheraton hotel were much to be preferred to the rigours of an overnight stay at QB.

The devotees of good wine and creature comforts who made up the PMC hailed from the overseas points of origin (namely Europe, the USA and Canada) of the three outfits that constituted the conflictive joint-venture partnership. They met in Chile on a quarterly basis, and that for me was at least three times a year too often. For their visits to QB the PMC normally took the early morning Ladeco flight from Santiago to Antofagasta and continued on by light aircraft. They then made the return journey from QB to Santiago on the same afternoon. Up at QB they conversed exclusively in English, chiefly among themselves as the crew didn't really count for much, and found as much fault as they could with as much of what they saw as was feasible in the limited time available.

On one well-remembered occasion, the sudden onset of a blizzard driven by a high wind trapped the PMC at QB, forcing them to stay for a night. During the storm the temperature dropped so low that diesel fuel jellified. In consequence, the power generator, responsible among other things for the camp's heating system, gave up on doing its job. If the PMC learned anything from the experience it was that they should be a lot more careful about watching the weather to avoid getting caught again in future.

The great unifying factor for the PMC at the project site was a desire to turn presence into absence. The whip it in, whip it out and wipe it aspect of PMC visits to QB offered a sure-fire guarantee that the members of the PMC had little or no appreciation of Puna beyond the meagre extent of what it could do to those exposed to it for only a few hours.

BEADY, THE RESIDENT Collahuasi project manager, who was based in Santiago and for whom I had the misfortune to work during the first year and a half of my assignment, exhibited no Puna symptoms of any kind on his own infrequent visits to QB.

He was, to my notion, a master of bombast equipped with few if any commendable elements of personal grace. His was the face that lunched a thousand chips. Beady was the type of person for whom "Hey, asshole!" wouldn't even have to come along as a wake up call. As a citizen of the USA abroad, Beady, who like myself was a Company assignee, demonstrated more than an appreciable number of the kind of public mannerisms that had so tarnished the image of his country in the eyes of the world at large.

Since Beady was a stranger to Puna symptoms on his own cognisance, he was disinclined to believe in the reported symptoms of anyone who, like me, did suffer from Puna. The single Puna-related incapacitation that I saw affecting Beady, demanding his urgent evacuation from QB to low altitude, was the pain of toothache greatly magnified by low atmospheric pressure. That was additionally an occasion on which I felt some sympathy for him, a sympathy that disappeared down along the cordillera track with him as he and his swollen jaw departed from QB in a cloud of dust.

BEADY WAS A HEAVY smoker, one of many with a grand smoking habit who visited QB during the period of my assignment. I noted a positive correlation between smokers and the mitigation of Puna symptoms. A smoker was much less likely to be affected by Puna than a visitor who didn't smoke. In virtually all Puna cases involving smokers that I came into contact with, the extent of the symptoms that they experienced was rarely much worse than mild.

This correlation allowed a reasonably confident prediction of the likely effect of Puna on anyone prior to his or her ascent to QB to be made. However, linking non-smokers to severity of Puna symptoms didn't always work. Puna for the latter was a uniquely individual and unpredictable affliction.

It seemed probable that smokers' lungs were conditioned by the smoking habit to extract and transfer oxygen into the blood more efficiently than "clean" lungs could. I had never smoked, but even though I couldn't test the theory out in practice, I could believe the evidence of my eyes, and that was good enough for me.

AND SO IT came to pass that when I got to QB, it was to find the Collahuasi project fitted out with a good crew altogether adapted to living and working at high altitude; a somewhat antagonistic PMC who seemed determined (come what may) to put in only minimal time (a mixed blessing) in the same location; and the heavily uncharismatic Beady, the project manager who felt, to all intents and purposes, as comfortable at high altitude as at low.

It was therefore not at all surprising for me to eventually conclude that Puna was regarded by just about everyone other than me as being little more than a footnote to a minor inconvenience.

The conventional wisdom for the project was that whoever got Puna, or alternatively whomsoever Puna got, should shut up about it and put up with it until Puna's full course had run out. There was an effectively institutionalised unwritten rule decreeing that, although an admission to being adversely affected by Puna ought not to bring down derision on the head of the afflicted, to be actually defeated by Puna was inconsistent with the macho element of Chilean culture. In this climate of opinion, those who succumbed to Puna weren't worth much.

My FIRST VISIT to QB and the Collahuasi project area lasted for eight long days. The visit, four months prior to my full-time assignment, was undertaken for technical familiarisation and, more importantly for me, to meet and get to know the members of the crew. The question of my suitability for such a working environment didn't arise.

For the visit, the journey from Santiago up to QB was broken by an overnight stop in a project-owned guesthouse located on the outskirts of an impressively unlovely mining town named Calama. The altitude of the guesthouse was approximately 2,700 metres above sea level. It was difficult for me to decide, in the event of a competition for grimness of appearance, whether the guesthouse or the town of Calama would have been awarded first place.

A night at the Calama guesthouse was intended, in all good faith, to kick off and ease travellers into the process of acclimatisation to increasing altitude. It offered rest at a half-way house prior to a following day's ascent to QB in a light aircraft coming up from Antofagasta for joining at Calama.

I developed a dull throbbing headache during the Calama stopover, although I was unsure at the time if the headache should be blamed on the stealthy feelers of impending Puna or on the utterly morose ambience of the guesthouse.

Others who took the same route may have had similar reservations, as it was not long after my one (and fortunately only) night of residence that the half-way house practice was abandoned, the given reasons for which welcome action were invested in reducing costs and travel time. Thereafter the thread of travel went directly up to QB from Santiago. The only breaks in the journey then involved transfer between aircraft at Antofagasta or between aircraft and road vehicle in Iquique.

A not insignificant benefit of flying directly to QB from Antofagasta rather than from Calama was that the flight time withstood in bumping and bucking through the boiling turbulence of the cauldron of air above the *altiplano* was minimised.

FOLLOWING THE NIGHT in the Calama guesthouse I set a comparatively grateful foot on the compacted dirt of the QB airstrip in mid-morning of the next day. This gratitude was solely related to the safe conclusion of a hair-raising, rodeo bronco-like flight up from Calama that I concurrently assured myself I was never going to repeat. Aeronautical terms such as pitch, roll and plunge had, on that flight, come to acquire whole new meanings for me.

On disembarking from the light aircraft I got an immediate feeling of disorientation. It washed over me in an instant. A sign adjacent to where the aircraft was drawn up informed me that the altitude at that very point was 4,400 metres. I had a dizzy surge of light-headedness. I seemed to lack the ability to hold my balance. I staggered when I walked. My mind drifted sideways like smoke in a light breeze. Thoughts that I was unable to focus on raced through my head.

I was forced into taking short and rapid breaths. My heartbeat speeded up to a rate that might have been double that of normal. For a moment it appeared that I was being systematically deprived of air. The moment passed, but only for a while.

The insistent, if generally manageable, headache that commenced in the Calama guesthouse intensified sufficiently to start causing me genuine distress. The pain of the headache was sharp. It shifted from the front to the back, from the top to the sides of my head. After installing its personality for a couple of hours the headache appeared to stabilise, at which point the pain eased to a level at which it was probably no worse than exceedingly unpleasant.

I boarded a pickup truck for transport from the airstrip down to the QB camp, where I was shown to my allotted accommodation for the duration of the eight-day visit. It was a three-room wood-framed cabin, shared with one of the crew. My state of mind didn't motivate me to admire the aesthetics of the cabin's furnishings and fittings, which was just as well as there wasn't too much to admire in any case.

To MY DISMAY, project-related working activities commenced at once. I was called to meet the project crew. During the round of introductions, I absorbed little and remembered nothing. I then had to sit through an inevitable presentation on the current status of the project. The words I heard slid through my ears, accumulating in my mind in the manner of fine sand poured on a coarsely woven screen.

I accompanied the crew to lunch at the camp canteen. I had neither the taste nor the appetite for food and was reduced to sitting through the meal in a fog of painful discomfort, trying to watch others eat. It was a tribute to the comprehensiveness with which Puna overwhelmed me that I was unable to appreciate the quality of the canteen food until later on. In fairness to Puna, however, it wasn't that much later on that the revelation dawned on me as to how supremely unpalatable the camp menu was.

Typical camp meals were high on carbohydrates, excessive to a fault on rough cuts of meat, and so low on fresh vegetables and fruit that the appearance of either on the table offered due cause for surprised comment.

As a direct consequence of the regular bill of fare, the members of the crew all appeared to suffer (to a greater or lesser degree) from a range of Puna-aggravated gastric complaints that covered the entire stop-go gamut from diarrhoea to constipation. They lived with stomach gripes, intestinal cramps, nausea, and the generation of copious quantities of internal gas that took no prisoners in attaining noisy freedom.

FOLLOWING THE LUNCH I didn't take, there were more project presentations for me to endure. As successive overhead slides were slapped down by their exponents onto the overheated glass of a projector in flourishes that stopped only just short of seeming triumphant, my feeling of instability sank ever lower. Towards the end of the infinitely drawn out afternoon I had difficulty in co-ordinating my movements. The headache reasserted itself and reached towards hitherto uncharted territory. I was confused, clumsy and unable to converse with any kind of fluency in English, let alone Spanish, not that there was anything new in that. At the same time I was plagued with disquiet that my performance as perceived by the project crew was not meeting their expectations, not to mention my own.

The prospect of putting in an appearance in the canteen for dinner in the evening was impossible for me to cope with. My sole objective was to somehow survive the working hours and have enough strength of purpose left at the end of them to be able to reach the cabin and retire early. That was the goal. The next day's events could be tackled when, or if, the next day ever arrived.

THE RESIDENT PARAMEDIC at the QB camp came from La Serena and was named Franklin. He visited the cabin to examine me in the evening and brought along with him a small cylinder fitted with a breathing mask attachment. A legend on the cylinder suggested that its contents were pressurised oxygen. He gave me instructions on using the apparatus. Breathing pure oxygen, said Franklin, would relieve Puna symptoms. Given the diminished condition that I was in, Franklin's advice fell on ears that were drowning under the surf-like pulse of a now monumental headache.

Oxygen cylinders were widely available around the camp for use as a counter to hypoxia. They were additionally fitted as accessories in the cabs of some of the project's pickup trucks. All the same, taking oxygen was regarded by most of the crew as a crutch to be leaned on only in cases of emergency. Their broad opinion seemed to be that those who grabbed for oxygen in the face of Puna were marked by a shameful weakness of character.

I might or I might not – I didn't really know – have managed to get a few short periods of sleep during the first night at QB. Time took on the pace of a geological era. If I had been so inclined I could almost have tasted the creeping passage of the hours. The night was sliced up by the blade of headache into a bitterly cold buffet of vividly unremembered nightmares and the kind of wandering hallucinations that were to become all too desperately familiar nocturnal features during each and every routine tour of duty that I was eventually to undertake.

The intensity of the headache became almost unbearable. I could hear my heartbeat trying to push its way out through my ears. Each heartbeat drove a marlinespike up through the top of my skull, which felt as if it was being splintered away, shard by bloody shard.

Elevating the head by sitting up eased the pain a little, but I didn't have either the strength or the resolution to remain seated for very long before the slough of despond dragged me down again.

I struggled to breathe, and although I attempted to use the oxygen apparatus for support, it didn't help me at all, and I had to abandon it. Of course, placing a bold, if not especially clever, face on my inability to benefit from the oxygen supply, I knew in my heart that I had really wanted to avoid using the oxygen. And then again, it didn't help a lot when it was subsequently discovered that the oxygen cylinder so thoughtfully provided for me by Franklin was empty.

I DIDN'T WANT to take any recommended anti-Puna remedies, well intentioned though the recommendations may have been. Whether or not the remedies might work for me was not an issue, but I thought that if I used them they would delay a natural cure for Puna that an eventual adaptation to high altitude might bring. However, when I was a couple of years into my assignment, I relented a little and was persuaded by Chilly Joe's chief medical officer to use the medication Diamox when commencing tours of duty at QB.

The prescribed routine for ingesting Diamox tablets was to take one in Santiago in the afternoon of the day prior to departure, one before going to bed that night, one on getting up on the morning of departure, and one immediately on arrival at QB. Diamox really helped to make my customary Puna-induced headaches less intense than they might otherwise have been, and that was no mean feat.

Anti-Puna remedies of a decidedly non-proprietary medicinal type were always available at QB for those who wished to try them out. Principal among these was a tea prepared from dried coca leaves, of which there seemed to be an unlimited supply on hand. I neither knew nor chose to find out where the coca leaves came from. Chewing coca leaves was in any case a long-standing tradition in the *altiplano* culture.

An alternative tea was prepared by infusing the vestigial globular shoots of a minute Andean plant known as *flor de puna*. Since water boiled at something like 73°c on the QB canteen's gas-heated stove (unless constrained in a pressure cooker), the success of any intensity of infusion of *flor de puna* (or any other form of tea) was open to debate. *Flor de puna* was a plant so minuscule in size and so well camouflaged in the fine-grained scree slopes where it grew that locating and picking even a tiny quantity called for the expenditure of a lot more energy than would ever be recovered from imbibing the eventual tea that it generated.

I tried out both coca tea and *flor de puna* tea. I found the cure-all reputation of the former to be overrated. *Flor de puna* tea demanded an act of faith as far as believing in its restorative powers went, and I just couldn't summon that up.

IN SPITE OF, or perhaps owing to, the torment of the first night at QB, it needed a major commitment on the morning of the second day of the eight-day visit for me to pull myself together. The act of lifting myself out of bed was an enormous challenge. I needed time to consider each sliver of movement before I could try to make it. Putting on clothes screamed out at me to slowly bend my contorted thoughts around each constituent action.

I was unable to climb over the barrier posed by breakfast. The world was dominated by pounding agonies jolting my head and coursing through what felt to be every muscle in my body. The best that I could do was to stagger as far as a chair in the cabin, where I sat for several hours while attempting to drag together the initiative to go on any further.

The headache persisted, in one form or another, through the full eight days of that first visit. However, once the first two days of the eight were behind me, the beating pulse in my ears faded and the hammer blows to the top of the head gave way to a rather duller form of pounding that liked to wander around wherever it chose to go. By the sixth day the itinerant inclination of the headache stopped and the remaining discomfort decided to become more generalised. By that time I had learned to co-exist with a permanent headache, by virtue of which achievement I believed that I was getting well on to the road of adapting to high-altitude living – that is, if you could really call it living.

LATE IN THE MORNING of the second day, the member of the crew (Jack by name) whose cabin I shared came along to where I was huddled in a chair, adrift in a maze of time. He invited me to accompany him on an afternoon orientation trip through the project area. The trip, he told me, would be made in a pickup truck, and so the need for me to do anything in the way of walking would be minimised. From the way

I was feeling, not having to do anything in the way of walking would still have been too much.

This invitation to make a field trip increased the sense of inadequacy in my being at such low ebb of spirit and ability when all around me were in such apparently good shape. I was well aware that I needed not just to show a willingness to share in the workload but also to be seen to be fully involved. Although all I wanted to do was to remain seated on the chair in the cabin, I drew on my inner resources and forced myself as best I could to accompany Jack on his field trip.

Lunchtime intervened and disappeared. I remained in the cabin. I took no lunch. Thanks to Puna, lunch held no attraction for me on that day either. The spur that enabled me to leave the cabin and reach the pickup truck for the field trip was none other than a sense of duty. I willed myself to do it, leaning on the crutch of an intense desire not to appear to be lacking in commitment. Having come so far, I just had to go further. I simply couldn't let Puna drag me down. I was engaged in a battle to resist a weighty burden of guilt and associated helplessness that were so much a part of Puna's plan of campaign.

It was perhaps just as well that I retained few firm recollections of that afternoon spent in the field with Jack. The field trip ended late in the evening. I was by then determined only to see it through, hour after hour, minute after minute, or second by second if that was what it took.

As the afternoon dragged on, the will to survive the day had almost deserted me. I was unable to get out of the pickup truck at any of the field stops that were made. Bitter cold invaded every aspect of my being. I was crushed by headache and muscular cramps.

The seemingly endless field trip drew to a close. The pickup truck returned to QB. I then needed assistance to walk from the vehicle to my room. I slumped in front of a gas-fired heater but was unable to get warm. A suggestion of pending dinner was received as if it were a thorn penetrating my flesh. I had eaten barely anything for almost two days. Moreover, I didn't much care if I never got to eat again. After a couple of hours I pulled myself to the bed. Facing the dread of the night ahead, I dropped into a dark pit of despair.

PUNA WAS A SCOURGE smothering me under a heavy shroud of imposed self-doubt. It imparted a total sense of wretchedness. It drained the cup of my spirit and poured hurt into the emptiness. It revelled in sowing seeds of lonely despair in all who came face to face with it in the remote outposts where it thrived.

The second night in the cabin offered me, if anything, a somewhat worse ordeal than did the first night. The enduring headache was accompanied not only by hallucinations but also with shivering chills alternating with feverishly pouring sweats.

Twenty-two years previously, on a darker continent, I had contracted malaria, the severity of which caused me to be hospitalised. During the second night at QB, I relived the worst of those malarial experiences and took them forward to levels I hadn't previously achieved.

At some time after midnight, Ricardo and Mario, members of the crew who were respectively camp administrator and camp manager, entered the cabin to check on my condition. They hummed, hawed and expressed a variety of concerns. Mario commented that should my health show no improvement by sunrise then I might need to be driven down to low altitude for recuperation. On hearing him, I was equally determined that an evacuation would not happen, irrespective of how stricken by Puna I might be. My objective was to fight the bout of Puna through to its conclusion, using whatever it took for me to beat it.

THE MANAGEMENT OF high-altitude working conditions and related occupational health problems were only going to realise success when the lessons learned from bitter experience were properly applied. The learning process was one of trial and error, and in that context I saw myself as an integral part of the trial side of the couplet. It was fortunate that I wasn't converted into an error of the kind that inevitably cropped up under a policy of getting the job done, come what may.

With the eventually more enlightened thinking that came later on with appropriate experience gained, any member of the crew, newly arrived or long-established, who exhibited Puna symptoms of even a moderate variety for more than a day or so was at once relocated to low altitude and was not permitted to return to the project site again. Had such a regulation been in place when I joined the project, my association with the project would have been of a rather short duration.

UPON THE APPROACH of sunrise in what was inching itself into becoming my third day of eight at QB, I once more struggled from the bed to the chair in the cabin and sat there until I could motivate myself to move on to reach the camp offices. The headache was still severe but was blessedly dropping to less elevated peaks.

From that point onwards both my general and my specific Puna symptoms gradually dwindled away. The headache shrank by degrees. My co-ordination crept back towards a semblance of normality, in spite of most muscles remaining weak and sore.

On the third morning, and not atypically on all subsequent mornings of the visit, my hands and face were noticeably swollen when I got up from bed. My eyes were especially troubled and stung constantly as if drops of vinegar had been surreptitiously slipped into them.

My appetite for camp food remained at rock bottom, although I was able to commence eating. The food contributed to substantial stomach gas, cramps and a rabbit-like stool, but I never felt nauseous, goodness knows how. Nausea was a Puna symptom to be chalked up on the list of the few that missed me as a target.

As my physical condition improved, I was able to spend time in the field as well as in the camp offices. In the course of the last couple of days of the visit I managed on balance to complete some constructive work. When the eighth day dawned I began to believe that I had my personal trial with respect to Puna under control.

In my mind I had just about defeated Puna. Or so I thought. I saw this as a significant achievement. However, I would not have wished my experiences to be repeated even on an enemy, nor were they experiences that I felt I would ever want to repeat on myself.

During the flight down to Antofagasta by light aircraft from QB when it was all over, the last traces of the headache vanished, abolished as if by a magical decree. Puna was a pugilistic champion at high altitude, but low altitude invariably knocked it down and out for the count.

IN SUBSEQUENT DISCUSSIONS in Santiago with Beady and with members of the PMC, I described my initial experiences with Puna. I didn't complain about the regrettable incapacity to cope. The quality of their responses made it clear how little they really seemed to care. It was curious to recognise how ready they all were to advise that putting up with Puna was "part of the job".

Under such circumstances, the evidence of personal incompatibility with working at the high-altitude environment of the project was rarely shown much sympathy by the PMC, let alone by Beady. Puna, after all, had to be experienced to be properly appreciated, and the PMC and Beady hadn't yet progressed that far in any long-term sense.

ONCE I WAS out of QB and separated from it by a vertical interval and horizontal distance incorporating oceans and continents, and when that great healer time had become part of the equation, the ravages of Puna seemed hardly worth recalling. My resolution never again to set foot in the *quebrada* of tears vanished as effectively as if it had been made on New Year's Day. Duty called. I slipped, almost without realising it, into accepting a permanent assignment to the Collahuasi project.

As it was, my concerns over the assignment were attached not so much to Puna as to what I regarded as two much greater evils, both equally unsavoury. The first involved the moral dilemma of privileged living and working in a country tramped beneath the iron boot of General Pinochet. The second was the requirement to report to Beady, who I had identified as dedicated to ready egocentricity and for whom I could summon up no vestige of respect. It was a case of Puna usurped by a pair of dictators. If only it could have been the other way around.

Chilean society could well have been modelled on either the South African apartheid system or Hitler's Germany. It comprised a minority upper class, which ruled the country and reaped rewards under Pinochet's dictatorial patronage, and a majority lower or underclass, whose purpose in life was to serve its masters and be poorly recompensed for the same. Those who objected to the inequality were often imprisoned, and in far too many instances they simply disappeared.

I was told that Chilean society embraced a substantial middle class, but between the upper-class minority and the lower-class majority I found no such grey area that I could recognise.

What I did find was that the majority was warm of character, hospitable in intent and a pleasure to associate with. Although, in accordance with Noel Coward's perception, the upper class not unnaturally had the upper hand when I arrived in Chile to take up my assignment, it became increasingly clear, as my assignment progressed, that the days of the upper class exercising the upper hand without contest were already numbered. Misgivings over residence in Chile were rapidly dispelled when I threw my lot in with that of the majority.

BEADY WAS LESS easy to deal with. Since he and I were the only non-Chilean nationals working for the project, it would have been reasonable to believe that some kind of bond should have existed between us. A common Company association should also have helped, although it had never offered any guarantee of co-operation anywhere else that I knew of.

My relationship with Beady was more about bondage than bond. Beady gave me to understand, as often as he could, not only that he had been instrumental in arranging my assignment to his (not the) project but also that he had the power to terminate the assignment at short notice.

It came as no great surprise to me that, as far as Beady was concerned, I was brought in not so much to provide him with assistance as to serve as a whipping boy to take the blame for any errors of judgement. This arrangement, coupled with the Chilean social issues and seemingly endorsed by the PMC, almost certainly contributed to my many feelings of Puna-magnified insecurity and guilt in existing on the fringe of an island of advantage in a sea of deprivation. If Puna was accomplished in making good seem bad, it was at its best in making bad seem so very much worse.

Beady left the project, under an inevitable cloud of his own making, a long year and a half after the start of my travails under his command. Well, I thought, life might not be so bad after all. His replacement was Casey, yet another American, a mining engineer of a most engaging character, and skilled in getting the best out of his people. Casey was associated with Stripes and thereby held no Company-sponsored axe to grind on my behalf.

Although Casey's arrival probably came too late to arrest the deterioration in my psychological condition, it bolstered my self-respect and was, I am sure, instrumental in drawing me back from the brink of breakdown.

TWO WEEKS AFTER I had taken up full-time residence in Chile, I commenced a schedule of regular fourteen-day tours of duty up at QB, interspersed by seven-day *descanso* periods down in Santiago.

Without fail, I always found it difficult to sleep during the night prior to heading north for a tour of duty. The passage of years only made it worse. Ultimately I had no ability to sleep at all on those specific nights and spent them sweating and trembling by turns, fearful of what lay ahead.

At the outset of the first tour of duty of the assignment, identical Puna symptoms to those that I experienced during the initial eight-day visit were repeated with an equal severity. So much for forgetting about them! However, in this instance the symptoms tapered off after only five or six days, following which I was (amazingly) free of headaches and able to move around with comparative ease.

It was possible that the intensity of the headaches overwhelmed concurrent Puna symptoms that I may have had and which, as a result, I then didn't recognise. If there were such other symptoms visited on me during the headaches I wasn't in any case predisposed to be aware of them.

I GOT LITTLE OR no genuine sleep at the QB camp on any night of that initial tour of duty, even when the Puna symptoms finally dissipated. I woke very frequently and didn't accomplish a lot more than dozing off lightly when I should have been slumbering. Sleep deprivation was a common Puna symptom that few could avoid.

The PMC, naturally enough in the comfort of Santiago, now and then discussed options aimed at improving the quality of sleep for those living (unlike themselves) up at QB. One of their schemes involved relocating the camp to an appropriately lower altitude. The benefits of the proposition, assuming decent access tracks, would need to be weighed against the debilitating effects on the crew of a daily yo-yoing commute between low and high altitudes.

Living in pressurised accommodation at high altitude was another plan investigated by the PMC. That alternative would in all likelihood have had even greater practical disadvantages than would the process of travelling up and down the side of the cordillera to the workplace. On the other hand, setting up a locally pressurised working environment, as for example within the cab of a truck or of an item of earthmoving equipment, sounded both logical and commendable.

AFTER THE FIVE to six days of Puna, few physical health problems remained at the end of my initial tour of duty. As the fourteen days wore on, I found myself looking forward to the end with an ever-increasing anticipation. Finishing off and returning home grew in importance as a key objective. Any thoughts that the whole process would have to be repeated again after a mere week of *descanso* were blocked out. All members of the project crew sustained themselves with similar aspirations.

When tours of duty were over, the outgoing members of the crew left QB in an instant. The worst thing in the world for them would be a suggestion that they needed to stay on at QB for a few more days.

In Chilean mining circles the duration of high-altitude tours of duty and related *descanso* varied greatly. A number of combinations were used, the Collahuasi project schedule of fourteen days on and seven off being just one incidental.

Alternative combinations were ten days on and ten off (in my opinion the best), four days on and four off (of dubious efficiency) and, in the case of the shaft-sinking contractor attached to the Collahuasi project, twenty-three days on and seven off (horrendous). Each of these had its adherents and detractors, apart from the twenty-three on and seven off, which seemed to number only detractors among those who had to follow it.

I believed that anyone could condition himself to work to any specific tour of duty schedule, provided that the schedule was precisely and consistently regulated. Maintaining a routine was of vital importance. Changes to established patterns of work were never welcome at high altitude, and, if they were made, then they were sure to increase stress levels in a crew in which levels of irritability, intolerance, indecision and inability to accept disruption were already drawn out by Puna into a fragile thread.

The golden rule for changes in high-altitude project working practice was to make one small amendment at a time and to let it take hold and establish itself before making another.

On returning to QB for a second tour of duty following the first *descanso*, I suffered from severe Puna symptoms for three days only. It seemed that things were looking up for me.

On every subsequent tour of duty during the following three years, Puna symptoms remained with me for between one and two days. I concluded that that was the best that I could realistically expect. Accepting it demolished the fundamental barrier to living with Puna on my own terms and allowed me to carry a fair share of physical activity without complaint.

Occasionally during the first couple of years I progressed so far as to play football for a QB team on a cleared dirt pitch at 4,150 metres of elevation, located down below the camp. In the first game I played I was only able to manage a breathless fifteen minutes of heart-sapping play. In a subsequent game I extended my range into participating all the way through to half-time, and from there I graduated to completing a whole game of two forty-five minute halves. My prowess was poor and for that matter I didn't even like football, but taking part was what it was all about.

UP IN THE area of the Collahuasi project I regularly climbed up and down the staged ladder-ways of mineshafts in pursuit of my job. The shafts were of both rather old and doubtfully newer construction. My deepest descent went 250 metres down into the defunct La Grande mine from a shaft collar elevation of 4,900 metres above sea level. Climbing out of the shaft at that altitude was a daunting task that it took in the order of an hour to accomplish. But I did it, and that really wasn't too mean an achievement under the circumstances.

In the deep parts of La Grande mine I usually developed a pounding headache, perhaps as a result of genuinely thin air in the old mine workings, since the headaches always faded when I returned to surface.

I climbed the shafts in increments of about ten metres, resting in between. An ascent of ten metres accelerated my heartbeat to a near drum roll and took my breath hostage. Ten metres not only made my bladder feel painfully full but also induced its contents to seem barely containable.

I FOUND, OR perhaps it was more of a perception that I seemed to find, a slight amount of relief from initial Puna symptoms when at the start of a tour of duty I travelled up to QB by road from Iquique rather than on the light aircraft from Antofagasta. The relief gained in this way may have existed more in the imagination than in reality, but for all that, highly nervous of the air travel, I elected to take the road route by preference.

Even if the journey up to QB by road gave me no more than a marginally improved physical condition, it at least let me reach QB at a happily advanced hour of the afternoon.

To arrive later rather than sooner at QB provided a genuine benefit. It virtually eliminated any requirement for me to do any work when I was at a state of lowered physical ability. It additionally implied that I could sleep (or go through a customarily disturbed first night scattered with hallucinatory dreams) shortly after arrival so as to get myself (hopefully) in the best (if that was an apposite word) possible shape to cope with whatever the next day brought along.

THE REAL FEAR for me in travelling by air up from Antofagasta to the QB airstrip was rooted in the light aircraft's final approach and eventual landing. The QB airstrip was buffeted by crosswinds, the direction and force of which were subject to dramatic change in the space of a moment. Far too many of the landings that I experienced as the passenger of an incoming aircraft were fraught with alarming incidents and threaded by moments of considerable anxiety. It was common for the aircraft to approach the QB airstrip wobbling so furiously that every attitude-warning signal bleated and blared like an orchestra dedicated to cacophony.

For landing at QB, the regular pilot (whose name was Flavio) made his final approach by flying directly at the airstrip's rising slope. There was no reduction in ground speed as Flavio had to be ever vigilant to the possibility of aborting a landing. Aborted landings were not unusual events and did nothing to inspire in me either a feeling of security or a sense of faith in Flavio's skill.

As a result of Flavio's special style of uniting his aircraft with the ground I reached a state of mind in which the absolute certainty of impending disaster at Flavio's hands was so intense that I needed to coerce myself to board the aircraft at Antofagasta. From the seeds of flying with Flavio grew far too many of the straws that sat on my camel's back load of Puna-exploited personal insecurity.

Flavio eventually resigned from the Antofagasta-based aircraft charter company to take a job with the Chilean national airline, LAN Chile. As a pilot with LAN Chile, Flavio enjoyed great success. He rose to the rank of captain, flying big passenger jets on international routes. I could only imagine my reaction on taking a seat on a LAN Chile flight and learning from the welcoming announcement that Captain Flavio was up there on the flight deck. Not a bad reason to avoid buying a ticket to fly with LAN Chile, I thought.

THE SEVEN DAYS designated for *descanso* between tours of duty were, on paper at least, intended to represent a well-earned break. *Descanso* was appreciated most of all for the opportunity it provided the crew for rest in the comfort of home, presupposing of course that the respective homes were indeed comfortable places to rest in.

Although I was not remotely as well paid as Beady, I was well enough paid for what I did for all that. I earned every peso and cent of it and in that respect had nothing to be ashamed of, yet the disparity between my remuneration and that of the crew members was such that I had great feelings of guilt. This was coupled with a need to justify myself, not least in the face of Diamond Jim's desire to save a few bucks.

As part of the justification I accepted that the project had to be able to count on my services at all times, as much during *descanso* as on tours of duty. I believed that my responsibility towards what was always an appreciably short-handed and workload-heavy project couldn't be reasonably suspended for one week in every three.

Consequently, I took to working at the project offices in Santiago during *descanso*. To begin with work took up two or three days, but as the months went by, time at the office seeped out to cover almost the whole *descanso* period. The work then took over weekends and spread through the few vacations I felt able to take. My actions were dominated by an anxiety that I shouldn't be seen to fall short in contributing all that I could to the project.

I was adamant only about not working on any afternoon prior to the morning's departure for a tour of duty. I spent those afternoons and subsequent evenings holding on to a link with home in an attempt, which came to be increasingly frantic as the hours slipped away one by one, to defer the dreadful moment when I would have to leave it all again. Time never seemed quite so precious as it did on those afternoons and evenings, nor did it ever slip away from me so capriciously.

The burning need to stay at home during those final afternoons overrode all other considerations. In cases when the afternoon fell on a formal working day, rather than during earned *descanso*, I took it as a half-day vacation in order not to break the vital routine.

At the start of *descanso* I generally landed at Santiago airport in good spirits. My practice on arrival was to go directly from the airport to the project offices to drop off the QB camp mail brought down with me, to debrief Beady (or Casey) on any highlights of the completed tour of duty and to collect any up-to-date information. In principle I wanted to reduce the self-imposed obligation for me to go into the project offices on the following day. It would have been good if the intention had worked, but it didn't.

Descending from high to low altitude for *descanso* caused no immediate physical distress. In the three succeeding days, however, I tended to become exceedingly tired from late afternoon onwards. Tiredness constrained my ability to work and so gave rise to deeper feelings of guilt. I had no desire for social contact. Fatigue was accompanied by apathy. Initiative drained away like water into sand. My limbs were weak, and my mind fluttered in disoriented directions.

These were all symptoms of what was sometimes termed "reverse Puna". Reverse Puna was the price to be paid by anyone recovering from recent Puna in a sub-Puna environment.

By the fifth day of *descanso* this endemic tiredness usually went away. It was replaced by a deepening sense of depression, not without a seasoning of desperation thrown over it, that only two days then remained before the next tour of duty was due to commence. An increasingly cold wind gusted through my state of mind as the years of assignment to the project went by.

As a counter to feelings of insecurity, I put together, involuntarily in their commission but quite deliberately through hindsight, a sequence of iconic actions by which I could stage-manage travel to and from QB.

It was essential to stick to an established routine without deviating. The more rigid I could make the routine, the more secure I thought I would (relatively) feel. That was the theoretical basis at least. Any diversion from the routine, particularly when it came unexpectedly, was able to raise a degree of anxiety that verged on panic.

For openers, I arrived very early at the Santiago airport to ensure a rapid and prompt check-in for the first Ladeco flight of the day to Iquique. Checking in early let me make a preferred selection from the flight-seating plan so as to sit as close up to the front of the aircraft as was feasible. A seat in row 1 was the real prize, but anywhere between rows 1 and 5 would be acceptable. I was really disturbed if I could only get a seat back behind the first five rows.

I preferred to travel on my own. That left me independent of a requirement to fall in line with the whims of travelling companions. On me I carried a number of good luck charms of both a religious (I didn't claim to be a religious type, but hey, when flying on a plane it was better to be a bit safe than a lot sorry) and a personal character.

I learned the individual registration numbers for the entire fleet of Ladeco aircraft. I was then able to identify each of them at a glance. Irrationally or not, I felt much better about boarding some of them than I did about boarding others, although I travelled with very little confidence even in those aircraft that I considered to be my "favourites". Flying in a Ladeco aircraft that I had an aversion to implied nothing less for me than an appointment with impending doom.

At the instant of take-off, commencing just as the wheels of the day clumped away from contact with the Santiago airport tarmac, it was my practice to count slowly from one up to two hundred with eyes tightly closed and hands clasped together. A casual observer might have thought that I was praying, and might have been right. At a given moment during the double century count, the "No smoking" sign bonged as it was turned off, a positive signal that up in the cockpit the captain was more or less happy with the way things had gone so far. That was all right then.

During the flight my heart shook with numerous adrenaline surges, jolted into alarm by such factors as changes in pitch or tone emanating from the engines, or the onset of turbulence, or odd nuances of aircraft movement, or variations from standard practice in the cabin crew's behaviour patterns. To name just a few.

On disembarking at Iquique airport, where, in spite of my catalogue of misgivings the Ladeco plane somehow always managed to arrive safely, my sole desire was to head off immediately for QB by road. Delays in getting through and out of Iquique made me fretful, and the longer a delay was, the worse the agitation became. Iquique was a city redolent with the odour of rancid fish and, in a gesture of certain proof that irony was by no means dead in General Pinochet's Chile, was hailed by its residents as "the pearl of the north".

THE ROAD OUT of Iquique in the direction of QB climbed the face of a near-vertical coastal escarpment that always seemed to threaten, not without some justification, to push into the sea the narrow strip of adjacent low-lying coast on which Iquique floundered. The implied threat was backed up by a vast and twisting sand dune, named Cerro

Dragon (not without reason), which thrust into the southern sector of the city along the base of the escarpment.

Once at the top of the escarpment the road ran due east inland through a rearing landscape that was as barren as it was surreal. Here and there the wreckage of an abandoned nitrate mine stood as a monument to failed enterprise. A short distance to the north of a supremely unprepossessing little dust-blasted town named Pozo Almonte, the road met the Pan American Highway. The route to QB then led south along the Pan American for eighty kilometres or so before diverting off to the left on a dirt-surfaced track to cross nitrate-scabbed, stony plains populated only by ephemeral dust devils and Inca ghosts.

The dirt track wended east towards the Paso Malo, a tight and precipitously sided rocky crack at the foot of a tight and savage valley (a *quebrada*) slicing into and up through the ramparts of the cordillera. On its long approach to Paso Malo the dirt track twisted between the ominously and ever-rising sheer walls of a canyon cut through cordilleran outwash gravels, the fruits of millennia of flash floods. Bracketed in the vehicle by the canyon, I sat in a stupor induced by heat, lack of sleep on the previous night and the creeping assault of Puna symptoms as the dirt track gained altitude.

A KILOMETRE OR two above Paso Malo the wedge-like declivity of the *quebrada* opened out into an extended and well-watered hollow, a virtual oasis alongside which stretched a small village of adobe-walled huts. The village was named Guatacondo. It was reputedly founded by Spanish troops commanded by no one less than the notorious conquistador Pedro de Valdivia. A bell in its ramshackle church bore a date suggesting that it was cast in the mid-eighteenth century.

Guatacondo's vital statistics were: altitude 2,500 metres, population 200 (give or take one or two). The population had probably varied little, either up or down, since the village came into being. The residents of Guatacondo specialised in growing small (hard, and to my taste barely edible) pears, pomegranates and *membrillos* (quinces) in tangled orchards untouched for very many years by pruning shears. One of their staple items of diet was rabbit meat. They held and bred rabbits in large, deep rectangular pits excavated in the centre of the village.

They (the population of Guatacondo, not the rabbits) were inbred through both isolation and choice. Strangers passing the village were shown the best of hospitality, but that was as far as it went. Strangers were expected to move on quickly. New blood was not welcome in that tribe of coarse-featured would-be grandees, who were convinced that the purity of their line spoke for itself.

There were several Guatacondites working for the Collahuasi project crew. Together – allegedly, I hasten to add – they formed a team as accomplished in the skills of warehouse depletion for domestic purposes as any that might be found operating in more civilised circumstances.

THE FIRST PUNA symptom to make itself known, at an appropriate juncture some 500 metres above Guatacondo, was pressure behind my eyes. This was accompanied by a stinging sensation around the eyelids. Once arrived, the symptom usually remained for up to two days. It sometimes gave me blurred vision from which I had great difficulty to refocus my sight. I didn't get associated ear blockages or earache, as did some other sufferers, which made one small blessing to be counted.

By the time that the track up the *quebrada* from Paso Malo was nearing QB I was experiencing light muscle pains, some misbalance, and the start of an all too familiar "mobile headache" that I knew was going to get a lot worse before it got any better.

For the first day of any tour of duty I had to will myself, not always successfully, to concentrate on performing specific tasks. Puna made memory not very retentive. To combat this I developed the habit of writing a detailed daily journal, recording what happened as and when it happened. The journal also gave me the opportunity to record whatever Beady said, as his edicts from Santiago tended to take on more shifting shades in his own memory than might appear on a chameleon stuck in a rainbow.

I made all such decisions as were required, although the process of decision-making was a lot less incisive at the project's altitude than it would have been down at Guatacondo, let alone in the pearl of the north. Courses of action took time to devise at QB. Thought was a ponderous commodity. Safe working on the project probably owed as much to good luck as to good judgement, given Puna's insidious ability to distort clarity.

On tours of duty the crew worked for a minimum of fourteen hours per day. Since unexpected disturbances of one kind or another during the night were not infrequent events, I had no desire to add to time spent in the crew's company by participation in the standard after-dinner recreational activities that consisted of watching either games of ping-pong or films on video that seemed to favour the work of Mr Chuck Norris. Once dinner was over I wanted only to be in my personal quarters at the earliest opportunity.

One of the greatest concerns involved either members of the crew or more casual or commercial visitors travelling up to QB with an estimated time of arrival after dark. I did my best to make it a rule that all such visitors must commence their journeys early enough to allow them to reach QB before nightfall. Unfortunately, such people tended to be non-compliant, and no amount of cajoling seemed to work to get them on their way out of Iquique at a suitable hour.

If the estimated arrival time of a visitor stretched out beyond an acceptable margin, there was an obligation to despatch a vehicle to search along the track for him. That was his due. All those who both lived and worked at high altitude looked out for each other at all times. It was vital to know where anyone was at any given moment. Those who leaned too far on the wrong side of advised ETAs could expect to get short shrift when they finally reached QB unless they had a convincing excuse to offer.

I QUICKLY LEARNED the habit of eating and drinking sparingly at QB, not least for the first couple of meals after arrival for a tour of duty. Given the quality of the food, that was not a difficult habit to adopt. Camp meals were classified by Casey, and not without some justification, as "gut bombs". They were the instigator of explosive intestinal battles in the war directed by Puna.

The effect of alcohol taken internally at high altitude on those who took it was considerably in excess of the effect of imbibing an equivalent quantity of the same down in the pearl of the north. Even a small quantity of alcohol swallowed at high altitude could be highly toxic. The ingestion of alcoholic beverages on the coast by anyone about to travel up to QB was strongly discouraged. The wilder personality-related characteristics that alcohol liked to draw out of so many of its adherents were greatly attenuated at high altitude, as if Puna hadn't already given enough unassisted cause for aberrational behaviour.

It was for good reason that the QB camp was kept officially "dry", a zone of soft drinks only.

ON THE MORNING after the first night of a tour of duty, apart from a headache, disorientation, puffy eyes, swollen hands and feet, and muscular pains and cramps, I was generally doing reasonably well. The headache usually drifted away in the course of the day, as did the various swellings. Muscular discomfort hung on for rather longer, but I could put up with that once the headache was over.

In the dry, cold cordilleran air and radiant sun, the skin on my knuckles, my lips and the corners of my mouth peeled, cracked and ran blood. Covering up to minimise skin exposure to the extent that it was feasible was the order of the day. The ultraviolet ability of the sun to flay skin must have been enhanced by dehydration. Using the proprietary remedy Vaseline Intensive Care Lotion on my hands and face helped to mitigate the effects of solar exposure. Sun-block lotions and creams didn't seem to work very well for me. What they did was to harden the skin and bring out a thick and fiery rash.

NIGHTS AT QB were always the worst prospects I faced. Puna incapacitated me on the first night of a tour of duty, so that was one down and thirteen to go. On the second and third nights, however, even though the Puna symptoms were eased, I got virtually no sleep at all. On the fourth night I generally managed to sleep a little in a kind of catch-up process, only to have a frustrating return to insomnia on the fifth night.

Paradoxically, by one of Puna's odd quirks, in the afternoons of the first four or five days of a tour of duty I all too often found myself fighting off waves of drowsiness. This somnolence was particularly bothersome if it came on when I was out in the field behind the wheel of a pickup truck. I then had to pull over and stop and doze until it was over.

Interestingly, and not without an ironically amusing angle to it as well, more than a few of the one-day, fly-in/fly-out management-associated visitors to QB were similarly affected. In the passenger seats of pickup trucks they slept their unwitting way through field inspection visits that they had presumably journeyed thousands of kilometres to undertake.

APART FROM THE previously cited Diamox tablets, I took no other formal medicines for the relief of Puna symptoms. Franklin offered me some sleeping tablets, but I was reluctant to start on that course.

There was, however, no alternative to using a nasal decongestant each night to assist with breathing. The relief provided was fairly short-lived, as my nasal passages dried out with what seemed like almost unseemly haste. When I blew my nose, the tissue always came away streaked with blood.

In the fourth year of my assignment, during which I was based exclusively in Santiago, I had great trouble in sleeping even at Santiago's limited altitude. One of Chilly Joe's staff doctors then prescribed a sleeping remedy for me under the local brand name of Zoltran. I took it regularly. Zoltran was beneficial in pulling me back on track with sleeping, although weaning myself off Zoltran was another story.

The inability to sleep properly at QB gnawed away at me, producing a feeling of increasing helplessness. By far the worst nocturnal symptom of Puna was what I came to identify as "nerve pains". These were crawling sensations of unbearable physical discomfort. They didn't crop up every night, and that was just about the only positive thing that could be said about them.

Nerve pains were located as a rule in my left leg. The right leg was by no means an immune zone, although both legs never seemed to be affected simultaneously. The nerve pain sensation was one of tension, sometimes dragging at the skin like the edge of a coffin on the floor of a rough crypt, or otherwise shivering with uncontrollable involuntary reflexes. The surface of the skin seemed as if it were being stretched towards a point at which it would tear.

Sometimes nerve pains extended themselves over the entire body, and were then at their most devastating in my arms, shoulders and scalp. The intensity of the nerve pains forced me out of bed. I pulled myself together as well as I could, which was not very well at all, and trudged around the QB camp in the dark for as long as it took the attack of nerve pain to subside.

Nerve pain was an important milestone along the road defining my relationship with Puna. I believed that it marked a dark watershed between a territory in which Puna affected me physically and the uncharted lands beyond where it impacted on me psychologically.

THERE WERE SO many occasions when QB received unscheduled visits from certain other residents of the *altiplano* that I lost track of their number. They almost always occurred late at night. These visits were generally related to Puna-related incapacities. The problems that the nocturnal visitors brought with them then became the project's responsibility to solve.

The most taxing of the visitors came from a large group of artisanal placer miners. They were engaged in working dry-stream gravels for gold at 4,700 metres of altitude, in a bleak and barren valley named Quebrada Chigglia, located about fifteen kilometres from QB. They were participants in a state-assisted employment scheme, the principal objective of which appeared to be the surreptitious manipulation and distortion by the state authorities of Chilean national unemployment statistics.

The gold miners of Quebrada Chigglia were a desolate collection of confused entrepreneurs. The philosophy under which they operated was one of every man for himself. The support, training, planning and supervisory facilities with which they were provided by their state sponsors were of such poor quality that the miners were, to all intents and purposes, not provided with anything at all.

They were known as *pirqueñeros*, working in groups of four known as *quadrillos*. If a *quadrillo* managed to win one gram of gold per day per man, it was doing quite well, although I knew of one particular *quadrillo* that took out over a kilogram of gold in a day, and that really wasn't doing too badly at all.

It was a measure of the casual approach to which Puna as an occupational hazard was taken in political as well as in corporate circles in Chile that such a harebrained employment scheme as that at Quebrada Chigglia ever came to be sanctioned. The scheme placed a large number of men in harm's way and then proceeded to ignore their plight.

Indeed, the whole scheme might not have been quite so much of a mess had only men been involved in it. When the scheme was finally disbanded, much to my relief, I was amazed to discover that upwards of 700 people required evacuation from Quebrada Chigglia, inclusive of many women, children and babes in arms. They lived among rocks and emerged from caves and hollows like wraiths.

The *pirqueñeros* digging for gold in Quebrada Chigglia were for the most part recruited as volunteers from the ranks of the unemployed in coastal cities. They were essentially all strangers to high altitude and therefore ripe for victimisation by Puna. Too many of them were brought in at night from Quebrada Chigglia to QB exhibiting appreciable Puna symptoms, made very much worse by exposure and hypothermia. More than a few *pirqueñeros* arrived at QB in an unconscious or comatose state, thickly wrapped about under their ragged clothes in tattered newspapers in an attempt to hold on to any minimal warmth that their poor bodies still retained.

As a matter of urgent priority, serious victims to Puna were evacuated down the cordillera in a pickup truck in order to lose altitude as fast as possible. Franklin accompanied the evacuee, with an oxygen cylinder (preferably fully charged) available at his side as a key accessory. The most rapid route to escape Puna's reach ran down the *quebrada* to Guatacondo and took about an hour. Time was critical.

One of Puna's *pirqueñero* victims out of Quebrada Chigglia was, on the clamorous insistence of his companions, evacuated to Calama. This involved a journey of four hours along the line of the cordillera. Altitude loss en route was slight and very gradual. The patient died in transit.

DURING MY SECONDMENT to the Collahuasi project three other deaths occurred, for which Puna was, if not directly responsible, at the very least a contributory factor in each instance.

One of the three unfortunates was an electrician employed by the project's shaft-sinking contractor, a company named Emmi. A pair of Latin gentlemen named Jorge and Jaime owned Emmi. They were highly accomplished in getting the job done tomorrow. On a certain day their electrician suffered a fatal stroke. A subsequent investigation showed that he had had a long history of heart disease and had forged a medical certificate in order to obtain his ill-fated job. It probably didn't help too much that Emmi's personnel camp in which he bunked was of the kind that anyone who had seen a showing of the film *The Great Escape* would have recognised at once.

The second fatality was a long-standing member of the project crew, incidentally a Guatacondite. He collapsed and died at QB one day while taking a shower. (The only showers down in Guatacondo fell occasionally from the sky.) A post mortem examination carried out in Iquique concluded that the cause of his death was carbon monoxide poisoning. The source of the toxic gas was supposedly a propane-powered water heater.

I carried out exhaustive tests for carbon monoxide within the allegedly deadly shower cubicle, but I was unable to detect as much as a trace of the gas from the heater, whether the shower was running or not. It emerged later that the deceased had, years previously, been diagnosed as having a heart condition. The record of this diagnosis had somehow slipped through the control net when the project employed him.

The third of the deceased was an experienced foreman employed by the project's diamond drilling contractor. He had many years of hardscrabble work at high altitude behind him. He appeared to be both physically and mentally adapted to employment on the *altiplano*. Until the day Puna finally caught up with him, he had (as far as was known) never exhibited the least Puna symptom. On that particular day he took to his bed, his state of health deteriorated overnight, and he died before he could be evacuated to safety. The cause of death was put down to heart and lung failure. This may have been so in a general sense, but I believed that his respective organs were in all probability weakened by lengthy exposure to high-altitude living.

It was the death of the diamond drill supervisor that, in my opinion, carried the most serious implications for all those who were ready to come up and work at high altitude. The longer-term effect of exposure to Puna on occupational health threw up questions that had so far barely been identified, let alone answered. Lengthy exposure to Puna might not, I thought, be particularly conducive to longevity.

If only Puna wasn't such a darned unpredictable creature!

I BECAME CONDITIONED to lying awake at night, straining my ears for the sound of approaching transport bringing in Puna cases from Quebrada Chigglia. My nocturnal thoughts were invariably pessimistic. A perception of a faint engine note in the far distance, wind permitting, was enough to throw me into a shivering state of tension.

The low mumble of QB's electrical generator was all too easily confused with the distant murmur of a vehicle engine. I tossed and turned to the nuances of the generator's tone, anxious to pick up assurance and doubled reassurance that the generator was actually running. The generator was a venerable unit that tended to give up and cough into silence a lot more often than was desirable.

I spent a period of two days alone at QB, during which I was so wracked with anxiety that the generator might break down that I visited the generator house obsessively. What I might have done if the generator had failed was best not contemplated. In its diesel-spattered surrounds I was compelled to make sure that it hadn't failed yet.

The rest of the crew were away from camp for the two days in order to cast mandatory votes in a national referendum to determine whether or not General Pinochet should be permitted to extend his autocratic presidential rule by a further seven years without having to undergo the undignified inconvenience of running for office against anyone else. In a "Yes" or "No" contest, Pinochet ran against himself, won a little over fifty per cent of the vote, and in so doing lost the race.

THE ONE TELEPHONE receiver at the QB offices communicated with the great exterior via a microwave link between a transmitter housed in a shack on a point of high ground just above the camp and an operator sitting in a rather more relaxed situation somewhere down in the vicinity of the pearl of the north.

I associated the telephone with the generator, since the latter charged the batteries that operated the former. A generator failure inevitably meant the loss of telephone service (notwithstanding light and heat), although the telephone service was apt to go down for other reasons as well, chief among which was being struck by lightning bolts of the ferocious breed that characterised the Bolivian winter.

For me the camp telephone represented a personal lifeline. It was a critical factor in easing the remoteness of the project area. My inability to use the telephone to make contact with home in Santiago on the many occasions when the installation was out of service, sometimes for the greater part of a tour of duty, gave me a piercing type of anguish that the passage of time did nothing to diminish.

When I first took up tours of duty at QB I made one phone call home to Santiago on each day. A few tours of duty later on I began making two calls every day, one in the morning and one in the evening. The number of daily calls subsequently increased to three. Towards the end of my third year on regular tours of duty I was phoning home as much as six times a day or more. The calls that I made were of short duration but were scattered over the extent of the day. These compulsive phone calls were the foundation pegs around which my whole day was constructed.

I took to lifting the telephone handset on frequent occasions during the day and again in the evening and so on into the night in order to hold on to the certainty that it was live. I simply wasn't able to go to my personal quarters in the evening without checking on the telephone, and even after I did that I felt obliged to return to it in the night to make additional checks, again and again.

Events that might have been considered trivial at sea level assumed a dramatically increased relevance at high altitude. Puna could transform minor irregularities into major issues. As my obsessive behaviour took hold, a feeling grew that I bore the sole responsibility for whatever happened to the project, irrespective of whether it was within or outside my control. When things went wrong, for any reason, I was filled with a sense of guilt that I had somehow fallen down on the job.

I took little or no pleasure in mealtimes, which I regarded as no more than punctuations in the sentence of a working day. It was probably a good thing that meals commenced at tightly specified times and were kept to a closely restricted duration. The crew adhered to meal schedules with a fervour that was almost religious. Any deviation from meal-time orthodoxy was certain to cause consternation.

Often after the lunch interval I felt as if I were being washed away in a flood of deprivation and isolation. I shed involuntary tears. I had to struggle to regain self-control. As the third year on the project progressed, maintaining stability in my mind on such occasions was so traumatic that I believed myself to be staggering on the edge of a precipice that I was almost ready to fall from.

There were many occasions on which I could not bear to remain in my quarters for even as much as an instant, afternoon and evening alike. The walls and the roof seemed to press in and down like a combined pit and pendulum intent on smothering and cutting through my heart.

During a fourteen-day tour of duty the crew took no days off work, apart, that is, from the first of May. International Workers' Day had to be observed. All the other good (or bad) days of the year were full working days as far as tours of duty were concerned.

The first of the two "weekends" in a tour of duty was a stretch of time in which most of the crew, not least myself, were able to find very little peace of mind. The first weekend came up after the initial Puna symptoms had dwindled, but there still remained, given the Wednesday mobilisation routine, the gulf of a whole ten days to get through before the next *descanso*.

As the following week eked out its course, there was a tendency for the crew to feel comparatively more at ease, only to find pressure building up once more with proximity to the second weekend, since by then the prospect of *descanso* was tangible. I wasn't alone in fearing that something unexpected might happen to cause the start of *descanso* to be deferred.

On the final night of a tour of duty, those scheduled to go out on the morrow were thinking of nothing other than the prospect of leaving QB. All were trembling with anticipation, although the desire to shake off the dust of QB implied no disrespect to the project. The compulsion to go was Puna-induced.

Those departing were anxious to be on the move well before dawn tinted the eastern edge of the black, star-pierced sky and brought the surrounding hills into sharp silhouette. My particular motivation was to get to Iquique airport as soon as I could, so as to claim a forward seat on the afternoon Ladeco flight to Santiago. I was reprising the outward travel routine, driven by an impulse to run no risk of missing the flight.

Following check-in at the little airport terminal out to the south of the pearl of the north I visited its cafeteria, where I habitually took the same seat at the same table and ordered and ate the same kind of sandwich each time. A deviation from this routine caused me to shake in agitation. When I got it right I felt moderately secure, but moderately secure was about all it was.

ON ONE DAY during a *descanso* in my third year on the project, I attended a seminar in Santiago on health and safety in the elevated parts of the cordillera. The main emphasis was on the activities, and the advance preparation for the same, of those who used the cordillera for recreational purposes. On that basis the relevance of the seminar to those who worked regularly at high altitude was questionable enough for me to be sceptical about its value.

By tradition, after-lunch sessions of seminars were soporific graveyards for speakers. However, shortly after lunch on that day I was shocked into paying a rare focus of total attention to a ten-minute presentation on the psychological effects of exposure to high altitude.

To my amazement, the presenter appeared to be talking about me. He was setting out, briefly perhaps, but certainly with clarity, many of the torments that I was going through at QB.

It was following this damascene revelation that my desire to be anywhere other than up at the project site must have started to conflict seriously with an ever-present sense of duty. I was deluged with thoughts of escape, of running away, no matter what it might take. The seeds of this inner struggle probably took root much earlier, but it had needed time for them to grow to a point at which they could no longer be suppressed.

I started to feel that I had insufficient willpower to continue working for much longer up at QB. I tumbled under an increasingly heavy burden of despondency. The gloom heightened a sense of guilt, and increased guilt brought me to ever lower depths. It was a truly vicious circle that I couldn't break out of.

Although Puna hadn't defeated me in the physical sense, it had drained my mental reserves, piece by fateful piece. My innate tendency to feelings of insecurity was the Achilles heel that Puna found and exploited to the last full measure.

Explaining the extent of my Puna-related difficulties to anyone who had either the authority or the interest to help never failed to be self-defeating. Members of the peripatetic PMC were never found wanting in showing a lack of enthusiasm to listen to anyone troubled by Puna symptoms. I attempted to handle the increasing trauma of the situation on my own, but it was a challenge I was unequal to meeting. On the last few of my tours of duty at QB I was failing to eat or sleep and I lost a great deal of weight.

Rationalising that if I could manage to get the Company, through the medium of Chilly Joe, to confirm a date for the completion of my assignment to the Collahuasi project, I would then have a target that I could steel myself to work towards, I submitted a request for advice. The request wasn't even responded to, let alone complied with.

Perhaps as a consequence – although I didn't really know for sure – I thought about the possibility of giving myself a self-inflicted injury that could gain me some extended time out of the Collahuasi project area. A desperate situation was calling for a desperate measure. The vital objective, thrumming through my mind, was to escape at all costs.

I stood at the side of a busy road in Santiago, watching the manic traffic whipping by and considering taking a knock (just a small knock was what I wanted) by stepping in front of a fleeting car or a hurried taxi.

I didn't do it, although I knew it was a close run thing. If I could have found an appropriate means to injure myself without any third-party involvement it might well have been another story. I didn't want to wish my troubles onto anyone else. A psychiatrist asked me, when Puna was all part of history and QB was a place I wouldn't go to again, if I had ever thought about suicide. I didn't know, but I didn't believe that I ever had. What I might have done if the tours of duty hadn't stopped when they did was best not thought about.

In the final days of my very last tour of duty there was little else that I managed to focus my mind on outside of the urgency of getting away. The word "escape" floated about in my head, the need to leave became all-pervading, and my emotional state broke down openly. This was obvious to the rest of the crew and was reported back to the Santiago office.

I received a phone call from Casey asking me to return to Santiago right away. He made the request with an ostensible reference to my being needed for a specific purpose in Santiago, although the fact of the matter was that my rapidly deteriorating mental state was finally being taken in hand.

In spite of a POW-like compulsion to break out of camp, part of me resisted Casey's request. I left QB with mixed feelings and many misgivings. I never went back again.

During the months that followed my return to Santiago I was sequentially referred to a bewildering array of medical specialists, in the course of which I underwent comprehensive physical, neurological and psychiatric tests. I was given a brain scan. I became familiar with the waiting rooms of various psychiatric institutions, inclusive of one particular snake pit in which I developed a high level of regard for the bizarre characteristics of my fellow afflicted and vice versa.

My physical status was diagnosed as good. Of course I knew that that would be the result all along, but it didn't prevent it being something of a disappointment. I secretly hoped that some facet of my physical condition might offer a bit of evidence to explain what Puna had done to me. In so doing it might then bring silence to what I believed, not without reason, to be some insensitive critics in the PMC.

The psychiatric diagnosis concluded that I was suffering from severe clinical depression, prone to acute anxiety attacks and exhibiting a marked guilt complex and sense of personal insecurity. These factors were considered by the psychiatrist to be rooted in my personality and psychological traits, induced to grow unrestrained and to be magnified and aggravated by Puna and the high-altitude environment.

The recommended treatment for my depression, which the psychiatrist considered was a reversible condition, was psychotherapy and the administration of anti-depressant drugs. Any return to the QB camp and the project site was ruled out. I commenced a regular programme of weekly psychiatric consultations.

AT THE INSTIGATION of one of my plethora of doctors, I was sent to undertake a series of specific tests at the Chilean Air Force hospital in Santiago. These were tests applied in the training of jet fighter pilots and were aimed at measuring capacity for flying at high altitude with and without oxygen support.

In many ways the tests at the Air Force hospital represented a last-ditch stand to demonstrate that whatever Puna was doing to me, it was real and therefore to be believed.

So it came to pass that at the Chilean Air Force hospital I sat in a hyperbaric chamber with the internal pressure simulating an atmosphere at an altitude somewhere between 4,500 and 5,000 metres above sea level.

During the session in the hyperbaric chamber the level of oxygen saturation in my blood was carefully monitored using an infrared sensor clipped to the right thumb. At the simulated range of altitude the sensor readings showed that blood oxygen count declined gradually when I was inactive and fell rapidly when I was given exercises to carry out. The rate of blood oxygen loss under the active condition was so precipitate that the tests were halted.

The doctor in attendance took the view that an abnormal level of blood oxygen was the fundamental cause of my adverse reaction to Puna. According to his opinion, oxygen that I breathed in at high altitude was expropriated by muscles rather than being absorbed into the blood. The outcome was instant hypoxia.

The doctor declared that my style of breathing was the principal factor contributing to my downfall. He recommended a programme of retraining in breathing technique, intended to maximise transfer of oxygen to the blood. Such programmes, he said, were generally applied to patients who had suffered heart attacks. A corrected breathing pattern, the doctor suggested, would direct inhaled oxygen to where it would do me the most good.

My psychiatrist accepted the Air Force doctor's diagnosis, but he saw no point in having me undertake a programme aimed at correcting the condition so as to enable a return to QB since he had already determined that I would not and should not go back.

The recommended programme to retrain me in breathing technique never took place.

A formal confirmation that my Puna problems had a clinical basis came as an enormous relief to me. At a single stroke it was as if a stony weight was lifted from my shoulders.

DURING THE TIME that I worked in Santiago following my escape from QB, I was oppressed by two key fears. The greater of these was that somehow I might be forced to visit QB once more. The other fear was that as an office-based regular in Santiago I was failing the project by not being present at the project site, where the real work was done.

Occasional, and no doubt well-intentioned, suggestions from one or other of my Santiago colleagues that I might make a PMC-styled one-day fly-in/fly-out visit to the QB airstrip filled me with black dread. A barrier against travelling to the project site rose up high and solid in my mind. I couldn't bring myself to think about such a visit. For a while I even developed an aversion to travelling anywhere at any time for any purpose, but later on that fell away.

THE WORK I did in Santiago gave me an opportunity to make a useful contribution to the technical planning and conceptual forward thinking for the Collahuasi project. It provided a real impetus in changing the project status from that of a modest mineral exploration venture into that of a world-class mining development. That, I thought, was an achievement that justified my having endured all that Puna had been able to do to me.

Not long afterwards, various corporate and institutional studies, in which Chilly Joe and the Company were numbered among the leaders, were undertaken, which considered the effects of Puna on occupational health in Chile. The answers that would be so essential in planning for the physical and psychological welfare of all those who involved themselves in future projects and developments on the high altitude frontier were at last being sought out.

I liked to think that my case history provided at least one of the fundamental stimuli for such studies, and if that was so – and I believed it was – that truly made it all worthwhile.

BUT SOMETHING ERE the end, some work of noble note may yet be done!

Other, that is, than saving Diamond Jim his few bucks.

That fiery question, the very same once allegedly put by HM QEII to HRH the CEO, and directly by me to a fuckin' mining engineer, remained to be answered.

What about the ore reserves?

What indeed!

The fact is that during my time on the Collahuasi project, a stage of the project at which ore reserves as such could be reliably estimated was never reached. On the other hand, the work that I did reached in the direction of ore reserves to the extent that it contributed to the identification of vast and attractive resources of copper mineralisation. My estimate for these available resources was in the order of four billion tons at an average copper grade of ± 0.9 per cent.

That was a world-class mineral resource!

The reaction of the PMC to my reporting the same was not, however, what I expected. They threw up their hands, expressed disbelief, ordered me to withdraw and scrap my report, and declared that such figures must never be mentioned again by me or anyone else, either in or out of their respective (but not especially respected) presences.

Perhaps the immensity of the reportedly available mineral resources was too much for them to grasp. A commonly expressed desire to promote a small-scale "starter project" development at Collahuasi may have loomed too large in their minds. Very probably the self-promoting interests of the three outfits that made up the joint venture and its PMC got in the way of common sense. They could handle equal shares of a small pie, but when the pie was bigger, each of them wanted the biggest third.

A FOOTNOTE TO this failure of reason came along a few years later, written in the pages of the celebrated weekly mining industry newspaper, the *Northern Miner*, published in Toronto. By then, Uncle Joe and Stripes were out of the joint venture, having sold their shares to Hawkspan and a newcomer, a second international mining company. Uncle Joe and Stripes each realised a price for their one-third shares that crowded on a couple of hundred million dollars.

Big money!

Not bad!

The relevant story in the *Northern Miner* reported that Hawkspan was proud to announce Collahuasi mineral resources of three billion tons.

Good for them!

Did they let me know that I was perhaps a little bit right all along?

No, they didn't.

Is any further comment necessary?

No, I don't think so.

− 9 −

A Short Walk in the Eastern Ghats

Much have I travell'd in the realms of clay,
And many goodly fields of bauxite seen,
Down many mined-out byways have I been,
Where dust and rubble dim the light of day.

Oft of one great resource had I been told,
That national agents ruled as their demesne,
Yet did I never tread Ghat ramparts green
Till Panchpatmali reared up, clear and bold.

Then felt I like some winner of a prize,
Fortuitous perhaps, tho' up my alley,
Or like stout Rao, when with bleary eyes
He peered at Galikondra from a stricken valley,
And I stood yielding in resigned surprise,
Silent in a gazebo at Chintapalle.

With apologies to Mr John Keats

I STOOD OUTSIDE the Taj Hotel in Hyderabad at 7.00 a.m. and viewed the immediate prospect. The only thing in sight that seemed to be both clear and cool was the hotel swimming pool, although I wouldn't have liked to stake good money on the clarity part.

As if to add substance to the pool, a reservoir formed a small lake-like feature further out in front of the hotel. There, the water was so dark-surfaced that it mirrored the haze hanging over the surrounding city. Every now and then, the surface of the reservoir dimpled and broke as fish rose to grab quick gulps of air. The air had the consistency of thin soup, flavoured, but not unpleasantly, with domestic smoke, traffic fumes and dust. I don't know if the fish found the air to their taste, but as beggars they couldn't be choosers.

Around the rim of the reservoir a scattering of herons and a whole squad of cormorants had staked out posts from which they could watch and wait for the right opportunity to decimate the smaller fry among the piscine population. A single stork stood among them, trying to appear aloof but managing to look rather uncertain as to whether it should be there or not. A bedraggled mongoose crept into view from behind one rock and disappeared again behind another.

It seemed that all creatures great and small knew their place in the local scheme of things, but then that was only to be expected. This was India.

UNLIKE THE PATIENT and eternally hopeful birds, I was able to retire to the inner precincts of the hotel, and that was what I did, heading directly to the restaurant. I ordered the *aloo paratha* with *dahi*, a blithely filled potato pancake served with yoghurt. At the Taj in Hyderabad they really knew how to set up an enjoyable breakfast.

Indian flute music was playing in the background. It made a perfect complement to my meal. A fellow-diner, whose credentials as an ambassador for his country of birth (which he would undoubtedly have referred to as the "Yookay") had evidently been left behind in that self-same country, requested a waiter in tones demonstrative of the fact that the spirit of the Raj might still have a spark of life left in it to "Turn down the noise! It is giving me a headache!" The waiter went away to comply with this offensive demand, no doubt wishing, like me, that he had the courage to dump a big bowl of *sambar* over that allegedly aching limey head, and shove a relative of the warbling flute up the retentive orifice located a metre or so beneath it.

I CHECKED OUT OF the hotel an hour or two later and took a taxi to the Hyderabad domestic airport where I was to take flight IC 561 of India Airlines to Visakhapatnam, the large port city in Andhra Pradesh state ("AP") on the east coast of India. Those who were familiars of Visakhapatnam referred to the city as "Vizag".

THE AIRPORT TERMINAL had seen better days, but so had I and so I couldn't complain. What the airport appointments lacked in cleanliness was more than amply compensated by the exuberance of the passengers and their camp followers milling in a rippling kaleidoscope of safari suits and saris, the loudness of some of which constituted a near environmental hazard.

Checking in for my flight was a relatively painless process once I managed to battle my way through the mob of porters, would-be porters, chancers, beggars, occasional well-wishers and the great ranks of the citizens of Hyderabad who had decided to lay siege to the gates of the airport on that day.

The road outside the entry doors to the airport terminal was kept open for the passage of traffic by a squad of paramilitary-styled policemen clad in pressed khakis, adorned with black berets on their heads and gripping long canes (known as *lathis*) that they employed to beat back any trespassers on the tarmac. Swinging *lathis* was an activity that the policemen appeared not only to enjoy but also to revel in, happy in the knowledge that they were able to lay about them with impunity and without a single motion in retaliation from those they were beating. Yet again it seemed that everyone knew his or her place in Indian society.

THE AIRCRAFT DESIGNATED to be flight IC561 was a Boeing 737, 200 series. It had once been new, but that was a long, long time ago. It was a museum piece. It looked forlorn from the outside and felt even more so on the inside. The interior fittings were drab, gloomy and so impregnated with the odour of local spices that breathing the cabin air made half a meal in itself. I boarded the aircraft with considerable reluctance.

I was allocated seat number 6D, sitting next to the good Doctor (of geological science) who was to be my companion for the trip to Vizag and parts beyond. His name was Emjee. He was formerly a highly placed official in the uppermost echelons of the Indian Geological Survey, who, on retirement from service, had set himself up as a geological consultant based in Hyderabad. Emjee specialised in providing advice on matters pertaining to the geology of bauxite and the exploration and exploitation of that very same commodity.

He must have been a lot older than he looked. Jet-black hair, whether or not aided by a skilful application of dye, could give that impression. On the other hand, disguising impairments in his physical condition was less easy for Emjee to manage. He was a fattish and rather squat man, although the features of his face were so finely drawn that they seemed at odds with his pudginess. Emjee had thin lips and a thin nose and drew breath through both of them in a hungry manner that did not portend well for any hill walks that lay ahead, notwithstanding the set of steps so recently ascended to board the aircraft.

Through those self-same tight lips Emjee discoursed at length during the entire flight from Hyderabad to Vizag. The flight lasted an hour, although it felt very much longer. I discovered that Emjee's favourite subject, perhaps the only subject he was truly interested in, was himself and the many great things that he had done in his life to date, some of which were probably true. Paying deference to Emjee's perception of his own importance shaped up as the sure way to get on well with him. No matter; his airborne monologue diverted my mind away from wondering whether or not flight IC 561 was going to reach Vizag or fall apart in the air on the way.

And yet, the flight to Vizag was not without one highlight in the excellent meal served on board, a mild vegetable curry with sour pickles, rice and yoghurt. Indian cuisine was so marvellously inventive when it came to vegetarian dishes that it was impossible to go wrong anywhere in selecting a vegetarian over a non-vegetarian option.

VIZAG, AS SEEN from the air, was a sprawling and supremely dust-ridden city of moderate size. Its immediate environment was prominently dotted about with diminutive rocky hills sparsely clad in dry bush. To the east lay the Bay of Bengal, sparkling under the sun. One large hill, smoothly rounded and extensive on top, looked out over the city on the north side. This was Kalaisha Hill, woven all over with public pathways and sprinkled with what looked like recreational facilities for the pleasure of Vizag families fancying a day out.

The city was dominated along its seaboard by a vast extent of dock, port and harbour installations. The port of Vizag was partly commercial and partly naval, India's key naval base in fact. The commercial side of the port complex was attested to by a multiplicity of wharves and sentinel-like silos backing onto tangled railway yards and flanked by huge stockpiles of chocolate-brown iron ore and black coal. In the midst of the drabness a stark white blossom surrounded storage silos from which alumina powder had been allowed to escape more often than it should.

The flight landed at Vizag airport on time. Emjee ceased talking about himself for just long enough to engage a taxi to take us to our hotel, the imperialistic-sounding Taj Residency. The taxi was a venerable Ambassador car, Indian made, sedate, functional to a fault and built as solidly as a tank – the true pride of Indian roads that didn't have a whole lot else to be proud about.

My chief impression of Vizag as observed from our taxi as we thundered in from the airport to the hotel was that if all the formally established shops and the many more much less formal vending establishments lining the road were to disappear overnight there would be very little left to excite a traveller's imagination. Vizag was a city in which the use of palm fronds as roofing material could never have reached its equal in heights of ubiquity elsewhere. Colour lay less in the flow of its sari-clad citizens, whether on foot or as fluttering back-seat passengers on mopeds, as in the truly staggering array of shop signs and advertising hoardings all couched in languages that were as attractive to look at as they were unintelligible for me to read. Small business entrepreneurs were legion in Vizag, and it was all too certain that more than a few of them must be regularly engaged in the business of sign painting.

The governing rule of Indian provincial advertising appeared to be that any space that could reasonably be covered must at once be taken up. In cases of doubt about what to put where, posters advertising the fruits of the Indian cinema, courtesy of Bollywood, must be slapped up on walls as the line of first defence. It was quite immaterial whether or not the posters reflected coming attractions to a nearby cinema.

Desolate cattle, which looked to be no more than tick-infested skins covering frames so emaciated that they formed object lessons in skeletal anatomy, plodded their zombie-like way wherever they chose to go, wandering onto and across roads at will, and more often than not giving up half way over and lying down on the tarmac. Traffic simply diverted around them. Black buffalo with shiny skins like polished gun metal added to the number of perambulating bovines.

The taxi driver handled the Ambassador with a deceptively patient demeanour. He draped one nonchalant hand on the steering wheel, and placed the other firmly over the horn button, which he pressed repeatedly. Although at the outset the repetitively volleying horn was an intrusive and irritating accompaniment to the ride, its application was so consistently brash that we did not have to travel very far for its insistence to come to seem quite normal. The vital function of the horn seemed to be to promote the avoidance of collisions with animate objects through a due warning process, and to a large extent it worked.

Every commercial truck carried a sign, directly painted on its rear end under the tailgate, inviting drivers of other vehicles desirous of passing it to "Please sound horn". No second invitation was necessary. Without a horn to press, any driver on the roads of India with thoughts of Formula One antics in his heart, and that meant all of them, would have been rendered impotent.

THE TAJ RESIDENCY hotel was an imposing, tower-like, step-faced edifice set on one side of a steep little hill leading down to the beachfront on the mighty Bay of Bengal. The hotel was another link in the chain that included the Hyderabad Taj and appeared to be of the same standard as the latter: two verging on three stars, no matter what the brochures might say to the contrary.

The proximate view of the sea that was obtained from a vantage point at the Taj Residency made the salty waters look a lot less azure and much less inviting to enter than did the more promising view from the aircraft incoming from Hyderabad.

Once Emjee and I were checked in at the hotel I thought that the moment might be opportune to review the trip that lay ahead of us over the coming week or so. The vital assumption was that Emjee already had some kind of plan in hand.

The Taj Residency was to be our base for the next few days, and thereafter we were due to travel to the north of Vizag to cross from AP into the state of Orissa. *En route*, we would be accommodated in a couple of guesthouses owned by certain of the companies with exploration and mining interests that we intended to call on.

The first of the guesthouses was located in Orissa on a breeze-blessed hill outside the town of Damanjodi. The second was trapped in the festering heart of a much less lovely town named Rayagada. From Rayagada we were to journey on to Orissa's capital city of Bhubaneswar, at the airport of which a flight (hopefully in an aircraft approaching a modest claim to modernity) could be taken to Delhi.

Both Damanjodi and Rayagada were *de facto* hill stations in the Indian highlands known as the Eastern Ghats. The Eastern Ghats soared up in a forested rampart-like spine running through both Orissa and AP, paralleling the coast and separated from it by a broad and fertile plain littered with rice paddies, studded with rocky hillocks, and marked by narrow roads rife with relentless traffic and teeming humanity.

The Eastern Ghats were only moderately mountainous, although the rising front that they presented to the plain and the coastline was nothing if not rugged, torn and gashed by the turbulent runoff of every monsoon that ever was.

Once, back in the mists of geological time, a vast plateau capped the summit of the Eastern Ghats. Currently, only isolated remnants abode as flat-topped and dendritic-edged reminders of the plateau's dissected glory, elevated a hundred metres or so above the surrounding terrain and standing at around 1,300 majestic metres above sea level.

What made the Eastern Ghats plateau remnants interesting to the Company, predilections of the Absolutely mandate notwithstanding, was the fact that the crystalline igneous rocks underlying them, petrologically defined as charnockite and khondalite, although it wouldn't have done to ask me which was which, were extensively altered to bauxite at surface. The plateau remnants were therefore capped by deposits of bauxite, some of which were huge enough to make acceptable projects for acquisition and exploitation.

Emjee told me that among his very many achievements in the days when he worked for the Geological Survey of India, the discovery, exploration and evaluation of the bauxite resources of the entire Eastern Ghats region were by no means the least. He managed to make the whole process seem to have been a genuine one-man show. There were no prizes for guessing the identity of the one man. The key to Emjee's success lay first and foremost in discovering the presence of bauxite on one of the plateau remnants. It was then possible to stand on that bauxite capping, turn through a complete circle, look at all the other surrounding plateau remnants fading off into the blue distance and decide that, all things being equal, the others had to have some connection with bauxite as well.

Exploration for bauxite in the Eastern Ghats had not exactly faded since the departure of its champion Emjee from the ranks of the Geological Survey of India. It had rather burgeoned out, as state and privately owned companies slid in on Emjee's coattails to take up exploration concessions and run their own specific programmes to properly evaluate the opportunities.

So far, if not necessarily so good, it had taken a mighty state-owned natural resources company to construct and operate the one and only bauxite mine in the Eastern Ghats, located on a plateau remnant known as Panchpatmali, near Damanjodi. This enterprising company ran an integrated undertaking, for as well as the bauxite mine it also operated an associated alumina refinery adjacent to Damanjodi at the foot of the plateau and a railway link down from Damanjodi to its all too visible alumina storage and shipping facilities at the port in Vizag.

The enterprise was national in constitution, produced alumina as its end-product and was an assuredly great company. Putting all these attributes together, it was logical that it should be known as Nalco.

Emjee and I were to visit the Panchpatmali mine to obtain an overview of what it might be feasible for a similar type of operation to achieve under the right circumstances on another plateau remnant. From a first-hand appreciation of Panchpatmali we would be primed to continue onwards to Rayagada to look at two more such plateau remnants named Kutrumali and Sijimali.

To date, Kutrumali and Sijimali had been subjected to an extensive exploration programme and might therefore present the Company with opportunities for investing in their further development. A technical team associated with a celebrated Indian industrial design and construction company (known as Ellentee) had carried out the said exploration programme. Ellentee was a fairly recent entrant into the world of mineral exploration and mining, but hey, so was the Company, relatively speaking.

Ellentee's field exploration office was located in Rayagada where, provided the monsoon season was not on, it occupied a small, sun-baked office block fronted by a dirt track spattered with dried cow shit. Kutrumali and Sijimali made quite a mouthful of words that didn't resound very well if they had to be repeated over and over again, and the project governing their exploration had come to be known as the much more free-flowing "Ellentee project".

THE ELLENTEE PROJECT, as with the Panchpatmali mine, was located in Orissa state. Down across the border in AP, the bauxitised plateau remnants of the Eastern Ghats marched on regardless, although in AP there had been little exploration of any kind for some time – probably not since Emjee's days in charge.

There was clearly a contrast between the respective situations in AP and Orissa that went beyond the requirement for visitors to AP to buy a licence permitting them to imbibe alcoholic beverages in the confined air-conditioned sanctity of the sort of hotel bars that managed to cast an air of sad desperation over anyone who opened the door and stuck his head in. No, the AP section of the Eastern Ghats was the stamping ground of an insurgent guerrilla movement, the membership of which was considerable enough for the movement (with its extreme left-leaning politics) to have conducted a local war with the Indian police and army for many years. Just how many had perished on either side along the way was not known. Numbers of dead never seemed to count for much in India, particularly when they concerned people at the lower end of the social ladder.

The guerrillas called themselves Naxalites. They did not look kindly on anyone who wished to explore for bauxite in their area of influence, and so, discretion being the better part of valour, exploration for bauxite in the Eastern Ghats of AP was on hold for the time being.

Emjee told me that there were no Naxalites active over the border in Orissa – at least none that he knew of. Whether or not this implied a Naxalite respect for state borders was a matter for debate. The regions around the bauxite-capped plateaux of Orissa were ripe with opportunities for the Naxalites to do what they did best, but for reasons of their own they hadn't yet chosen to do it. In any event in Orissa there could be found a whole directory of more or less peacefully intentioned NGOs to keep any pot of dissent bubbling until the Naxalites decided to intervene.

Emjee planned a quick visit for us to have a look at the Chintapalle district bauxite plateaux in the Eastern Ghats of AP, well into Naxalite domain, so we would see what we would see, and I didn't doubt that it would be nothing much – of Naxalites, that is. Certainly I hoped so.

FOR DINNER ON our first evening in Vizag, I joined Emjee on the open-air balcony restaurant of the Taj Residency, looking down towards the beach. The air had a soft and balmy warmth to it. There were no mosquitoes – a great bonus for me, as any mosquitoes in my general vicinity were never backward in coming forward to seek me out.

On a waiter's recommendation I dined on tandoori lobster accompanied by tandoori-baked *roti* bread and had no cause to regret it. Emjee opted for a *thali*, a row of vegetarian offerings lined up in small metal dishes around the circumference of a large plate, accompanied by rice and curds. With the daintiest of touch, Emjee selected and combined morsels from the dishes using the fingers of his left hand, and mixed his choice upon a side plate with his fingertips before scooping up and transferring the dripping rice-fixed mess to his eager mouth.

I slept well and was ready for breakfast at sunrise on the following day. A buffalo plodded up the hill outside the hotel as I opened the curtains of my room on the morning. For breakfast I had two small tomato and onion *upathams*, or patties, plus a bowl of *sambar*, a liquid delight of fiery spice and flavour, to dip them in. Pastes of ginger, coriander and coconut, providing all the colours of the Indian flag, were provided as condiments, but I can't say I really cared for any of them.

EMJEE HAD PLANNED an in-and-out visit to the Orissa sector of the Eastern Ghats for the day. It involved a journey of a hundred kilometres or so out of Vizag to view the Anantagiri plateau group of bauxite deposits, all allegedly discovered by Emjee himself. We travelled out in a chauffeur-driven Ambassador car, over-conspicuously white in colour as far as I was concerned.

The road we took traversed the coastal plain to meet the foothills of the Eastern Ghats about eighty kilometres out. On the plain the road followed a railway track (or vice versa) in its near vicinity to the extent that the two criss-crossed one another. The road was fringed with tall and stately palms. Bolder men than me were engaged in cutting fronds from the summits of the palms. Their disregard for their own safety was matched only by their lack of concern for the well-being of those who stood below to collect the severed bounty that crashed down around them from above.

The road was not short of traffic; whether two-legged, two-wheeled, four-legged or four-wheeled, it was all grist to the mill. The closer the road came to a town or village, the greater was the swarming orchestration of traffic practically overwhelmed by the sad music of humanity.

Within the towns and villages the crush on the road was a searing epidemic in which far too many threads of life seemed to be unravelling, while the flames of saris burned bright. Cows, buffaloes, high-wheeled and overloaded ox-drawn carts, bicycles, rickshaws, mopeds, commercial trucks, the hale, the sound and the wrecked all vied for a place in the tumult, opening up to the approaching cacophony of a vehicle horn and immediately closing in again behind as the vehicle moved on through. Our white Ambassador made its way through the town of Parvatipuram as completely engulfed in a solid mass of flesh and dust as if a monster had swallowed us in one gulp.

Overtaking was a discarded art, supplanted by an imperative to avoid forcible vehicular impact with anyone or anything along the way. I wondered where the multitude was going and whatever it was going to do when it got there – that is, if it ever got there in the first place.

We approached the front face of the Eastern Ghats. It was covered with the kind of dry and brittle brush that looked as if it was waiting far too anxiously for the arrival of the next monsoon. The brush didn't look in any way primeval, or for that matter even primary, but it had nevertheless managed to get itself declared part of a national forest reserve. Perhaps the declaration was a political ruse designed to deter the teeming population on the plain from taking up residence on the side of the Eastern Ghats, and if that was the way it was, well, it seemed to be working.

The Ambassador wound its way up along the narrow, twisting Ghat road that rose from the plain. It was a slow process. Overtaking was precluded not only by an insufficiency of space but also by the constant hazard posed by trucks advancing downhill in their customarily confrontational manner, generally heaving into sight when least expected.

Such trucks were the quintessential carriers of Indian freight. Virtually all of them had a nominal carriage capacity of about ten tons. However, in India any recommended capacity was a commodity ripe for squeezing well beyond its limits prior to being then squeezed once again. The trucks were brightly and colourfully painted, adorned with personalised and religious motifs and slogans, all of which no doubt reflected the preferences of the driver behind the wheel. Some trucks were so heavily decorated that they became aggressively mobile works of art in their own right.

At ten tons, it was not that the trucks were so very large, even though they made a more than threatening match for any car. It was just that there were so many of them. Given India's vastness and the associated intricacy of the road network, the number of trucks plying freight on a national count must have been truly astounding. They promoted a vast support and service industry in which relief drivers, helpers, loaders, unloaders, artists and painters, cooks, tea makers and mechanics, combined with the untold host of hangers-on that such Indian endeavours attracted, must in all likelihood have been numbered in millions.

THE AMBASSADOR MANAGED to reach the Ghat village of Anantagiri without mishap, although any one of its passengers could have been forgiven for believing that the advent of a mishap was only a matter of time. Anantagiri was a small village bursting at the seams with population. To the west and north, hill after hill lay in ranks, fading into the hazy blue distance.

Emjee called a halt about ten kilometres on the far side of Anantagiri, on a hill overlooking a valley terraced at the bottom with rice paddies and on the slopes with plantations of small coffee trees. Directly across the valley to the north stood a hill known as Ratnakondra (translated as "blood-red hill", according to Emjee). The flat summit of Ratnakondra, a remnant of the great plateau of the Eastern Ghats, hosted a bauxite deposit of the same name.

A lateral slope of another such plateau remnant named Galikondra (meaning "breezy hill") rose from the edge of the road immediately behind where the Ambassador was parked on the south side of the valley. A rough track, the construction of which Emjee claimed to have managed for exploration access twenty years previously, connected with the road and wriggled up to the top of Galikondra. Time had been just as kind to the surface of the track as it had to the physique of Emjee.

We took the track and walked up to the Galikondra plateau, which was almost entirely vegetated by dwarf palm trees, none more than a metre high. The dwarf palm was a plant, Emjee told me, which grew only on bauxite. As an aide to bauxite exploration the dwarf palms seemed to be second to none. In the absence of anything better their little fronds were cut and used locally for roof thatching. The fronds looked flimsy, but I supposed that if there was enough of them on a roof – and there seemed to be no shortage of supply – then at least the milder downpours of the monsoon could be kept at bay.

From the top of Galikondra we could clearly see Ratnakondra standing at a precisely equivalent elevation across the way, and beyond that, across a gap of twenty kilometres, the third of the Anantagiri plateau group named Chittangargli. Emjee didn't enlighten me on how Chittangargli translated into English.

He directed my attention to some trench excavations, dug (beyond doubt by others) during the exploration programme supervised by Emjee on Galikondra. The trenches were almost (but fortunately not quite) obliterated by the climatic ups and downs featured in the most recent couple of decades. We found the trenches by almost (but again not quite) falling into them. It proved less easy to locate associated exploration drill-hole sites, but by virtue of wandering around in circles through the dwarf palms we eventually managed to stumble across a site marker. Emjee appeared relieved, as he was effusively anxious to declare the magnificence of his works.

He was an ebullient guide, casting out information in a near gabble. Had the Sermon on the Mount been delivered at a similar pace the world would never have known that the poor in spirit were blessed for theirs was the kingdom of heaven. Such beatitudes fit the society of India like a well-meaning velvet hand in an ironic glove.

I had to ask Emjee to repeat himself more times than I would have wished, and far more times than he was happy to be asked. Making regular references to him as a world expert on the bauxite of the Eastern Ghats helped to control his spate of flow. He was quite satisfied in his own mind that he was indeed the pre-eminent authority in the field, and he revelled in confirmation of the same from others.

A SMALL, THIN boy appeared alongside us at the trench. He was carrying a plastic bag containing bottles of water. He was dressed in a pair of ragged shorts and a dirty shirt hanging open due to the fact that it lacked any buttons. The boy was a hill dweller, hired for the moment by the driver of the Ambassador, on the instructions of Emjee, to perform the essential role of water bearer for the visit to Galikondra.

Carrying our own water up the hill would have presented us with no hardship. India had struck again. We were there to penny fight and Aldershot it. I didn't find out the little boy's name, but had it been Gunga Din it would have come as no surprise.

Emjee characterised to the little boy as "tribal". By formal convention in Orissa State the hill people of the Eastern Ghats were always referred to in this way. Indian society was as distinctively stratified as any formation of geological sediments, but even on that consideration I found the "tribal" sobriquet uncomplimentary, and Emjee's invocation of it cast a slight cloud over the visit to Galikondra.

We descended from Galikondra down the exploration track, trailed by the small boy. I assumed that he was to be recompensed for his services but I wouldn't have bet on it. I was realising that with Emjee's approach it was always going to be double drill and no canteen.

In the Ambassador we drove down to the foot of the valley below Galikondra to halt under a shady tree alongside a trickling spring to eat a lunch packed for us earlier that morning, or it might have been the previous night, at the Taj Residency. The lunch was exceedingly so-so — so much so-so as to preclude any requirement for its description. On second thoughts, it must have been prepared the previous night, or maybe even the night before.

Setting aside my package of lunch, I walked a short distance back up the road to have a look at a small Hindu shrine cut into the valley slope. The custodian of the shrine, named Sankar, was on duty at the time and welcomed me effusively. I left him forty rupees, which was all the money I had on me, and in return for that, Sankar daubed a red spot between my eyes. Insubstantial though the daub was, I could feel its presence for as long as it remained. Later in the afternoon I developed a headache that I attributed to the red spot, although the sun may not have been guiltless in the matter.

FOLLOWING A LUNCH that never was, we returned to Anantagiri village along the valley past Galikondra and then diverted along a road that led us to a precipitously deep limestone gorge some eight kilometres to the north of Ratnakondra, in which the curious phenomenon of the Barra caves was located.

The Barra caves, more appropriately described as immense caverns, were entered through sink holes accessed along a wooden walkway that appeared to be holding on to the rim of the gorge by much less than a wing and a prayer.

We were conducted through the caverns along a predetermined route by a retainer who appeared to be as ancient as the cavern itself. Concretions of precipitated secondary limestone bulged from the cavern walls. Each concretion seemed to have a name and a history. The caverns were a natural wonder. It was equally natural to wonder why they were not better maintained. A mighty host of bats twittered eerily up in the roof of the caverns seventy metres above us.

From the Barra caverns we returned to the Taj Residency in Vizag on roads everlastingly cluttered with human, bovine and mechanical obstacles. Our driver, through expert manipulation of the Ambassador's horn, managed to involve the vehicle in no more than twenty near misses, which by local standards was not bad, as was also the Andhra Pradesh chicken curry that I had for dinner at the Taj that night.

ON THE FOLLOWING day Emjee scheduled a visit to the Chintapalle district in the Naxalite territory of the AP sector of the Eastern Ghats. We set off in the Ambassador at 8.00 a.m. following a breakfast of another *upatham*, carrying onion only this time, with *sambar* on the side.

Inside the Ambassador, Emjee was as garrulous as ever. His rapid-fire delivery provided me with information that might or might not have been useful. I would never know of its ultimate quality, as it was impossible either to remember it or to write it down in time. It began to dawn on me that Emjee regarded knowledge as power. Perhaps he was feeling that he had gone as far as he could in testing the limits of his personal confidentiality code and had released as much information to me as he could. I didn't want to press him too hard about it.

I asked Emjee if he would be disposed to lend me one or other of the summary reports on the bauxite resources of the Eastern Ghats that I knew he had in his personal effects but which he was guarding with such commendable zeal. We arranged that I would meet him at an appointed hour in his room at the Taj the next morning, assuming that we were to return alive from Chintapalle to Vizag in the meantime. Emjee said that at the proposed meeting he would show me a report and would "read it out slowly" so that I could actually take some notes. Clearly we were progressing.

THE DRIVER STOPPED the Ambassador in front of a paint-peeling shrine on the outskirts of Vizag. He got out and went in, ostensibly to offer up a prayer for a safe journey. I hoped that whomsoever he was praying to was not only listening but also prepared to comply. We all got a red spot daubed on the centre of our foreheads from a priest who seemed to specialise in the art. That particular red spot did not give me a headache, probably because it was so badly needed.

We took the main road leading due east from Vizag, along which avenue of steady hazard the Ambassador managed to negotiate its reckless way though the essentially uncharming little towns of Anakapalle and then Tallapalem, from where it branched off through extensive groves of thatching palms towards a much larger centre of cattle-leavened hot humanity named Narsipatnam.

I came to realise that the reason why the roads were constructed so narrowly was to relieve the driver of having to make a decision as to which side he should drive on. The paramount rule of the road was that if you drove fast enough and directly enough at the clogging multitude of people, animals and multifarious varieties of transport, then, assuming that your horn was blaring loudly enough, a gap would open ahead of you just in time for your vehicle to be inserted. It was a game in which all involved were participants, and it seemed to work, apart from all those mangled instances we saw when it obviously hadn't.

The road began its ascent of the Eastern Ghats about twenty kilometres past Narsipatnam and climbed steadily through a sequence of sharp hairpin bends. The state forest was thick and mature on the face of this part of the Ghats, with an abundance of tall trees.

At the top of an escarpment we passed through Lammasingi, from where we ran thirty kilometres on to the town of Chintapalle, central to the region of Eastern Ghats bauxite plateau remnants in AP. Our final destination was twenty kilometres beyond that, following a climb up a second escarpment through the villages of Gudem and Saparella, which, together with another village named Jerrell, had given their good names to three bauxite deposit groups in the general area. They were pleasant villages of little square houses under red-tiled roofs. The population, which may or may not have contained members or fans of the Naxalite persuasion, appeared on the face of it to be devoted to tending to the orderly coffee and teak plantations that surrounded the villages. It all seemed too tranquil for insurgency to be a local issue.

THE END OF our outward journey came at a rounded height of land on which a government agency had erected a small gazebo-like shelter for the benefit of travellers, like us, who wished to sit and either admire the view or keep a sharp lookout for Naxalites. The surrounding vegetation was burned off over an extensive area, perhaps to deny advancing Naxalites any cover.

From the gazebo the view to the south covered a range of flat-topped hills. From my experiences with Emjee at Galikondra on the previous day I was able to recognise each and every one of them at a glance as bauxite-capped plateau remnants. Since Emjee's preference was to make as much use of the shade within the gazebo for as long as he could, it fell to me to scout around the height of land to the north to have a look at other plateau remnants out in that direction. It took me an hour or so and was well worth the effort.

The consistency of the catering staff of the Taj Residency was manifest in the quality of the predatory packed lunch that Emjee had set out, waiting for me when I returned to the gazebo. A litter bin set on an adjacent post provided the packed lunch with a merciful despatch.

For our return to Vizag we "came out by the same door as in we went", as Oumar Khayyam so aptly put it. With respect to Naxalites the day was uneventful enough to be slightly disappointing. They must not have wanted to bother us, or maybe at the timing of our visit the day was just too hot. The greatest dangers we had faced were from road traffic.

Our return to Vizag was characterised by a requirement to stop for lengthy periods at three separate railway crossings for the same train to pass by each time. The train, which was so long that I got lost on each of the three occasions that I tried to make a count of the number of items of rolling stock, clanked along so slowly that grass might have grown with impunity ahead of its wheels. The crossings were like dams spreading a stalled flow of pedestrians and road traffic back into the far distance.

I WENT DOWN for a walk on the beach at Vizag in the evening, inserting my presence into a shifting parade of like-minded residents of the city. Any thoughts of maintaining anonymity were as short-lived as an Emjee lapse into modesty. I was accosted with great frequency. Some of those who approached me were motivated by simple curiosity, but most of the others came desiring a little, or a lot would be better, of my money. The production of a ten-rupee note from my pocket in an attempt to stave off a particularly persistent individual put me under attack by a rapidly advancing host of her ragged army of associates.

It was fair to describe the beach as sandy, but charitable opinion could not be extended far enough to characterise it as clean. A viscous runnel of raw sewage cut a gully in the sand that was fortunately narrow enough to step over. A used hypodermic syringe lay nearby. I resolved never to go barefoot on that beach. For that matter I had already decided that beach life in Vizag was not for me in any shape or form.

FOR DINNER AT the Taj Residency following my retreat from the beach, I asked the balcony waiter, with whom by now I was on the closest of personal terms, to serve me up the hottest dish (hot in terms of spices, that is) that the menu offered, irrespective of what it was. He came along with jumbo prawns, very well spiced rather than supremely hot, yet making a wholly acceptable means of rounding off another day in a place somewhere short of paradise.

THE NEXT MORNING brought along with it the promised opportunity at last to obtain some genuine data on the bauxite resources of the Eastern Ghats from one of Emjee's reports. The prospect felt almost too exciting to be true. After a breakfast of *masala rawa* (a rice pancake) and two green bananas covered with honey I went along to Emjee's hotel room with a growing sense of pending privilege.

With the preliminary niceties out of the way, and the quality of Emjee's health clarified, Emjee picked up a folder lying on his tangled bed, opened it, cast his eye on whatever was exposed within and rattled out a plateau-remnant specific list of relevant AP bauxite resource figures while I endeavoured, with mixed success, to take notes. Emjee declined to deal with the respective figures for Orissa on that occasion, claiming that it would be more appropriate for him to read out that section of the document contained in the folder in a day or two, when we were staying at one or other of the Damanjodi or Rayagada guest houses.

Emjee stressed that the figures he was giving me were provided in confidence. I told him that he was a far superior geologist to me, but even so I could assure him that I really knew how to protect confidences. Emjee agreed with me that he was at the peak of his profession, and I nodded my head sagely as he expounded on a few more of his many self-perceived virtues.

We then talked for a while about the standard of driving on Indian roads, with highly focused attention on my part to the performance of the driver of the Ambassador. Emjee waved his right hand languidly. Our driver, he informed me, was a city driver using city-driving techniques out in the country. Was that a good or a bad thing? Emjee didn't seem to know; although I thought it much more likely that in contrast to me, he didn't give a shit about it one way or the other.

The meeting in Emjee's room lasted about an hour and may well have contained a few currants of value within the stodgy dough of its greater substance. It broke up, much to my relief, in order to allow us to make a visit, arranged by Emjee, to the Vizag Port Authority offices to meet the port president. This celebrity appointment would be followed by a tour of the port facilities. The rationale behind this was that if the Company was going to participate in an Eastern Ghats bauxite project, mine bauxite and go on to refine bauxite to alumina, it would be essential to have somewhere appropriate to ship the final product out to a world anxious to receive it. That meant that the port of Vizag could not be overlooked.

The Port Authority building looked moderately clean on the outside but rather less so inside. A sign on a wall within the unimposing entrance to the building advised, "Do not shed blood, shed hatred". The sign ought to have served as a motto for the conduct of the port president but didn't. It did not specifically rule out other bodily fluids, although the drab internal stairwell was somewhat less streaked with meteoric brown spit marks and not quite as redolent of urine as was common in such buildings containing significant numbers of clerical staff.

Emjee and I waited in a large and gloomy retaining area to be summoned to the port president's august presence. The carpet was a shade of red that was unpleasant enough to suggest that too much unwiped footwear had trodden its thin pile. On the walls around us hung portraits of Tagore, Ghandi, Nehru and Mrs Indira Ghandi, plus a framed twelve-month calendar that was current ten years ago.

Time clearly meant not very much to the port president. After we had hung around the waiting room for an hour we were ushered into his office by a minion whose deferential attitude suggested that the port president held the power of life or death over him.

What the port of Vizag appeared to have conferred on its president was a quality of intense disagreeability. The president may have grown ever more obnoxious as he shouldered the daily exigencies of his job, but then again he may have been a complete asshole right from the word go, which is what I suspected to be more likely. There were not many such in India, but when they cropped up they were assholes of the first water, almost invariably abusing positions of considerable authority.

In our ten-minute meeting with him I do not think that the port president deigned to look at us for as much as an instant. He slumped his glowering presence behind his desk, set his mouth into a disdainful sneer and flicked through files while Emjee talked to the open air about the objectives of our visit to his port. The port president's singleminded interest appeared to be to let Emjee run out of steam before dismissing us back to the oblivion that he no doubt hoped we had come from. Even though Emjee's capacity for monologue would have been the envy of Johnny Carson, Emjee needed interjections of flattery to keep the tide running and he wasn't about to get any of that from the port president.

At a prearranged moment, when Emjee was visibly flagging, and I was only barely resisting an urge to tell the port president that he could shove his port up his presidential rear end, the office door opened and another gentleman entered. He, it emerged, was the port secretary, named Reddy. The president summarily turned us over to Reddy and we left the office with him, without being given the opportunity to thank the port president for nothing.

Placing us in Reddy's hands was, however, the port president's finest gesture, as Reddy proved to be a wholly co-operative antidote to the courtesy call on the port president, assuming that courtesy could be used as a qualifier in that poisonous context.

Reddy, a rather thin gentleman of uncertain age, although not young by any means, was amenable to answer any and all questions we had and offered us a tour of the sectors of the Vizag harbour, designated as East and West, by waterborne launch. We accepted eagerly.

Reddy told us that there was a critical shortage of open wharf space in the port. Only two unsecured berths were left in the West harbour, and none at all in the East, owing to rapid industrial expansion during the last decade and consequent demand for facilities. He was refreshingly frank about it. Emjee and I, he said, were merely the latest in a line of commercial types who had come to the port preaching big ideas and grandiose schemes that had all turned out to be a lot shallower than the minimum dockside draft. I didn't recall Emjee being so far grandiose about anything other than himself, but perhaps I was distracted into missing something when we were back in the smouldering atmosphere of the port president's office.

What it amounted to, said Reddy, was that whatever we might choose to tell him about our intentions, the Port Authority would have heard it all before and would be disinclined to believe it. I could relate to that completely. In a country where cows were sacred, Reddy was unable to use the word bullshit in a definitive sense, but I needed to have no such reticence.

A PEARLY DRY season haze lay over the harbour for our launch-borne voyage around it. We gave Reddy our passports for photocopying, filled in some forms and waited a little while for the deputy chairman of the Port Authority to return from what had no doubt been a rather good lunch, as his validating countersignature on our papers was deemed essential. Thereafter we were issued harbour entry passes and were ready, with Reddy, to be steady and to go. The entry passes indicated that we were assigned VIP status. I couldn't imagine the port president agreeing to it.

From the Port Authority building we drove to the port gates along a road fringed by evilly stained concrete walls that looked mean to the point of wretchedness. The most popular human activity in that festering gully, to judge from the evidence presented so prolifically along the foot of the walls and in more than one instance in the road itself, was vested in having a shit. The only problem that I could see for those who emerged from the port to engage in this activity was to locate a place for their feet that someone else had not already crapped on.

Inside the port the situation was somewhat improved. While we waited for the launch to arrive I talked to some port workers who were evidently taking an early afternoon tea break. One of them, who said he was a foreman, took charge of me and invited me to have some tea with him in a nearby canteen. I didn't expect the canteen to be in pristine condition, and I was not disappointed. The tea was excellent, served in a glass, hot, sweet and thick, made with a lot of milk, and containing subtle overtones of ginger and other spices that I could not name.

I thanked the foreman profusely for his hospitality, which resulted in his insistence that I take a second glass of tea. He said that Indian people were big on hospitality but small on money. It was the most telling remark I had heard so far that day.

OUR TOUR OF the harbour was made on a slim launch that dated from colonial times and which would not have looked out of place in a marina at Monte Carlo. It was decked over with a brightly coloured awning under which we all sat. The launch chugged sedately around the commercial wharves, passing the entry to a big Indian Navy base, and headed through to a construction dockyard alongside floating cranes. From there we slipped into the outer harbour, guarded from the open Bay of Bengal by two long breakwaters. It was a hugely impressive harbour, capable of berthing ships of up to 35,000 tons. Photography was not permitted.

Within the great stretch of the outer harbour the fish population was under threat from a host of small motor-driven fishing boats, oar-propelled pirogues and sail-rigged feluccas. Two dolphins broke water near our launch (or maybe it was one dolphin twice), intent on not letting the fishermen catch every fish in the harbour.

In the background a great ship stood against a wharf receiving a load of iron ore, generating in the process an immense cloud of billowing red dust that appeared to be taken by the wind in the direction of one of the lesser slums of Vizag. It was the type of slum that sprang up around most industrial sites in India and where, as far as the authorities were concerned, the feelings of its residents counted for less than nothing.

ON OUR RETURN from the harbour tour, although it was getting to be a little late in the afternoon, a quick bite to eat in the canteen was mooted. I took a stuffed *brinjal*, or aubergine. I didn't dare to ask what it was stuffed with, but whatever it was, I enjoyed it.

For what remained of the afternoon we paid a visit to Nalco's sector of the port complex. It was well organised, and we were given a cordial reception at the administrative office block by the manager of the facilities, yet another doctor of geological science who in this instance went by the name of Venka. Geologists rarely made good managers of anything, but to his credit Venka may have been made of sterner stuff. It emerged that he had worked for Emjee during those halcyon days of exploring for bauxite up in the Eastern Ghats. It was a relationship destined to do our visit no harm at all, provided that Venka still knew his place.

Venka was a man equipped with the kind of flowing corpulence that made a moon-cast shadow of Emjee's modestly advanced style of rotundity. Not that I would have liked either of them to sit on me. Venka gave me the impression that for him, not only were visiting representatives of other companies grist to his mill but there was also nothing that they could tell him about their intentions that he hadn't heard and disbelieved before.

Whatever else Venka may have been proficient at in the line of his profession, he was a smoker of considerable note. In the half hour or so that Emjee and I spent in his office facing up to his voluminous presence across a desk that was far too neatly arrayed to suggest the imminence of urgency, he puffed and dragged his way through at least half of a packet of twenty State Express 555s that lay within easy reach. On a shelf behind his desk a well-stocked carton containing more packets of the same brand suggested that Venka was set for the afternoon.

As a host, Venka was charming. His deliveries were always courteous and highly obsequious when directed towards Emjee. His personal secretary, a little man sparking with nervous energy, was kept busy plying us all with tea. In between times Venka sent him on various errands within the building under instructions that he barked out in a rather harsher tone than I would have chosen to use. I suspected that the secretary, named Harikumar, was the one who did the real work in keeping Venka's endeavours afloat, while Venka flopped back like Jabba the Hut and watched it all happen.

Venka managed to pull himself to his feet in order to guide us on a short tour of the slice of Nalco's port empire that he governed. The core of his demesne was a tightly enclosed railway terminus where rolling stock bringing alumina powder down from the Damanjodi refinery was automatically unloaded and whence the product was conducted by a steeply inclined modern cable belt conveyor to a concrete storage silo, the height and circumference of which were almost as breathtaking as the blizzard of alumina spillage that surrounded it.

We moved on from the railway terminus down to the dock, passing a big circular steel tank on the right-hand side. On and over the tank, a swarm of the labouring classes had taken up positions in an apparent competition to determine which one among them could best defy gravity without being burdened with artificial support. Their common task was the receipt of a ship's fluid cargo of concentrated caustic soda. The corrosive liquid, eventually destined for onward transfer by rail tanker trucks to the refinery at Damanjodi, was discharged into the steel tank from a cracked rubber hose. Drops of it flew around like bullets seeking targets. None of the workers was equipped with any conventional safety apparatus or protective gear that I could see. Few of them could even boast of any kind of footwear. Rubber gloves were unknown and shirts were no less conspicuous in their absence.

When we were in the administration block I saw a large sign bearing the proud claim that Venka's employer was an ISO 9002 certified company. ISO certification was supposed to credit the holder with the assurance of having attained an internationally recognised level of operating excellence, including compliance with the norms of worker safety, environmental protection and social policy. In my experience ISO certification also implied in many cases that its certifiers were gentlemen who believed in the tried and true maxim that every company had a price it was willing to pay.

According to my observations, common labourers in India were generally drawn from the very bottom of the social heap, were deemed dispensable by those who employed them, were shown where they were required to work and were then ignored. The basement level of ISO certification was well above their heads.

It was clear to me that on this understanding Venka saw nothing amiss in the desperately unsafe practices that were all too obvious within his sphere of supervision. From the vantage point of his superiority, mere labourers were such inferior chattels that their existence could be dismissed.

If that was the way it was when you worked in India, then the hell with it I thought.

EMPLOYING THE NIXON principle laid down when the President of the same name was asked why for his second term he had again chosen Spiro Agnew to be his running mate and he replied that you didn't break up a winning team, I selected jumbo prawns *masala* once again for dinner at the Taj Residency that night. I had much less cause to regret my choice than did Nixon to lament his or, for that matter, for Agnew to lament being chosen.

My friendly waiter had come through again, but he was much less happy with my breakfast selection on the following morning when I poured some honey over three little *idli* cakes that he brought to me. The *idli* (which he recommended) were stark white sponges made from steaming rice flour dough. Their taste was so stupefyingly bland that something drastic had to be done to save the day. The *idli* soaked up the honey wholesale and were, I thought, much improved as a result.

The waiter strove to conceal his displeasure over such an outlandish assault on traditional Indian cuisine but was unequal to the task. I apologised for the affront, but at least I had made the *idli* palatable and, who knows, perhaps a new fashion in breakfasting on *idli* was born.

In view of the *idli* incident, it was then perhaps just as well that Emjee and I were leaving the Taj Residency after breakfast for Damanjodi and parts beyond. Still, in view of the considerable number of hotel staff who came along to bid us farewell, including my waiter, I assumed that the one breach of protocol over the *idli* was forgiven. It all went to show that a stranger in a strange land could never be too careful.

WE TOOK TO the road with the same Ambassador, the same driver, the same speed, and the depressingly same expert techniques of sounding the horn and leaving no more than the width of a coat of paint between passing pedestrians and transforming them into victims. The road led along the coast past Kalaisha Hill and onwards through a large town named Vizianagaram prior to making the plains crossing towards the Eastern Ghats. Emjee pronounced Vizianagaram as if he were trying to dislodge from his throat a fragment of underdone *aloo*.

One of the Ambassador's tyres was quite a lot balder than even Ghandi in his heyday. My comment on the tyre, omitting any slighting reference to the Mahatma, was brushed aside with a by-now customary wave of Emjee's hands. It didn't help that the road across the plain was not only rough but unpleasantly undulate. It took no time at all to discover that the Ambassador would benefit from a set of new shock absorbers, if it had any old ones in the first place.

The driver stopped to take tea at a teahouse in a small plains town named Saber. The streets of Saber were so jammed with the familiar mix of shuffling humanity and cattle pulling things, pushing things or generally getting in the way of things while wandering and messing randomly in all directions simultaneously that stopping for a while seemed a reasonable option.

I was keen to have some tea, but Emjee advised me not to partake in Saber on grounds of a lack of hygiene that he didn't really have to elaborate on. Since he was the fount of local wisdom I went along with his viewpoint, albeit reluctantly. What I did, while the driver sipped his murky brew, was to wend my way along the road for a short distance to stretch my legs – no mean achievement in the midst of a madding crowd that I wished I was far from. My presence excited amazement rather than curiosity in the breasts of many members of the mob. They stayed their passage and gazed as wide-eyed and open-mouthed at me as Hoagy Carmichael's Old Music Master might have done.

Across a shallow roadside ditch conducting a slowly seeping liquid of an evilly olive-green hue, the blackened remnants of a long line of recently burned out shacks still cast a few tendrils of smoke from where groups of people milled and kicked disconsolately at the cinders that may once have been their homes, not to mention former members of their families.

The driver, when he had finished his tea, told me that the conflagration had depleted the population of Saber by at least eleven. Emjee listened and shrugged his shoulders. Everything was relative and life went on. By Indian standards, eleven down didn't rate much of a mention.

WE CLIMBED THE Ghats over a good road engineered, so Emjee told me, by a German named Sanke. As a not unsurprising consequence there were few hairpins on the way up. The settlement on the road at the border crossing from AP into Orissa was named after Mr Sanke, and once we were there Emjee was agreeable to our taking tea, much to my delight.

A good deal of the pleasure of tea taken in Indian roadside teahouses lay in the ritual of its preparation. The more ramshackle the teahouse, the better the whole experience was. The boiling of the water and milk, the sprinkling of the condiments, the technique of pouring from one vessel to another, the foamy head and the uniform colour of the rich brew redolent of the heart soil of India all made the moment for me one of intense pleasure. One glass of tea was never enough. Bollywood music crackling from a patched-up portable radio in the background was the perfect accompaniment.

FROM SANKE THE road rose through rolling open country, heavily cultivated with rice, other cereals and an occasional patch of commercial forestry darkening the lower slopes of prominent plateau remnants standing here and there. The bauxite-capped plateaux were like high floating carpets, which were not going to be unchallenging to gain access to. We made a short stop to take a distant look at a plateau named Pottangi, which (it went without saying) had been explored for bauxite under Emjee's supervision, prior to making our final run into Damanjodi.

The town of Damanjodi lay on the moderate slope of a long hill that rose as if it were intent on getting as far away as it could from the vast alumina refinery complex nearby. The refinery was stuffed into a hollow folded in towards the towering bluffs of the Panchpatmali plateau, whence the life-giving bauxite descended to it down an impressively engineered conveyor system. Damanjodi was a company town, and that explained why there was only a small horde thronging its main street. Everyone else who might otherwise have been there to join in the fun presumably had either a job or an alternative sense of purpose, such as giving support to an anti-Nalco non-government organisation. Of such NGOs there were many.

The guesthouse where Emjee and I were to be accommodated for two nights, courtesy of Nalco (so now was not the time to start discoursing on the rights and wrongs of NGOs), lay just out of town, adjacent to a main road where it peaked up in sentinel fashion in a cleared area on top of a thickly forested rounded knoll. The forest surrounded the cleared area like a monk's tonsure.

Bears were reputed to wander around its crackling floor at night, offering the opportunity of an exciting experience to those who chose to come up the curling driveway to the guesthouse on foot at a late hour. The recommendation was to stay off the driveway after midnight, although if you couldn't bring yourself not to comply and happened to meet a bear, you could be comforted by the fact, advised to me by Emjee, that if the bear attacked you it would intend only to maim and not kill you.

The clearing around the guesthouse was coated with a well-tended lawn splashed all about with bright flowerbeds. It commanded panoramic views of the surrounding district and featured a lookout point over the most pleasing prospect, that being the one facing in the opposite direction to Damanjodi and the refinery.

When we arrived at the guesthouse, a major exercise in interior redecoration involving impressively large numbers of lightly clad artisans was in progress. Anyone capable of holding a paintbrush looked to have one in his hand, with which he was slapping paint on walls, ceilings, staircases, doors and floors, although I don't think that all of the paint on the floors, while certainly prolific, was altogether intentional. The quality of my room was somewhere on the basic side of austere; however, it contained a bed and a noisy air conditioner in a port on a wall, and that was good enough for me. No doubt any one of the spattered painters would have considered it palatial.

My luggage was borne to the room by guesthouse retainers who, willing or otherwise, were not about to let me carry anything for myself. I had almost given up on the battle to handle my own suitcase, but since I hadn't yet adopted the truly Indian practice of strolling idly along behind an elderly porter bent double under the burden of both my effects and an impending hernia, my fight went on, unsuccessfully as usual.

We were called for lunch almost immediately. It was a rather ample repast, consisting of rice, *roti naan*, *dall*, vegetables, chicken more lightly spiced than I would have preferred and, horror of horrors, some fried chips. Perhaps the presence of the chips explained why the association of spices with the chicken was so cursory.

In mid-afternoon we repaired to Nalco's main administration office block, which stood uncomfortably close to the refinery gates. The purpose was to attend a brief meeting with both the deputy general manager of the entire Damanjodi-based enterprise and the general manager of the mining sector. They would then know who we were and vice versa. All I could hope was that their memories would be better than mine.

Permits were required to get us up onto Panchpatmali and into the mining area the next morning. Although our completion of the requisite forms involving a host of personal details proceeded in a timely manner, processing the forms thereafter was characterised by neither urgency nor haste, in spite of, or perhaps because of, the small army of clerks who gave it their undivided attention.

I had omitted to bring my passport with me and so needed to return to the guesthouse to extract it from the suitcase in which it was locked. On arriving at the guesthouse I discovered that the key to the suitcase was in my briefcase back at the administration block and therefore I had no alternative other than to return to the block with my suitcase and open it there.

Emjee and I waited in the office of the personnel manager for the permits to arrive. Time seemed bound in chains. Personnel departments were run solely for the benefit of those who ran them, and making meaningful conversation with their proponents for a couple of minutes, let alone the couple of hours that we were allocated, was a taxing challenge. Even Emjee's talent for monologue began to falter prematurely. The problem was that the personnel manager not only didn't know Emjee but also committed the cardinal sin of blowing his own personal trumpet, eclipsing Emjee from the word go. It was a near fatal mistake from which conflict was only just averted by the arrival of our visiting permits as dusk was falling and all seemed lost forever. The permits were a quality of mercy that dropped into our midst as the gentle rain from heaven.

We were cleared to return to the guesthouse, to dodge any bears that might be lurking around the driveway on our way and to have dinner. The dinner came a little later than was desirable but was worth it when it came: okra, *dall*, chicken stew, and rice and *roti naan* again.

It was unfortunate that I did not enjoy a good night. There was an overpowering smell of paint in the air for one thing. The bed felt uncomfortable, which it was, and unclean, although it probably wasn't. The long night was, however, pleasantly offset by the cool of dawn, in which the hills looked clear and crisp against a lightening sky.

AFTER BREAKFAST EMJEE and I set off in the Ambassador to visit the Panchpatmali mine. The excellent access road wound along the wall of the plateau, taking advantage of ridges and gullies, in a steady climb of some fourteen kilometres. The views over the rolling blue expanse of the Eastern Ghats were spectacular. A precipitous drop always lay on one side or the other of the road right up to the final cutting leading to the mine offices at the summit.

The top of Panchpatmali was twenty kilometres long and averaged eight hundred metres wide. It made a sitting target for sun and monsoon alike and hosted a genuine world-class bauxite resource. The bauxite was mined at an annual rate of about 2.4 million tons, which meant, on the assumption that the resource estimates were correct, that mine life was good for a few years yet.

We were shown around the mining operations by Ceejay, the mine manager. He was an affable gentleman of few words, which made a pleasant change. He knew Emjee and seemed happy to let him make the running. During the visit, Ceejay took us to the bauxite production benches, to some mined-out areas under rehabilitation via revegetation and to the primary crusher alongside the head sheave of that very grand cable belt conveyor down to the refinery. I thought it all looked fairly reasonable at face value, and what I saw of the infrastructure certainly compared favourably with one specific Company bauxite mine that I knew.

It was interesting to note the extensive planting of trees that was being carried out within the scope of the land rehabilitation process on top of Panchpatmali – interesting because trees were not otherwise an original feature anywhere on that over-exposed plateau. Perhaps Nalco knew something that nature didn't.

However, safety considerations, irrespective of potential hazards, were no better for labourers on Panchpatmali than they had been at the port down in Vizag. The labourers were men, women and – as if it weren't bad enough that there were women – also children. The women clutched ragged saris about their persons to try to prevent stray ends getting caught up in static or mobile machinery. Children wielded shovels and carried rocks. I realised why the taking of photographs was prohibited by management.

I wondered, not for the first time, if there could ever be a more inappropriate garment than a sari for a woman to wear when she was about her everyday activities, let alone when undertaking heavy industrial labour. Local colour aside, a sari seemed to me to be a garment designed by men solely to bind a woman into a place of submission.

I FELT, AT the risk of offending our hosts, that I had to question a corporate philosophy under which labourers were required to work in highly dangerous conditions in the absence of a single shred of protective gear. The discussion with Ceejay and Emjee that followed the question was extremely clinical and very matter-of-fact. The labourers that I had seen were unskilled workers, I was told; and in any case, virtually all of them worked for contractors and were therefore the contractors' responsibility. So that was all right then. Additionally I learned that most of the labourers were the so-called tribals who didn't know any better. I didn't hear any qualification that they were non-persons but don't doubt that I could have winkled that out had I persisted.

I then asked how this situation could be held to be compatible with the much-vaunted ISO 9002 certification? Well, of course, since the labourers didn't work directly for Nalco they weren't part of the audit that led to the certification, which had focused more on the ever-ready availability of Nalco's operating procedures manuals. It was clearly all a matter of priorities. The clinching argument that placed my concerns in perspective pointed out that twenty years ago, industrial safety standards in Europe were rather slack. Following that riposte, my head might have been bloody, but it was unbowed.

An afternoon tour of the refinery complex down at the other end of the belt conveyor didn't shape up as a thrill in prospect, although it did appear to contain the potential to complete a rounded picture of what Nalco was all about, inclusive of the Vizag port and the mining operations up on Panchpatmali. We were shown around by Sanjit, who bore the grand title of plant manager.

We had a look at the red mud disposal area over to the west of the refinery. This unctuous waste product of the refining process, consisting of the portion of the raw bauxite that was not alumina (rather a lot of it really), was impounded behind the most enormous rock-faced dam that it had ever been my fortune to encounter.

On returning to the refinery offices from this masterpiece of engineering in the fervent hope that it was not going to collapse and release its red flood on the district, at least while I stood in its shadow, we were given an overhead slide-assisted talk on the refinery process by the selfsame deputy GM we met on the previous day, although I still couldn't remember his name. I also can't remember if I was successful in fighting off an urge to fall asleep during his discourse, probably because I wasn't.

We then moved on with Sanjit to have a look at some of the sectors of the refinery that the deputy GM's presentation had endeavoured in vain to inform me about. These sectors included (I wrote their names down in a notebook as we saw them, wondering why I hadn't done the same for the deputy GM's name) the bauxite discharge; the stacker and stockpile area; the great ball mills in which the bauxite was reduced to slurry; the solution and precipitation tanks; and the alumina filters.

Directly underneath the rapidly spinning ball mills, their unprotected heads scant centimetres away from the blur of blunt instruments that were the protruding ends of the huge mill liner bolts, barefoot men and women fought to control spillage using either worn-out shovels or their hands. To judge from the stalagmitic accumulations of muck that surrounded them, their battle was far from being won.

I asked about the refinery's safety record, assuming that there was one. Some South African mines recorded "fatality-free" rather than "accident-free" days, and I felt that the former might be applicable to the operations around Damanjodi. I would have been surprised if the number of days for either of the two eventualities had ever risen to double figures.

I was told, well, the record wasn't good, particularly when it was applied to those who had "no safety sense". The implication was that tribals fell into that category, although since I had already learned that tribals didn't count it might have been churlish for me to suggest that some form of instruction aimed at helping them to appreciate the hazards of their work might have been in order.

ON THE WAY back to the guesthouse Emjee and I made a short diversion to have a look at a Hindu temple standing alone on a nearby hill. The temple's marble walls seemed to light up the encroaching forest that surrounded them. I was met with great enthusiasm by the temple's attendants and was led into the precincts, minus my shoes and socks, for an anointing with yet another red spot and the added bonus of a small portion of banana and some sweet rice pods to eat as part of the ceremony. I couldn't imagine such a classy style of welcome taking place at any Christian church.

It was a working temple and its exterior grounds were replete with a sufficiency of working beggars, lank-haired hangers-on and wild-eyed aesthetes. A beggar with legs withered to stubs clawed what was left of him along the ground in my direction. His arms were muscular, and his torso would have suited a weight lifter. A desperately wizened woman, who, in the manner of the filthy rags she was draped in, could have been of any age, shuffled along behind him. Her right arm was thickly wrapped about with a grimy bandage through which blots of something unpleasantly yellow seemed to be seeping.

I gave them both some money, for which act I was severely admonished by Emjee, perhaps with justification. The alacrity with which every other beggar in sight made a sudden beeline for me was remarkable and at the same time rather scary. I moved away from this posse of the halt and the lame with as much despatch overlain with decorum as I could.

A vendor of pressed sugar-cane beverages, prepared while-u-wait, then stood in my path and told me that he was about to make a drink for me. I declined his offer very politely. His portable drink-making unit had a lack of salubriousness written across it in letters of fire. However, he would not be deterred and grabbed my arm to draw me towards the side of his apparatus, which consisted principally of a handle-operated roller press into which stalks of raw sugar cane were fed for the liquor to be crushed out of them. The liquor dribbled from the press and trickled down along a metal slide from which it was funnelled into a receptacle over a filter cloth that looked as if it had been torn from the garments of the poor woman I had so recently met up with.

The vendor thrust the ends of a couple of long sugar-cane stalks in between the rollers and began cranking the handle to feed them through before I had time to hesitate any further. The two stalks were induced to pass the roller press a few times, doubled over after each transit so that ultimately they were reduced down to a fibrous wad and all the contained juice was collected in the cloth-covered receptacle. For the penultimate and ultimate pressings a chunk of ginger and half a lime were introduced to the equation.

My eager benefactor reached into a cavity beneath the press and produced a large glass tumbler. He dipped the tumbler into a bucket of opaque water and, with a swirl that was almost triumphal, considered the glass washed in accordance with the exacting standards of his trade. He filled the tumbler with the sugar-cane extract from the receptacle and handed it to me for my delectation.

I held the drink in my hand and looked at it in the fading light while contemplating whether to do the sensible thing or to do what was right under the circumstances. I chose to follow the latter course of action and drank down the draught, thinking that if it were done when 'tis done, then 'twere well it were done quickly, and hoping that I was not once again commending the ingredients of a poison'd chalice to my own lips.

The flavour was quite delicious. Although I might well regret it later, I didn't regret it at all then.

Dinner at the guesthouse that night seemed to have slid downhill as far as its chief characteristics were concerned. It was a vegetarian affair of *dall*, vegetables and fried *roti*. Perhaps the regular chef had gone home.

I went to bed in the committed belief that there was a time bomb ticking in my bowels, ready to explode at an inopportune moment. That it didn't was the result of pure luck. The temple gods must have smiled on me, encouraged by the alms I bestowed on the beggars.

For the following morning I ordered early morning tea but got coffee. On the other hand, when I saw both tea and coffee standing in cups side by side they looked and smelled about the same, so I supposed I should have felt good about it.

I thought I would be adventurous at breakfast and go for a poached egg, as last night's *roti* was a presence that had yet to leave me. Two eggs were put in front of me, both fried. It was clearly time for the dust of Damanjodi to be shaken from our feet and for us to continue onwards to Rayagada and Ellentee.

Rayagada was separated from Damanjodi by a hundred and twenty-five kilometres of circuitous road that twisted south to Similigurha (fifteen kilometres), northwest from Similgurha to Koraput (twenty-five kilometres), and finally northeast from Koraput to Rayagada (eighty-five kilometres).

The road unwound through rolling hills, dry fields and patches of forest. Mango trees were plentiful and already flowering profusely. There were glimpses on the side of three more bauxite-capped plateaux named Kakirigoma, Karikuma and Kurangumali. Emjee needed no invitation to hold forth on their prospective merits, although all of them could have fitted into a single lobe of Panchpatmali and left room to spare.

The countryside that surrounded the road appeared to be well tended and populated almost exclusively by the ubiquitous tribals. The tribals may not have known a lot about industrial safety but they were obviously dab hands at agriculture and could, I thought, have taught Nalco a thing or two about care for the local environment. They were not particularly attractive-looking people, although that was a sentiment that no doubt rested purely in the eye of the beholder. It may have been the thick gold rings hanging from the septa of too many tribal noses that didn't do it for me in the appeal stakes.

We stopped for tea at a place named Laksmi, taking advantage of a roadside teashop that catered for the truck-driving trade. The tea was as excellent as ever. A line of blackened pots over a roaring open fire cast an odour of magically spiced dishes into the tearoom. The chef was an elderly wizened man clad in a tee shirt that might once have known days when it had a legible identity and a piece of threadbare cloth posing as a sarong that could easily have been as old as he was. He invited me to sample the food – wonderful concoctions of tomatoes, *dall* and, rather unusually, cabbage. I would have been happy taking a meal in a place like that.

RAYAGADA WAS A widely sprawling collection of crumbling buildings and fetid streets lined with vital shop fronts and choked with people shuffling to nowhere as aimlessly as they could. Its alleged population was around a hundred thousand, and most of them seemed to be out and about in the streets to greet us when we arrived. To judge from the number of dazzlingly colourful processions preceded by bands of musicians specialising in cacophony that thrust their way through the throng looking like crocodiles invading a reedy swamp, the wedding season was running in full spate.

A dust-ridden mass of humanity crowded on and around a shiny mesh of railway tracks and the main road route through Rayagada, which were more or less one and the same thing. Trains festooned with hangers-on and flanked by brightly decorated freight trucks clanked through the hymenopterous throng of pedestrians. Gaunt cattle were so adept at getting in the way of vehicle transport that there must have been a conspiracy at work.

The Ellentee guesthouse where we were to reside was less easy to find than I hoped the Ellentee bauxite project was going to be. We located the guesthouse, with the helpful advice of two or three shopkeepers, up along one narrow side road and then into another, branching to the left while skirting an open sewer. The guesthouse was a grimy yellow block set a short distance in on the right, across the sewer behind an impressive fence of wrought iron.

Any expectations of what might be found inside the guesthouse were not high, but once I entered I saw that it was both clean (a word that until then I believed I would never use in the same context as Rayagada) and comfortable. The stairway and balustrade up to the first floor, where the guest rooms were located around a central lounge cum dining area, was constructed of cool white marble, as was the footing of the first floor itself. The quality of the guest rooms and their internal appointments was groping in the direction of Taj Residency standards. From that first impression, memories of the guesthouse at Damanjodi were shouldered to one side.

As we deposited our suitcases in the rooms allotted to us, another wedding procession made its blaring way down the street outside. I wished the bride and groom well in my heart and hoped that they managed to negotiate the sewer without incident.

Teekay, Ellentee's Rayagada-based project manager, arrived at the guesthouse to greet us. He was accompanied by Jeekay, his mining engineer. Put together, the two names suggested a comic double act.

Teekay was short and square of body. The bluntness of his shoulders was offset by the sharpness of a face from which his nose was a projectile in waiting. A quiff of black hair drifted across his forehead in the manner of an approaching monsoon. One of Teekay's eyes had a mild cast that gave him a slightly crazed look. If he was perhaps a little too deferential towards Emjee and me to start with, his manner was pleasantly open. It seemed that we became old friends in an instant.

By contrast, Jeekay was young, lithe and exceedingly handsome. It was tempting to contemplate that he had film star looks, although, to judge from that multiplicity of posters advertising local cinema attractions that were not only a ubiquitous but also an unavoidable feature of my travels in India to date, genuine Bollywood heroes tended to be overweight, greasy, and fitted with the kind of faces that you didn't want to come across in a dim street late at night. On the other hand they probably looked their best in the dark. I imagined that Bollywood heroes were sprinkled with a seasoning of repellence in order to present heroines in their most attractive light.

We partook of lunch with Teekay and Jeekay in the guesthouse. It was excellent fare prepared by Hemant, the splendidly jovial custodian of the guesthouse. The menu, comprising *dall*, chicken, vegetables and *roti*, was fast becoming standard fare.

After lunch we all travelled over to the Ellentee offices in Rayagada, in which we were fortunate to be guided by Teekay, since we would never have discovered our own way through the maze of festering streets between it and the guesthouse. The offices were located in a building faced with crumbling concrete and backing onto a large barn sheeted over with corrugated metal. Inside the barn were stored the two tractor-mounted sampling drills that Ellentee used in the pursuit of its bauxite exploration programme, together with an accumulated and exquisitely inventoried mass of remnant samples taken and prepared from the drill-hole cuttings. Retention of the sample remnants allowed the sampling results to be recreated in terms of value and location, making a hugely valuable record for the advantage of an investor.

Our first action was to inspect the barn and its contents and to be suitably impressed by the same. We then moved to the office block where Teekay made a presentation on the bauxite exploration programme over Kutrumali and Sijimali, the two plateaux outside Rayagada for which Ellentee owned the state concessions. It was alleged that Ellentee's work had demonstrated bauxite resources of hundreds of millions of cumulative tons on Kutrumali and Sijimali. A mining feasibility study, of sorts, had already been carried out. There were plans drawn up for a mine, a refinery, a dedicated town site, a railway branch line, red mud lakes and a dam on a local river to ensure a sufficiency of water supply. So, apart from the fact that exploration activity was suspended for the time being owing to lack of funds to take it any further (and hence Ellentee's increasingly desperate quest for a participatory partner), it was all go really.

Before proceeding any further, it seemed that it might be worth the effort to make sure that Kutrumali and Sijimali actually existed. To that end Emjee, Teekay, Jeekay and I were driven forty-five kilometres out to the north of Rayagada in two vehicles, one being the Ambassador, to have a perceptive look.

Not far from Rayagada we drove through a company-owned town named Jaykaypur, which from its appearance and not least its appalling smell, was devoted to the production of paper pulp while at the same time being opposed to the well-being of those unfortunate enough to live in and around it. It needed just one glance at Jaykaypur to convince me that in India further industrial disasters of the Bhophal type were not only likely, they were inevitable.

The site of Ellentee's proposed refinery, from which a distant view of Kutrumali's bauxite-topped, table-like summit was possible, was set squarely in very well cared for tribal land close to a neat little tribal village named Kalyansingaparam. In order for Ellentee (and any future partner) to construct a refinery, some fifteen hundred tribal families would need to be relocated. It seemed to me that this presented what might be a near fatal flaw for the project. But no, it wasn't that way at all, Teekay told me: the tribals were all on Ellentee's side and, moreover, had been fully briefed on their impending relocation.

I didn't want to disbelieve Teekay, but as I had also heard that there were tigers and leopards living up on the Kutrumali plateau I assumed that, faced with such predators, all pigs in the vicinity had learned to fly. All the same, Teekay and his team had done a commendable job and, on the face of it, could well have managed to develop a social policy that Nalco might have learned something from and that the lords of Jaykay-pur could only dream about. I didn't want to be cynical of course.

That night we all met in the Ellentee guesthouse once more, this time for dinner. Teekay and Jeekay arrived much later than planned. Hemant finally served dinner at 9.40 p.m., by which time I was so agitated over the distant culinary prospect that I was starting to believe that food in any form might never appear at all.

Teekay gave me some very useful written information on the Ellen-tee project bauxite resources in the privacy of my room and asked me to handle it with discretion and not let Emjee know that I had it. Teekay knew a lot more about Emjee's habits than I did, although I was rapidly learning, and so I could respect the request.

ON THE FOLLOWING morning I got up at 5.15 a.m., precisely as "bed tea" was delivered to my bedside by Hemant. After I had drunk the tea, or rather poured it away as it was so ferociously tart, I thought I would step out into the pre-dawn streets of Rayagada and take a short walk in the anticipation that the numbers of people about at that hour might not be quite so overwhelming as they would be later on. Those people who were in evidence – and there were already a lot more than a few of them – were mostly huddled in and around doorways looking like bundles of sinister rags.

An impression of my having wandered onto the set of a cheesy Hammer horror film was suddenly compounded by the appearance of a file of chanting women led by two shaven priests, one of whom was beating a drum in time with the chant while the other clutched a bell-like instrument that he clanged in a random manner. The procession had an intense poverty and a crazed religious fundamentalism written across it in equal measures. It tramped by me close enough to curdle my blood. Charles Dickens' Fat Boy would have admired its ability to make flesh creep. My hair stood on end. I watched the file go and hurried back to the guesthouse.

Now THAT WE had viewed the rim of the Kutrumali plateau from a distance, it behoved us to make some kind of effort to drive in and actually set foot on it. That would at least ensure that what we saw from the refinery site was not just a haze-induced mirage. Unfortunately, Teekay advised, the intervention of a couple of monsoons in the period since the cessation of formal exploration activity on the heights of the plateau had not improved the quality of a bulldozed access road that had never been particularly good, even when it was first put in.

Since driving was out of the question, walking in to Kutrumali had to be the order of the day. An expedition was planned. Accordingly, Teekay, Jeekay, Emjee and I (and a not insignificant number of assistants) jammed ourselves as best we could into two jeep-like vehicles, both of which were the property of Ellentee. Thus equipped, we set off for Ellentee's mothballed exploration camp at a locality named Sunger, well outside Rayagada and set more or less equidistantly from Kutrumali and Sijimali.

On the way out of Rayagada, two more jeeps joined our convoy. These were crammed with policemen, at least twenty altogether. All were armed with rifles. A sprinkling of relatively high-ranking officers was included among the squad for good measure. The rifles were of post-Indian Mutiny issue, perhaps by not too many years. They did, however, look a little too effective to me, and I would have preferred that the policemen had stuck to chasing Naxalites rather than drawing attention to our expedition through such an obviously high profile.

The policemen were coming along, Teekay announced, to guard and protect us against any dissident tribal elements that might object to our crossing their land. It was not, he hastened to add, that the tribals were anything but friendly to Ellentee's interests. However, I supposed there could, as Jack Hawkins put it so succinctly in *The Bridge on the River Kwai*, always be the unexpected to contend with.

343

WE FIRST TOOK the road to Koraput and branched off to the right about twenty kilometres out of Rayagada to head the thirty kilometres or so north to Sunger. Our combined party, as it advanced along the road to Sunger, was quite large enough to kick off a local war and, at a pinch, to stand off a siege of the Sunger camp should that prove necessary. Teekay said that the Sunger road was going to be a bad one to travel along, although the degree of badness I thought depended entirely on the relative standards that it was judged against. By the time we arrived at Sunger, my opinion of the narrow strip of road we had come along was that its surface could have been a lot worse.

Along much of its length the road was under steady repair by team-like bands of tribals. Each band might well have been family specific. The men shovelled dirt, and the women loaded and hauled the dirt away in dish-shaped wicker baskets borne on their heads. Each band appeared to be responsible for keeping a couple of kilometres of road in passable order.

The extent of manual labour involved in road reparation was impressive. At intervals along the verges neatly squared-off piles of meticulously sized pieces of road stone sat like graves of lost hope, interspersed with tightly deposited banks of crumbling brown laterite. The rock-breaking experts looked to be all children.

Road building was an art form. The hand-sorted chunks of road stone were laid down and fitted individually into a firm mosaic. The edges of the mosaic were lined with laterite, which was then tamped down into a solid frame pounded into submission by the whole band acting in rhythmic concert with long, flat-ended logs. The final touch was to place a thin layer of laterite on the surface of the newly created road stone mosaic and to beat the laterite into the interstices to guarantee a totally locked system with an integrity that would hold at least until the next monsoon came along.

THE ROAD INTO Sunger twisted and turned through a rolling terrain of open valleys and smooth-topped hills. The valley bottoms were covered with rice paddies, and although the season was dry, the few paddies that counted on irrigation looked fresh and green under a growing crop. It struck me that the very best direction for foreign aid into India to take would be to promote the development of irrigation systems in rural areas.

The Sunger exploration camp lay in a slight depression alongside the road, flanked all around by rounded hills. It was enclosed within a tall wire mesh fence capped by razor wire. The entry gate was just wide enough for a single jeep to slip through and hopefully avoid getting its doors scraped *en route*. The camp was established in the form of a large U-shaped conglomeration of corrugated metal-clad quarters surrounding a central square that featured a couple of strategically placed mango trees and a neatly tended garden characterised by hibiscus and roses.

The expedition's convoy having entered the confines of the camp, the party piled out and milled around for a moment, waiting for someone to take charge. The contingent of policemen, who were clearly at Sunger not for the first time, gravitated in the direction of what turned out to be the section of the corrugated metal-sheeted edifice in which the camp cook plied his trade. The policemen were an active refutation of the understanding that there was no such thing as a free lunch.

On close inspection, whatever lay behind the metal sheeting all around the camp's internal perimeter appeared to be much more significantly ventilated than one might have expected it to be. Windows were minus most of their glass, and the metal sheets forming the walls and doors were decorated with so many gashes, obviously made forcibly, that it was impossible to count them.

I enquired as to the intent behind this disfigurement and was told, not without some reluctance to tell me on the part of the teller, that an NGO-instigated mob of tribals had undertaken a night-time rampage against the Sunger camp, and presumably whatever the camp stood for, while employing a range of bladed instruments with which they could make their feelings known. Looking at the damage, I had a feeling that great rage had had a hand in there somewhere. There was some consolation in learning that property and not people had been the object of the rage. They didn't touch the mango trees or the roses, and that had to count for quite a lot.

The attack did not correspond at all with an allegedly willing relocation of fifteen hundred tribal families from the vicinity of Ellentee's proposed refinery site. Moving that many people was likely to be an uphill battle that I wouldn't have wanted any part in. My perception of the extent of tribal delight with Ellentee's ambitions was growing more muted by the hour. However, the inclusion of the small army of policemen in our expedition to Kutrumali suddenly began to make some sense.

Fortified with tea, the invading tribals having spared enough of the camp crockery for that key purpose to be inviolate, the expedition set off once more. In the case of the policemen some comestibles were consumed along with the tea. Where food was concerned, the policemen demonstrated that the availability of crockery was a non-essential.

We drove a short distance back along the road in the direction of Rayagada before moving off to the left along a track that ended in the heart of a small village named Mandidisi, tight to the edge of a rocky-floored river crossing. On the far side of the river was the pathway we were to take in order to walk in to the Kutrumali plateau.

A few policemen approached Teekay at Mandidisi to complain that they had not received their fair share of food back at Sunger. There was a slight delay while Teekay tried in vain to placate them. Only the eventual tabling of a hearty lunch was going to do that I thought. The expedition was turning into even more of a circus than it had seemed to be at the outset.

We eventually started walking, about thirty of us altogether, a late lunch having been promised at Sunger on our return. We made our way down through Mandidisi's mean single street, which was coated with a thick deposit of cow shit stamped smooth. We stumbled across the river, stepping from rock to rock to avoid wet feet, mostly successfully, and took the pathway up the hill and so to parts beyond.

Kutrumali was approximately ten kilometres distant from Mandidisi. Emjee dropped out prior to the completion of the first kilometre, a victim to the heat of the day and that lack of resolve which was a not infrequent associate of obesity. The pathway was rubbly and uneven, rising and falling with the terrain, although it managed to avoid any significantly steep gradients until we arrived under the shadow of Kutrumali.

We crossed hard rolling hills and slipped along valleys floored with terraced rice paddies and hemmed about with massive mango trees. On the way, the party began to string itself out as more and more of its members, chiefly numbered among the higher-ranking members of the police presence, fell like Emjee by the wayside.

At the foot of Kutrumali those who were still part of the expedition consisted of Jeekay, Teekay (by that time one of the walking wounded but to his credit unwilling to throw in the towel just yet) and six policemen, all constables. Three of the six policemen balked at the thought of ascending the long and powerfully steep slope of the Kutrumali plateau. They decided to wait in the shade of a mango tree near a compact tribal village for the return of those of us who took on the ascent of Kutrumali.

As we approached the tribal village a horde of villagers surged out. I hoped that their intention was to greet us, but since they surged as quickly back again when they saw that policemen were among our company, I was destined never to know for sure.

The three remaining policemen stuck with me. We forged on up the gradient and reached the flat summit of Kutrumali well ahead of Teekay and Jeekay. Our arrival point was on a heavily forested western lobe of the plateau. We emerged from the trees into open, short-turfed plateau grassland. An eagle slid by overhead, and the air was full of the song of larks.

Teekay and Jeekay eventually joined us. We were a final group of six out of the original thirty. I thought the occasion called for the planting of a flag but had to settle for a look at an exploration pit dug by Ellentee to expose the full section of residual bauxite, which was twenty-nine metres thick at that point. We additionally managed to get a good view of the Sijimali plateau, separated from Kutrumali by a very broad and very deep declivity floored by rice paddies.

HAVING ESTABLISHED THE existence of bauxite on Kutrumali, it was time to make our return journey to Mandidisi. Teekay was by then having a lot of trouble with his right foot. He made a slow and painful descent from the plateau to where the three police constables were continuing to take their ease under the mango tree of their choice.

We were a flagging procession drawn out over several kilometres, an ignominious retreat in all but name. I was the first to reach the four parked vehicles at Mandidisi. The rest of the party came in, either limping or staggering, at intervals over the succeeding hour. My legs were trembling and my feet ached, but otherwise I was in better shape than many of the others.

It seemed a reasonable supposition that all members of the Kutrumali expedition were pleased to return to Sunger camp. In our absence, Hemant had come up from Rayagada in a fifth vehicle and had clearly been busy preparing the kind of meal that the policemen were so eager to partake of, consisting of stringy local chicken, rice, *dall* and *roti*. The police had done their duty as they saw it, and since the expedition hadn't been subjected to a single assault by agitated tribals, I had to concede that they had done their duty as I saw it as well.

We returned to Rayagada at 6.15 p.m. Teekay and Jeekay recovered enough from the exigencies of the day to come along to the guesthouse for dinner again, and Hemant was on his best form in serving up *brinjals*, fried green vegetables, stewed chicken, tandoori chicken and *roti*.

My final thought on retiring for the night was that I needed to get some laundry done tomorrow – or perhaps today, as it was late enough at the time.

By 6.45 AM on the next day, at which hour Emjee and I left Rayagada in the Ambassador bound for Bhubaneswar, the principal city of Orissa State, the streets of Rayagada were assuming life. Itinerant cows and buffalo were on the move, rickshaws were out hunting for marks on their way to work. Teekay came along to say goodbye, and told me that he normally jogged through the streets of Rayagada before the sun came up. He was a better man than I was. I hoped that the road would always rise to meet him.

The Ambassador followed a winding route that on the average headed due west from Rayagada and on over the lip of the Eastern Ghats. It was a narrow strip of much patched road threading its way through a seemingly continuous gauntlet of road repair bands, most members of which were fully involved as part and parcel of the universal game of near misses.

We stopped on the face of the Ghats to take tea at Toptapani, a small collection of shops seemingly built of, and certainly selling, mud culled from a sulphurous hot spring that they surrounded.

Beyond that, on the coastal side of the plain at the town of Brahmapur, made memorable for its crowds and not much else unless it was the lunch we took at a truck stop restaurant on the northern edge of the town, we turned northeast along the main road to Bhubaneswar, our final destination in Orissa prior to shipping out by air to Delhi.

Not the least virtue of the lunch, a wonderful chicken curry served with red pepper and ginger pickles, was to take my mind off the prospect of Bhubaneswar airport where, when the time came, an aircraft of Indian Airlines would be waiting in undoubted decrepitude for my reluctant feet to board it.

– 10 –

A Rendition of Feelings

There's a rickety rackety guesthouse to the north of Ho Chi Minh,
  There's an unexploded bomb above the door.
There's a broken tap, cold dripping on the side as you come in,
  There's karaoke on the upper floor.

There's coffee on the hills, roots set in bauxite 'neath the soil,
  There's a pre-dawn wakeup mandate, blasting song.
There's the flow of turgid rivers through the fields of loving toil,
  There's a cheerful little town they call Dac Nong.

There's a sawmill, scented lumber, creamy sawdust, fragrant day,
  There's a restaurant upon a dusty street.
There's a will to set aside that once there was the USA,
  There's a nation that will never know defeat.

With apologies to Mr J. Milton Hayes

THE COUNTRY THAT I was going to was named Vietnam.
Vietnam was, for me, to borrow an expression applied by Mr Neville Chamberlain to another situation in another place in another age, a far-away country with a people about whom I knew nothing. Fortunately I had none of Neville's cited quarrel with any of those people, and although some contextual involvement with digging trenches in Vietnam could be anticipated as being consistent with my job, trying on a gas mask as Neville did was likely to be no more than a remote possibility. It was peace for my time.

As a name, Vietnam was unreservedly iconic. It evoked a kaleido-scopic range of images distorted as much by the shimmering heat of wars past as by the base fog of associated propaganda past and present.

My state of ignorance concerning the country could be easily cor-rected, but in order to ensure that the remedial process was sound, I first of all had to place my feet on Vietnam's well-tested soil.

THE FIRST STAGE of the journey to Vietnam took me on a non-stop flight in a Cathay Pacific aircraft from London's Heathrow airport to Hong Kong. The route taken by the aircraft cut a southeast diagonal over Europe, bent more or less to the left when it reached Turkey and then bore directly towards Hong Kong over parts of Iran, Pakistan, northern India, the Himalayas and a whole swatch of China.

The scheduled flying time from London to Hong Kong was eleven hours and forty-two minutes. It was announced as such prior to the departure of the aircraft from Heathrow airport. I wondered for a while how on earth the amount of time that it took to go half way around the world could be so precisely determined when there was so much in terms of weather, headwinds, congested skies (and a number of other eventualities that it was best not to dwell on) that could get in the way.

It then occurred to me that the estimating technique employed by flight planners had much in common with the methods applied by those of us who estimated ore reserves. In both cases, faced with a vir-tual minefield of potential hazards, we balanced the evidence against the risks and gave it our best professional assessment prior to placing our necks and reputations on the line. All the same, the announce-ment of the flight time would have resounded much more credibly in my ears if the captain had rounded it off and quoted it as being about twelve hours. The best estimates always had to contain some room for manoeuvre.

Thoughts of the unexpected engaged my mind with some urgency as the aircraft made its final approach into the airport at Hong Kong. By then I had given up worrying about just how long the flight would last. Half a day in the air had been quite long enough.

We dropped towards Hong Kong in one of those alarmingly fast approaches that seemed destined to be aborted. Low clouds drifted like grey shrouds over the dark sea beneath. Glimpsed through a window on the right-hand side of the cabin, the early evening streets of the city of Hong Kong were neon-crusted canyons flicking by like the spokes on a bicycle wheel in a beam of light.

To encourage the passengers, immediately following the touch-down the captain announced that a sudden deterioration in the local weather, incorporating an abrupt reversal of wind direction, had forced him to make a tail wind-driven landing. As if to confirm these glad tidings, rain commenced pounding the by then thankfully landed aircraft so aggressively that it endorsed the sense of weather that really didn't welcome our presence.

The aircraft taxied on a long, slow and winding way through crowds of parked up counterparts. Perhaps the captain was hunting for a space large enough to stop in, as the route of the wandering aircraft felt as if it was being made completely at random. Maybe a good ramble was a Chinese tradition to celebrate an unpropitious arrival.

The quest for a parking bay eventually paid off. We passengers then waited for a patience-straining extended interval for permission to disembark, during which time the airport authorities must have been anxiously seeking the availability of a bus capable of fighting its way to us through the continuingly dense downpour.

THE METEOROLOGICAL INCLEMENCY ensured that my connecting flight (number VN 793 of Vietnam Airlines) from Hong Kong to Hanoi in Vietnam was the subject of yet another of the "late arrival of incoming aircraft" announcements so beloved of those who were charged with devising excuses for flight delays. However, where flying was concerned I always believed in the maxim of being better late than never. Arriving was always to be preferred to travelling.

Flight VN 793 was a happy revelation. The aircraft was a brand new Airbus A320, sparklingly clean and blessed with a supremely welcoming cabin crew clad in distinctive pink uniforms.

It took about an hour to fly to Hanoi from Hong Kong. The service in the cabin was impeccable. An excellent dinner was provided, offering a choice of a fish and rice dish or beef noodles. I selected the former and was delighted with what I got.

As we approached Hanoi the passenger seated next to me, who from his features appeared to be of Chinese extraction, looked through the side window and exclaimed, "It's raining in Hanoi!" This observation was something of an exaggeration, but I could forgive him for it. He sounded too excited to be worried by the prospect of later disappointment. Most of the rain in the region of Hanoi must have gone up to Hong Kong for the day, as all that was left of rain in the surrounds of Hanoi when we disembarked was a light sifting drizzle.

Hanoi customs and immigration officials were courteous, correct and very efficient. Their counterparts at entry ports to the USA could have benefited greatly by learning from them exactly how arriving passengers should be properly treated. On the other hand, the USA had already been taught a fair amount from prior associations with certain Vietnamese agencies, even if along the way its presidents seemed to have learned little from the experience.

ANOTHER GENTLEMAN WITH oriental features, a Vietnamese on this occasion, was waiting for me at the exit of the airport terminal. I was attracted to his vicinity by virtue of a rectangle of white board he was holding up with my name written out on it in black marker. Well met, he led me to a vehicle parked not too far away. The vehicle was one of Daewoo's more upmarket models. In it, he drove me into Hanoi to the Daewoo Hotel – same manufacturer, same class – where I was to stay. The dark of night, the lightly falling mist and my being tired out by flying to the point of perplexity all combined to provide me with no impression whatsoever of what the part of the city of Hanoi that we drove through looked like.

In the foyer of the Daewoo hotel, which was such a luxurious and modern-looking establishment and blessed by so much inherent local character and the grace of a friendly welcome that even with a large measure of disorientation I knew I was not in London, Mr Yi, the manager of the Daewoo organisation in Vietnam, was waiting for me.

There seemed to be an awful lot of Daewoo in the air.

DAEWOO WAS IN fact the essential motivator for my visit to Vietnam. Although that Seoul-based South Korean outfit was best known as a manufacturer of automobiles and electronic goods, diversification into pretty much any other area of industry, heavy or light, was not ruled out by its directors if a good deal could be made along the way. Uncle Joe tried out the same thing once upon a time. Forestry, fishing, hotels (clearly) and mining (where the Absolutely mandate brought me in) were all grist to the Daewoo mill.

Yi was of Korean (South presumably) nationality, a Daewoo man to the centre of his being, short, plump and full of drive and bustle. He was a man with a mission and inscrutable with it, and he was to be my guide and associate in Vietnam. He had my visit programme planned down to a fine art. A short while in Yi's company, even late at night after a long plane journey, made the all-conquering worldwide spread of South Korean industrial endeavour seem entirely logical.

According to Yi, "Daewoo" translated into English as "Great Universe". Modesty was clearly not part of the relevant corporate vision. The Daewoo office building, in which Yi held court with me on the following day, was situated only a short walk away from the hotel across an open courtyard. The building was so festooned both internally and externally with the corporate logo as to suggest all the obsession of a love affair.

The logo was even pressed into the surface of the fine white sand-filled receptacles adjacent to the lift doors, inviting the attention of anyone brave enough to disfigure it with a cigarette butt. No corner inside the Daewoo office building was so remote that it wasn't commanded by the benevolent yet imperial big brother scrutiny radiating from at least one of an all too prolific distribution of hanging portraits of the president of the Great Universe.

Outside of its hotel and car sales business in Vietnam, Daewoo had made a specific diversification into the country's slowly germinating mining industry, allegedly involving an exclusive deal with the Vietnamese government. The terms of the deal had many of the hallmarks of a sprat used to catch a mackerel. It had quid pro quo written all over it.

For the government's part of the deal, Daewoo was required to explore and exploit a bauxite deposit near the town of Dac Nong, close to the national border with Laos in the Southern Vietnamese Highlands up to the north of Ho Chi Minh City.

For Daewoo, plans for expansions in its core business in Vietnam were sure to be favourably regarded by the government following a successful outcome to the Dac Nong bauxite project. Progress towards the outcome, however, was not yet as substantial as the government would have liked it to be. Daewoo just might have promised the government a little more than its embryonic technical understanding of the nuts and bolts of the mining industry would permit it to deliver.

Daewoo's principals were therefore worried. They wanted a partner with a main line of business in mining to assist them in making a professional evaluation of the bauxite project up at Dac Nong. The Company, all being well, was up for it as a realistic candidate to take up that partnership option. The task of making a field assessment of the bauxite project was allotted to me. Once it was done I was scheduled to head up to the distant north where the dusk went down like thunder out of China cross the bay, and there in the vastness of their Seoul redoubt to brief Yi's masters on the conclusions of the field visit.

FOLLOWING MY ARRIVAL at the Hanoi Daewoo hotel, I was tired enough to get some sleep in spite of jet lag, and woke to the sound of the alarm clock that I had set to go off at 6.40 a.m. The window of my room was at the front of the hotel, overlooking a number of boulevards radiating out from the hub of a great roundabout that already formed the eye to a vortex of swirling mopeds and bicycles that grew ever more dilated as I looked on. It was fascinating to watch the intricacy of patterns as the two wheelers converged from all directions and interwove in a multiplicity of barely avoided collisions.

The day outside was dry and even a little hazy after the drizzle of the night before. The city spread out like a low-slung drift of yellowing concrete presided over by the front of the hotel.

An English-language newssheet, headed "Vietnam News", was shoved into my room under the door. The second page carried a letter that was evidently written by an American resident down in Ho Chi Minh City. The letter contained words that read as a strong attack on the driving standards on Vietnam's roads. Its author compared local driving conditions with those back in the USA. I admired his nerve. He claimed that the streets of Ho Chi Minh City were safer during the infamous (my word, not his) war than they were at present. I wondered how he knew about that and how comfortable he might feel to be asked how he knew.

The Daewoo hotel was characterised by the highest of quality. For breakfast I took a thin, *bouillon*-like soup loaded with rice noodles and thin-cut beef strips. Finely chopped onions, tomatoes and fresh chillies were available for adding to the soup to suit individual taste. It made an excellent start to the day.

YI CAME ALONG at a pre-decreed hour of 8.35 a.m. to conduct me to the offices of the Vietnamese state mining corporation, more conveniently known as Vimico, for an introductory meeting. As far as the exploration and exploitation of bauxite went, Vimico handled matters for the government. The meeting agenda, Yi claimed, would take in some extended formal niceties and a general briefing from a Vimico senior geologist on the current status of the Dac Nong bauxite project.

Afterwards there would be an opportunity to review some relevant maps and documentation on the project. Knowledge of the Vietnamese language might well be an asset in this regard. That left me out in the cold right from the word đi.

We were driven to the Vimico office building in (*pause for fanfare*), a Daewoo car. The car threaded its way through what was to me an increasingly confusing maze taking in least ten kilometres of Hanoi's back streets. Fortunately, both Yi and the driver knew the way.

The successive thoroughfares that we passed through appeared to be in competition with one another as to which of them was able to line its edges with: the most roadside kiosks vending things to eat (among which comestibles noodle dishes and rainbow-like arrays of fruit took pride of place); the greatest abundance of bars specialising in the practice of karaoke; the most extended display of shop fronts; and the mightiest flood of bicycles that could fall just short of seizing up into a solid mass while carrying potential customers to the vendors. On the way, respite from the commercial tide came when we crossed a great river on a long bridge formed of steel girders on which rust, redolent of conflict, had long since assumed command.

The internal ambience of Vimico's offices was both hot and humid. This must have reflected the predilections of those who toiled within. As a consequence everything I touched felt rather damp. Even the pages of the few documents that I managed to lay my hands on seemed clammy. As was normal on so many similar occasions, a lot less information was made available, whether by accident or by design, than was desirable to the cause of gaining an enlightened understanding of the ins and outs of the project in focus. I was used to this state of affairs, and so it didn't bother me too much.

Any initial release of information to interested parties, particularly when state organisations were involved in releasing it, was usually very selective. It was necessary to work towards getting a look at the documents that mattered by building a relationship of trust with those who held them sacrosanct. The process took time – fair enough when time was available – but unfortunately there wasn't always enough of that commodity in hand to break down the invariable barriers of suspicion that marred the first occasion of asking.

We met with two Vimico officials in a well-appointed (if dank) meeting room. The senior of the two was either the Deputy Director or one of a lesser band of deputy directors. His slot on the organisation chart was not clarified. The other was a geologist named Cheung. Between us all there was sufficient linguistic common ground in both English and French to permit reasonable communication. To cap it all, and thereby ensure that no turn remained unstoned in plugging critical gaps, Yi brought along an official interpreter, a very pleasant Vietnamese girl whose command of English was better than mine.

Cheung was probably aged somewhere in his early forties, but he had the kind of thin, hungry and weather-beaten look that was timeless. His eyelids were so tightly pinched that they appeared to be as good as shut. I felt that living off the land would be instinctive to him. A handful of rice, and Cheung would march a trail all day.

Among the subjects that the discussions at the meeting dealt with were the Vietnam Mining Act where it touched on mining and exploration concessions; the geology and estimated Dac Nong project bauxite resources (allegedly tonnages of washed bauxite in nine figures – allowing for a desperately low percentage recovery from the raw bauxite in the ground); bauxite processing and pilot plant tests that had already been carried out by Hungarian agencies; and a summary of exploration and project evaluation results that seemed to have been derived not only by those same Hungarians but also by a Russian mission.

Both of the cited parties from behind the former iron curtain, Cheung told us, had held on to quite a lot of the results generated by their work, to the extent that no one at Vimico had much of an idea as to where those data were currently being held. A guess could be hazarded that either Moscow or Budapest would be not improbable locations. Whatever the event, the information was a long way out of reach for present purposes and therefore could be cheerfully not worried about for the time being.

Cheung said that the main bauxite deposit in the Dac Nong district, which we were to visit in the field, was named "First of May" or "First

May" or otherwise "1-5". The numerical title sounded too inspired by Western convention for my taste, and I resolved never to use it.

The formal proceedings of the meeting at Vimico lasted for almost exactly two hours. I assumed that this was Daewoo precision laid on by Yi.

Afterwards, Cheung told me that he had studied geology at a Russian university, from where he returned to Hanoi in 1973. At that time the war with America was still raging, although very much on the verge of moving towards the end game. Cheung's most vivid memories of the war were of Hanoi being bombed from the air. He said that the trauma of those days gave him cause for a while to think that North Vietnam might not win the war, but the moment passed, and he never doubted the inevitability of eventual victory again.

What impressed me most of all was the total lack of animosity towards Westerners that was demonstrated not only by Cheung but also by all the other Vietnamese, North and South, whom I met during my visit. The Vietnamese were a truly magnanimous people. The hospitality they showed me was exemplary. Any invader would have to be deluded if he thought that he could subdue a country blessed with a people replete with so much spirit.

WITH THE MEETING over, we all repaired to a Japanese buffet restaurant for lunch, offering grateful thanks to the Great Universe for footing the bill. In the restaurant we came face to face with an almost bewildering assortment of fresh fish, shellfish, meat and vegetables on display from which we were invited to make personal selections. I chose scallops and tiger prawns, which a chef then grilled for my delectation on a large steel hotplate before my very eyes. I was very taken with the fiery substance of the chopped red chillies that were available on the side. Certain items referred to as *sushi* were brought along separately and unbidden. Where *sushi* was concerned I was neither a connoisseur nor an admirer. Green tea was poured in such profusion into cups that were not permitted to be empty for more than a second that the volume of the brew threatened to overtake my capacity to drink it down.

THAT AFTERNOON, ACCOMPANIED by Cheung, Yi and I visited the Ministry of Industry building in Hanoi to meet an alleged Deputy Minister. The visit was arranged by Yi as a courtesy gesture to raise the

Ministry's awareness that Daewoo had firm intentions in hand regarding development of the First May bauxite deposit. I didn't yet quite know what those firm intentions were, but presumably Yi did and that was what counted.

The Deputy Minister, for such he was, claimed that a great deal of the Dac Nong bauxite project data were being held somewhere in Hanoi. That was not quite the message received from Vimico at our meeting that morning, although the Deputy Minister did seem to agree with Vimico that there were definite gaps in the availability of the historical record that needed to be bridged.

From the Deputy Minister I obtained a copy of the 1996 Vietnam Mining Act setting out standard procedures for the acquisition of exploration licences. Although he didn't say it in as many words, I also obtained a very clear impression from him that his Ministry was flat broke. Whereas the Ministry was ever ready with open arms and the vast reservoir of goodwill typifying Vietnam and its people to welcome a foreign investor, the Ministry's assistance involving paying for anything in any size, shape or form was not on the agenda.

At the close of the afternoon, Yi, Cheung and I flew down to Ho Chi Minh City from Hanoi in another of Vietnam Airlines' new Airbuses. For that matter, the aircraft we flew in might have been the same as the one I came in on from Hong Kong. Be that as it may, Vietnam Airlines possessed an up to date fleet of aircraft that would have been the envy of any national carrier anywhere.

Ho Chi Minh City was formerly known as Saigon. The change of title was made to honour that great and victorious national leader of wars fought against various western colonists, invaders and combinations of the same. For all that, few Vietnamese that I met during my visit ever chose to call the city by anything other than its original name. Some traditions died hard. I thought I might as well fall in line with popular opinion.

On the flight to Saigon, the choice of which meal to go for would have been familiar to Mr Hobson, as beef noodles was the only dish on the menu. The beef noodles were not quite as good as yesterday's fish and rice but were very acceptable nevertheless.

Flying south from Hanoi placed the right-hand side of the Airbus in the glow of a brilliant sunset that held on for a satisfyingly long portion of the two-hour flight. The temperature at Saigon airport on arrival was 29°C. Our bags appeared on the carousel with almost stunning promptness. Cheung got hold of a taxi to take us to the New World Hotel Saigon, a brash and hulking building dominating an area of the city known as downtown District 1.

Saigon was nothing if not a vibrant city: livelier by far than Hanoi. Its streets glittered with raw neon and were tightly crammed with traffic in which four-wheeled vehicles lay as virtually stalled boulders in a smoking white water rapid of fast-flowing mopeds.

My HOTEL ROOM was on the tenth floor. I found sleep that night eluding me and thereby was wide awake at 3.30 a.m. and motivated to get up at 4.00 a.m. At that morosely small hour of the morning the front concourse of the hotel that I looked down on from the window of my room was lined with arms-porting uniformed policemen. Perhaps a head of state was about to arrive at or to check out of the hotel, feet first for all I knew.

I breakfasted on noodles and vegetables at 6.00 a.m., being the very first customer into the hotel restaurant once an eager waiter flung the doors open to me. Following breakfast it was then my turn to check out of the hotel, still feeling tired to the bone, to travel with Yi and Cheung up to Dac Nong and the area of the First May bauxite deposit. The day was fine, dry and sunny, auguring well for the trip. The policemen were gone.

We travelled in a four-by-four Mitsubishi pickup truck, courtesy of Vimico's Saigon-based administration and driven by a Vimico driver. If Yi was upset over being compelled to travel in a vehicle that Daewoo had not manufactured, it said much to his credit that he didn't show it.

The way out of Saigon was slow going owing to the phenomenal numbers of bicycles and mopeds on the roads. Each and every one of them was a potential hazard on two wheels. They turned the roads into obstacle-festooned computer games. Few of the mopeds bore less than one passenger on the back seat – many carried more than one, and three passengers were not uncommon. Cheung said that accidents were commonplace, which didn't surprise me at all. Near accidents slipped by us at the rate of several every second.

More by luck than through skilful negotiation the Mitsubishi gained the outskirts of Saigon without engaging in a single impact. Provided that this happy state of affairs could maintain itself in the (by then) much diminished two-wheeled traffic melee, it would take us about four hours to reach the final destination in the Dac Nong district.

At no point on the trip north from Saigon were we out of sight of people, dwellings, or agricultural development. The fields were beautifully and lovingly tended. The countryside shone with the pride of those who not only cared greatly for it but had also shown themselves more than competent in fighting to hold on to their birthrights. Many of the fields spread like green carpets around a central cluster of the tombs of the ancestors of those who still worked the land. The presence of the tombs in the living fields seemed totally appropriate to the circumstances of a people who viewed the land as extensions of themselves.

According to Cheung, one great problem on the land was a current plague of rats. The government had placed a bounty on the rodents, manifest in a fixed rate paid per rat's tail delivered to any one of a number of designated collection points. Around eight million tails had been handed in so far, but still the rats were roaming the fields and eating the crops in untold numbers. In the absence of a suitable Vietnamese pied piper, cats, dogs and snakes were engaged as the key rat control measure. Cheung said that it was recently reported in a Hanoi newspaper that 171 kilograms of snakes was released into fields in the vicinity of Hanoi. It begged the question as to who weighed them. I had a mental picture of streams of snakes being discharged from sacks while every rat and person within a radius of a hundred metres from the serpentine emancipation legged it as fast as possible in the opposite direction.

The great problem exercising local minds was that the flesh of each of the three species of rat-hungry predators featured in gourmet dishes on the menus of many popular restaurants throughout the country. There was additionally a thriving culinary export trade in live cats, dogs and snakes to China. It all presented a major dilemma for the authorities to cope with. There were few votes to be gained by closing down snake restaurants, let alone similar establishments catering for those who favoured dining on cats and dogs. Unfortunately, rat restaurants lacked any general appeal. A heated debate was likely to rage on.

THE ROAD TO Dac Nong was paved for the first eighty kilometres out of Saigon up as far as the little town of Dong Xoi. Beyond Dong Xoi the remaining one hundred and twenty kilometres that we travelled were generally under some form of repair or construction. There would be a good road all the way to Dac Nong one day, but that day was clearly not yet. Brown laterite, dug from the hills, was used as road fill, and the dark and tightly crystalline basalt that underlay the laterite was crushed for ballast.

As the road gradually gained in elevation, rice and maize crops gave way to rubber tree and coffee plantations. We drove through long sections where it seemed that virtual forests of young coffee seedlings were planted wherever a space could be found to dig them into. The incidence of growing coffee made a good cue for us to stop at a roadside coffee house for a cup of the beverage of the same name. The taste was as strong and as dark as the soil that nurtured the beans.

Cheung said that during the war with the Americans, the Viet Cong controlled most of the area that we came through from Saigon. The infrastructure that had existed then was light and was only now being upgraded. He led me to understand – or maybe I assumed what I wanted to assume – that the Americans had never been in control of very much of the country, North or South, even at the height of the war. Cheung told me that the Americans operated from fortified bases out of which they spread like reluctant ripples and back to which they moved again in the face of determined opposition. Most of the damage done to rural areas by the Americans was carried out indiscriminately from the air through dropping bombs, napalm and the infamous Agent Orange.

I REMEMBERED A tale I once heard in Quebec in Canada alleging that the defoliation capabilities of Agent Orange were originally tested on some of the more deciduous regions of the remoter backwoods of that extensively forested province. It wouldn't have done to carry out such tests anywhere down in the forests of Canada's big neighbour to the south, or so the story went. Canadian trees were expendable.

As if to compound the felony, the province of Quebec was regularly invaded from the south by many aircraft bearing colourfully uniformed and heavily armed good old boys from the USA. The aircraft were chiefly single-engine, float-mounted planes, more of a hazard to those who flew in them than to those who might have peered up at them through the traceries of Agent Orange-denuded branches below.

The good old boys were, when they weren't draft dodgers, hunters of the moose. They stepped out from well stocked bush camps bristling with hunting rifles and fishing rods, making forays that were just as nervous in execution as any military patrol from a fortified base in Vietnam would have been. Of what lay in the woods in wait for them, they knew not.

In a bar up in the Quebec mining town of Chibougamau, a mine surveyor of my acquaintance (named Rod) once fell into conversation with some members of such a hunting party. Rod sensed free drinks and fair game, and when asked by them what he did for a living he enhanced his cause by telling the hunters that he was an Indian fighter. They engaged his services on the spot. Rod said he could have named his own fee. He visited their camp, disappeared for a while, then returned and assured them that he had eliminated all hostiles from the general area. The hunters were then able to wander at will, without fear of being shot at by anyone apart from other hunters.

The word got around down south. Rod's Indian fighting skills were so much in demand by hunting parties up from the USA, and his reimbursement was so lucrative to boot, that he took his vacation in moose season and became a full-time Indian fighter for hire. He was so effective in his work that no party that he sold his services to was ever bothered by marauding Indians. The US Army in Vietnam could have used a man like Rod, although they probably wouldn't have paid him as well as the moose hunters did.

WE DROVE ON over a fair and rolling land, up past Doc Phong, through deep and geometrically precise road cuttings and over a brand new bridge across a river where the ruins of its war-damaged predecessor formed a decaying monument away on one side.

The pleasantly pretty little town of Dac Nong was draped over two neatly rounded hills. Prior to checking into a local guesthouse where we were due to spend the night, we stopped at a restaurant in a dusty street on our way through town to have lunch. The restaurant had been invaded by more than its fair share of the dust, but under the superficial grime lay a welcome oasis serving food cooked to order that I found wonderful. We were served greens, beef noodles, rice and pork with chillies. I doubted that a more enjoyable lunch was served anywhere else in the country at that given moment.

THE GUESTHOUSE THAT we were to stay in was large and rickety, constructed almost entirely of not particularly well-maintained wood. A large and allegedly unexploded bomb, dropped by the Americans without good intent and no doubt retrieved by the Viet Cong as a heaven-sent gift, was mounted in pride of place directly over the principal entry to the guesthouse. I didn't like to ask whether or not the bomb was yet defused but guessed that perhaps it wasn't.

The guest rooms were small cubicles, separated by thin wooden panelled walls. There was a tap providing cold running water for those who wanted to wash themselves. The beds were low and hard, each enveloped in a serviceable mosquito net. It was all most adequate. There was a rudimentary dining room at ground level, and from it a flight of stairs led to an upper floor where it was advertised that a couple of chambers were fitted out with all that was necessary for guests and visitors who, irrespective of their ability to carry a tune, fancied their chances in the field of karaoke. As one who had yet to sample such delights, I made a mental note to investigate the karaoke option at a suitable juncture.

WITH THE ACCOMMODATION arrangements complete, we boarded the Mitsubishi once more to be driven thirty kilometres or so outside of Dac Nong to look over the general area underlain by the First May bauxite deposit. Rather too much of the route we took followed a track of the kind that the wet season would not treat with kindness when it came.

The First May bauxite deposit was covered by a flat, park-like expanse set in an extensive, open region characterised by short, brittle grass and studded with clumps of tall woodland. Occasional rough, rain-torn gullies choked with brush wriggled off from one edge in the direction of Laos.

The First May exploration programme had been carried out using manually excavated pits rather than by indulging in any form of mechanical drilling to intersect the bauxite. The pits were about a metre square in cross-section, nominally dug at a grid spacing of two hundred metres. One line of pits was, however, dug at intervals of a mere fifty metres to provide a closer distribution on which both to improve confidence in the lateral continuity of the bauxite and to extract a pilot sample for processing.

Back at Vimico's offices in Hanoi I was reliably informed that the pits were all backfilled, but there, standing among them, it was patently obvious that, fortunately, that was not so. The exposed walls of the still open pits gave an opportunity for me to view bauxite sections at first hand.

The First May exploration work as carried out was neat and of a good standard. My concern over the future of the deposit was that no matter how well it might have been explored, the reported quality of the raw (unwashed) bauxite was too poor to feel commercially viable. More detailed exploration could certainly be undertaken, but I didn't think it would improve the situation much.

In the near vicinity of the line of pits spaced at fifty-metre intervals a sawmill was screeching as it made significant inroads on some of the locality's formerly standing trees. The sawmill building was sagging at the seams, looking as if a selection of the cut timber stacked in piles around it could have been employed with advantage to shore up its listing frame. The clean scent of freshly cut wood caressed the warm air and lay like a benediction on the crackling grass.

The sawmill workers downed tools and came flooding out to greet us. They were many. We were kings for the day. They could not have been more enthusiastic to see us or more hospitable in their approach, but then, I was learning that the people of Vietnam were like that.

WE RETURNED TO the guesthouse in the evening, and from it, after a brief interval to tidy up, we went back into Dac Nong to have dinner at the same restaurant where we took lunch. The chef fried some small potatoes and served them up as an accompaniment to rice, strips of beef with garlic greens and boiled bananas. The proprietor sold me a packet of locally grown coffee beans. I was coming to think that if Daewoo and Vimico wanted to make the best of the First May bauxite deposit they should plant coffee beans on it.

Back at the guesthouse after dinner I heard the loose notes of an unfamiliar tune escaping from one of the karaoke rooms. I climbed the stairs and cracked open the door to peer in at whatever spectacle was about to present itself. The room contained a long red leathery sofa fronted by a low table, as long as the sofa or maybe even a little longer.

Both sofa and table were crowded close to a large television monitor, on the screen of which the words associated with the tune were unravelling at a rate that was evidently challenging the three Vietnamese gentlemen seated on the sofa, each wielding a microphone in one hand and a glass of beer in the other, to keep pace.

The low table was laden with bottles that had once contained the beer that was now contained within the three chorusing gentlemen. There was no space left for any more bottles on the table, full or otherwise. In any case the chorus of three demonstrated by its demeanour that its members had imbibed sufficiently to render the arrival of any more beer redundant to the cause of getting drunk.

The trio turned as one to look at me as I peered in on them. One of them leapt to his feet, knocking an empty bottle off the table as he did so. The bottle rolled under the television set. He grabbed my arm and pulled me into the room, drawing me over to the sofa, where he pushed at me to sit down. There was plenty of room for four of us on the sofa. As if simultaneously triggered, each of my now three companions thrust his beer glass in my direction. In order not to disappoint any of them I swallowed a slug from each glass. The beer was at room temperature and did not appear to have travelled well.

One of the three picked up a folder and riffled through it. He selected a page and handed the folder to me, pointing at it with an index finger as he did so. The folder contained a list of the hundreds of songs available on the karaoke machine. Most of the numbers were Vietnamese, although the chosen page somehow specified a limited number of English language songs.

The former holder of the folder punched a number into a remote control unit and handed me his microphone. The opening words of "Autumn Leaves" appeared on the screen. I missed the opening bars, but managed to insert myself into the flow eventually and sang the song through for them. My singing was consistent with the quality of the bauxite of First May.

Following the fall of "Autumn Leaves" I was anxious to quit the room but was impressed into vocalising "I Get a Kick Out of You" as an encore. That was more like it. Karaoke began to grow on me. I gave my companions a rendition of "Perfidia", always a favourite of mine, and followed it up with a tasteful rambling through "Feelings", on which I was at my most impressive in foundering on the high notes. "Feelings" brought down the curtain rather than the house. There could be no capping it, even through the auspices of the much-loathed karaoke standard "My Way".

"Feelings" was a mainstay of the elevator school of music that stalked business travellers around the world with such implacability. No hotel from three stars and counting upwards ever failed to shove "Feelings" at innocent guests trapped in its public precincts and helpless to do anything about it. To that illustrious list of hostelries favouring "Feelings" could now be added the Dac Nong guesthouse with a welcoming bomb poised over the front door.

THE THRILLS OF my night were not yet over, as the door to my room slipped shut behind me when I stepped out to utilise the cold-water tap to wash up and clean my teeth once the karaoke session was finally consigned to the dustbin of history. I was locked out, left to hunt through the dark grounds of the guesthouse on bare feet and minus a shirt to seek out the roaming custodian of the guesthouse's master key and persuade him to let me back into my room. I was lucky not to tread on anything squishy soft or anything that might otherwise be prepared to bite me.

Such bites as I suffered were left to occur later on in my bed. The mosquito net did its job in repelling mosquitoes but proved to be no deterrent to ants. The night was hot enough to turn sheets and blankets into an unnecessary burden, which was just as well as there weren't any of them on the bed. Whoever was resident on the other side of the pervious panel that formed one wall of my room was far more accomplished at snoring than I was at carrying a karaoke tune.

At 5.00 a.m. precisely the incessant snoring from next door met its match in the tones of stirring music that belted out over the guesthouse from the direction of Dac Nong. If this was intended to be a communal wake-up call, implying alarm or a summons to indulge in the practice of tai chi, it was supremely effective. It was far more comfortable for me to give up and get up than to try and stay in bed and fight a losing battle against such high-decibel odds.

AN HOUR OR so later we went to have breakfast at our by now well-accustomed restaurant in Dac Nong. Omelettes were prepared, noodle soup was delivered in great bowls, plates were set out piled with freshly made baguettes, hot from the oven, steaming with fragrance as the bread was broken.

It was a pity that we weren't staying another day in Dac Nong, the chef said, as he had dog available on that evening's dinner menu and would have been happy to reserve the choicest portions for us. I struggled to contain my lack of disappointment.

Cheung announced that he had spent a fair portion of the previous night in the company of members of a Dac Nong police squad. The police were allegedly upset by their failure to be informed in advance in writing that a foreigner (me) would be visiting their sphere of influence. I didn't know if Yi was also classed as a foreigner, although he probably was. The written advice was a legal requirement according to the police. They felt obliged to issue Cheung with a formal complaint related to the offence. It was a good job they hadn't been subjected to "Feelings". Cheung said he had to pay what was euphemistically referred to as a fine, which was probably what the whole episode was about in the first place.

WE CHECKED OUT of the guesthouse, took a final look at the bomb embellishing its superstructure and departed for the return journey to Saigon. Cheung planned an initial detour to the north to drive by Gia Nghia, another of the Dac Nong group of bauxite deposits (seven altogether) dominated by First May.

We slipped through splendid coffee plantations along roads made easy by an advanced state of upgrading. The Gia Nghia bauxite was distributed along a sequence of elongated ridges separated by wriggling valleys. Most of the valley slopes were planted with coffee seedlings.

My recall of the return journey to Saigon was that it was a long and winding road. It was also very hot. I found the heat debilitating and spent most of the journey in a lack-of-sleep induced stupor, floating in a sea of rolling thoughts, in which my perception of bauxite opportunities was totally eclipsed by the relative importance of coffee to the regional economy.

WE REACHED THE edge of Saigon at 1.00 p.m., just in time for lunch. Cheung selected a restaurant. He appeared to know it well. The restaurant was a large and complex *al fresco* establishment, with tables set out under advantageous shady trees to bask in the glow of bright banks of bougainvillea. On the side, a wide and turgid river slid past. Rafts of water hyacinths, some small and some not so small at all, moved slowly along the river, smoothly borne in the brown flow. A few items of flot-sam that it was better not to think too much about bobbed and dipped as they were carried downstream alongside where we sat.

Cheung placed the order for lunch, calling for fish soup to commence with, to be followed by some assorted snake dishes as an integrated main course. I couldn't applaud his choice, although I imagined that it was made in the spirit of an implicit challenge and was determined to rise to it. I expressed joy with fingers crossed.

Cheung said that he was not a great lover of snake meat as he had been compelled by necessity to eat so much of it during the war that he had tended to lose his taste for the delicacy. He had my sympathy, as I went through a similar experience with tripe. Cheung allowed that he was willing to make a small sacrifice and eat snake on this occasion for my benefit, although I wasn't sure that if the tables were turned I would have been able to reciprocate with tripe.

Our intended lunch, a black reptile in the order of a metre long that I thought could have been a cobra, was brought to the table for Cheung's inspection and approval. At the sight of its writhing coils, Cheung smirked and nodded enthusiastically to the bearer, employing all the unctuous mannerisms of a practised wine snob.

The eager bearer held on like grim death to the neck of the strug-gling snake while a waiter laid the paraphernalia of pending ceremony on our table. This consisted of a large block of hardwood stained with what looked suspiciously like venerable blood, a wicked looking cleaver, a jug of rice wine and a fluted glass tumbler.

The condemned reptile was stretched out on the block of wood, and with a flourish that was so rapid it would have been missed had I blinked, the snake-bearer released one hand to grab the cleaver. With a gleam and a hiss of the blade the snake's head was severed from its body. That made one less snake for the rats of Vietnam to have to worry about.

Taking up the body of the snake by its tail end in one hand, the bearer hung the upper end (minus head) over the fluted tumbler and, by drawing his other hand down along the snake's body in a style that would have been familiar to anyone experienced in milking a cow, he induced a rather impressive quantity of snake's blood to accumulate in the glass receptacle.

When it seemed that the snake was wholly desanguinated its corpse was laid out on the wooden block once more, and the cleaver was then employed to slit it all along the mid-point of the belly scales. With more glee than was desirable under the circumstances, the bearer plucked out the snake's heart and liver. After a short rummage, he then withdrew a pea-like object that shaped up as being the bile duct. He nicked the bile duct with the cleaver and squeezed the viscous, evilly green contents that emerged into the dark blood resting for the moment in the fluted tumbler.

The snake's heart, to my profound dismay, was dropped into a steaming bowl of fish soup that had been brought along to our table in the meantime. A plea entered my head that it must not be me who would find the snake's heart in his portion of soup. It wasn't, because Cheung got the heart, which the hot soup had more or less cooked right through for him. However, I was not to escape altogether as Cheung extracted the heart from his bowl, cut it into three pieces and regaled both Yi and myself with a piece. All that was lacking was the presence of Mr Wackford Squeers to declare, "Here's richness!"

The separated liver and chopped up carcass of the snake were whisked away by a waiter to a place where they would no doubt be appropriately prepared for our delectation.

Meanwhile, back at the table, the bottle of rice wine was opened and a large portion of its liquid contents were decanted by another waiter, skilled in the task, into the mixture of blood and bile in the fluted tumbler. The waiter swirled the fluted tumbler around a few times to blend the cocktail and poured an equal measure of the result, neither shaken nor stirred (or for that matter licensed to kill) into three wine glasses that he fetched for us. We were each handed one of the charged glasses. Cheung proposed a toast to all of us. Yi proposed a toast to the First May bauxite project. I proposed a toast to the people of Vietnam. Given the intensity of the moment, it was not surprising that a toast to Daewoo was overlooked. With duty done, we downed our bloody draughts in unison.

I was hoping against hope that my third of the blood, bile and rice wine cocktail would stay down in me, and fortunately it did. I didn't taste it at all. One thing I became accomplished in when I attended primary school was swallowing a daily spoonful of cod liver oil without any trace of it ever touching my taste buds. That childhood skill stood me in good stead at the snake restaurant on the outskirts of Saigon.

Unfortunately, it was not quite that easy to swallow solid pieces of snake in the same way, but I did my best. The availability of chillies on the side for liberally masking association was never felt to be more welcoming than on that occasion.

From lunch we returned to the New World Hotel Saigon where I was allocated a day room to use while I waited to check out later that night prior to flying with Korean Airlines out of Saigon up to Seoul, the home of Daewoo's imperial base.

Just as I was finishing sorting out my papers and a few specimens of First May bauxite that I had collected from the excavated material dumped around the exploration pits during our visit to the deposit site, Cheung came to the room to invite me to accompany him to a nearby Saigon market. I was keen to buy a Ho Chi Minh tee shirt and had no hesitation in accepting his offer.

I felt perfectly secure on our walk to the market but was distressed by the large number of children who came to me begging for money. It was a situation impossible for me to react to in any constructive way, and it filled me with a sense of helpless frustration. I contemplated going back to the hotel to avoid it, but didn't.

Getting to the market involved crossing a road rife with hurtling traffic and ill-equipped with traffic lights. Residents of Saigon performed the science of nonchalant crossing with great aplomb, born to it no doubt and never missing a step as mopeds brushed them front and back. Cheung pranced over the road, evading four-wheeled vehicles as if he were a matador and they were charging bulls. I waited for a break in traffic that seemed unwilling to arrive, lacking the nerve to make an assault on the far shore. At a moment when the traffic thinned I gathered my courage to make a precipitate dash and only escaped being run down by the skin of my teeth. I was relieved by this success but was already worrying as to how I was going to make the return trip.

The Saigon market was designed as a seemingly infinite labyrinth of narrow alleys lined by tiny kiosks that all appeared to be absolutely devoted to the sale of clothing. There were more than enough tee shirts on offer in an extensive enough set of designs to suit any aficionado of those useful garments. The art of salesmanship associated with the hardest of sell and the sunniest of smiles was the order of the day.

"Can I buy a tee shirt, please?"

"How many tee shirt you want?"

"Only one."

"OK, but how many tee shirt you want?"

"That one!"

"Yeah, how many tee shirt you want? This good one! This also good one!"

"All right, I'll take two then."

"Yeah, sure, now how many tee shirt you want?"

I somehow managed to end up buying a total of nine tee shirts, one of which actually bore a picture of Mr Ho Chi Minh himself. I gave two of them away. It had been a satisfactory visit to the Saigon market for someone, but I was not sure that that someone was me. Laden with the tee-shirt bounty I was so busy wondering how I had managed to acquire all these items that I didn't really want that the return journey across the frightening road posed no terror. To that extent, the tee-shirt episode was a bit less of a debacle than it might otherwise have been.

WE ATE THAT evening in a restaurant named "W". The W might well have stood for "Why", but as to why, I didn't know. W wasn't a letter that featured in the Vietnamese language. The restaurant specialised in seafood but had some other traditional Vietnamese dishes of a meatier type on offer as well. To get the best of both sides of the menu I chose crab soup, tiger prawns and a portion of pork with vegetables. It was my intention to pay the bill, but since I had left both my money and my credit card in the safe deposit box in the day room back at the hotel, I had to borrow the necessary funds, including the tip, from Yi.

Travelling representatives of the Company were recognised masters of reluctance to reach for a tab, although in this instance my failure to cough up on demand was inadvertent. That was my excuse, and I was sticking to it.

I paid Yi back when we returned to the hotel. It didn't help the state of my liquidity to have Cheung present me a little later with an invoice for a hundred and twenty dollars related to the provision of various Vimico services rendered during the First May visit, including the transportation there and back in the Mitsubishi. I wasn't sure if it was up to me to cover it, although I did, only realising afterwards that it had virtually cleaned me out.

All the same, I had just enough money left to pay for a taxi to the Saigon airport, and so I departed, with much regret, from the New World Hotel Saigon at 10.30 p.m. I left Yi and Cheung in the hotel lobby. Both of them were by then a lot richer than I was in all ways other than in memories.

THE FLIGHT UP to Seoul, numbered KE 682, took place in an Airbus A300-600 of Korean Airlines. The aircraft departed from Saigon for a scheduled four and a half hours long flight at 1.05 a.m., only twenty-five minutes late. A short night that was doomed to seem long stretched ahead. I was not conscious of cutting it down with a single moment of sleep.

I tried to think about what I could tell the representatives of the Great Universe that I was destined to meet later on that same day. They were no doubt already trembling in their dreams up in Seoul, fingering the logo and figuratively clutching the edges of their corporate seats, anticipating my every utterance on the undoubted merits of the First May bauxite deposit. It wasn't that the deposit lacked bauxite, it was just that the bauxite it didn't lack wasn't very good bauxite. It was explored well enough, but so far not wisely enough. Rather a lot more exploration was required to support any plans for a feasibility study leading to mine development.

The good old fall-back position of all those who, like me, worked at the front end of the mining business – namely, that when in doubt, propose that more work should be done – immediately suggested itself.

The breakfast served on the flight was Korean noodles served in a plastic bowl. I didn't try to eat the bowl, but if I had it might have tasted better than the noodles that it contained. I was missing Vietnamese cuisine already.

WE LANDED AT Seoul airport at 7.30 a.m. Local time was two hours ahead of Saigon. At 2°C the ambient temperature was by contrast a long way in arrears. The city of Seoul loomed beyond the airport in sere chill under a clear sky, a hugely sprawling monstrosity for which manufacturers of concrete had much to answer. Without question I had travelled far from the golden apples of the sun. I did have the foresight to have brought a jacket with me, but it performed only marginal service in mitigating the penetrating nature of southern Korean cold.

Waiting for me in the airport arrivals hall was a bulky and unconditionally bland-faced emissary from the Great Universe, a corporate stalwart named Jae-Keun. I was totally unsurprised to be led by Jae-Keun to a parked example of Daewoo's latest example of automotive design. I could smell the newness of this masterpiece even before I reached it.

Seated in its agreeably balmy interior, I was driven by Jae-Keun into the centre of the mighty city, where I was dropped off at the entrance of the Seoul Hilton hotel. On the way, Jae-Keun told me that Seoul was a city of twelve million people. Looking around, all I could think to add to that was, and the rest. I was not too tired to conclude that however many people Seoul contained, there were an awful lot of them. There was also an awful lot of Seoul.

The drive in to the Hilton took an hour on roads crammed with what I first of all assumed was early morning rush-hour traffic. Later on I realised that such volumes of traffic were no more than par for the trivial round, not to mention the common task. The loaded roads were, no more and certainly no less, a crawling paean to the South Korean car manufacturing industry.

There was not a single moped in sight.

THE SEOUL HILTON hotel was a monolithic grey building of undeniably stark proportions. Advice from Jae-Keun that the hotel was Daewoo-built and Daewoo-owned did no more than confirm what would have been a reasonable surmise. Behind the hotel, down at the foot of a shallow slope of frost-bitten garden, stood a similarly sharp-edged and hulking construction decorated with that grandly wrought logo that made no secret of the fact that it contained Daewoo's corporate centre – the very place where Jae-Keun told me I was expected for a meeting with the First May project team in the afternoon.

I checked into the Hilton, where, thanks to mine hosts, Room 708 was already reserved for me. I went to the room and attempted to rest but couldn't, and so it was with no small sense of relief that I descended to the lobby to meet Jae-Keun once more at 1.45 p.m. and make the crossing with him to the Daewoo centre.

Together we walked down a broad flight of steps and threaded along a path through the sloping garden. In the garden there was no plant that was not withered to a rustling brown by the cold or any shrub that was not devoid of leaves. We passed a broad pond in which large orange and white carp were rising and sinking with metronomic regularity. I expected that the carp were checking the surface of the water to make sure that ice was not forming on it.

Jae-Keun's first order of the afternoon at the Daewoo centre was to lead me to a large auditorium, buried deep down in the basement of the building, where I was left to sit alone and view at least the first ten minutes of a colourful half-hour video presentation outlining the diverse and stellar qualities of the Great Universe. The sleep that had eluded me back at the hotel showed no reticence in joining me for most of the final twenty minutes of the show. Fortunately, I woke abruptly as the lights went up at the end, trusting as I did that I was not about to be questioned on what I thought about what I hadn't seen.

Jae-Keun then took me from the auditorium up to a meeting room on an elevated floor of the centre, in which eight members of the impressively titled Daewoo Non-ferrous Metal Business Development Team were already gathered and waiting for me to join them. The eight may have made up the whole Team, but even if they didn't, they were more than enough to be going on with.

My first thought on casting an eye over the assembly of Team members was that in spite of my jacket and unwillingly knotted tie, I had fallen dramatically short of meeting the accepted South Korean business dress code by many an Irish mile. I stood in the midst of the Team looking, and feeling, like a poor relative. Dark suits were obviously mandatory wear. The Team members stood in a row, each seeming to have been cloned from a prototype model cobbled together in a secret Frankenstein-styled laboratory in a part of the Daewoo centre subject to restricted access. If the dire day on which dark suits fell out of fashion were ever to arrive, then the conduct of business in Seoul would be a spent force.

Handshakes as a means of welcome were out. Back slapping embraces were so unthinkable as to be abhorrent. Any hint at flesh-pressing contact was untenable. The greeting convention consisted of a formal bow made from the waist with the arms held stiffly at the sides. The rule seemed to be that angle of inclination of a corporate back should not exceed twenty degrees from the vertical position.

Business cards were produced with triumphantly snapping flourishes. I got eight cards. The Team members got only one each, but

I wouldn't have liked to conclude that the advantage was mine.

We sat around a large oval table. The Team leader for the day, identified as such not only by the fact that he did most of the talking but also by the deference shown him by the other seven, requested me to set out my opinions on the First May bauxite deposit for the Team to consider. This I did. The Team was unable to disguise its lack of exuberance for what I had to say. It additionally seemed surprised not to have received a glowing report on the project from me. I wondered what kind of advice Yi could have phoned through while I was in the air.

My remarks provoked a circuitous debate that came no closer to resolution at the finish than it had done at the beginning. The order of service was a sequence of drawn-out harangues. Each one of the eight ground his very own axe. It was clear to me that the Team in Seoul hadn't progressed nearly as far with the First May evaluation as Yi led me to believe they had done when I was in Vietnam. It might have helped the Team's cause if a few of them had flown down to Vietnam rather more often than they had (or hadn't) so as to get a first-hand look at the project they were supposed to be planning.

By consensus, the Team seemed to want to place the onus on me to give them ideas and make some decisions. Much to my perturbation, I discovered that this kind of buck-passing strategy was applied by the Team as more or less standard practice in dealing with Vimico's First May development expectations. The Company was being identified as Daewoo's rabbit in the hat. I struggled to impress on the Team a critical need for more detailed exploration to be carried out on the First May bauxite deposit, in order to underpin confidence in future development options.

The collective mind of the Team was motivated solely by a deadline for it to produce a positive recommendation on the First May project for delivery to Vimico by the end of the year. That might have been all right if only the deadline date weren't a mere month and a half away.

The Team leader said that Daewoo could get hold of all the First May project information currently in the hands of Hungarian and Russian agencies for me to review. I noticed that he didn't add how soon this happy state of affairs could be realised. I said that I would do all that I possibly could to comply with a prompt review when I received the data, acting within the constraints of the opinions that I had already expressed.

The meeting ended when the joint will of the Team to keep it going faded away. Its thrust dwindled and expired with something of a whimper at about 5.30 p.m. Since some form of decision was considered opportune, one such was made to hold another meeting on the following day. By this means the threat of reaching a conclusion was effectively deferred. The purpose of the next day's meeting would be to discuss a plan for ongoing action. For the moment it was better to travel hopefully than to arrive, or so it seemed.

A second decision, one in which I didn't participate and that I didn't much welcome when it was made, was that all of us should head out into the heart of Seoul for dinner that evening. Ah well. I returned to the Hilton and was collected for the great banqueting excursion an hour later.

SINCE WE WERE nine in number, we were driven in a fleet of three cars (no prizes for guessing the make), locked tight into Seoul's perpetual flood of traffic for much more than an hour. At long last we arrived at what was supposed to be the selected restaurant and turned out not to be. We found that out immediately on entering. The fixtures and fittings of the erroneous restaurant were Japanese and, rather appealingly, the background music on offer as we strode in and crept out again was "The Colonel Bogey March", otherwise famed as the theme from the film, *The Bridge on the River Kwai*. I kid you not. Seoul was added to a list of cities in which the quality of Murphy dropped as the gentle rain from heaven.

I sensed, from the glowering looks that the dark-suited Team member responsible for making the dinner reservation received from the Team leader, that the former might well be preoccupied on the morrow with preventing his head from rolling. We returned to the fleet of Daewoo cars and drove ever onwards to eventually locate the correct restaurant, named the "Samwon Garden", on the second try. I had long since passed the point of accepting that Seoul was a city I would willingly choose to live in.

DINNER AT THE Samwon Garden was styled as Korean fare. A small, charcoal-fired griddle was set up as a central fortification on our table, besieged by a host of small dishes containing chunks of raw fatty beef and various vegetable offerings, some of them raw and some lightly boiled. The guiding principle was that all diners selected the bits and pieces from the dishes they desired and cooked their selection on the griddle to suit personal taste. We were all provided with huge paper bibs to place around our necks. Dark suits had to be protected from spitting fat at all costs.

Bowls of limp cabbage marinated in something that contained enough garlic to make even a Frenchman throw up his hands and run in the direction of a church screaming "Sanctuary, sanctuary!" were served to us. Described as *kimchi*, the treated cabbage was a Korean speciality, a dish of national identity. *Kimchi* might not have been the most wretched thing I had ever attempted to eat anywhere, but it was quite close enough to the nadir to get in the way of my remembering what the direst actually was.

The favoured beverage accompanying such delights was local beer. The beer was not for sipping. Our glasses were filled, repeatedly so. "Bottoms up!", or the Korean equivalent of the same, was called out with each filling, and it was then implicit that the contents of one's glass must be drained off in one go. Any struggle to comply that I might otherwise have felt was mitigated for me by a fervent compulsion to wash away the deadly taste of the *kimchi* by fair means or by foul.

THE EARLY MORNING of the following day was once more grey and overcast. It suited my mood. The aftertaste of *kimchi* had seized my tongue in a grip of steel, and given that Daewoo was totally responsible for it, invoking a steely grip seemed not inappropriate. The atmosphere in the public areas of the Seoul Hilton was equally in tune with the overcast skies, suffused as it was with piped-in classical music numbers composed by ponderously named and long-dead Europeans. "Feelings" failed to materialise for once. There was no chance presented there for me to continue to hone up my karaoke skills.

Breakfast in the imposingly sombre hotel dining room offered me a choice between a Western and a Korean-styled menu. I decided to break with my usual practice of eating the food of the country that I was in and to declare no contest by going directly for the Western. Whatever was presented as being Korean on a Korean menu was best left to be ordered and eaten by someone of Korean nationality.

AT 10.00 A.M. Jae-Keun came to the hotel lobby yet again to take me to the location of the planned "action" meeting with the Team in the Daewoo centre. The eight dark suits gathered around me in the manner of a ring of crows ready to peck at carrion, or otherwise a convention of undertakers anxious to produce a tape measure and estimate the quantity of timber that would be needed to make a casket for me. The clothing ensembles in view might have been the self same that I saw yesterday, but I couldn't have sworn to it. Although there were no evident spots of fatty beef juice on any lapels, the big paper bibs would have taken care of eliminating that eventuality.

Following a session of creakily hinged bows in greeting all round, we got on with the discussions. The Team leader expressed reluctance on the part of the Team to recognise that the First May bauxite project still had a lot of ground to cover on the road to development. The part of my gut feeling that was not still reeling from its assault by *kimchi* led me to advise the Team that the poor quality of the bauxite was the fatal flaw that was likely to sink the whole thing. They didn't like hearing that at all. I added that we should all be prepared to make a joint effort to give the project the best shot that we could. The Team then reacted more favourably.

The prime task identified as facing the Team was to bring together all relevant information on the First May bauxite project in one place, pulling it in from its currently widespread set of locations around the world. My view was that the place of central collection should be Hanoi. The Team thought that Seoul was to be preferred. The Team leader agreed that Daewoo Corporation would use all of its widespread international influence to pursue the information, track it to its lair, trap it and bring it back alive. Leading on from there, once a comprehensive appreciation of all the exploration and evaluation work carried out so far was obtained, a decision on how much more such work was needed could be made. And there, which was palpably an unsatisfactory juncture for the Team (but what the hell, there we were and that was it), we let it lie.

The Team took me to a staff restaurant on the ground floor of the Daewoo centre for the final lunch of my visit to Seoul. Not unnaturally, the style of cuisine on offer was Korean. My heart sank. We were served semi-raw vegetables that were absolutely coated with minced garlic, and strips of *kimchi* as thin as they were bitter. There were, however, other vegetables, more acceptably fried in batter, and two kinds of hot *tofu*-littered soup. And throughout lunch there was an incessant pouring of beer into glasses accompanied on each occasion with a

"Bottoms up!" admonition that courtesy directed me to obey. I was not used to taking beer in any form at lunchtime but was willing enough to break with tradition to kill the meal as painlessly as I could. Crossing a road to visit a Korean restaurant went on my inventory of options to be avoided at all costs.

After lunch the minutes of the morning's "action" meeting were ready to be signed by those among the bottoms-up brigade who could still distinguish which of the double dotted lines was the correct one to sign on. A re-read of the blurry-looking minutes seemed somehow superfluous.

STEADY RAIN WAS falling as I weaved across the withered garden back to the Hilton to collect my personal effects and check out. Jae-Keun was delegated to return me to the Seoul airport through the rain in another Daewoo car. I noted somehow that this one was an "Arcadia" model. The road to the airport was anything but Arcadian in character. Traffic crept with the speed of a millipede, almost welded into a single dragging entity between the hotel and the airport departures terminal.

I was scheduled to travel all the way back to London on Cathay Pacific aircraft, with a transit stop to change aircraft in Hong Kong. From Seoul to Hong Kong I was allocated a seat in the first-class cabin. The cabin attendants were so over-attentive to my limited needs that I believed they might well have been trained in the science and art of feudal serfdom.

Their well-nigh overwhelming attention made me feel rather uncomfortable, although on the way down to Hong Kong there was an extended period of turbulence in which the cabin crew was required to sit down and fasten seat belts like the rest of the passengers, so that made a small mercy of sorts to be thankful for. The only item worth remembering about the dinner menu in flight was the soup, and even then I couldn't remember what sort of soup it was.

Our final approach into Hong Kong's airport was not quite as rapid as it was on the flight I arrived in when I was destined to go on to Hanoi. However, an abrupt banking movement of the aircraft shortly before touchdown was not lacking in a capacity to alarm, which was just about *déjà vu* all over again, I thought.

A Seminal Team

On one side lay blued ocean, and on the other
Lay a dun river, and the sun was full.
And of a sudden, lo! The turgid flow
Rippled the greening groves of mangroved shore
Where black-clawed roots grasped at the drift.
From out the slanting tide there hove a smiling craft,
Stem white as samite, stern mystic, wonderful.
And all the deck was gay with rev'ling forms,
Their numbers all a-babble in tune with tinkling glass.
Until the captain's hand coursed motors full
Into the Magdalena. Like some demented fowl,
That fluted a defiant song in face of sense,
She laid her churning wake across the ebb.
And found, at curling crest of chance-struck bank
Her mort d'artère. Long stood the Knights
Of Seminar, reliving faded memories, till her hull
Made shift in grip of new ascending flow.
Then, cross the mere, their wailing died away.

With apologies to Alfred, Lord Tennyson

A CATALYTIC SPARK, struck at the property of the Company's nickel mining and refining operations in northern Colombia, ignited a blaze of inspiration from out of which the Seminar leapt like a salamander.

At the moment of enlightenment I was standing outside the glassed-in front entry doors to the site's administration office block, attempting to talk to Ricardo, the operations manager.

THE HILL THAT gave the said operations not only their sense of purpose but also a title sprawled in all its dark promise about a kilometre to the rear of the admin block. Its name was Cerro Matoso. The nickel mining and refining operations thereby took the same name (with a formal SA added for luck) and were referred to for convenience as "Cerro".

The hill was formed from a durable plug of deeply crystalline nickel-iferous peridotite – one of the most basic of the suite of intrusive rocks and far more resistant to erosion than were the surrounding softer sediments into which the plug was intruded.

The hill rose out of a rolling savannah on which the great deep-cut meanders of the Rio Uré were flung about like an unwanted lasso. One brash curve of the river dared to clip a flank of the hill to form a rare, although rather unimpressive, bluff.

The surface of the hill, benefiting from exposure to the process of tropical weathering over a geologically inspired time frame, was transformed into a skin of laterite a few metres thick. The chemistry of the peridotite alteration process incorporated removal of the dross and retention and consequent enrichment of the better parts. Much of the silica was got rid of by solution leaching; most of the iron was pulled together in a hard superficial capping of ferruginous oxides; a gradational profile of brown and green saprolitic clay separated the hard cap from the virgin peridotite as if it were the filling in a chicken and avocado sandwich; and the original trace quantities of primary nickel sulphide minerals were turned into secondary garnierite, thereby ensuring the bona fides of the saprolite to be a nickel orebody.

RICARDO, WHEN I chanced to meet him on that fateful occasion, was about to make use of a boot-cleaning machine, a rotary brush mounted unit placed in a strategically prominent location on one side of the admin block's entry doors. I had already referred my boots to the attention of the machine. Its purpose was to remove the worst excesses of mud from the footwear of those seeking access to the admin block, and in this capacity it worked well enough for those who bothered to use it.

The defining term of "seminar" intruded into my opportunistic conversation with Ricardo in the assertive manner of the great billowing dust-laden plume that we could see rising to impressive altitudes from the refinery dryer discharge stack over there on the left. As with the plume, our seminar-hinted discourse was destined to flee downwind and cast its shadow on all that lay beneath.

The thought of arranging an event to be known as a seminar was tentative at the outset. We could perhaps have considered it in terms of a gathering or an assembly or a conclave or a congregation or a rally or a reunion or whatever the hell else a thesaurus might be able to cough up on demand. However the word "seminar" came and stood at once at the bold head of the queue. A seminar it was to be: a meeting of people of like mind and common discipline for the purposes of discussion and, hopefully, consensus.

CERRO WAS BY no means the least of the group of remotely located mines that received my personal and technical ministrations, whether they liked it or not, under the umbrella of the Absolutely mandate. Within the gamut of their respective standards and quality, the field and operating techniques practised within them, and their specific performance criteria, there were far more contrasts and differences than similarities. What the mines all shared, however, was a desire on the part of the majority of their people to do all they could to the limit of their ability to make their working places the best possible under prevailing circumstances.

Assistance in promoting this laudable aim fell well within the scope of the Absolutely mandate, which meant that for the group of mines as a whole I was something of a common factor. I showed up at the various gates once or twice a year, sometimes to help, sometimes (depending on whose opinion was sought on the property) perhaps also to hinder. By and large, though, I thought that my visits were progressive. In spite of the instinctively knee-jerk opposition from generally conservatively minded managements, standards of best practice in the disciplines of mining geology, mineral resource and ore reserve estimation and mine planning were getting to be installed in the overall operational consciousness, not to mention the conscience, bit by bit.

I hoped that those whom I worked with on the mines were helped by me, much in the same way as I learned from them. I imagined that we all got something from the deal. Unfortunately, it often seemed that the wholehearted co-operation extended to me during visits was like a lake which sank into a desert when I left the mine sites and when those I left behind went back to confronting their day-to-day working priorities. The road to progress was only paved by the essential medium of regular face-to-face contacts.

Not to put too fine a point on it, I was one of a very few representatives of the Company's central office who came along and spent time measured in rather more than hours (or at best a day) with people working at all levels on the mines. It was always certain to me that although the people I worked with were diverse in terms of nationality, culture and social and professional aspirations, they had so very much to offer one another. A shared distaste for those who controlled their destinies from afar was always a pretty good motivator for unification.

To achieve a genuinely Company-wide team spirit transcending continents, I thought that there was much more to be gained by direct personal communication between the various parties than there was through the occasional showing-up on site of an itinerant go-between like me. I was keen to get a circle of contacts together, and on the shoulders of that thought, the seminar sat like the child borne by St Christopher on his medals.

So AS TO have something to say, I voiced my thoughts to Ricardo. He was responsible at Cerro for both the mining and the refining operations and possessed just about the most energetic approach to his job of anyone I ever met in the empire of the Company. People of Ricardo's standard of excellence were all too often taken for granted by those who employed them. Once the inevitable point was reached at which their dynamism was judged to represent a threat to someone or other's ambitions, they were usually shunted so rapidly off to one side that they were effectively derailed. Ricardo was, so far, a survivor.

The comprehensive scope of Ricardo's job guaranteed that his attentions were spread thin on the ground. That made him a difficult man to get hold of. Any opportunity to beard him in his den had to be taken when it came up, especially in connection with matters concerning the mining side of his duties. In Ricardo's cake, mining was the crumbs left on the edge of his plate by the refinery cake.

In the time-honoured Company tradition of an executive management dedicated to homage before the altar of a so-called "bottom line" at the foot of which logic was all too often sacrificed, Ricardo seemed to feel at home. He adhered to the quasi-religious myth, spread by a sermonising management, that since the cost of running Cerro (capital and operating) was allocated an almighty proportion to the refinery and a paltrier sum to the mine, his own proportional attention to mine and refinery needed to be divided equivalently.

In the order of service at this perilously unbalanced shrine of worship the management's creed was written on tablets of stone (peridotite maybe). Management believed in serving mammon and thereby was suffused with the faith that whatever happened to the Cerro mine would have such a negligible impact on the bottom line that the mine could more or less be left to look after itself.

The consequence of this blinkered rote, the cumulative result of many years of short-sightedness, was a sure under-investment in mining activities. "Best performance" on the mine was thereby condemned to be "best under the circumstances" and not "best of kind".

It was all too obvious to me that the safe and effective performance of the Cerro refinery was totally reliant on the chemical grade specifications of the saprolitic nickel ore delivered to the refinery from the mine. The inter-dependence of mine and refinery didn't seem even to figure in management's thinking, no matter how frequently entreaties were made by concerned parties for management to give it some form of attention. Management played a numbers game in which eyes on the greater glorification of the refinery marked the one card deemed worth holding.

WHEN I MET the elusive Ricardo in the vicinity of Cerro's boot cleaning machine I left him with no alternative other than to direct some momentary attention to the mining side of his area of responsibility. We talked about the work I was doing at Cerro. I told him that I thought there was a need for Cerro's management to give mine planning a little more of the kind of material support that always seemed to be forthcoming where the refinery was concerned.

I then said that if mine planners and mining geologists from all around the Company's operations were ever to come together in one place, then much that would be positive for them, their parent operations and the Company as a whole was bound to happen. Not the least advantage of such a gathering would come through sharing experience and thereby identifying solutions to hitherto intractable technical problems.

Ricardo was surprisingly quick to agree with me. He said that he could easily relate to solving technical problems as he was faced with more than his fair share of those every day. He was also no doubt anxious to get away from me and back to matters pertaining to the refinery. Ricardo told me that if I could come up with enough of the right kind of people who would be interested in attending a seminar on mine planning and mining geology (*the* Seminar – the term was thereby coined), then Cerro would host and fund the event. As one who was well accustomed to having ideas rebuffed as a matter of pure principle I was not quite able to credit what Ricardo had just said. I asked him to confirm it. He did, we shook hands to seal the deal, and to all intents and purposes the Seminar was on.

THERE WAS OF course a great deal more involved in holding the Seminar at Cerro than simply flying in a bunch of like-minded guys for a few days and then sending them all home again. The overriding consideration was security. Security governed all comings and goings to and from Cerro by people from foreign points of origin. Colombia was distinguished as the world's top-ranking country for socially and politically inspired mayhem of all kinds, in which extortion, robbery, kidnapping and murder were not least among the chosen.

Some of the perpetrators of Colombia's violence sought financial gain, a lot of others were keen to take political advantage; but far too many, it seemed, lashed out just for the hell of it, simply because it was what they did best.

A multiplicity of guerrilla factions, individually organised, although sharing a single-minded resolve to overthrow the democratically elected Colombian government no matter what the cost to life, limb and the national economy might be, seemingly ranged at will and did their worst throughout most parts of the country. Within a land-locked mountainous area reputed to be the size of Switzerland, guerrillas ran a state within the state, a cloud cuckoo land in which the legally constituted authorities were scarcer than cuckoo clocks.

The snag with guerrillas was not that they were led (as they were) by clinically insane fanatics but rather that their political leanings ran the whole gamut of wings from the extreme left edge to the far right tip. One and all, each guerrilla faction appeared to abhor every other faction with quite as much venom as they hated the Colombian government. All of them were ever ready to eliminate the opposition wherever they found it. And as far as the opposition went the scope was so breathtaking broad as to spoil them for choice.

The most notorious of the guerrilla factions were the Revolutionary Armed Forces of Colombia (the FARC); the National Liberation Army (the ELN); and the Paramilitaries (factions with no shared acronym to unite on, although in their case they made up for it by being perhaps the most vicious of the lot). The Paramilitaries were allegedly a species of anti-guerrilla death squad associated with and thereby tolerated by the Colombian National Army (the EN), although no one sitting in an official position to know if this was or was not the Paramilitary's *raison d'être* was ever going to admit anything.

The guerrillas favoured hit and run tactics conducted from bases established in mountains, dense forests and thick jungle. The name of their game was to emerge under cover of night, hit selected targets hard and run home fast. (That was close to being an executive management technique.) Violence from all the armed factions, including the EN, seemed to be as mindless as it was bloody.

Perhaps more so than any other country on the face of the earth, Colombia offered to its people and its visitors an unrivalled opportunity to meet up with the wrong people in the wrong place at the wrong time. Personal precautions aimed at the avoidance of such encounters could only go so far. A disciplined practice of personal conduct or *modus operandi* was essential for reducing the risk of the worst happening when least expected.

Insidiously woven through this whole sorry mess were the evil tentacles of the drug trade cartels, with which nefarious multinational business the name of Colombia was essentially synonymous. The guerrilla factions were involved to the hilt with the cartels in satisfying the developed world's craving to get a kick from cocaine. Mere alcohol didn't satisfy them at all. It was by no means their idea of nothing to do. Anyone who stood in the way could rest in the sure knowledge that being mown down by an appropriately explosive means was an ever-present option.

All in all, this was a pretty mixture into which to drop an international Seminar on mine planning and mining geology.

ON THE OTHER hand, the life-and-limb risk for the Seminar wasn't all burdened with doom and gloom. The overwhelming majority of the good people of Colombia wanted to do nothing more than play out decent lives in a climate of peace and harmony in place of taking the role of innocent bystanders on the shore of a sea of troubles. There was no consolation in knowing that theirs was the fate of so many others in a world cursed largely by the existence of politics and religion. In Colombia, the experience of decades of civil conflict had led the general population to adjust the habits of its daily life to generate an eye of eerie normality within the hurricane of violence swirling around them.

From foreign visitors the people of Colombia merited no less than beaming admiration. Colombians were among the most friendly and hospitable of people. It was as if the dark side of the image of their country had drawn them to compensate by over-emphasising its bright face. The people of Colombia were the positive side of the country, and to be with them was always more than enough to warm the heart.

CERRO'S WELL-ESTABLISHED security practice for visitors arriving in Colombia at Bogotá international airport from more (or sometimes, but not very often, less) peaceful countries of origin, enclosed the visitors in the protective carapace of a virtual cocoon for the duration of their visit. Once the attention given by Colombian customs officials to the arriving visitor's luggage had run its perfunctory course, assuming for the process that the luggage was not still sitting at another airport, Cerro's security department, purring like a well-oiled machine, took both the visitor and the luggage over. The incoming visitor could lean back and relax like Prince Prospero in his castle while, without, the red death held dominion.

The advantaged visitors were met by members of Cerro's department of trained security personnel at the airport arrivals gate. Cerro's security department was an elite, dedicated, strong and skilful policing organisation in its own right. Although I never saw any open evidence of arms being borne by any of the Cerro security personnel who picked me up at the airport, I could not but note that the wearing of the kind of craftily cut suits or baggy bomber (unfortunate term, that) jackets capable of shrouding a multitude of sins was *de rigueur* for them even in the warmest of temperatures. All in all, they were invariably a lot better dressed in all respects than I ever was.

Visitors were driven away from the airport in a Cerro-owned top-of-the-range four-by-four pickup and taken directly to the Tequendama hotel in downtown Bogotá. The Tequendama was a salubrious establishment set in an unprepossessingly seedy locality and had been selected as a suitable place to contain the visitors presumably on account of its proximity to Cerro's Bogotá offices located across the way. Its high-rise opulence soared like an unassailable cliff set in a sea of under-privilege and seemed to me to present an open invitation to any denizen of the street who might entertain malicious intentions for the type of guests that the hotel attracted. However, apart from having a few windows broken once in a while by the occasional car bomb in its general vicinity, the walls of the Tequendama hotel were probably rarely violated by malefactors.

The hotel lobby swarmed with slick-looking, sharp-suited individuals, strutting their stuff like bantam roosters. If these characters weren't on the make they were in the wrong place.

IN AN APARTMENT block, standing tall on the far side of a courtyard to the rear of the Tequendama, Cerro maintained a luxurious sixteenth-floor apartment where Company directors and their ilk were wont to reside when in town. In spite of its exclusivity, on a couple of occasions I got to spend a night in the apartment. (There must have been a mix-up over the bookings.)

On the second of these occasions I was brought to the apartment by Cerro security staff after an arrival in Bogotá on an early morning scheduled flight up from Montería following a ten-day visit to the Cerro property. Given the hour, the apartment was but recently vacated after a previous night's stay by one of the Company's executive directors and his wife and had yet to be attended to by a cleaner.

When I unlocked and opened the apartment door the odour that greeted me was a raw assault on my every sense. Its foul reek was so solid that the thought of getting hold of a machete from Tequendama room service to cut my way through it wouldn't have been unreasonable. Inside the apartment every ashtray overflowed with cigarette ends. So many used cups lay in various attitudes of crusting abandon on tables, on chairs, on the floor (and as an afterthought in the kitchen sink) that washing up had clearly not been a popular activity for either the executive director or his wife. Sloppy wet towels lay wherever they had no doubt been thrown, in corners, on the bed, on a dressing-table and trailing out by the bathroom door. The bed was unmade to the extent that it must have taken both purpose and calculation to achieve its disastrous appearance.

The cleaner came in behind me. I felt sorry for her and deeply ashamed at how the credibility of the Company's image must have shaped up in her eyes. She flung open every window in the apartment to let the cleansing wind course through the precincts, all to no avail against the resistant vileness of the atmosphere. Nor was the passage of further time a particularly great decontaminating agent.

Maybe the cleaner was accustomed to confronting such vistas of executive director-inspired mess, the one quite as abominable as the other. What kind of people were they? And for that matter, the same consideration could be applied to their wives. The recently checked-out couple were obviously well matched. I shook my head. The Company's birthright might have been sold for a mess of potage.

SAFELY CHECKED IN and accommodated at the Tequendama hotel, a visitor was at liberty to move around freely for the duration of his allotted stay, as long as he remained inside the hotel. Cerro security regulations did not permit a visitor to leave the hotel unless accompanied by one or more of Cerro's security department personnel.

The visitor's exit from the Tequendama hotel normally took place at a very early hour on the morning after the arrival of the night before. No matter how small that hour, the effect of jet lag, enhanced by Bogotá's light headache-inducing altitude, would ensure that the visitor was up and running and ready to be conducted back to Bogotá international airport for a connecting flight north to the eventual destination of Cerro's mining and refining operations.

The Cerro security people did not leave the visitor's side until he or she (or It in the case of a certain executive director, not to mention his wife) stepped through the airport departure gate en route to the waiting aircraft.

Designated transportation often featured a light aircraft operating as a charter between Bogotá and an airstrip constructed just outside the buoyantly rural delights of a formerly mud-spattered town named Montelibano, adjacent to which was the dedicated town site serving the Cerro nickel mining and refining operations.

Montelibano rested easily on a bend of the great Rio San Jorge in Cordoba province about four hundred kilometres to the northwest of Bogotá, a flight of an hour and a half over FARC-infested mountains and wriggling, greenly mysterious valleys. The investment by Cerro in local infrastructure and related social support facilities, coupled with a consequently induced invasion of Colombian entrepreneurs whose spectrum of enterprise was matched only by the breadth of their political leanings, had succeeded in replacing Montelibano's claim to be Cordoba's number one shit hole with its pride in being a bustling market town ripe with quality of life.

From the airstrip near Montelibano, which boasted a concrete sur-face, arriving passengers were conducted for a kilometre or so in secure transport to Cerro's town site. The closed vehicles drove through nar-row alleys, probably under the tight-eyed scrutiny of the representatives of more than one guerrilla faction in town to do their shopping.

Twenty or so kilometres to the southwest of Montelibano there was an alternative airport associated with the large provincial town of Caucasia in Antioquia province. Cerro used the Caucasia airport prior to the construction of its own airstrip at Montelibano. Scheduled air services came down to Caucasia from Medellin, although Cerro's pas-sengers very rarely used these, the security risk outstripping the relative convenience.

The regular alternative to light-aircraft charter flights to Monte-libano from Bogotá was the scheduled Avianca air service from Bogotá to Montería. I preferred this to the charter route. Montería was a beautiful provincial city located a hundred and forty kilometres to the northwest of Montelibano along a good road.

Secure transport notwithstanding, that much open road could easily be reckoned as being not without risk to travellers. However, for most of its length, the Montería to Montelibano road ran through grand savannah vistas of lushly rolling cattle country, finca upon finca, haci-enda after hacienda. Of encompassing guerrilla-friendly mountains there were none.

Those who wished ill to travellers on this road were therefore burdened by a lack of viable topography to retreat to and hide in. Cerro considered the road to be "safe" to the extent that such a term was applicable in the context of travel in Colombia. The surrounding region might well be rife with the usual plethora of so-called "incidents" incorporating shootings, knifings, arson and an occasional small massacre to keep it all going, but at least the road, said those who knew about those things, was "safe".

About half way between Montería and Montelibano the road snaked through a rambling town of crumbling buildings named Planeta Rica by a founder with a clear sense of irony. The stock in trade of Planeta Rica was vested in preparing and selling various forms of fruit juice, freshly pressed to the order of the eager public. It was a matter of some regret that Cerro security regulations did not permit any passing vehicle that I was a passenger in to pull up and partake of this delight.

CERRO'S TOWN SITE at Montelibano was contained behind an impressively high mesh fence reinforced at the top with a ravel of razor wire. Heavily armed and smartly uniformed guards, all of whom were members of the security department, manned the entry gates. Additional members of the same gang occupied guard posts dotted around the town site, from which, day and night, they conducted rifle-porting foot patrols. All too often I found their presence to be a little too overt and menacing for my taste.

Visitors to the town site, like me, were lodged in a guesthouse that merited a grading of at least three stars and were fed at the restaurant of Cerro's Club Katuma, reached from the guesthouse by crossing over the main road from Montería into Montelibano using a meshed-in (not forgetting the razor wire) footbridge. The proximity of the guesthouse to the bridge naturally led to the guesthouse being called "Casa Puente".

THE MINING AND refining operations were located twenty kilometres outside Montelibano. A wide road floored with compacted ferruginous hard cap (stripped from the top of the nickel orebody draped over Cerro Matoso) connected the town site with the operations area. The road surface was smooth and sure. It held its quality even when rain fell. Rain was a frequent and torrential event that was invariably greeted with dismay by those involved with handling the softer saprolitic clays of mine production.

Visitors were transported between town site and operations at the start of the working day and then back again at the end. Modes of transport included a number of four-by-four pickups, an escorted minibus, or a regular local bus service dedicated to carrying the Cerro staff. My preference was to travel under the anonymity afforded by the bus service.

Any association with armed escorts always seemed to me to raise the profile of whoever was being escorted and thereby to attract the attention of miscreants in a way that was too inviting to the latter to be desirable to the former – although, since I was never offered an escort, I couldn't speak from experience.

NOTWITHSTANDING THE WIDESPREAD incidence of violence in the surrounding region, the Cerro operations, the attractiveness of which as a likely target went without need for further qualification, were (curiously perhaps) never directly touched by guerrilla activity. I rationalised that this resulted from Cerro's commendable reputation as a local employer and general benefactor to the welfare of the citizens of Montelibano.

In spite of all that, nothing could be taken for granted. In Colombia, knowing who was who (even if you weren't a gringo) was never easy, and precisely what lay around the next corner was impossible to predict. Cerro's security cocoon could be relied on to take as much care of the unexpected as it could, but it could offer no dead-cert guarantees.

Those who were taken care of needed to observe the rules and let Cerro do the rest. It took me a few trips in and out of Colombia to grasp this, and it was only when I understood what protection it gave me that I came to properly appreciate the days I spent in the country. At the same time, even with enhanced feelings of comfort regarding my personal security, I didn't ever stop feeling too upset to leave Colombia for an onward destination, unless (but that's another story) that onward destination was Caracas.

IF THE GAME of the Seminar was to be played, it was entirely up to me to kick the ball, handed to me by Ricardo, all the way down to the goal. Before anything else would happen, I needed to deliver my side of our handshake deal – namely, to identify and confirm an adequate number of interested would-be participants.

I planned to break up this first part of the Seminar process into three linked phases involving (a) establishing ground rules, (b) submitting the ground rules to the mine managers from whom the initial expression of interest had to be obtained, and (c) confirming, in concert with Cerro, the minimum numbers on which a go or no-go decision would be taken. The execution of the three phases was characterised by lobbying, by cajoling, by persuading and, where necessary (as it all too often was in Company matters), by begging.

A go decision was to be based on a minimum of eight confirmations of attendance. Eight didn't sound like an awful lot, but it would be enough to satisfy the objectives of the Seminar. After a plodding beginning from which the bounty of co-operation fell from the mine managers as if it were no more than a light mist, the mist merged into a drizzle, the drizzle intensified into rain, and on once despondent slopes a little stream began to trickle, gained pace and waxed as a mighty flow. The number of participant confirmations escalated to thirty-two as the concept of a Seminar involving a meeting of minds in a commonality of technical and personal co-operation came to excite imaginations and override earlier misgivings.

The ground rules called for participants to be responsible for their own air fares between their points of origin and Bogotá. The participants would also need to fund personal expenses in Colombia, not least among which were likely to be impressive bar bills. They were advised that immediately following their arrival at Bogotá international airport the Cerro security machine would take charge of them and that they would be wholly subservient to its rules. All forms of transportation, accommodation both in transit and at the town site near Montelibano, meals and Seminar accoutrements and facilities were to be paid on Cerro's account.

The Seminar was scheduled to last for five days, comprising three and a bit days of conference at Club Katuma, which would also incorporate a visit to the mining and refining operations, and an added bonus (thanks to Cerro's generosity) of one and a bit days of excursion to the fabled Colombian city of Cartagena on the Caribbean coast.

AN EVENT HELD under Company auspices of the kind typified by the Seminar was normally supported by a formally allocated budget. In the specific case of the Seminar the assurance of funding applied, in that formal sense, only to the portion of the Seminar arranged to take place within Colombia. The mine managers outside Colombia were obliged to dig deep into the dusty recesses of their respective pockets to come up with the means of sending their delegates to Bogotá. Having done so, their policy was best summed up in terms of being "this far and no further".

That left a lot of bits and pieces still to be covered. Small-print items were voluminous. To take care of such requirements, and equally to set up the dreaded contingencies without which no budget would ever be complete, I laid down my Company credit card as the foundation stone.

I was only too well aware that if I attempted to run the arrangements through "proper channels", the plan for the Seminar would at best be subject to severe delay and at worst be deferred indefinitely. The powers that be would be certain to jockey for personal kudos in the event that they smelt a successful event in the making or would join a stampede to trample the Seminar into the mud in an instant if they sensed that it would fail. Self-respecting Company executives rarely came to a party that was not calculated to promote their own interests at the expense of others. The "Hey, asshole!" brigade was always looking for the main chance.

AT THE END of the day, to borrow a verbal tic that such rectal brigades larded through their regular deliberations (I once counted that expression used a hundred and fifteen times during a single meeting through the course of a morning), it occurred to me that I had yet to advise my Johannesburg-based boss, the instigator of the Absolutely mandate, on what I was doing. I knew in my heart that I had committed a sin of commission in putting off telling him about the pending Seminar, principally because I had little doubt that he might not be backward in trying to stop me going forward. Faced with no alternative but to let him know, I took the plunge.

Much to my surprise, not to mention relief, he seemed to favour the idea of holding the Seminar. However, he decreed, Colombia was not an appropriate country in which to host it. No, no, he declared, the Seminar must take place in a safe country – such as, he added, South Africa. That, according to him, was his final word on the matter.

Unfortunately for the welfare of his point of view, Colombia, through the good offices of Cerro, already counted for a great deal more than half of the Seminar equation. To switch horses in mid-stream would, in a word or two, throw a fatal blow at the Seminar's future and, much worse that that, would form a breach of faith with Cerro that I wasn't prepared to countenance.

Well, as the General Manager of Avoca Mines always said when he sat on the horns of a dilemma, piss on it and something will happen. If I was required to be in the Seminar for a rand I might as well be in it for a peso. I decided to shelve my boss's South Africa or bust edict and press on with the plan to stage the Seminar at Cerro's Club Katuma on the assumption that the event was going to be a success. That being so, my boss would, in the manner of a wooden rocking horse, be unlikely to give a shit about the venue. If the Seminar didn't work out quite so well in Colombia, it would be hardly likely to have a different outcome in South Africa.

It was then that the burden of managing the Seminar single-handedly became too much for me to carry. I was fortunate to be able to engage the assistance of a currently under-used and generally under-appreciated (much as we all were) secretary named Ariane from the Company's head office. She showed her mettle and at once took firm control of the Seminar co-ordination and organisation both in and out of Colombia. She was instrumental in pulling the arrangements together. Through her, the Seminar participants finally came to know who among them had to be where, when they had to be there, where they were coming from and how they were travelling in order to arrive in Bogotá at the right time.

A week or so prior to the scheduled commencement of the Seminar, Ariane flew out to Bogotá and onwards to Montelibano in order to draw the remaining loose strings together. It was as well that she did, as the strings linking the Club Katuma end were not only loose but also tangled. The quality of her work on bringing the Seminar to realisation made a major contribution to her transference afterwards to a position in the Company's public relations department. It took a special kind of talent to justify selection for polishing up the Company's image.

The mine planners and mining geologists who signed up to participate in the Seminar came from projects and mines in which the Company was a leading light in Australia, Brazil, Canada, Chile, Colombia (of course), Cuba, Ghana, Indonesia, the Netherlands, South Africa, Suriname, and the United Kingdom.

These participants came to the Seminar primed to make presentations (what else) and to contribute to discussions and debates on a host of issues relating to their professional disciplines, their parent organisations, the commodities produced by their mines (bauxite, copper, gold, lead, nickel, manganese, silver and zinc) and the countries and cultures they represented.

Yet was there evidence of serpents in the lawn of accord, for numbered among the participants were two general managers of mining operations. Not only were they GMs, which ranked them an imperious cut above what I thought was desirable if the Seminar was to enjoy an informal atmosphere characterised by constructive dialogue, but they were GMs of South African mines, and in principle that association set them out as a beyond-the-pale breed apart.

Within the tight universe of the mining industry and all its works there were no individuals guaranteed to be more punctilious of attitude, more authoritarian in demeanour or more demanding of deferential obedience from those subservient to their command than the GMs of South African mines. Their role model was Captain Bligh of HMS *Bounty*. Such men turned the quality of aloofness into an art form that royalty could only envy.

Casualness in or out of the workplace, whether in terms of dress code or form of address code, in operating procedures, command structure, reporting relationships and liberality of outlook in any size, shape or form, did not feature in a South African mine GM's phrase book. Live and let live represented, to each and every one of them, an attitude of mind that only lesser mortals indulged in.

The GMs of South African mines ruled their demesnes not unlike black-browed latter-day Homers. On executive thrones they sat in palatial splendour behind respectively vast expanses of polished desk, issuing directives from hands that the rod of empire might have swayed, or staked with ecstasy the living liar. They stood at the apex of kingdoms of fear of their own creation and revelled in their dominion over all. And to cap it all, they insisted on the wearing of ties as inviolate badges of office.

A prime objective of the Seminar was the stimulation of free-flowing discussions in a relaxed setting. The Seminar was designed to generate ideas and draw the participants away from the constraints of the workplace into an open forum of community and co-operation.

Would the presence of two GMs of South African mines be conducive to realising these ideals? Was a bear Catholic? Or for that manner, did the Pope shit in the woods?

Worthy though the two South African GMs might be (at least according to their respective opinions of themselves), I didn't want this pair of luminaries to attend the Seminar and so did my best to deter them. My level of success had much in common with that of a certain King Canute facing a rising tide. Neither of the duo evinced a single iota of willingness to be put off, and so, in spite of my own misgivings, their names went down on the list of confirmed attendees. It seemed that if I couldn't fight 'em, I had to let 'em join. If they were the rogue bulls that I perceived them to be, the onus was on them to adapt to the movements of the common herd.

THE SEMINAR PARTICIPANTS dribbled in to Bogotá airport in a scheduled sequence of arrivals spread over at least a day or so. Cerro's security co-ordination was impeccable. The arrivals fell into the all-enveloping protective welcome, in which embrace they were whisked off to the temporary containment pen that was the Tequendama hotel. A mass evacuation to Montelibano was the first appointment for the morrow.

The quality and effectiveness of the arrivals exercise ought neither to be underrated nor to remain unsung in the magnificence of its safe marshalling of an assembly of innocents, near-innocents and a few of the usual suspects in a zone of almost-war.

The Cerro security regulation requiring incoming participants to remain within the holding precincts of the Tequendama hotel was rigorously applied and adhered to, reluctantly or otherwise, by all save three of the band. It was ever thus. The errant group all related to a prominent South African manganese mine, comprising a GM, Coen by name, and two of his acolytes.

Coen was a native speaker of Afrikaans. This personal linguistic attribute was superbly advertised by both the fleshy coarseness of his face and an impressively pendant belly (in the development of which so much beer had been invested that Coen's nether regions existed in a permanent state of shadow). Coen's short-sleeved shirt formed more of a tribute to the built-in safety factor of the thread holding its straining buttons in place than to the skill of its tailor. A corporate tie, an arrow-straight device slanting down from bulging neck to swelling navel, completed his assembly.

The Coen-directed trio, whose flight touch-down into Bogotá had been made some hours ahead of my own, were out on the town when I got to the Tequendama. I was weary from my flight in from London, but not so much so that I wasn't both worried and upset by Coen's profligacy. This, I thought, was exactly what South African GMs brought to the party. The Seminar was out on a thin limb already by virtue of taking place in Colombia and being supported by not much more than faith and hope and the charity of a Company credit card that was thinner than an executive director's smile. We just didn't need an overbearing bunch of lost plattelanders from the northern Cape of South Africa to provide the opportunity for an incident to occur.

OF COURSE, COEN and his two boys weren't the only participants of obdurate persuasion that the Seminar could lay claim to. A mining engineer from Suriname, delegated to participate, told me when I met up with him beforehand in his benighted country of nationality that he was going to hit the streets of Bogotá if he felt like it and that was that. I let him know that he could do what he liked, but if he did wander anywhere without the authorisation and protection of Cerro security, then he could just keep on going right back to Bogotá airport where he could catch the first flight out of Colombia that would take him to wherever the hell he had to go to pick up a connection to Paramaribo.

There weren't many such connections, so he wasn't spoiled for choice. I didn't know if he took my words to heart or not. I was never any good at laying down the law. In the event he stayed put in the Tequendama according to the rules. Maybe he just didn't feel like an excursion into the streets of Bogotá.

THE CORPULENT COEN and his two adventurous disciples returned to the Tequendama at a relatively timely evening hour. It was still early enough for them to demonstrate that their capacity for the consumption of Colombian beer had at best been barely dented during their external peregrinations. They proceeded to test the ultimate limits of their ability to contain beer with a vigour that merited awe rather than admiration.

I was so relieved to see them intact that I did little more than remind them of the rules they had agreed to observe, and which they had recently trodden on with varying degrees of heaviness. The mild admonition bounced off the three in the manner of a golf ball hurled at a brick wall. My still-water opinion on the character of GMs of South African mines ran so deep that its surface was not so much as rippled.

ON THE FOLLOWING morning the Seminar participants gathered together in the hotel lobby at an hour that was almost painfully close to dawn. At a given signal, involving a contingent of Cerro security personnel taking on the role of ushers, the participants moved to the mean street outside. There, a small fleet of impressive looking four-by-four pickups was assembled for the purpose of conducting the participants to the out of the way corner of Bogotá airport specifically dedicated to the arrival and departure of light charter aircraft. Four such aircraft were there, ready and waiting, to fly everyone onwards to Montelibano.

A pressing problem for the moment was that the airport was shrouded in rather thick fog. No aircraft of any stature was about to move on the ground or land from the air while the fog held on, and hold on the fog did for so long that it began to look as if the first day of the Seminar presentations at Club Katuma was likely to be placed in some jeopardy.

On the credit side, although the presentations would be valued in the experience of those who gave them, those to whom the presentations were given would not all be quite so enthralled. Presentations were generally designed to reveal the presenter and his or her material, irrespective of its relative merits, in the best possible light. Tastefully designed overhead slides offered highly skilled illusions directing the audience's attention away from an array of shortfalls.

The enduring benefit of the Seminar was set to be in the personal and working relationships that it would build between participants. That required a lot of talking and not a little bullshitting, some of which could be achieved equally as effectively at a fog-shrouded airport as anywhere else.

The foggy delay extended itself through all of three hours. Although the fog might have caused the British Museum to lose its charm, by all measurable criteria its durability provided a constructive contribution to team building. The participants were able to unite in a shared disdain not only for the reduced visibility outside but also, and rather more militantly, against the strikingly unpretentious interior facilities of the charter airline company's waiting room. In fairness to the waiting room, however, its lack of decor might not have tested the patience of a single flight's complement of passengers delayed for maybe twenty minutes, particularly if any of the passengers had an affinity with residents of the mythical Sparta.

The close confines of the waiting room were conducive to conditions promoting personal interaction akin to the intimacy of a London Underground train carriage at the height of the rush hour. The waiting room did its job so well in this regard that I entertained a sneaking suspicion that the fates had played a hand rich in aces in arranging the fog for the Seminar's benefit. The participants were destined to be late on the ground at Montelibano, but for all that they were going to arrive as a more integrated group than might have been the case had the departure from Bogotá not been delayed, the incidence of the two GMs notwithstanding.

A reduction in the opacity of the fog owed more to the effect of fading than of lifting as the morning advanced. The four charter aircraft were finally boarded by the participants and readied for departure once visibility had improved sufficiently for air traffic control to manifest optimism in getting flights away. The four aircraft taxied out, one by one, to insinuate themselves as best they could in an immense departure queue of aircraft of every conceivable size and shape designed for international, national and merely local destinations. The sequence of departing aircraft was dovetailed with a steady stream of arriving flights, some of which had been in a holding pattern up above the murk for long enough to carve a rut in the sky.

The big jets took precedence in the pecking order for departure. Little charter aircraft were taught to know their place in the scheme of things. As a consequence, the first of the Seminar charter flights out of Bogotá had arrived at Montelibano, dropped off its load of participants, and taken off again for its return flight before the last of the four had received its air traffic control clearance for departure from Bogotá.

THE SEMINAR WAS coming together. In spite of a tardy arrival at Montelibano, the actual proceedings of the first day were not destined to be a total write-off, even if a late *al fresco* lunch at Club Katuma was consumed much less rapidly than scheduled, probably because rather more Colombian beer was imbibed than was intended.

Beer at lunchtime was a beverage incompatible with an after-lunch attention span of anything greater than minimum duration. Of course, quite irrespective of the intake of such liquid refreshment, the first hour of the afternoon session of any seminar anywhere was a lost cause for the presenter unfortunate to be on stage at that time. For that matter, some post-coffee mid-morning presentations were not much less soporific either.

In mid-afternoon the Seminar participants assembled for the opening session in the Club Katuma restaurant, the accoutrements of formal dining having been removed from the premises for the occasion. As it was, the restaurant was rarely used for the purpose suggested by its name, as the serious business of eating (and drinking) was an activity undertaken in the great outdoors under a covering of dusty thatch exposed on one side to the over-warm waters of a swimming pool.

The participants sat around the outer edge of a horseshoe arrangement of tables, facing each other across a narrow expanse of no-man's land within which the moderator or presenter of the moment was free to wander about at will in a vain quest to demonstrate a telling point. The facilities for projecting visual aids, and the screen on which those masterpieces of overhead slide complexity were to be projected, were set up at the open end of the horseshoe. At the rear, in behind the toe of the horseshoe, a couple of so-called simultaneous translators hid away behind a perforated wooden screen. They were determined to convert spoken English to unintelligible Spanish (and not unnaturally vice versa) to their own entire satisfaction, if not to the gratification of any of the participants.

At the epicentre of the toe of the horseshoe, Coen, who less than a day previously had sought out certain of the fleshpots of Bogotá on his own lamentable initiative, smothered a chair with his overflowing ass and raised a sense of dubiety in the hearts of all who looked on that the integrity of the chair would be equal to the challenge so posed. His two associates flanked him, one on the right and one on the left. Their three corporate ties hung in parallel, making an inviting wicket that anyone present would not have been averse to hurling a bread roll at. I couldn't work out if aggression was oozing from them like sweat or if sweat dripped from them aggressively. Whatever it was, all three seemed to sit there like the very antithesis of three wise monkeys, almost desperate to declare their superiority.

That wouldn't last long.

WHEN PEOPLE BLESSED by a large measure of mutual goodwill formed the majority of a group, then the less well-intentioned minority was faced with the options of either shaping up or shipping out. A benevolent majority was a guarantee that the whole was much more than the sum of its parts. And so it was.

In the course of the next two days, the Seminar proceedings took pride of place. Among the highlights, debate on the various presentations proved rather less than easy to get going in plenary sessions; the Cerro mining and refining operations were visited; a major depletion was recorded in Club Katuma's stock of beer (and its wine cellar, such as it was, fared not dissimilarly); meals were taken; evening receptions were enjoyed; and conviviality reigned.

THREE SPECIAL FEATURES of the success of the Seminar proceedings that impressed themselves on me involved, significantly enough in two of the cases, the South African GMs.

The first of these merited citations commemorated the beef-burdened Coen's burgeoning joviality, which culminated in the phenomenon of his appearance in public without a tie to mar the mighty aspect of his frontage. Although Coen never quite went on to become one of the boys, he came pretty close to achieving that ideal state of grace in spite of his background.

The second commendation involved the impromptu discussions that broke out all around like flowers in springtime. These mostly involved no more than a few participants around a table sharing their thoughts over coffee or a beer. The participants were all the time getting to know one another and forming relationships that would stand strong long after the Seminar was over. Between themselves they ensured that the lift of a phone or the click of a mouse would give them all the future bridge-building materials they needed.

The third of the awards involved the second of the South African GMs, Jacques by name. I saw Jacques sitting in earnest discussion with a Ghanaian geologist and an Indonesian mining engineer. Each was clearly appreciating the company of the others. I sensed goodwill flowing from and between them in vital waves. This little tableau provided me with the definitive image symbolising what the Seminar (and not forgetting the Absolutely mandate) was all about. National and cultural constraints were unlocked with the common-ground key of shared aspirations.

I didn't imagine that my boss was likely to be displeased with a positive outcome to the Seminar. The fact that it was successful in Colombia effectively buried Colombia as an issue.

AND SO IT came to pass, once the proceedings around the Seminar horseshoe at Club Katuma were over and done with, that a reasonably well-bonded body of participants, acceptably pulling together in one direction in the pursuit of a collective cause of shared professional values, departed from Montelibano in search of greener pastures and stiller waters.

It was a matter of regret to some of the departing participants that in spite of their best efforts Club Katuma had yet to be drunk dry, but, much to their credit, they were philosophical about that particular failure. You won some, you lost some, they reasoned.

The spirit of the Seminar would go forth and sow good seeds, they believed. More than a few hoped that future wins would eclipse future losses. Most participants were primed to renew combat with adversaries that included competitor organisations and certain elements of the Company's executive management.

The destination for the participants, flying out of Montelibano in mid-morning, was the beautiful port city of Cartagena, where a relaxing excursion of a day or so was planned. Cartagena's coral block fortress redoubts had deterred the incursions of pirates for some centuries, and on that basis the participants were on a hiding to nothing if they hoped to make a real impression on that beach-girt metropolis.

Naturally enough, most of the intrusive pirates, buccaneers, freebooters and the associated likes of Sir Francis Drake, seafarers all, hove into sight from the Caribbean out to the west of Cartagena. Their present day-FARC *et al* counterparts were landlubbers by contrast and so might well be expected to have a presence either in or behind Cartagena. Although there was no obvious threat, security on the Seminar's visit to Cartagena continued to be applied to the letter by Cerro.

Following installation of the participants in a Cartagena hotel of

Cerro's choice, a short supervised excursion along the sea front, taking in a host of shops and kiosks selling souvenirs and artisanal works of art (and craftiness) took place. The gentle people and lively colour of the city formed an enduring image of all that was great about Colombia.

When darkness loomed and the time came for everyone to be taken back to the hotel, one of the participants, a geologist named Alan, affiliated to the small gold mine managed by Jacques near Barberton in South Africa, took substantial umbrage with me when I stopped him making his return on foot. In the absence of anyone from Cerro security immediately available to authorise Alan's perambulation I decided to err on the side of caution.

Alan's response offered me a forcible reminder, as if I didn't know it already, that South Africans were far less concerned with the perils of unknown streets than I was. As in the then current social and political climate of South Africa it was well nigh impossible to find anyone of any skin tone who had not so far been touched by violent crime, Alan's reaction shouldn't have been surprising. It seemed that I had inadvertently introduced a note of discord into what was hitherto an increasingly close harmony ensemble.

COEN, NOW TIELESS to a fault, girded in a garish shirt that might have tented up a family of vagrants on any beach in Hawaii, and wearing a pair of khaki shorts capable of forming the groundsheet to the said tent with material to spare, was (unlike Alan) most amenable to being driven back to the hotel. Coen was actually generating empathy.

Coen's casual attire assumed the status of a great boon when a heavy-footed attempt to dance with a juiced-up complement of participants along the edge of the hotel swimming pool placed him a lot closer to the rim of the pool than he intended to be. He toppled into the pool with all the grace of the statue of a fallen dictator following the latest revolution, to create the vortex of an almighty splash and a radiating tidal wave that may well be remembered in Cartagena to this day. It was a baptism of resurrection. The water washed away many more shreds of Coen's uneasy crown of GMness in the glorious process of changing him from being one of them to becoming one of us.

Coen's feel-good factor seemed to have arrived to stay. He declared that he (or rather his expense account) would stand the cost of all drinks for the participants at dinner that night. He was clearly bolder than I had up to then given him credit for being. My sorely tested Company credit card was already lined up for the edible portion of the dinner bill as well as for paying the extras to hotel costs not covered by Cerro. Coen's bonhomie threw my drowning credit card something of a lifeline. For that relief was due much thanks.

THE DINNER IN question was held in an open-air restaurant located on top of one of the battlements of Cartagena's city walls, a few kilometres from the hotel. In my diary I recorded my share of the meal as "beef and potatoes". It was clearly not memorable.

A serious assault on Coen's contribution to the liquid bill of fare commenced when the beef and potatoes were no more. Coen didn't appear to have regretted his renaissance as a man whose generosity was as ample as his girth, as he was instantly in among the wine and beer bottles with the best of the advantage takers.

I declined to hang on with the die-hard drinking contingent for any longer than a token period and elected to return to the hotel together with one of Cerro's participants. If nothing was ventured nothing would be gained. We elected to drive back in one of Cartagena's celebrated horse-drawn open carriages, sometimes referred to as Victorias.

Travelling in a Victoria was an attractive prospect for the two of us. The horse, carriage and driver had all seen better days, but then, as I was constantly reminding myself, so had I. The outfit clattered away from the foot of the rampart underlying the restaurant and threaded its way through an utterly charming network of narrow colonial streets, overhung by ornate balconies dripping with flowers.

Once under way, it suddenly occurred to me that this mode of transport was not exactly consistent with the security norms that I was such an avowed advocate of. I was well able to talk the talk, but I wasn't walking the walk. In that respect I came as close to sharing certain of the values of some of the Company's executive directors as I was ever likely to. It did me no credit.

Much to my dismay, the Victoria emerged from the warren of colonial streets to confront once again the very rampart on top of which the evening dinner was consumed and where the post-prandial session funded by Coen was, to judge from the audible clamour from the summit, well in progress. Leaning over the battlement and looking directly down on the clip-clopping Victoria were two of the Seminar participants. I was horrified to note that one of them was Alan, whose planned stroll along the sea front I had foiled earlier on in the day.

I made a point of seeking Alan out on the following morning to offer him a profuse apology for my Victoria-based conduct unbecoming. I was as abject in defeat as Alan was magnanimous in victory.

Following his return to South Africa after the Seminar on a flight connection through Miami, Alan was hospitalised with a serious blood clot in one of his legs. He was off work for a number of months. No direct linkage of the symptoms was made with either his attendance at the Seminar or his long flight there and back. Deep-vein thrombosis, otherwise DVT or "economy class syndrome", was not at that time generally recognised as a hazard of long-distance air travel, but there seemed to be little doubt in hindsight that DVT was what afflicted Alan. A brisk walk along the Cartagena sea front might have done him some good after all.

NATURALLY ENOUGH, BREAKFAST for me on the morning after the dinner included a large dish of humble pie. It was not the first time that I had eaten this dish, and if I could have found someone willing to take a bet that it would not be the last time either I would have been on to a sure thing.

The day was bright and blue. The Caribbean nodded and danced like a field of sunflowers. We were all due to make a return flight to Bogotá that evening using scheduled air services prior to going our separate ways at the closure of the Seminar, but between now and then the participants had a full day's excursion to enjoy. Arranged by Cerro, the said excursion was to the Islas de Rosario, an idyllic cluster of tiny islands set in the glowing sea an hour or so's run southwest from Cartagena. We voyaged thither in a motorised launch appropriately named *Sonrisa*.

Sonrisa skimmed over the water like a cresting bird, out between the fortressed jaws of the Boca Chica, leaving the serrated skyline of Cartagena's Boca Grande astern. As the coastline receded behind *Sonrisa's* creamy wake, even the least hint of the FARC felt a million miles away, and the ELN and the whole gamut of the paramilitary stamp seemed as ephemeral as the early morning mist on the distant hillcrests.

The participants disembarked on an island that was perhaps the mainstay of the Rosario archipelago. There we could swim with

impunity in the clear and balmy water around the shores, appreciate an impressive array of marine life in a natural aquarium, watch
a dolphin jump and soar at the behest of a slim and neatly bikinied
young lady who hailed from Brazil, and pick up (for a price) from as
engaging a bunch of laid-back vendors as anyone could wish to meet,
items wrought from red coral and cultured pearls and designed largely
to adorn necks and wrists. Marine life, not least among which was a
species of lobster, also featured prominently on the luncheon menu.

THE HOUR OF day scheduled for the return voyage of *Sonrisa* to Cartagena was 1.30 p.m. This requirement fell into the best-laid schemes of
mice and men syndrome, as – why not? – it was subject to delay. It
was not that the delay was excessive, nor would it have been important
had not 1.30 p.m. been the latest time for us to leave in order to ensure
that the evening flight to Bogotá out of Cartagena could be caught
comfortably. Charter flights might have no other alternative than to
wait for passengers, but Avianca was not of their ilk, foggy conditions
notwithstanding.

Sonrisa moved away from the island shortly before 2.00 p.m., full
throttle in force as soon as the dock was cleared. The good ship ruled
a dead straight white wake on the canvas of the Caribbean, heading for
Cartagena.

Facing time constraints, the captain of *Sonrisa*, who gave every
impression of knowing the local waters like the back of a hand,
although not necessarily his own hand, appeared to have decided that
he knew a short cut home and, moreover, was well up for taking it.
Whether or not he took the short cut following consultation with the
Cerro regulators on board or simply handled it on his own initiative
was destined never to be a matter for owning up to.

The captain's action involved pointing *Sonrisa* at the turgid mouth
of the Magdalena River under full power. The captain reckoned not
with the fact that the said river was only as deep as the state of the
tide permitted it to be. That particular tidal state was one of ebb. The
mud-laden river water was dropping even as we looked at it. Banks of
riverbed sediment, consisting of gooey pulp held together with a minimum of sandy content and enough rotten vegetation to be liberal in a
political context, were rising to break the surface in shoals.

One such bank intervened to impede *Sonrisa*'s course, causing the launch to come to a rather abrupt standstill that in one impetuous moment threw more than a few of its passengers into supine positions on the deck. The captain, who appeared still to consider himself not short of a ceremonious trick or two, juggled the motor controls to and fro, alternatively attempting to plough ahead through the bank and then pull back from it. *Sonrisa* oscillated furiously and irretrievably immured itself in the Magdalena's sucking grip.

ALTHOUGH FEW OF the Seminar participants were equipped with much maritime experience, they were, one and all, able to rest assured at that moment that a similar allegation might well be applied to the captain. It was, however, universally appreciated that time and tide waited for no man, and the logical extension of that relevant observation by Robert Burns decreed that *Sonrisa*, temporarily rechristened *Tristeza*, was going nowhere until the ebb finished and the succeeding flow rose to an appropriate depth.

Such a moment was a few hours away at best. Avianca could count on being short of thirty or so passengers on its flight to Bogotá that evening. On the other hand, even if nothing could be done to genuinely alter our marooning, there was nothing to be gained by anyone in actually doing nothing.

The thought of taking action seemed to infuse itself osmotically into the souls of many of the participants in a single moment of time. They leapt overboard one by one, exhibiting a kind of spontaneity normally associated with sinking ships and rats.

The fallen depth of the Magdalena River ranged from knee to waist, depending on the incidence of hollows, or up to the neck and above in the case of potholes. The consistency and colour of the water was not unlike that of French onion soup minus the *croûtons*, bleeding out towards a healing sea.

To begin with it was not clear what the great leap forward into the murky waters was intended to achieve. In one sense it lessened the load bearing down on *Sonrisa*'s keel, not least where Coen was concerned. Coen was one of the vanguard over the top, intent to his deep core on being one of the boys.

A large launch stuck as fast as *Sonrisa* (or *Tristeza*) required more than a token reduction of passenger complement to budge its keel. The subsequent endeavour by the river-bound group to apply its combined strength to shifting the hull by a centimetre or two was proof of this reality, but what was raised to the nth degree was spirits.

If the heaving and shoving resulted in *Sonrisa* moving by as much as a millimetre, such a measure of success was not perceptible. Yet, as a team-building process it was all without precedent in its magnificence. The struggle in the Magdalena River enshrined the glory of the Seminar for evermore. Its sense of common purpose united the participants as much in congeniality as in co-operation, cementing bonds that would carry and spill over into benefits for both personal and working relationships.

As an ultimate curtain call for a great event, the grounding of *Sonrisa* could not have been bettered. There were one or two who claimed that the incident in the Magdalena was arranged by rather more than pure fate.

I wouldn't want to disillusion them. Absolutely not!

Or better yet, Absolutely!

Revelation

And they showed me a corridor, and along it the doors were seven in number, and they were closed each one, and I beheld them. And I opened the first door, and I heard, as it were the sound of vainglorious thunder, the first of the four housemen of the executive committee saying, come and see.

2. And I came and saw, and beheld a white desk, and he that sat behind it wore a bow tie, and an airline ticket was given unto him, and he went forth to be conquered.

3. And I opened the second door, and I heard the second of the four housemen of the executive committee say, come and see.

4. And I came and I beheld that he who lodged within bore features red flushed by costly products of the grape, and the power was his to wipe all good projects from the earth, killing them one and another, and there was assigned by his minions unto him a great four-letter word.

5. And I opened the third door, and I heard the third of the four housemen of the executive committee say, come and see. And I came and I beheld, and lo his brow was black, and he that bore it held the careers of far too many balanced in his hand.

6.	And I heard a voice from without in the midst of the corridor call out the price of a measure of gold, and the worth of three measures of copper, and cry on anew to hurt not the oil and the wine.

7.	And I opened the fourth door, and I heard the voice of the fourth and chief among the four housemen of the executive committee say, come and see.

8.	And I came and I saw. And behold a pale houseman, and the name that sat on him was dearth, and shell followed with him.

9.	And power was given to them all four, over the whole part of the earth, to deceive with words redolent with the droppings of male kine, to dissemble with blunders, and with ignorance, and with the connivance of their own kind.

10.	And I opened the fifth door, and I saw within a great oval table, and all around it stood the souls of those cast into outer darkness for their words of truth, and for the testimony to incompetence of the four executive housemen that they bore in witness.

11.	And they cried out to me as one with a loud voice saying, how long, by all that is holy and true, can the excesses of the beasts that dwell behind the four doors escape the hand of justice?

12.	And white bound redundancy packages were given unto every one of them, and it was said unto them that they were banished to a dry land of early retirement where the prophecy of the casting aside of them and their colleagues should be fulfilled.

13.	And I opened the sixth door, and lo I beheld a great commotion, in which photocopies flowed, black as sackcloth of hair, and scarlet blood fell on the carpet.

14.	And in every corner was much coffee sipped, even as the rumourmongers cast timely gems into the hungry void, shaking complacency as with a rushing mighty wind.

15.	And I opened the seventh door and beheld that a faint light of hope glowed within. And I beheld the cohorts of the four executive housemen departing to be defenestrated apace as the judgement scroll unwound and moved their blind ambition and arrogant demeanour to a place of merited torment.

16. And he who was chief among the four executive housemen, and his three disciples and the indolent directors, and the rich men and the mighty men and the captains of industry were humbled, and hid themselves in their dens and lay behind the rocks they once crawled out from under.

17. And they cried out for a sanctuary to hide them from the faces of those their greed had destroyed, and from the wrath that was to come. And their bondsmen were freed to hold dominion over them.

18. For the great day of wrath will come, and who then among them shall be able to stand?

With apologies to St John the Divine

Lightning Source UK Ltd.
Milton Keynes UK
UKOW04f0026281117
313449UK00001B/12/P